A Taste of Tomorrow

Maeve Thornton

Published by Maeve Thornton, 2024.

This is a work of fiction. Similarities to real people, places, or events are entirely coincidental.

A TASTE OF TOMORROW

First edition. October 6, 2024.

ISBN: 979-8227612236

Written by Maeve Thornton.

Chapter 1: A Recipe for Change

I stand in the bustling kitchen of Luna's Sweet Retreat, the smell of vanilla and fresh pastries surrounding me like a warm hug. As the head pastry chef, I've dedicated my life to this small, charming bakery tucked away in a corner of Charleston, South Carolina. The walls are painted a soft, buttery yellow, and the air is thick with the warmth of ovens and the laughter of customers as they greet one another over steaming cups of coffee. My station, a chaotic haven of flour, sugar, and tempered chocolate, feels like an extension of myself, a place where I've crafted hundreds of cakes and pastries, each one a little piece of my heart served on a plate. However, after years of pouring my soul into confections that never quite seemed to satisfy my creative spirit, a wave of dissatisfaction washes over me.

It was during one of those typical Southern afternoons when the sun blazed high and the humidity clung to your skin, that I found myself wandering home along King Street, the cobblestones warm beneath my sandals. My mind drifted like the scent of magnolia blossoms carried by the breeze, thinking of the evening's special—lavender lemon tarts, a nod to summer. As I turned a corner, I stumbled upon a vibrant art gallery, its windows showcasing a stunning collection of desserts crafted into works of art. The pieces sparkled under the gallery lights, each one more breathtaking than the last. There were sugar sculptures resembling delicate flowers, intricate chocolate filigree, and cakes that seemed to defy gravity. I felt a tug in my chest, a flutter of excitement mixed with longing, as a seed of inspiration was planted deep within me.

The gallery was a kaleidoscope of color and creativity, a stark contrast to the warm tones of my bakery. I pushed through the door, a soft chime announcing my arrival, and was immediately enveloped by an atmosphere charged with passion. The walls were adorned with vibrant canvases that portrayed everything from abstract landscapes to whimsical interpretations of life in Charleston. As I wandered further inside, I found a cluster of exquisite dessert displays, their artistry invoking emotions I hadn't felt in years. I reached out, fingertips grazing the delicate sugar petals of a floral cake that was almost too beautiful to eat. In that moment, I understood; it was time to infuse my work with a new purpose, to create pastries that weren't just delicious but also visually arresting.

With a newfound determination, I returned to Luna's Sweet Retreat the next morning, the aroma of fresh bread mingling with my ambition as I kicked off my shoes and donned my apron. The kitchen buzzed with the usual energy—Marisol, my right-hand woman, was expertly frosting a batch of cupcakes, the vibrant colors reminiscent of the rainbow that often graced Charleston's skies after a rain. Her laughter rang out, light and infectious, and I couldn't help but smile, the thought of change bubbling in my chest. I approached her, a spark of excitement in my eyes.

"What do you think about changing up our menu a bit?" I asked, my voice barely above a whisper, like the very idea of it was a secret waiting to be revealed.

Marisol paused, her spatula hovering above a cupcake, the rich chocolate frosting glistening under the fluorescent lights. "What do you have in mind?"

I hesitated, the words struggling to form in my mind as the visions from the gallery swirled around me. "I want to incorporate art into our pastries. I want to make them stunning, something people can't help but photograph and share."

She blinked at me, her brow furrowing in thought. "You mean like the gallery? But Luna's is known for comfort, for those cozy, familiar flavors..."

I couldn't deny that she was right. We were beloved for our chocolate chip cookies that tasted like childhood, and the pies that evoked warm family dinners. But somewhere beneath my skin, the artist within me stirred, urging me to break free from tradition. "I know, but what if we could blend both? Comfort and creativity? Imagine a blueberry pie, but the crust is a delicate lattice that mimics the way light dances on the water at sunset. Or maybe a cheesecake that looks like a blooming garden. It could change everything."

The gears in Marisol's mind turned visibly as she considered my proposal. "That does sound kind of amazing," she finally conceded, a smile creeping onto her face. "But we'll need to practice. I mean, we can't have customers taking pictures of something that looks like a train wreck!"

Laughter erupted from both of us, the tension in the air dissipating like sugar dissolving in warm tea. With every passing moment, the vision of what I could create began to crystallize in my mind, the prospect of a new chapter in my culinary journey fueling my determination. We spent the day brainstorming, sketching out ideas for vibrant pastries and cakes that would be as much a feast for the eyes as they were for the palate. Flour flew and butter softened as we experimented, my heart swelling with hope and excitement.

That evening, as the sun dipped below the horizon, casting a golden hue over the quaint streets of Charleston, I stepped outside for a breath of fresh air. The warm breeze carried the sounds of laughter from nearby restaurants and the distant strum of a street musician's guitar. In that moment, I felt alive—imbued with the conviction that I was on the brink of something transformative, ready to infuse every pastry with a piece of my heart and soul.

As the sky turned to twilight, I could almost see the vibrant creations that awaited me—the desserts that would not only delight taste buds but also evoke joy and inspiration in the hearts of those who savored them. Change was on the horizon, and I was finally ready to embrace it, ready to blend the familiar sweetness of Luna's Sweet Retreat with a splash of vibrant artistry, creating a culinary symphony that would resonate through the streets of Charleston.

I returned to the bakery the next morning, feeling as if I had unearthed a part of myself that had been buried under layers of flour and sugar. The kitchen welcomed me with its familiar hum—a comforting soundtrack of whirring mixers and clinking utensils. As I slipped into my apron, I glanced around at the vibrant mosaic of colors and scents, my heart racing with a mixture of trepidation and excitement. Marisol had her sleeves rolled up, and together we began the intricate dance of creation, testing new flavors and designs, painting our pastries like the artists we aspired to be.

We spent days in this whirlwind of creativity, each session revealing something new. I would start with sketches, vibrant ideas splashed across paper—an explosion of colors, flavors, and textures coming to life. The combination of raspberry and lime, for instance, became a tart that shimmered like a summer sunset, its crust a delicate golden hue that crumbled beautifully beneath the first bite. Marisol, with her uncanny ability to infuse joy into every dollop of frosting, transformed the simplest of cakes into whimsical creations, swirling clouds of pastel colors reminiscent of cotton candy.

Word spread quickly about our experiments, and soon our regulars were buzzing with anticipation. Old Mr. Johnson, who had been a loyal customer for nearly a decade, walked in one afternoon, his white hair tousled and a permanent twinkle in his eye. "What's cooking, ladies? Smells like magic in here!"

With a wink, I led him to the counter, unveiling a shimmering blueberry pie topped with edible flowers that seemed to bloom right off the crust. "This, Mr. Johnson, is a taste of summer!"

His eyes widened, and a chuckle escaped his lips. "You girls are up to something! It's like you're painting the bakery with flavors!"

Encouraged by his enthusiasm, I felt the weight of my dreams lifting, and for the first time in a long while, I found myself truly excited about the journey ahead. Our loyal patrons were intrigued, delighting in our adventurous creations, and as we decorated the pastries with bursts of color and artful designs, I noticed a palpable change in the atmosphere of the bakery.

The corners of Luna's Sweet Retreat glowed with a new energy. We adorned the space with splashes of color—bright flowers in vases atop every table, the walls filled with playful illustrations of our confections that seemed to dance with life. The hum of conversation grew louder as curious newcomers joined the chatter of our regulars, each one eager to sample the masterpieces emerging from our kitchen.

Then came the day when I decided to host a grand unveiling, an event to showcase our new line of pastries. I printed flyers, each one bursting with colors as vibrant as our desserts, and invited our cherished customers and the surrounding community to experience the magic of artistry and flavor combined. Marisol and I worked tirelessly to prepare, setting up tables outside the bakery adorned with white linens and sprigs of mint, the Charleston sun casting a warm glow over everything.

As the sun began to dip low in the sky, painting the horizon in shades of orange and purple, I felt a rush of nerves. I stood behind the tables, my heart racing as the first guests began to arrive. People wandered over, drawn in by the enticing aroma and the promise of something new. Families, couples, and friends gathered, their laughter mingling with the sounds of the bustling street, creating a symphony of excitement.

The moment I unveiled our centerpiece—a towering cake that resembled a cascading waterfall, draped in sugar flowers and edible gold leaf—was electric. Gasps filled the air, eyes wide with wonder as they marveled at what could only be described as a piece of art. I couldn't help but feel a swell of pride as I served slices of the cake, each one a blend of rich chocolate and light vanilla, accompanied by a dollop of lavender cream.

"Tell me this isn't the most incredible thing you've ever tasted!" a woman exclaimed, her eyes gleaming as she savored her first bite.

As the crowd devoured our creations, I felt a warmth spreading through me, a confirmation that I was on the right path. Each compliment washed over me like a wave, carrying with it the affirmation I had longed for. With every laugh and cheer, the bakery transformed into something alive—a haven where people not only came to satisfy their sweet tooth but also to share joy, laughter, and stories.

But even amidst the celebration, a whisper of doubt crept in, nagging at the edges of my happiness. What if this newfound success was fleeting? What if, just like the summer rainstorms that swept through Charleston, it would all wash away, leaving behind only the remnants of what could have been? I shook my head, refusing to let negativity taint this moment.

With Marisol by my side, we toasted to our success that night, raising our glasses filled with sweet tea, the clinking echoing through the warm summer air. "Here's to new beginnings!" she exclaimed, her eyes sparkling with ambition and promise.

"Here's to change!" I replied, feeling a surge of hope as I clinked my glass against hers. The laughter around us blended into a melody, and I felt the weight of uncertainty lift, if only for the moment.

As the evening wore on and the stars twinkled like sprinkles on a cake, I stood back to observe the scene unfolding before me. Friends gathered around tables, sharing stories and smiles over decadent pastries, the joy evident on their faces. The bakery had become a canvas, and the community, our artwork, vibrant and alive. I had taken the leap into a new world, embracing not only the artistry I craved but also the connections that blossomed with every shared dessert.

In that moment, I realized that this journey was not just about transforming pastries; it was about creating a space where people could find happiness and connection. The art I longed to express transcended the mere act of baking; it was about nurturing relationships, celebrating the beauty of life, and welcoming everyone into a vibrant tapestry woven with sweetness and love. The bakery was no longer just a job; it had become my heart, my home, and my canvas for change.

The bakery thrived in the weeks that followed, with the tantalizing aroma of creativity wafting through its doors. Our new line of desserts attracted a diverse crowd—families celebrating milestones, couples on first dates, and tourists enchanted by Charleston's charm. Each day felt like a festival of flavors, and I relished every moment spent behind the counter, serving slices of joy to eager patrons. Marisol and I expanded our repertoire, inventing pastries that told stories through taste. Each creation became a chapter in a shared narrative, our little bakery an epicenter of laughter and delight.

One evening, as the sun dipped low, casting an amber glow over the cobblestone streets, a distinguished man in a tailored suit stepped through the door. He exuded an air of sophistication that immediately captured my attention, and my heart raced with anticipation. His hair, silver like the finest dusting of powdered sugar, framed a face lined with both wisdom and warmth. He approached the counter with a confidence that suggested he was accustomed to indulging in the finer things in life.

"Good evening," he said, his voice smooth like the dark chocolate ganache I had just made. "What do you recommend for someone who appreciates artistry in every bite?"

Caught off guard, I smiled, searching for the right words as I glanced at the display case, filled with my latest creations—pistachio macarons, marbled cheesecakes adorned with edible flowers, and an elaborate torte resembling a painter's palette. "Well, if you're looking for art, I'd say the raspberry-lavender tart is a must. It's delicate yet bold, a perfect balance of flavors that surprises the palate."

He nodded appreciatively, and I felt a flutter of excitement as I carefully plated the tart, my hands steady, a contrast to the whirlwind of emotions swirling within me. As I presented it, I noticed his eyes sparkled with intrigue.

"I must say," he began, his gaze still fixed on the tart, "there's a certain magic in how you've transformed this dessert into something almost... tangible."

My cheeks warmed at the compliment, and a strange sense of kinship flickered between us. "I believe every dessert has a story, and I aim to tell that story with each bite."

With a smile, he took a forkful of the tart, his eyes closing for a moment as he savored the flavors. When he opened them again, I could see genuine admiration shining through. "You have a gift. I'd love to discuss your vision further; perhaps we could collaborate on an exhibition that marries art and culinary creations."

My heart raced at the prospect. This distinguished gentleman, who seemed to embody the essence of Charleston's artistic soul, wanted to partner with me? "That sounds incredible!" I replied, my voice bubbling with excitement. "I'd love to explore that idea."

We spent the evening talking about our passions, sharing dreams and inspirations over the remaining pastries, and I learned his name was Samuel. He was an art curator with an eye for beauty in every form, and as he spoke about his experiences, I felt as if I had found a kindred spirit. Samuel proposed that we hold a showcase at the gallery, a night dedicated to desserts as art, an event that would bring the community together in celebration of creativity.

Days turned into weeks, and the plans unfolded beautifully. Samuel became a fixture in the bakery, often found sketching designs or tasting our newest creations, his presence a comforting shadow. The idea of blending our worlds ignited a fire within me, pushing me to craft desserts that would tell a story not just through taste but also through artistry. We worked tirelessly, fine-tuning every detail, transforming my small bakery into a vibrant workshop filled with color, creativity, and camaraderie.

As the day of the exhibition approached, I felt a thrill mingled with anxiety. Would our community embrace this new venture? The thought of presenting our work to an audience sent ripples of excitement through my veins. I found solace in the fact that Marisol, always my rock, stood beside me, her laughter a steady anchor in the whirlwind of preparations. Together, we painted the walls of the gallery with splashes of color, showcasing the textures and designs of our pastries.

On the night of the event, the gallery glowed under twinkling lights, a breathtaking backdrop for the desserts that adorned the tables like jewels. Guests began to arrive, their chatter a chorus of anticipation, and I stood nervously behind the table, watching as people marveled at the creations we had poured our hearts into. There were mini cheesecakes layered with hues of lavender and blue, delicate meringues shaped like blossoms, and a magnificent cake designed to resemble a vibrant sunset.

Samuel floated through the crowd like a conductor, drawing attention to the art of the desserts, weaving stories of inspiration and creativity. I caught snippets of laughter, applause, and excitement, my heart swelling with pride. The evening danced on, each bite a note in a symphony of flavor, each moment a stroke of color on the canvas of our collaboration.

As the crowd savored our creations, I overheard whispers of admiration and delight. "This is not just a dessert; it's an experience," one guest exclaimed, and I felt my heart lift at the affirmation. I had taken a leap into the unknown, and the embrace of my community felt like a warm hug, a confirmation that I had created something meaningful.

With every passing hour, I reveled in the joy of our success, but as the night unfolded, something shifted. The crowd began to swell, and a new energy crackled in the air. I turned to find a familiar face—James, a childhood friend I hadn't seen in years, weaving through the throng with a wide grin.

"Is this really you?" he exclaimed, his eyes sparkling with surprise. "I heard about the exhibition, and I had to see it for myself!"

I felt a rush of nostalgia wash over me, memories of our youthful days spent exploring the streets of Charleston flooding back. "James! I can't believe you're here!"

We embraced, laughter spilling from our lips as we exchanged stories of our lives since those carefree days. He leaned in closer, his voice dipping low. "I've always known you were destined for greatness, but this—this is extraordinary."

Our conversation flowed easily, the years apart fading into the background as we spoke of dreams and aspirations. It felt as if a door had been opened to a time when everything was possible.

With Samuel beside me, our collaboration not only created desserts that delighted the senses but also reawakened connections I thought had been lost. I realized that this journey, this blending of art and pastry, had drawn people together in ways I had never imagined.

As the evening reached its crescendo, Samuel raised his glass, his eyes shining with pride. "To new beginnings and creative partnerships! May we continue to inspire and uplift each other."

The clinking of glasses filled the air, a harmonious sound echoing through the gallery, and in that moment, I felt a profound sense of belonging. Luna's Sweet Retreat had transformed into more than just a bakery; it had become a sanctuary for creativity, a place where art and flavor danced together, a celebration of life itself.

As laughter and joy mingled in the warm Charleston air, I took a moment to reflect on the path that had led me here. From the simple confines of a bakery to a vibrant world filled with colors and flavors, I had unearthed not only my passion for pastry but also a renewed sense of purpose. The sweet aroma of change lingered around me, a reminder that sometimes the most beautiful creations come from daring to embrace the unknown.

Chapter 2: Beneath the Surface

The kitchen hummed with life, a cacophony of sizzling pans and the rhythmic thump of dough being kneaded. I could feel the heat rising around me, not just from the oven but from the growing excitement in the air. With each rise of the dough, my heart soared higher, anticipating the coming days of the baking competition. This was it—my moment to shine, to finally prove that I belonged in the culinary world. The scent of sugar and butter wrapped around me like a warm embrace, a promise of sweet triumph. I could almost taste the victory as I lined up my ingredients, each one a crucial piece in the puzzle of my ambition.

My small kitchen, tucked away in a vibrant neighborhood near the heart of Nashville, overflowed with the vibrant colors of summer. The sun poured through the window, painting everything in golden hues, reflecting the pride I felt in crafting delectable pastries. The whimsical décor—a mix of rustic farmhouse charm and modern flair—set the perfect backdrop for my culinary journey. From the chalkboard wall, scrawled with the day's baking plans, to the mismatched vintage plates lining the shelves, everything felt alive, an extension of my creative spirit.

It was in this haven that I met Ethan Walker, a name that would soon taste as sweet on my lips as the pastries I was preparing. He burst into my life like a splash of color on a gray canvas. His gallery, nestled just around the corner, was an eclectic mix of local artists and culinary masterpieces, a place where food met art in a deliciously vibrant dance. When I first entered, the air was thick with creativity, the walls adorned with canvases splashed in every imaginable shade, a feast for the eyes. And then there was Ethan, standing in the center like a maestro conducting a symphony, his passion as contagious as the aroma of freshly baked bread wafting through my kitchen.

Our introductions were like a playful pastry toss, unexpected yet thrilling. His smile was a mix of mischief and charm, a twinkle in his eyes that felt like a shared secret. "You must be the one stirring up all this competition," he said, leaning against the counter with an effortless grace that made my heart flutter. There was something about the way he held himself—confident yet approachable, a blend that invited conversation. "I've seen your creations; they have a flair that's hard to ignore."

His words were a sweet compliment, coating my insecurities in a sugary glaze. I felt a spark of connection as we began to share our stories, both of us drawn to the art of creation, though from different angles. His past as a pastry prodigy colored his insights, and I listened, enraptured, as he spoke of the struggles and triumphs of culinary artistry. The way he described each dish made my mouth water; his passion radiated like the warmth from the oven, enveloping me in a world I longed to explore.

We started collaborating, our late-night brainstorming sessions morphing into something more than just flour-covered hands and ideas bouncing off the walls. In the glow of my kitchen lights, we would laugh, mix batter, and throw around wild ideas for pastries that would steal the show. Each evening became a blend of laughter and creativity, a canvas where we painted our dreams with powdered sugar and chocolate ganache. With every whisk and fold, the tension between us simmered just beneath the surface, a thrilling current that neither of us dared to acknowledge.

I watched as Ethan maneuvered around my kitchen with a blend of confidence and artistry, each movement deliberate and fluid, like a dancer in the spotlight. He would reach over to sprinkle flour onto my cheek, a playful gesture that made my heart race. His laughter was infectious, filling the room and lifting my spirits even on the days when self-doubt threatened to overshadow my ambition. There was an undeniable chemistry between us, an electric undercurrent that crackled in the air whenever our eyes met, igniting something deep within me.

As we pushed through the late nights, the flour dust seemed to settle not just on our countertops but on our hearts. The stakes grew higher as the competition approached, each day marked by increasing pressure and the weight of expectations. My pastries transformed from mere recipes into vessels of hope, each one carrying a piece of my dreams and fears. Yet, amidst the chaos, Ethan remained my anchor, his unwavering belief in my talent grounding me.

I found myself grappling with an unfamiliar conflict—was my focus shifting from the competition to this budding connection? I would catch him studying me while I worked, a look of admiration in his eyes that made my cheeks flush. The way he effortlessly transitioned between chef and confidant made the line between ambition and attraction blur. Did he feel the same magnetic pull, or was it merely my imagination concocting a fantasy amidst the stress of baking?

With every passing day, the kitchen became our sanctuary, a sacred space where dreams rose alongside the pastries we created. The vibrant world around us faded as we focused on each delicate layer, every sprinkle of sugar, and the intricate dance of flavors. The competition loomed like a storm cloud, yet here, in this bubble we'd crafted, it felt distant, a mere whisper compared to the laughter and the flicker of something deeper between us.

But as the final days approached, the weight of reality began to settle in. I had come too far to let distractions derail my journey. My heart ached with the decision looming ahead, torn between my fierce ambition and the intoxicating allure of a connection I wasn't sure I was ready to embrace. Each pastry I crafted held the echoes of my dreams, yet Ethan's laughter lingered like the aroma of freshly baked bread, irresistible and warm, beckoning me to explore a world I hadn't dared to envision.

In this vibrant world of culinary creativity, I stood on the precipice of something monumental. Would I allow myself to dive into the depths of this connection, or would I rise above, fueled solely by ambition? The choice felt both exhilarating and terrifying, a testament to the power of dreams, love, and the tantalizing dance of destiny.

As the days rolled on, the baking competition loomed closer, casting an ever-growing shadow over our late-night sessions. Each moment spent with Ethan seemed to sharpen my focus, yet the very spark that ignited my passion for pastry also stirred a tumult of emotions that I struggled to navigate. In my kitchen, amid the flour clouds and sugar dust, he was both a muse and a distraction, igniting a flame that warmed my heart while simultaneously fanning the flames of my ambition.

Our collaborative efforts turned into a delightful dance, each of us effortlessly twirling around the kitchen, bouncing ideas off each other like the joyful sounds of a bustling café. I began to notice the way Ethan's hands moved, skilled and confident as he demonstrated techniques that seemed to transform the mundane into the extraordinary. The way he shaped dough, creating curves and edges with a precision that made my heart flutter, was a work of art in itself. With each playful nudge and floury toss, he coaxed laughter from me, a reminder that joy and passion were meant to coexist.

One evening, as the sunset spilled golden light through my kitchen window, we were caught in the throes of creativity, throwing out ideas for our signature dessert. The walls reverberated with our laughter, and the atmosphere crackled with unspoken tension. Ethan suggested a lavender-infused crème brûlée, the kind that whispered of warm summer evenings and the intoxicating scent of blooming flowers. I could already envision it—the delicate purple hues, the silky custard, and that satisfying crack as a spoon pierced the caramelized sugar crust. I could hardly contain my excitement.

"Lavender, huh? You really know how to elevate the ordinary," I teased, raising an eyebrow. "But do you think people will appreciate that kind of flavor?"

Ethan's gaze bore into mine, playful yet serious. "It's not about what they think. It's about what we feel. If we create from our hearts, they'll taste the love infused in every bite."

His words struck a chord deep within me, a reminder of why I had fallen in love with baking in the first place. It wasn't merely about competition or recognition; it was about the joy of creation, the delight in sharing something beautiful with the world. The warmth of his conviction wrapped around me, and for a moment, I could envision a life where our passions intertwined—his art and my pastries, a perfect duet.

As the night deepened, we dove deeper into conversation, weaving tales of our dreams and fears. Ethan spoke of his journey, how he had once dazzled audiences with his culinary prowess, only to retreat into the shadows after a series of setbacks that had left him questioning his path. There was a vulnerability in his voice that captivated me, making him even more endearing. I found myself wanting to shield him from the doubts that haunted him, just as I longed to shield my own heart from the distractions that danced around us.

In return, I shared snippets of my own struggles—the long nights spent perfecting recipes that sometimes crumbled, the moments of self-doubt that clawed at my confidence. Yet, as I spoke, I could feel the weight of my fears begin to lift. There was something about Ethan that made me want to reach for my dreams, to take risks I had previously shied away from. He made it seem possible to break free from the confines of my self-imposed limitations.

The kitchen became a sanctuary, a place where we could escape the pressures of the outside world. The sounds of our laughter mixed with the whir of the mixer, creating a melody that was uniquely ours. Yet, in the quiet moments between our bursts of creativity, the silence would pulse with unacknowledged longing, a shared glance or an accidental brush of our hands igniting a flame that simmered just beneath the surface.

I watched him one night as he meticulously plated a chocolate tart, each element placed with an artist's precision. The way his brow furrowed in concentration, the slight curve of his lips as he tasted the ganache—it was as if he were painting a masterpiece with chocolate rather than brush strokes. I couldn't help but feel drawn to him, my heart racing as if caught in a whirlwind. The familiar tug of ambition warred with an equally strong desire to lose myself in the moment, to savor this connection that felt both exhilarating and terrifying.

The tension reached its peak one evening when we found ourselves in the glow of candlelight, the remnants of our baking strewn about like confetti from a celebration. The air was thick with the aroma of vanilla and cinnamon, mingling with an electric anticipation that buzzed between us. Ethan leaned in closer, his voice a soft murmur that sent shivers down my spine. "You know, I never thought I'd meet someone who understood the passion behind this craft. You've reignited a spark in me that I thought had gone out."

His words hung in the air, heavy with meaning. I felt the heat radiating from him, the unspoken connection threatening to boil over. My heart raced, caught between the urge to step forward into that warmth and the instinct to hold back, to protect the fragile dream I was so close to achieving. "Ethan, I—" I started, my voice barely a whisper, yet the words felt like a heavy weight on my tongue.

But before I could finish, the sudden ringing of my phone shattered the moment, pulling me back into the reality of the looming competition. I glanced at the screen, a flurry of notifications reminding me of the tasks that awaited me, the pressure mounting like a soufflé on the brink of collapse. I excused myself, scrambling to regain my composure as I answered. Yet, even as I spoke, my thoughts remained tethered to Ethan, to that moment suspended in time where ambition and attraction danced tantalizingly close.

As the days raced forward, the reality of the competition cast a shadow over our culinary escapades. I poured my heart into my creations, fueled by Ethan's unwavering support. Every pastry became a love letter to the journey I had embarked upon, and with each bake, I could feel my resolve solidifying. Still, the tension between us loomed larger than life, a silent acknowledgment that lingered in the air, teasing us both as we navigated the delicate balance between our budding connection and the fervor of competition.

In this vibrant world where sugar and ambition intertwined, I found myself caught in a whirlwind of emotion. My heart and mind wrestled for dominance, each moment filled with the sweet taste of dreams waiting to be realized and the intoxicating pull of a connection that could change everything. The competition was on the horizon, but so was something deeper, something that felt just as vital. With each passing day, I felt the stakes rising—both for my pastries and for the uncharted territory of my heart.

As the competition approached, each day became a delicate balancing act of ambition and desire, the very essence of my baking journey. The air buzzed with excitement and trepidation, filling my kitchen with an energy that pulsed like a beating heart. I had adorned my workspace with notes and sketches, a chaotic tapestry of my culinary aspirations. Ingredients lay scattered, each bag a promise of flavors yet to be unlocked, the scents of fresh herbs and zesty citrus mingling in a tantalizing dance.

Ethan remained a constant presence, a warm glow that lingered like the sweet aroma of vanilla. He would often drop by unannounced, armed with quirky culinary tools and ideas that made my heart skip a beat. One evening, as I measured flour with meticulous precision, he tossed a box of vibrant edible flowers onto the counter, their colors a vibrant explosion against the stark white backdrop of my kitchen. "Imagine a lemon tart adorned with these beauties," he suggested, his voice a melodic whisper that filled the room with warmth. "A taste of summer on a plate."

I could hardly contain my enthusiasm. The idea unfurled in my mind like a blooming garden. "It's perfect! The tartness of the lemon, the sweetness of the flowers—it's a marriage made in culinary heaven!" I felt a surge of inspiration, my heart racing at the thought of creating something truly special. Together, we began crafting, our laughter mingling with the sound of whisking, the crunch of the knife slicing through fruits, and the soft thud of butter hitting the warm pan.

But beneath the laughter, the undeniable tension persisted, an electric charge that crackled in the spaces between us. I caught myself stealing glances at Ethan when he wasn't looking, observing the way his hands moved with effortless grace, or the way he bit his lip in concentration. There was a magnetic pull between us that felt like the gentle tug of a rising dough, both enticing and tantalizing. I sensed that he felt it too, the way his eyes lingered just a moment longer when our hands brushed, a shared spark igniting the air.

As our days blurred into a whirlwind of creativity and late-night brainstorming, I began to feel a sense of urgency settle within me. The competition was no longer just an opportunity to showcase my skills; it had morphed into a test of everything I believed in. Would I allow myself to be vulnerable? Could I step into the spotlight, not just as a baker, but as someone willing to explore the depths of a connection I had never anticipated?

One fateful evening, after a particularly long day in the kitchen, I found myself alone with Ethan, the flickering candlelight casting a warm glow around us. We had just finished a trial run of our signature dessert, the lemon tart adorned with edible flowers. The flavors danced on my palate, a symphony of sweetness and tang, yet my thoughts were miles away, tethered to the palpable tension simmering just beneath the surface.

"Can I be honest with you?" Ethan's voice broke through my reverie, low and sincere, the playful mischief replaced by something more profound. "This competition, it scares me. I've seen how fiercely you approach your baking, how much it means to you, and it makes me wonder if I still have that passion in me."

His vulnerability struck me like a lightning bolt, a raw honesty that resonated in the depths of my heart. I had always admired his confidence, but hearing him admit his fears made him all the more human. "You have that passion, Ethan," I replied, my voice steady, grounding us both in the moment. "It's in every dessert you create, every idea you share. You have the gift, and I believe in you."

For a moment, we sat in silence, the weight of my words hanging in the air, thick and rich like a chocolate ganache. The flickering candlelight danced between us, casting shadows that mirrored the myriad of emotions swirling in my heart. But the silence was pregnant with anticipation, the air thickening with unspoken words. As our gazes locked, I felt the distance between us evaporate, the yearning surging to the forefront, demanding acknowledgment.

Ethan took a step closer, the warmth radiating from him enveloping me like a comforting blanket. "You're more than just a talented baker, you know," he murmured, his voice barely above a whisper. "You inspire me to create, to push boundaries. I want to be part of your journey, wherever it leads."

Before I could respond, he closed the gap, his lips brushing softly against mine, igniting a fire within me that burned brighter than the flames of my oven. It was a kiss that tasted of sugar and longing, a sweet melding of our dreams and aspirations, a promise wrapped in the delicate folds of hope. As we pulled away, reality came rushing back, the competition looming large like a storm cloud threatening to rain on our moment of bliss.

The next few days passed in a blur of heightened emotions and fervent baking. The tension between us had transformed into an exhilarating dance, each touch a reminder of our budding connection. I poured my heart into my pastries, imbuing them with the essence of what we were becoming—an intricate tapestry of flavors and feelings.

However, the looming competition loomed like a shadow, casting doubts and fears that I had to confront. I spent sleepless nights perfecting my recipes, each ingredient carefully chosen, each technique meticulously executed. The stakes felt higher than ever, and with every moment spent in the kitchen, I wrestled with the duality of my ambitions.

One evening, as I prepared for the final stretch leading up to the competition, I found myself reflecting on the whirlwind of emotions that had swept through my life. I stood in front of the mirror, my apron dusted with flour, hair slightly tousled, and for the first time, I didn't just see a baker. I saw a woman on the precipice of embracing her dreams, with someone equally passionate by her side.

The day of the competition arrived with a fervor that electrified the air. The venue buzzed with energy, the scent of baked goods mingling with the anxious anticipation of competitors and judges alike. As I set up my station, I caught a glimpse of Ethan across the room, his eyes locking onto mine, a reassuring smile gracing his lips. In that moment, the weight of the world seemed to lift, and I felt emboldened to chase my dreams.

With each dish I prepared, I poured every ounce of my heart and soul into my creations, determined to make a mark. And as I glanced at Ethan, I realized that no matter the outcome, I was already a winner—my passion for baking reignited, my heart open to possibilities, and the promise of something beautiful just beginning to unfold. In the symphony of flavors and dreams, I knew that together, we would navigate whatever challenges lay ahead, ready to embrace the sweetness of life that awaited us.

Chapter 3: Whispers of Doubt

The sun hung low in the sky, casting a golden hue over the cobblestone streets of our small town, where the whispers of the farmers' market danced on the breeze, inviting us in like old friends. My heart thrummed in rhythm with the bustling energy around me, a perfect backdrop for what felt like the beginning of something extraordinary. I scanned the colorful stalls overflowing with vibrant produce, artisanal cheeses, and flowers that seemed to shout their beauty in unison, their scents mingling like old secrets shared among lovers. It was a scene straight out of a postcard, yet here I was, weaving through the crowd, holding Ethan's hand, feeling like a protagonist in a romance novel yet uncertain of the plot twists lurking just ahead.

Ethan, with his easy laughter and warm, deep-set eyes, appeared to fit seamlessly into this picturesque tableau. As he paused at a stand bursting with heirloom tomatoes, I watched him pick one up, rolling it between his fingers as if it held the answers to the universe. "Look at this one! It's perfect," he said, grinning at me, and for a moment, the world around us melted away. I smiled back, drawn to the way he seemed to illuminate everything in his orbit. But just as quickly, the moment shattered when he turned to discuss the vendor's selection, a shadow flitting across his face, replaced by a tightness in his jaw that didn't go unnoticed.

The vibrant life around me faded slightly as Sarah's warning echoed in my mind. "He's trouble." I shook my head, willing her voice to dissipate like the steam rising from the fresh tamales sizzling in their pots. I had come to trust Sarah's instincts, her ability to see through façades that most people, including myself, often overlooked. Yet here I was, irresistibly drawn to the very thing she cautioned me against. I pushed the thought aside, determined to focus on the moment, but a nagging feeling settled in my stomach, twisting uncomfortably, like the roots of a weed entangled with the flowers I sought.

As Ethan chatted animatedly with the vendor, I couldn't help but notice the way his laughter sometimes didn't reach his eyes, those deep wells of emotion that seemed to harbor secrets. A pang of doubt shot through me, a sharp contrast to the warmth radiating from the stalls laden with produce. I took a deep breath, inhaling the scents of cinnamon and fresh bread, trying to anchor myself. After all, he had invited me out today to share something he loved, and I was determined not to let my insecurities spoil it.

"Have you ever tried a tomato like this?" he asked, his enthusiasm contagious as he handed me the fruit, its skin gleaming under the sunlight. I took it from him, feeling the weight in my palm, and nodded, forcing a smile. "Not one this pretty, that's for sure." We both chuckled, and in that moment, the doubt momentarily faded, replaced by the thrill of the unknown, the delicious sense of adventure coursing through me.

We wandered further, losing ourselves in the sights and sounds, Ethan stopping every few steps to sample a new flavor or admire a piece of handmade jewelry. I reveled in his presence, the ease of our laughter mingling with the chirps of nearby cicadas, the air heavy with the fragrance of blooming flowers and freshly harvested produce. Yet, every now and then, my gaze would catch his distant stare, like he was glimpsing something far beyond the market, his laughter slightly forced, an echo of something deeper lurking beneath the surface.

When we finally came across a stall selling artisanal lemonade, I ordered us each a cup, the cool liquid a perfect antidote to the warm afternoon. As I took a sip, I felt the refreshing tartness dance across my tongue, a burst of sweetness that made me giggle. "Now, this is what summer is about," I declared, raising my cup to him. He mirrored my action, but his eyes were still clouded, a storm brewing behind that charming facade. "Yeah, I guess so," he replied, but the edge in his tone sent a shiver down my spine.

"Ethan, are you okay?" I asked, the question slipping from my lips before I could catch it. He hesitated, and for a heartbeat, the laughter and chaos of the market fell away, leaving just the two of us standing beneath the canopy of intertwined branches, their leaves whispering secrets. His gaze shifted, his smile faltering as if he was about to reveal a truth that could shatter everything.

"Yeah, just...thinking," he finally replied, but the way he looked away, the tightness around his lips, told me it was much more than that. I had a choice now, to press further or to let it go, to seek the truth or to remain blissfully ignorant. I wanted to trust him, wanted to believe in the whirlwind romance that felt like a dream, but the shadows in his smile seemed to flicker and dance just beyond my reach.

As we continued to stroll through the market, I couldn't shake the feeling that beneath the surface of his charm lay something more complicated. Each laugh, each glance shared, felt imbued with unspoken words, truths cloaked in mystery. The market buzzed around us, a vibrant tapestry of life and laughter, but I found myself standing at the edge of a precipice, staring into the unknown, my heart pounding with anticipation and fear alike.

A burst of laughter nearby pulled me from my thoughts, the sounds of children playing, parents chatting, and vendors hawking their goods swirling around me. It was a world alive with joy, yet here I was, caught in the crosshairs of doubt. I couldn't help but wonder, was I chasing a mirage, or was Ethan truly the captivating soul I wanted him to be?

The clamor of the market swirled around me like a vibrant painting come to life, colors splashing across my vision as I maneuvered between booths. Ethan's laughter, a melody against the backdrop of chatter and clinking jars, tugged at my heart. Yet, beneath his charming surface, the feeling of unease nestled deeper, like a stubborn splinter refusing to dislodge. I caught a glimpse of him speaking to a couple who owned the local bakery, his hands animatedly gesturing as he shared an inside joke. The warmth in his voice was infectious, and for a moment, I was caught up in the spell he cast over everyone in the vicinity. Still, those shadows loomed—glimpses of a darker undertow hidden beneath his radiant exterior.

As we approached a stand adorned with a patchwork of fragrant herbs, I plucked a sprig of basil, inhaling its earthy aroma. "This could be perfect for that pasta dish I've been dying to make," I said, half-heartedly trying to distract myself from the thoughts that swirled like autumn leaves in the wind. Ethan leaned closer, his shoulder brushing against mine, the warmth igniting a spark that momentarily lit the doubts flickering in my mind.

"Basil, huh?" he mused, a playful smirk dancing on his lips. "I have a secret ingredient that could take your dish to the next level." His eyes twinkled with mischief, and I couldn't help but grin back, surrendering to the playful banter that often felt like a refuge from the growing storm of uncertainty.

"What's that?" I prompted, tilting my head in feigned curiosity, desperate to draw him into lighthearted conversation.

"Love," he replied, his tone teasing but with a genuine warmth that sent a thrill racing through me. But the moment hung, suspended in air, and as his gaze flickered past me toward a distant corner of the market, I felt that familiar chill creep back in.

"Ethan," I began, feeling the weight of my own curiosity, "what's on your mind?"

His response came in a hesitant sigh, the kind that spoke of burdens unshared. "Just...thinking about some things."

"Care to share?" I pressed gently, the urgency of my need to know slipping from my tongue before I could reel it back.

He turned to me, the sunlight catching the golden flecks in his eyes, but the shadows loomed large. "It's nothing, really. Just stuff from my past. Nothing worth worrying about."

The revelation caught me off guard. I felt my heart tighten, caught between wanting to pry deeper and respecting his boundaries. I held his gaze, searching for the truth hidden within. There was a flicker of something vulnerable behind his charm, a glimmer that made my chest ache. But then, as quickly as it appeared, the moment retreated, swallowed by the buoyant laughter of nearby children chasing bubbles that glistened in the afternoon sun.

Our playful banter dwindled, replaced by an unspoken tension as we wandered deeper into the market. I couldn't help but feel as if I were chasing shadows—trying to grasp something elusive, yet the threads seemed to slip through my fingers, leaving only a lingering sense of uncertainty.

We eventually reached a corner where a local artist displayed her vivid paintings of landscapes and cityscapes, each canvas alive with color and emotion. One piece in particular caught my eye—a tumultuous sea crashing against rugged cliffs, the deep blues and grays contrasting with the warm tones of the setting sun. "This one is stunning," I murmured, stepping closer to admire the brushstrokes that seemed to tell a story all their own.

"Yeah, I love how chaotic it is," Ethan remarked, his voice softening as he stepped beside me, shoulder brushing against mine. "Like life, you know? Beautiful, messy, unpredictable."

I turned to him, intrigued by the depth in his words. "And you think life is chaotic?"

He shrugged, his gaze drifting toward the canvas. "Sometimes. You can't really control the waves, can you? You just have to ride them."

The metaphor hung in the air, resonating with the turmoil within me. I wondered if he was talking about more than just the art.

"Is that how you see it?" I asked, my voice barely above a whisper, the vulnerability in the question raw and unguarded.

He hesitated, his eyes narrowing slightly as he studied me. "It's just something I've learned over time." The shadows returned to his face, and I felt a pang of regret for probing deeper. I wanted to know what had shaped him into this beautiful, complicated person, yet I was terrified of the answer.

"Maybe the waves are what make us stronger," I suggested, my heart pounding as I turned the conversation back to something lighter, something I could control. "Like in surfing. You have to fall a few times before you really catch the wave."

Ethan chuckled, and the sound was a balm to my fraying nerves. "True, but it's the getting back up that counts."

As we continued to meander through the stalls, sampling peaches and homemade jams, I watched Ethan closely, studying the way he interacted with the vendors, how he genuinely engaged with them, a hint of something reminiscent of tenderness in his voice. I was enchanted, but I couldn't escape the shadows, the whispers of doubt that still clung to the edges of my mind.

A few minutes later, we found ourselves by a stand selling fresh-baked pastries. The scent wafted through the air, sweet and buttery, wrapping around me like a comforting hug. I ordered a flaky croissant, its golden layers glistening with promise. As I took my first bite, the pastry crumbled in my fingers, a delightful mess that mirrored the chaos swirling inside my heart.

"Delicious, right?" Ethan said, watching me with an amused expression as crumbs decorated my chin.

"Absolutely," I replied, attempting to clean up my mess, laughter spilling between us like the sunlight bathing the market. But just as quickly as the moment blossomed, it dimmed when I caught a glimpse of something shadowed in his gaze again—a fleeting thought darting behind those expressive eyes, something unspoken, untold.

"Ethan, what's really bothering you?" I asked again, more insistent this time, my heart racing with the urgency of knowing him fully.

He hesitated, and the weight of silence stretched between us like a taut string ready to snap. "It's complicated, really," he finally said, his voice low.

"Try me," I urged, leaning closer, feeling a connection that transcended words, an unspoken understanding that felt almost magical.

He let out a slow breath, running a hand through his tousled hair, the sunlight catching the strands and illuminating the softness of his features. "I guess I just want to make sure I'm not dragging anyone down with me."

The heaviness of his words settled around us, and I felt an unexpected warmth fill the space. "You're not dragging me down, Ethan. I want to be here."

The openness hung in the air, a moment where vulnerability danced dangerously close to hope, and I wondered if perhaps we were both riding the waves of uncertainty together, navigating a storm we had yet to name.

The tension in the air thickened, swirling around us like the aroma of cinnamon mingling with the sweetness of ripe strawberries at the next stall. I took a moment to absorb the reality of our surroundings: couples strolled hand in hand, families laughed over shared treats, and laughter mingled with the distant sound of a local musician strumming a guitar, his voice a melodic embrace that echoed softly through the market. Yet here we were, standing at the precipice of something undefined, our laughter painted over a canvas of uncertainties.

Ethan shifted slightly, his posture tense yet somehow elegant, as if he was a figure carved from the same marble as the statue in the town square. He had a way of grounding the space around him, transforming the mundane into something extraordinary, yet the shadows in his eyes told another story. "I guess I've just been running from my past," he confessed, the weight of his words pressing down like the humid air around us. "There are things about me I'd rather not bring into your world."

His vulnerability struck a chord within me, resonating like a haunting melody. "But isn't that what makes us who we are?" I ventured, instinctively reaching for his hand, intertwining my fingers with his. "We all carry stories. They shape us, but they don't have to define us."

His gaze softened, but there was still a flicker of resistance lurking behind it. "Maybe. But some stories can drag you under."

In that moment, I felt a pang of longing to unravel the threads of his narrative, to understand the shadows that haunted him. But just as quickly, I was reminded of Sarah's words, her worry lingering like a faint echo. I wanted to assure her, to tell her that I was fully capable of discerning what was safe, yet the question clawed at my resolve: Could I truly navigate the depths of Ethan's complexities without getting lost myself?

We resumed walking, the vibrant market unfolding before us like a living tapestry, each stall a story in its own right. As we approached a booth draped with colorful scarves, I felt a shift in the energy around us. The vendor, an elderly woman with twinkling eyes and a welcoming smile, beckoned us closer. "Come, come! Choose something that speaks to you!"

Ethan hesitated, his focus shifting from the scarves to the vendor, and I watched the internal battle play out in his expression. "You should pick one," I encouraged, hoping to lighten the mood. "It's a perfect way to add some color to your wardrobe."

His lips curled into a hesitant smile, the shadows briefly receding. "Alright, but only if you choose one too."

As I sifted through the vibrant fabrics, each one alive with its own story, I felt a spark of excitement. I found a deep emerald scarf, its rich hue reminiscent of the forest after a rainstorm, and held it up, imagining the warmth it would bring against the chill of autumn. "What do you think?" I asked, holding it up to my face.

Ethan's eyes lit up, and for a fleeting moment, he looked genuinely pleased. "That one suits you perfectly. It brings out the color in your eyes."

"Flattery will get you everywhere," I teased, draping the scarf around my neck. I watched as he searched through the scarves, and when he finally chose a bright maroon one, I couldn't help but laugh at the contrast. "Are you sure you can pull that off?"

"Watch me," he grinned, wrapping it around his neck with a flourish that made me giggle. The moment felt lighter, the weight of our previous conversation drifting like dandelion seeds on the breeze.

We paid for our scarves and continued wandering, the market alive with a blend of colors, sounds, and scents. Yet, even as I reveled in the moment, the undercurrent of doubt clung to me like an unshakable shadow, whispering that perhaps I was still ignoring the warning signs. The idea of unearthing Ethan's truths was both thrilling and terrifying, a tantalizing dance on the edge of a cliff.

As the sun began to dip lower in the sky, casting long shadows across the market, I noticed a local bakery stall at the far end. The tantalizing scent of freshly baked bread wafted toward us, drawing us in like moths to a flame. "We should grab something sweet," I suggested, my mouth watering at the thought of pastries.

"Only if we can share," Ethan replied, his playful tone returning as we approached the stall. The baker, a jovial man with flour-dusted hands and a welcoming grin, offered us a selection of treats, each one more decadent than the last. I settled on a chocolate croissant, its flaky layers beckoning me closer.

As we stood there, indulging in our pastries, Ethan seemed to relax, the tension dissipating like the steam rising from a cup of hot coffee. "You know," he said between bites, "this is the best thing I've done all week."

I couldn't help but smile, feeling the warmth of his compliment seep into my bones. "I'm glad I could help make your week a little sweeter."

Just then, the sun slipped below the horizon, painting the sky in hues of orange and purple, the world around us transforming into a magical realm. The market glowed under strings of fairy lights that twinkled to life, illuminating the laughter and conversations of friends and families.

Yet, even in this picturesque moment, a cloud lingered over my heart. Ethan's laughter was infectious, yet I couldn't shake the feeling that something was still lurking beneath the surface. I had seen the complexity in him—the hesitations, the shadows in his smile—but there was also a genuine connection that I didn't want to lose.

As we finished our treats and began to wander toward the exit, I caught sight of a local art installation, vibrant murals depicting scenes of life in our town. The colors bled into one another, creating a tapestry of experiences and emotions that mirrored our own journey. "Look at that!" I exclaimed, pulling Ethan toward the wall. "Isn't it beautiful?"

"It really is," he agreed, his eyes tracing the artwork with a mix of admiration and something deeper. As we stood before the mural, I felt an urge to ask him about his story, to dive into the depths of his past, but I hesitated. Instead, I decided to share a piece of my own. "You know, I've always thought of art as a reflection of who we are. It captures moments, feelings... It makes everything feel alive."

Ethan turned to me, a thoughtful expression crossing his face. "That's a beautiful way to look at it. I think that's what makes connections so special. They're like those murals—layered, complex, and vibrant."

I met his gaze, heart pounding as I felt the unspoken understanding wrap around us like the colors of the mural. "Then maybe it's time we start sharing those layers."

His expression shifted, the shadows returning momentarily before he took a step closer, closing the distance between us. "You're right. I think it's time."

In that moment, under the flickering lights and vibrant murals, I sensed a shift, an opening—a door to the depths of his past that I longed to explore. And as we stood together, surrounded by the beauty of our small town, I couldn't help but wonder if perhaps the waves we were riding would lead us both to shores we had yet to discover, weaving our stories together like the threads of a tapestry.

Chapter 4: Recipe for Heartbreak

The lights of the competition venue blaze above me, a constellation of hope and anxiety illuminating the polished hardwood floors that gleam like freshly unwrapped candy. It's the kind of day that swells with promise, the air tinged with the sweet notes of chocolate and the sharp, citrusy scent of lemon tarts waiting to be assembled. My heart races as I move through the chaos, weaving between camera crews and judges who parade around like triumphant monarchs in a culinary kingdom. Each tick of the clock sends a pulse of urgency through the room, as if the very walls are holding their breath alongside me.

I stand at my station, surrounded by a kaleidoscope of ingredients—ripe berries in every shade, chocolate tempered to a glossy sheen, and pastry dough that has been coaxed into delicate shapes. The centerpiece of my creation, a towering chocolate sculpture, rises elegantly, its curves echoing the grace of a dancer mid-twirl. Inside, the vibrant fruit tarts wait like hidden treasures, promising bursts of flavor with every bite. I can't help but glance toward Ethan, who stands on the sidelines, his expression a canvas painted with encouragement and pride. His dark hair is tousled just so, and the way he leans forward, almost breathless with anticipation, sends a thrill through me.

But just as the warmth of his gaze washes over me, it's interrupted by a flurry of whispers that dance through the air like unwelcome confetti. "Did you hear about Ethan?" one contestant murmurs, her voice dripping with intrigue. "He had a restaurant, but it fell apart. Something about betrayal... It's all anyone can talk about."

The words slice through my focus, leaving a raw, jagged edge in their wake. Betrayal? My heart stutters. My hands, steady until this moment, tremble slightly as I reach for my spatula, a fine tool that suddenly feels foreign in my grip. I've always prided myself on my ability to create beauty and flavor, to translate emotion into edible art, but now I feel as though I'm standing on quicksand, every part of me wavering as the ground shifts beneath my feet.

I catch a glimpse of Emma, the source of the whispers, her confidence radiating from her as she shapes a perfect crème brûlée. The golden custard glistens under the bright lights, and I can't help but feel a pang of envy mixed with resentment. She's the kind of contestant who thrives on competition, a fierce warrior in an apron, and here she is, casting shadows over my brightest moment. My thoughts spiral like a tornado; the delicious tarts and the carefully crafted chocolate tower blur as doubt takes root.

Suddenly, the venue feels stifling, the air thick with a cocktail of tension and uncertainty. I glance around, trying to ground myself in the vibrant chaos. The hum of conversation, punctuated by bursts of laughter, melds with the clanging of pots and pans—a symphony of culinary ambition. Yet, I feel isolated in this bustling world, my dreams inching away as I grapple with the gnawing fear that perhaps Ethan, with his charming smile and magnetic presence, is not the ally I thought he was.

My mind races back to the fleeting moments we've shared—the way he leaned in close, the warmth of his voice as he shared cooking tips that felt like secrets meant just for me. It's impossible to reconcile the tender moments with the idea of betrayal. I force myself to focus on my creation, the beauty of it, the intricate detailing that has consumed my waking hours.

"Just breathe," I whisper to myself, casting a glance at Ethan, who seems to sense my unease. He catches my eye and gives a slight nod, the corners of his mouth curving upward as though he understands my turmoil. In that moment, I want to believe that he's different, that the whispers are merely smoke, illusions that can't touch the truth of who he is.

With renewed determination, I dive back into my work, carefully assembling the tarts and placing them within the chocolate shell. Each movement becomes a meditation, a way to drown out the chaos around me. The other contestants, driven by their own ambitions, whirl around like fireflies in the summer dusk, their laughter ringing through the air, a soundtrack to my internal struggle. But as I pipe the delicate pastry cream into each tart shell, I can feel the weight of uncertainty press against me, demanding my attention.

Time slips away, hours collapsing into minutes as I place the final garnish on my masterpiece. The judges are making their rounds, their discerning eyes scanning the creations that surround me, and I can feel the electricity in the air—the palpable thrill of competition mingling with the bittersweet taste of anxiety.

I glance back at Ethan. There's something in his gaze that pulls me toward him, a flicker of understanding that goes beyond words. As the competition builds to a crescendo, I silently plead for clarity, for resolution. The whispers may haunt me, but the choice remains mine. I can either succumb to the weight of doubt or embrace the passion that brought me here in the first place.

With a final flourish, I present my creation, my heart pounding in my chest like a war drum, ready for battle. The world around me fades as I step forward, drawing strength from the very essence of what I've crafted—a delicate balance of flavors and textures, a representation of my journey. I hope, against all odds, that it's enough to silence the whispers, to rise above the shadows of uncertainty. And as I take a deep breath, the excitement mingling with the remnants of doubt, I realize that whatever happens next, this moment is mine.

As the judges begin their meticulous examination, my heart performs an awkward tango between hope and despair. Each step they take toward my creation sends a fresh wave of adrenaline coursing through my veins, invigorating yet terrifying. Their expressions are unreadable, masked behind a facade of professionalism that feels almost impenetrable. I watch as they lean in closer, scrutinizing the interplay of chocolate and fruit that I've crafted with the utmost care. The silence stretches, each tick of the clock echoing louder than the last, amplifying the tension that hangs in the air.

Ethan's gaze doesn't waver; he remains anchored in his spot, an unwavering lighthouse amidst the swirling fog of uncertainty. His presence is a balm, a soothing reminder that not all is lost, yet the whispers nag at me like a persistent itch. I catch fragments of Emma's words floating in and out of my thoughts, accusing shadows that loom over the sunlight of our budding connection. The betrayal, the past—those words claw at my confidence, threatening to unravel everything I've fought for.

The first judge, a formidable woman with striking silver hair that cascades like a waterfall down her back, extends a hand toward my sculpture. Her fingers brush against the chocolate, and I can't help but hold my breath. It's a small gesture, but the weight of it feels monumental, as if she were deciding the fate of my culinary dreams with that delicate touch. She lifts a piece of chocolate, allowing it to glisten under the bright lights before taking a bite. The moment stretches, every second heavy with anticipation, and I feel as if the entire room has paused, holding its breath alongside me.

Her expression transforms as the flavors unfold—an eruption of surprise and delight dances across her features, followed by a contemplative nod. The relief floods through me, but the shadows lurking in the corners of my mind refuse to fade. I catch Ethan's eye again, his supportive smile emboldening me. But the gnawing suspicion creeps back, begging to be acknowledged. Is he just a figment of my hopeful imagination, or could he be hiding the very truths I dread?

One by one, the judges taste my creation, their critiques veering from the technical to the poetic. They discuss the balance of sweetness and acidity, the craftsmanship of the chocolate, the vivid colors of the fruits. Yet I remain ensnared in my web of uncertainty, my mind swirling with doubts and fantasies, crafting a narrative that spins too fast for me to grasp. Emma's voice echoes in my ears, and I wonder if she's somehow entangled in the storyline of my life, casting herself as the antagonist.

As the tasting concludes, I feel a mix of pride and vulnerability, like a tightrope walker who has successfully navigated a treacherous path but still has to make it back. The judges confer among themselves, their serious expressions a reminder that the moment of judgment looms closer. I shift my weight from foot to foot, each step a reminder of the hours I spent perfecting this masterpiece, of the moments of doubt and inspiration that fueled my creativity. I picture my small kitchen, the hum of my oven, the way the ingredients came together like a carefully orchestrated symphony, and I realize that no matter what happens next, I poured my soul into this.

Finally, the lead judge steps forward, her gaze piercing as she meets mine. "Your creation is exquisite," she begins, her voice a melody laced with authority. "The balance of flavors is impressive, and the execution is masterful." Relief washes over me, warm and enveloping like a hug from an old friend. But then she pauses, and my heart stutters. "However, we must consider not only the presentation but also the story behind the dish."

Her words hang in the air, a tantalizing mix of promise and peril. As she continues to speak, I realize that the very essence of my dish—the love, the struggle, the triumph over self-doubt—has become entwined with my personal narrative. But what story do I tell? The joyous moments with Ethan, the playful banter, or the darker whispers of betrayal and heartbreak? I want to share it all, to expose my vulnerabilities, but the fear of judgment looms large, ready to snatch away my courage like a thief in the night.

In that moment, a connection sparks between me and Ethan across the bustling room. He smiles, not just with his lips but with his entire being, and the warmth of it seeps into my bones. The doubts still swirl around me, but they begin to lose their grip, melting away like chocolate on a warm day. Suddenly, the competition feels less like a battleground and more like a celebration of passion, resilience, and, dare I say it, love.

With newfound clarity, I step forward, ready to speak my truth. "This dish is a reflection of my journey," I begin, my voice steady and firm, resonating through the tension in the room. I share the story of my late-night baking sessions, the struggles I faced in finding my voice in a world that often feels stifling. I weave in tales of small victories and the thrill of discovering new flavors. And yes, I touch upon the swirling emotions that accompany every bite, the sweetness of connection and the bitterness of uncertainty.

As I speak, I catch Ethan's eye again, his gaze unwavering, a reminder that vulnerability can be a powerful ally. The competition fades away; it's just me and the audience, my heart laid bare. The judges nod thoughtfully, their expressions shifting from scrutiny to appreciation. I can see them absorbing my words, letting them mingle with the flavors on their palettes, allowing my story to resonate with their own experiences.

When I finish, the room erupts in applause, and I feel a swell of gratitude that threatens to burst from my chest. In that moment, the doubts that haunted me begin to dissolve, replaced by the shimmering realization that I have created not just a dish, but a connection—between myself and those around me, between the flavors I love and the stories that shape me.

The judges deliberate one final time, and as they speak, my heart races anew. The world is not just a place of competition but a canvas for expression, a melting pot of experiences that can inspire and unite. I take a deep breath, letting it all wash over me, ready to embrace whatever comes next. After all, sometimes, the sweetest victories come from daring to be vulnerable.

A cacophony of applause reverberates through the air, mingling with the scent of melting chocolate and fresh fruit. The judges' deliberation feels like a tide pulling me in multiple directions—relief, hope, anxiety, and the ghostly tendrils of doubt that still linger in the back of my mind. I allow myself a small smile, buoyed by the reception, yet I can't shake the feeling that a storm brews just beneath the surface. Ethan's encouraging smile remains a steadfast beacon, but the rumors weigh heavily on my heart like a leaden anchor.

As the judges gather at the front of the stage, their expressions are serious, each face carefully schooled in neutrality. They confer in hushed tones, glancing occasionally at the other contestants, and my mind races through the implications of what they might say. I've always thrived on the thrill of competition, the sharp edges of excitement, yet today feels different, tinged with an unsettling mix of vulnerability and tenacity. I run a hand through my hair, feeling the soft tendrils slip between my fingers like the fleeting moments of confidence that have eluded me.

Amidst the excitement, I scan the audience, my heart racing when I spot Emma again. She's standing with her fellow contestants, her arms crossed defiantly, as if she's guarding a treasure that only she knows exists. The way her lips curl into a smirk as she meets my gaze ignites a flicker of animosity within me. I know this competition is fierce, but there's an undercurrent of rivalry in her demeanor that feels personal, as if she's weaponized the rumors surrounding Ethan to take me down a peg. The thought of her using his past against me gnaws at my resolve, but deep down, I know that I must find a way to stand tall.

The judges' voices finally break through the haze of my thoughts. "It's not just about taste," the lead judge states, her tone firm but fair. "It's about the story you tell through your food. The emotion behind your work." My heart swells at her words, each syllable striking a chord that reverberates through me. This is why I cook; it's more than mere sustenance—it's a language, a form of expression that transcends the ingredients themselves.

As they begin to announce the finalists, the world around me blurs into an indistinct swirl of color and sound. When my name is finally called, it feels like a jolt of electricity, a pulse of life surging through my veins. I'm suddenly thrust into the spotlight, the dazzling glow of the stage lighting casting my shadow across the floor. I rise to my feet, my heart pounding in rhythm with the applause, and I take a moment to breathe, letting the reality wash over me.

Ethan stands among the audience, his face lit up with genuine pride. His eyes sparkle like stars against the backdrop of the venue, and I can't help but feel the warmth of connection envelop me. Yet, the specter of doubt still lingers, and the shadows of Emma's whispers dance at the edge of my consciousness. I turn my focus inward, grounding myself in the moment, savoring the triumph as if it were the sweetest chocolate ganache.

As I take my place among the finalists, the atmosphere shifts. It feels charged, crackling with excitement and unspoken competition. The other contestants stand beside me, their expressions a mix of determination and vulnerability, each one a narrative unto themselves. The camaraderie feels electric, but so does the tension, weaving an intricate tapestry of ambition and dreams.

The final round commences, and we're tasked with creating a dish that embodies our unique culinary perspective. The clock ticks down, and I'm drawn into a whirlwind of flavors and creativity, every pulse of time urging me to dig deeper, to unearth the essence of what

I truly want to convey. I sift through my ingredients, my mind racing with possibilities—how do I encapsulate my journey, the essence of resilience, and the courage it takes to follow one's heart?

Suddenly, a burst of inspiration strikes. I envision a dessert that symbolizes not just sweetness but also the bittersweet moments that have shaped me. I decide on a deconstructed pavlova, with a cloud of meringue that represents the lightness of hope, nestled atop a tart citrus curd that embodies the tang of struggle. Each vibrant berry that adorns the dish is a reminder of the beauty found even in moments of despair, a visual representation of the complexity of emotions that swirl within me.

As I work, I can feel the adrenaline pulsing through me, heightening my senses. The kitchen is a symphony of sounds—the rhythmic chopping of fruit, the crackle of sugar caramelizing, and the distant hum of the audience murmuring their anticipation. Each sound blends into the other, creating a melody that resonates with my heart.

I catch sight of Ethan again, standing at the edge of the crowd, his presence a reassuring anchor. He raises an eyebrow, a subtle sign of encouragement, and I can't help but smile. It's as if he understands the rollercoaster of emotions I'm navigating. In that moment, I decide to let go of the worries that have clouded my mind. I won't let Emma's words define my experience. I refuse to let the shadows of doubt dull my light.

With renewed determination, I pour my heart into the final touches of my dish. I create a delicate spun sugar nest to cradle the meringue, adding a whimsical touch that echoes the dreams I've fought to nurture. Each element I place on the plate is intentional, a reflection of my journey, my trials, and my triumphs. I imagine the judges tasting the combination of flavors and textures, and I hope they can sense the love that underpins each bite.

As I plate my dessert, I feel a wave of calm wash over me, the anticipation morphing into a sense of clarity. The last moments of the countdown loom, and I give my dish a final flourish, stepping back to admire the creation before me. It stands as a testament to my resilience, a symbol of everything I've learned, every tear I've shed, and every moment of joy I've savored.

The moment of truth arrives as the judges come forward, their expressions unreadable yet intent. I hold my breath, offering up my creation as an invitation, hoping they will taste not just the flavors but the story woven into every layer. Each bite is a leap of faith, a vulnerability exposed before the audience and the world.

As they taste, I can see the wheels turning in their minds, the pleasure flickering across their faces, and I feel my heart swell with hope. I catch Ethan's eye again, and this time, it's a look that says it all—a mixture of pride, admiration, and something deeper. In that fleeting moment, I realize that the whispers of doubt may never fully vanish, but neither will the strength I've found within myself.

And as I stand there, vulnerable yet empowered, I know that regardless of the outcome, this experience has changed me. It has stitched together the fabric of my dreams, pulling in the threads of resilience, creativity, and connection that weave a brighter tapestry of possibility. The stage lights shine brightly, illuminating not just the competition but the journey of a girl who dared to dream and create, who stood up against the shadows and emerged, if not victorious, then undeniably transformed.

Chapter 5: Sweet Temptations

The soft glow of candlelight danced across the walls of the gallery, casting playful shadows that seemed to sway in rhythm with the steady beat of my heart. It was the kind of place that breathed art, where every brushstroke and sculpture whispered stories of the soul, and where I found my own spirit unfurling, eager to embrace this intoxicating blend of creativity and uncertainty. Ethan was there, as he had been so many times before, a steady presence amidst the vibrant chaos of our collaboration. His laughter rang out like a melody, lifting the air with the promise of inspiration.

We were knee-deep in preparations for the gallery opening, a date that loomed closer with every tick of the clock. The heady aroma of freshly baked pastries wafted through the space, mingling with the scent of turpentine and the faint musk of old wood. I had arranged for a local bakery to supply an array of desserts, each piece more exquisite than the last, adorned with delicate icing flowers that looked almost too beautiful to eat. They would serve as both art and temptation, a fitting tribute to the theme of the night—Sweet Temptations.

I stood in front of my latest piece, a large canvas that felt like an extension of my very being. Bold strokes of crimson and gold merged with softer hues of lavender, creating a mesmerizing dance that spoke of longing and desire. As I stepped back to admire my work, Ethan leaned against the wall, arms crossed, his gaze fixed on the canvas with an intensity that made my breath hitch. There was something captivating about the way he saw me, as if he could decipher the secrets hidden within my layers of paint and emotion.

"It's stunning," he finally said, breaking the silence, his voice low and rich like dark chocolate. "You've captured the essence of the theme perfectly."

I turned to him, a warm flutter igniting in my chest. "You think so?" I asked, trying to mask the tremor of vulnerability in my tone.

"Absolutely," he replied, pushing himself off the wall and stepping closer. The space between us shrank, filled with an electric tension that was both thrilling and terrifying. "It's raw and beautiful, just like you."

My cheeks flushed at his words, and I could feel the heat creeping up my neck. It was moments like these that made me wonder if he felt it too—this unspoken bond that drew us closer, like two magnets pulled by an unseen force. But the shadows of doubt loomed in the background, threatening to snuff out the flicker of hope ignited in my heart. I knew that the closer we drew, the higher the stakes became.

"What if I mess this up?" I blurted out, my voice a mere whisper as I tore my gaze from his. "What if the opening night doesn't go as planned?"

Ethan's expression softened, his eyes a kaleidoscope of warmth and understanding. "You won't mess it up," he assured me, his hand gently brushing against mine, sending a jolt of electricity racing through my veins. "You've worked too hard, and this piece is a reflection of that dedication. Just remember, the art is meant to evoke emotions, not perfection."

His reassurance enveloped me like a warm embrace, momentarily easing the tight knot of anxiety coiling in my stomach. As the evening progressed, we continued to dive deep into our work, our laughter mingling with the rich tapestry of aromas swirling around us. The world outside faded away, and for a time, it felt like it was just the two of us—a duo lost in the creative whirlwind, crafting our own story amidst the chaos.

As night fell, the gallery transformed into a haven of enchantment. The candles flickered like stars in a velvet sky, illuminating the artwork in a soft, intimate glow. Each piece seemed to come alive, whispering secrets to those who dared to lean in closer. The delicate clinking of wine glasses and the low hum of conversation filled the air, creating an atmosphere that was both electric and serene.

Ethan and I flitted through the crowd, our hands often brushing against one another, sending tiny shivers of delight coursing through me. He introduced me to potential buyers and art enthusiasts, his words weaving a spell that drew people in like moths to a flame. I watched him engage with others, his passion contagious, and felt a swell of admiration for the man who had not only become my collaborator but had also captivated my heart in ways I never thought possible.

Then came the moment when our gazes locked across the crowded room. It was a fleeting instant, yet it felt like time had paused, the world around us fading into a distant murmur. In that shared silence, I saw something reflected in his eyes—an understanding, a connection that transcended words. I couldn't deny the magnetic pull between us, nor could I ignore the tremors of fear that threatened to unravel everything we'd built.

The night carried on, each passing minute bringing a mix of exhilaration and dread. As I engaged with guests, I caught glimpses of Ethan's unwavering support—a nod here, a smile there—as if he were anchoring me amidst the tempest of emotions swirling inside. But just as the gallery opened its doors to the world, a part of me remained tethered to the uncertain future looming on the horizon.

The opening was a success, drawing in a throng of admirers, all captivated by the beauty we had crafted together. Yet amidst the applause and praise, my heart ached with an impending sense of change, as if the very fabric of our collaboration was about to unravel. I couldn't shake the feeling that the night held secrets, dark and twisted, waiting to unravel in the most unexpected ways.

Ethan caught my eye once more, and with a mixture of hope and trepidation, I ventured into the night, knowing that whatever happened, I was ready to embrace it, if only to see where this tumultuous path would lead us.

The opening night was a kaleidoscope of emotion, with laughter ringing like chimes throughout the gallery, mingling with the sweet melodies of a string quartet nestled in the corner. The air was thick with the aroma of freshly baked goods, a tempting mix of chocolate ganache and almond pastries, enticing guests to indulge. I stood behind my featured piece, watching as people wandered between the paintings, their expressions a blend of curiosity and awe. Yet, as much as I longed to bask in the success of the evening, my heart felt heavy with an unshakeable sense of foreboding.

Ethan was there, his presence a grounding force amidst the swirling chaos. He moved effortlessly among the crowd, charm radiating from him like a sunbeam cutting through fog. I marveled at how he transformed into this charismatic figure, captivating art lovers with anecdotes and insightful commentary about the pieces on display. Each laugh he shared seemed to create ripples, drawing people closer, but it was his eyes—dark, smoldering, and filled with an undeniable spark—that truly held them captive.

I caught snippets of conversations, the buzz of excitement that filled the room. "Did you see the way she layered those colors?" "It's like the canvas is alive!" "I need to get one of these for my collection!" Each compliment felt like a warm caress against my soul, yet it was bittersweet, tangled with the anxiety that had become a constant companion. With every praise, my joy was shadowed by the weight of the unsaid, the unacknowledged tension that crackled between Ethan and me.

As the evening progressed, I found myself slipping into the background, watching as the gallery came alive without me. I was just a spectator now, observing the very creation that had once consumed my thoughts and emotions. I could see Ethan moving, always just out of reach, weaving through the throng with effortless grace. I longed to join him, to experience the joy of this moment together, but there was a barrier, an invisible wall built from our unvoiced fears and doubts.

Amidst the buzz of celebration, I caught sight of a familiar face, a gentle reminder of my past. Mia, my college roommate and confidante, approached with a radiant smile, her presence a balm for my restless heart. "You did it! This place is stunning," she exclaimed, her voice ringing with genuine delight. Her hair, a cascade of sun-kissed curls, bounced with each step as she pulled me into an enthusiastic embrace.

"Thanks, Mia! I couldn't have done it without Ethan," I admitted, glancing around for him. "He's been an incredible support."

Her eyes sparkled with mischief. "Oh, is that what we're calling it? Support?"

I couldn't help but laugh, shaking my head. "You know what I mean! He's been there every step of the way."

"Sure, sure," she teased, nudging me playfully. "Just remember, sweet temptation comes with a price." Her words hung in the air, a cheeky wink toward the simmering chemistry that was becoming harder to ignore.

As the crowd shifted and swirled, I felt the tug of longing pulling me back toward the center of the room. The string quartet played a sweet serenade, and I took a deep breath, letting the music wash over me. I needed to reclaim my moment, to step into the light that was now glowing warmly around my creation.

With renewed determination, I moved forward, weaving through clusters of guests until I found Ethan, who was engaged in conversation with an older couple. I approached just as he gestured toward my painting, his hands animated as he spoke. "And this piece, in particular, is a reflection of her journey—how art can be a conduit for our innermost feelings, a bridge connecting us to our truest selves."

His words struck a chord within me, igniting the passion that had fueled our late-night sessions. I could feel my cheeks flush with warmth as I stepped into the circle, catching his gaze, which was laden with unspoken understanding. "You're making me blush," I quipped, feigning modesty while truly savoring the way he held my work in such high regard.

"Just speaking the truth," he replied, his voice smooth and inviting. The couple smiled, clearly charmed by the dynamic unfolding before them. I could see their admiration for Ethan, and perhaps for me, reflected in their eyes, which only intensified my gratitude for the partnership we had forged.

Once the couple wandered off to explore more of the gallery, the moment hung delicately between us. I could feel the magnetic pull drawing us closer, and as if compelled by an invisible force, I stepped toward him, the space between us crackling with anticipation. "I couldn't have done this without you," I said softly, my voice barely above a whisper.

Ethan reached for my hand, his touch sending warmth spiraling through my core. "We did this together. You have a gift, and tonight the world gets to see it."

His praise enveloped me, but the weight of our unspoken feelings lingered like an uninvited guest at the feast. I wanted to explore the depth of his gaze, to unravel the mystery that flickered there, yet an undercurrent of fear threaded through my heart. What if this night marked the pinnacle of our relationship, a peak we could never ascend again?

The night unfolded like a dream, yet each laugh, each compliment echoed with the potential for heartbreak. As the clock ticked toward midnight, the guests began to thin, but the warmth of the evening remained like a cozy blanket draped over our shoulders. I leaned against the bar, stealing glances at Ethan as he spoke animatedly with the remaining art enthusiasts, his enthusiasm like a flame flickering in the wind.

Just then, a gust of cool air swept through the gallery as the door swung open, drawing my attention. A tall figure entered, his silhouette stark against the warm glow of candlelight. Instinctively, I held my breath, a sense of foreboding rising within me. It was Marco, my former mentor and a force in the art world, known for his discerning eye and formidable presence.

"Ah, what a delight to see the gallery alive with such talent," he boomed, his voice reverberating against the walls like a thunderclap. His eyes scanned the room, landing briefly on me before shifting to Ethan, assessing, judging. The smile on his face didn't quite reach his eyes, and I could feel the atmosphere change, thickening with tension.

Ethan stepped forward, his posture shifting slightly as he extended his hand to Marco. "Thank you for coming. I hope you enjoy the pieces on display."

As they exchanged pleasantries, I felt a knot form in my stomach, a sense of apprehension creeping in. I knew Marco's opinion carried weight, and I couldn't shake the feeling that he might see something in Ethan that could threaten the delicate balance we'd created. The night's triumph felt precarious, teetering on the edge of a cliff.

I took a deep breath, willing my heart to steady, and reminded myself that regardless of Marco's opinions, I had poured my heart into this night, and no judgment could overshadow the beauty we had created together. I was determined to navigate this unexpected storm with grace, ready to stand beside Ethan, facing whatever challenges lay ahead, no matter how sweet or bitter the temptation.

The atmosphere shifted the moment Marco stepped into the gallery, like a shadow unfurling itself across a sunlit room. His presence commanded attention, and the murmurs of guests faded to a respectful hush. As he approached, the air thickened with anticipation, and I instinctively straightened, trying to shake off the unease that settled in my chest like a heavy weight. I caught Ethan's eye, and the fleeting connection between us felt like an anchor in the swirling sea of uncertainty.

"Impressive," Marco declared, his gaze sweeping over the room before landing on my painting. "I've always believed in the power of youth to invigorate the art scene, but tonight, you've truly outdone yourself." His words dripped with the kind of thinly veiled condescension that only someone of his stature could muster, and I fought the urge to bristle.

"Thank you," I replied, forcing a smile as I stepped forward to reclaim my voice, my pride flaring up like a match struck in the dark. "I appreciate your feedback. Art is about evoking emotion, and I hope my work resonates with the audience tonight."

Marco raised an eyebrow, a smirk curling at the corners of his lips. "Resonates, indeed. The question is, will it sell? That's the true test." He glanced around as if assessing the worth of the room, his expression shifting from amusement to something sharper, more scrutinizing.

Ethan's posture tightened beside me, his hand instinctively brushing against my arm, a silent reassurance that ignited a flicker of warmth in my belly. I could see the tension in his jaw as he shifted his weight slightly, stepping closer to me. "Art can't always be measured in monetary value, Marco," he countered, his voice steady. "Sometimes, its worth lies in the connections it fosters."

"Ah, the romantic ideal," Marco chuckled, but there was an edge to his laughter that felt like a knife slipping through the fabric of the evening. "But as you'll learn, my dear Ethan, the art world thrives on more than just sentiment. It requires savvy, strategy, and sometimes, a bit of ruthlessness."

I felt a chill at his words, a stark reminder of the world we inhabited. I had always known that art could be a double-edged sword, capable of bringing beauty and despair in equal measure. Yet, standing there, I was struck by the reality that surrounded us—one that seemed to promise fleeting joy while lurking with the threat of inevitable disappointment.

Ethan's eyes darkened for a moment before he regained his composure, his gaze steady as he met Marco's challenge. "Perhaps," he replied, his voice low, "but true art transcends commercialism. It speaks to the human experience, igniting passion and provoking thought. Isn't that worth pursuing?"

The tension hung between them, palpable and thick, like the scent of frosting in the air. I watched, heart pounding, feeling caught in a tempest of conflicting emotions. I wanted to jump in, to diffuse the prickling unease, but words danced just out of reach, and all I could manage was a small, encouraging smile toward Ethan.

"Enough of this," Marco said abruptly, dismissing the tension with a wave of his hand, as if the air itself were inconsequential. "Let's move on. The real intrigue lies in how the rest of the night unfolds." With a final glance at my piece, he turned, leaving an uneasy silence in his wake.

As the conversation resumed around us, I could still feel Marco's words clinging to my skin, heavy like an unwanted coat. I turned to Ethan, who was watching me with concern etched into his features. "Don't let him get to you," he said softly, his voice low enough that only I could hear. "Your art is your voice, and it deserves to be heard."

His words washed over me, soothing the frayed edges of my anxiety. "You're right," I admitted, drawing a deep breath, letting the rhythm of the evening reclaim me. "I won't let one person's opinion dim the light of what we've created."

With renewed determination, I made my way through the remaining guests, eager to soak in their reactions and allow their enthusiasm to lift me once more. I lost myself in conversations, recounting the inspirations behind each piece, feeling the warmth of connection bloom within me. Laughter bubbled up from corners of the gallery, sweet and effervescent, creating a tapestry of voices that filled the space with life.

Amidst the chaos, I caught sight of Mia, her enthusiasm unwavering, bouncing over to my side. "You know, I've been talking to some collectors, and they're genuinely interested," she said, her eyes wide with excitement. "Your pieces are resonating with them, and I can feel the buzz in the air."

"Really?" My heart raced at her words, a blend of hope and disbelief fluttering within me. "That's amazing! I wasn't sure how tonight would go."

Mia placed a hand on my shoulder, her grip firm and encouraging. "You've put your heart into this. You deserve every bit of recognition that comes your way."

As she spoke, I glanced back toward Ethan, who was still engaged in conversation, his presence a beacon of support. I felt a surge of gratitude for him, for the way he had encouraged me to break free from my insecurities, pushing me to create boldly and authentically.

Just then, a tall woman with cascading chestnut hair approached, her expression a blend of curiosity and admiration. "Excuse me, I couldn't help but notice your work," she said, her voice smooth like silk. "It's captivating. I'm Sophie, an art consultant. May I ask about your process?"

"Of course," I replied, my heart fluttering at the unexpected opportunity. As I shared my creative journey with her, I felt the warmth of possibility enveloping me, igniting a fire within. This was what I had dreamed of—sharing my passion, connecting with others who appreciated the beauty of artistic expression.

With each passing moment, I felt the night's earlier tension dissipate, replaced by a rising tide of excitement. Laughter echoed, wine glasses clinked, and the gallery felt alive with the pulse of possibility. I glanced at Ethan, who caught my eye and grinned, his expression brimming with pride. In that moment, I realized that despite the looming uncertainties, I was exactly where I needed to be.

As the evening drew on, I found myself gravitating back to the center of the room, the hum of conversation fading into the background as I lost myself in the atmosphere. The golden candlelight flickered softly, illuminating faces filled with wonder, and I felt a sense of belonging wrap around me like a warm embrace. This was my world, vibrant and unpredictable, each stroke of paint a reflection of my journey.

In a corner, Marco lingered, observing with a cool detachment that set my teeth on edge. I could sense his skepticism, the undercurrent of doubt that tried to seep into the fabric of the night. But I was done allowing his words to hold power over me. This was my moment, and I refused to let anyone dim the light I had fought so hard to cultivate.

As the night wound down and guests began to take their leave, the atmosphere shifted to one of camaraderie and celebration. Ethan stood by my side, our shoulders brushing as we shared quiet laughter, the bond between us deepening in the shared triumph of the evening. The gallery was a tapestry of memories now, each thread woven with passion, determination, and undeniable connection.

"I'm so proud of you," Ethan said, his voice barely above a whisper as we surveyed the room, now filled with remnants of the celebration. "You poured your soul into this, and it shows."

I turned to him, feeling a wave of emotion crash over me. "I couldn't have done it without you," I admitted, my voice thick with gratitude. "You believed in me when I struggled to believe in myself."

His eyes sparkled, and in that moment, the tension from earlier faded into nothingness. "We're in this together," he assured me, and

I knew in my heart that whatever challenges lay ahead, I would face them by his side.

As the last of the guests trickled out, a sense of possibility hung in the air, electrifying and sweet, a prelude to whatever awaited us on the horizon. And in that enchanting world, filled with the lingering echoes of laughter and the soft glow of candlelight, I realized that love and art, when intertwined, could create the most extraordinary masterpiece of all.

Chapter 6: Cracking Under Pressure

The gallery thrummed with an electric energy, a palpable excitement that danced in the air like the bubbles in the champagne flutes raised by elegantly attired guests. Soft light spilled from the hanging chandeliers, glinting off the polished marble floor and illuminating the bold strokes of color on the canvas that filled the walls. Each piece, a riot of emotion captured in vibrant hues, beckoned patrons to explore the depth of the artists' souls. The air was heavy with the mingling scents of fresh paint and expensive perfume, an intoxicating blend that made my heart race with a mixture of anticipation and anxiety. This was it—my moment to shine, to bask in the glory of my hard work and creativity.

Yet, as I stood there in my carefully chosen dress, the fabric clinging to me like a second skin, a disquieting sense of unease wormed its way into my chest. I scanned the crowd, my eyes searching for Ethan, hoping to find him amidst the sea of faces. The longer I searched, the more that knot of apprehension twisted tighter. When I finally spotted him, it was not the confident, supportive partner I adored who met my gaze but a man encased in an air of distance, his focus entirely consumed by Emma, my former mentor.

Their conversation appeared heated, too intense for the festive atmosphere swirling around us. Ethan's brow furrowed, his eyes dark with contemplation, while Emma gestured animatedly, her red lips forming words that I couldn't hear over the buzz of laughter and clinking glasses. A part of me wanted to brush it off, to revel in the beauty of the night and the successes I had worked tirelessly to achieve. But as I watched, a bitter taste coated my tongue, souring my joy and drawing my gaze back to them like a moth to a flame, spiraling into a vortex of jealousy that burned hotter with each passing moment.

I tried to shake it off, forcing myself to mingle with guests, to laugh, to talk art and dreams and everything in between. But every time I laughed, every time I turned away from their whispered conversations, that twist in my gut flared again, each flicker of resentment feeding on my insecurities. I smiled through it, feigning interest in compliments thrown my way, but all I could think about was the invisible chasm widening between Ethan and me, stretching like the vast desert sky overhead.

When the gallery finally began to clear, my heart thudded with the weight of what I was about to do. I approached him with determination, the familiar rhythm of my breath betraying the turmoil beneath the surface. "Can we talk?" I asked, my voice barely rising above the fading music, trembling as the words escaped my lips.

He turned to me, the light catching the angles of his face, but the warmth I'd come to expect was absent. He nodded, his expression inscrutable, and together we slipped into a quieter corner of the gallery, away from the jubilant crowd that had once felt like a celebration.

"What's going on?" I demanded, my heart racing as I tried to keep my voice steady. "You've been distant all night, and it's not just the art."

Ethan crossed his arms, his eyes narrowing slightly. "You wouldn't understand," he replied, a coldness creeping into his tone that stung worse than any harsh critique I'd ever received.

"Try me!" I urged, my frustration bubbling to the surface. "I've poured my soul into this, and I need you here with me, not hiding behind your walls!"

"Walls?" he echoed, his voice low, tinged with an edge of defensiveness. "You think I'm hiding? You think I'm not proud of you?"

"Then why do you seem so afraid?" The question burst from my lips before I could stop myself. "What are you so worried about?"

A flicker of pain crossed his face, and for a moment, I saw the vulnerability lurking just beneath the surface, waiting for the right moment to break free. "I can't afford to fail again," he confessed, his gaze dropping to the ground, shame hanging in the air like a thick fog. "You don't know what it's like to stand on the brink of everything you've ever wanted and watch it slip through your fingers."

My heart ached at his confession. I took a step closer, reaching for his hand, but he flinched back, retreating into himself. "I'm not your past," I whispered, my voice trembling. "Let me in. I want to be here for you, to help you, but you have to meet me halfway."

He shook his head, the pain in his eyes transforming into a resolute barrier. "I don't want to drag you down with me," he said, each word steeped in regret. "You deserve better than my failures."

"That's not how this works!" My voice cracked, emotion swelling within me, desperate to breach the walls he'd built. "We lift each other up! You can't just shut me out because you're afraid of what could happen."

But he didn't respond. Instead, the silence hung heavy between us, a chasm forged from his fears and my frustration. I felt tears prickle at the corners of my eyes, blurring the gallery around us, transforming the vibrant colors into a washed-out canvas of despair. I wanted to shake him, to make him understand that together we were stronger, that love was meant to weather the storms of life, not crumble under the weight of doubt.

In that moment, everything shifted. I saw him—the man I loved, the man fighting his own demons, trapped in a cycle of self-imposed isolation. I took a deep breath, searching for the right words to reach him. "Ethan, if we can't be honest with each other, what's the point?"

I implored, my voice softer now, laced with the raw vulnerability I felt inside.

Still, he remained distant, a statue forged from stone, unwavering in his resolve to keep me at bay. And just like that, my heart began to crack under the pressure of his silence, splintering into a million shards of uncertainty and longing, each piece a reminder of the connection I yearned for but felt slipping away.

The tension between us hung in the air like the fine mist of a summer storm, palpable and heavy, with an undercurrent of frustration crackling like static electricity. I studied Ethan's face, hoping to find a glimmer of the warmth and affection I cherished, but his expression remained a mask of stubborn determination. With each passing second, the distance between us widened, an invisible rift forged from fear and unspoken words.

"Ethan," I whispered, desperation creeping into my voice as I tried to breach his fortress. "I'm not just your partner in this. I'm your teammate. If you're scared, I want to be scared with you." My heart beat rapidly, each pulse echoing the sentiment I yearned to express. "I won't let your past dictate our future."

For a heartbeat, I thought I saw a flicker of something—an acknowledgment of the bond we shared, a flash of hope that perhaps I could reach him. But then he turned away, focusing instead on the wall behind me as if it held the answers to everything. I was left standing in a whirlwind of confusion and vulnerability, wishing he could see just how fiercely I cared.

"Sometimes, it's easier to be alone," he muttered, almost to himself, a deep resignation in his tone that pierced through the atmosphere like a dagger. The realization that he believed he was better off isolated sent a wave of frustration crashing over me. I wanted to scream at him, to shake him from this self-imposed exile. But instead, I felt the ache in my chest deepen, threatening to consume the remnants of my resolve.

"Ethan," I began again, softer this time, as if speaking too loudly might scare him away entirely. "You're not alone. You have me. And I can't promise that everything will be perfect or that we won't face setbacks, but I can promise that I will be here, standing right beside you."

The silence stretched between us like a taut wire, and I could feel my heartbeat thrumming in my ears. Every moment felt like a countdown to an inevitable explosion, a moment when he might finally crumble under the weight of it all.

Finally, he turned back to me, his expression softening ever so slightly. "You say that now, but what if I drag you down with me? What if my failures become yours?" The raw honesty in his voice sent a shiver down my spine.

"You won't," I replied, an unexpected fire igniting within me. "You're not going to fail. Not this time. We're in this together. You've shown me that you're capable of so much more than you think."

He opened his mouth to respond, but the words caught in his throat. For a moment, I felt as though we stood on the edge of a precipice, teetering between vulnerability and guardedness, the chasm of doubt threatening to swallow us both whole. I could see the walls he'd constructed, towering and unyielding, but the more I peered into his eyes, the more I realized they were constructed not just from fear but also from a profound sense of love—a love that both terrified and exhilarated him.

"Let me help you," I urged, reaching out for his hand again. This time, he didn't pull away. Our fingers touched, and a warmth surged between us, threading through the seams of our uncertainty. "Let's face this together. We're stronger together, remember?"

The corners of his mouth twitched, almost a smile, but his eyes remained clouded, still wrestling with the demons of his past. "You make it sound so easy," he said, a hint of incredulity lacing his words. "Like I can just forget everything that's happened."

"Not forget," I corrected gently. "Learn from it. Let it shape you, but don't let it define you. You've got this, Ethan. You just have to let go."

In that moment, the atmosphere shifted. The air was charged with something more than just unspoken fears—it was laced with the potential for healing, the promise of understanding. Slowly, he nodded, the fierce storm within him settling just enough for a glimpse of clarity to shine through.

"I wish I could believe that," he confessed, his grip tightening on my hand. "But every time I think I'm ready to move forward, something pulls me back."

"That's just life," I countered, my heart racing as I felt the tension between us ebbing away, leaving a fragile connection that pulsed with hope. "It's messy, and it doesn't always go according to plan. But it's also beautiful and worth fighting for."

A flicker of understanding passed between us, and for the first time that night, the heavy weight of doubt lifted slightly from my shoulders. The gallery around us faded into the background, a colorful blur of laughter and art, as I focused solely on Ethan.

He sighed, the sound a mixture of relief and surrender. "I just don't want to disappoint you," he said, his vulnerability laid bare before me.

"You won't," I promised, squeezing his hand tighter, willing him to believe me. "I don't need perfection. I need you—flaws and all. We're in this together, remember?"

The silence that followed was filled with unspoken promises, a delicate truce forged in the heat of our emotions. Ethan's expression softened, the storm clouds in his eyes clearing just enough for me to catch a glimpse of the man I loved beneath the weight of his fears.

"Okay," he finally murmured, his voice barely above a whisper. "I'll try."

In that moment, I felt a surge of joy wash over me, mingling with the relief that coursed through my veins. The gallery opening hadn't gone as planned, but perhaps it was a beginning of sorts—a new chapter forged from honesty and shared vulnerability.

As we stood there, hand in hand, the world outside continued its bustling rhythm, but in our little corner of the gallery, time felt suspended, infused with possibility. I was no longer just the artist; I was a partner, a confidante, and together, we would navigate the uncertain waters of our dreams and fears. The night might not have unfolded as I envisioned, but it held the promise of something far more valuable: the chance to grow together, to face our fears, and to build a future unfettered by the shadows of the past.

As the evening wore on, the noise of the gallery faded into a low hum, a backdrop to the whirlwind of thoughts that swirled in my mind. I stood beside Ethan, my heart still racing from our confrontation, feeling the warmth of his hand in mine. It felt like a fragile truce, a delicate bridge over the turbulent waters of our emotions. Yet, the laughter of other guests echoed around us, vibrant and carefree, as if to mock the heaviness that lingered in our space.

The remnants of the opening night buzz filled the air with the scent of rich, velvety chocolates and the crisp notes of white wine. The gallery's walls, adorned with brilliant artworks, seemed to pulsate with life, each piece telling a story that I desperately wanted to share with Ethan. I wanted to turn to him and discuss the intricate details of the brushstrokes, the emotions behind each piece, but the heaviness of his unvoiced fears loomed like a dark cloud, smothering the light of the night.

"Let's go outside," I suggested, my voice barely above a whisper. The thought of stepping into the cool night air felt like a lifeline, a way to escape the lingering tension inside. He hesitated for a moment, uncertainty flickering in his eyes, but then he nodded, and we slipped out the glass doors that led to a small courtyard filled with blooming night jasmine. The sweet, intoxicating fragrance enveloped us, a stark contrast to the anxiety that had woven itself into our earlier exchange.

The courtyard was bathed in moonlight, the silvery glow casting soft shadows across the cobblestone path. I took a deep breath, allowing the fragrant night air to fill my lungs, hoping it would somehow cleanse the remnants of our argument from the space between us. Ethan leaned against the cool stone wall, his posture relaxed but his gaze distant, still lost in the labyrinth of his thoughts.

"Look at the stars," I said, trying to redirect the tension. I pointed toward the sky, where a tapestry of stars twinkled like diamonds scattered across dark velvet. "They're like the artworks inside—each one unique, yet they all belong together in this vast universe."

He followed my gaze, and for a moment, the weight of his fears seemed to lift as he marveled at the celestial display. "It's beautiful," he admitted, his voice softening. "But it's also overwhelming. So many stars, and I can't help but think about how small we are in comparison."

I stepped closer, my shoulder brushing against his. "Maybe that's what makes us stronger," I countered gently. "We're tiny, but we're capable of making an impact. Every star shines with its own light, and that's what counts."

His eyes shifted from the sky to me, and I could see the flicker of something deeper behind the shadows—curiosity, perhaps, or maybe a hint of understanding. "You make it sound so easy," he murmured, a faint smile tugging at the corners of his lips. "But I don't want to be just another star that fades away."

"No one ever is," I insisted, my voice earnest. "You are Ethan Prescott. You are so much more than your past. You've helped people through their struggles; you've inspired them. Don't you see how brilliant that is?"

The vulnerability that had once clouded his eyes began to dissipate, replaced by a flicker of warmth. "You always know just what to say," he replied, his voice steadier now, as if my words had anchored him, bringing him back from the edge of his fears.

A teasing grin danced across my face. "It's my job as your partner to keep you grounded. Just like it's your job to keep me sane when I'm drowning in paint and deadlines."

Ethan chuckled softly, and the sound was like music, a balm to the frayed edges of the evening. "Maybe we should make a habit of this—stepping outside, away from everything."

"Absolutely," I agreed, feeling a surge of hope bubbling within me. "But first, I think we need to clear the air about Emma."

The mention of her name caused a flicker of tension to return to his features. "I didn't mean to make you feel uncomfortable," he said quickly, defensive again. "She was just offering some advice—"

"Advice?" I interrupted, my heart racing. "Or was it something more? I saw the way you two were talking, and it felt charged. I want to trust you, but I can't shake this feeling that there's more to it."

His eyes widened, surprise mingling with concern. "It wasn't like that. Emma and I go way back. She's always been supportive, but she's also someone I'm trying to distance myself from. I don't want to be that person again—the one who relied on others for validation."

"Then why did you let it feel like that tonight?" I pressed gently. "I need you to be honest with me, Ethan. I can't be a part of your life if you keep things hidden."

He sighed deeply, the air escaping his lungs like a deflated balloon. "I know. I should have told you. I guess I was just caught off guard. Seeing her reminded me of a time when I didn't believe in myself, and I didn't want to drag you down with my insecurities."

"By not sharing, you're dragging me down too," I countered softly, my heart aching for the man standing before me. "We're in this together. Remember?"

As I spoke, I watched the light slowly return to his eyes, a flicker of recognition igniting behind them. "You're right," he admitted, his voice heavy with the weight of realization. "I shouldn't hide things from you. I want to be better. For us."

With those words, the tension in the air shifted once again, and it felt like a dam had broken, allowing the flood of honesty and connection to wash over us. I stepped closer, closing the gap between us as I searched his gaze for reassurance.

"I don't want perfection," I murmured, resting my forehead against his. "I want you to be real, flaws and all. That's what makes you who you are."

He nodded, his breath warm against my skin. "Okay, I'll try. I promise."

As we stood together beneath the canopy of stars, I felt the weight of our earlier argument dissolve into the night. There was still work to be done, still walls to dismantle, but in this moment, the air was charged with a new promise—one of vulnerability and shared dreams. I breathed in the scent of jasmine, savoring the beauty of the moment, and for the first time that night, I felt a true sense of peace settle over us.

With our hands intertwined, we turned back to the gallery, ready to face whatever came next, united against the shadows that had once threatened to pull us apart. The night was still young, and as we stepped inside, I couldn't shake the feeling that this was just the beginning of a deeper connection, one that would be forged through honesty, love, and the courage to face the past together. In that vibrant space filled with creativity and hope, I felt a quiet strength blooming within me, a belief that we could navigate the complexities of life hand in hand, painting our own story against the backdrop of a world waiting to be explored.

Chapter 7: Rekindling Flames

The gallery stands as a beacon against the dusk, its stark white façade glowing softly in the fading light, a contrast to the chaos brewing inside my heart. I push through the glass door, the familiar jingle announcing my entrance, yet it feels as if I've entered a different world—a realm where art and emotion collide in a swirl of vibrant colors and profound silence. The scent of linseed oil and fresh canvas fills the air, wrapping around me like an embrace, reminding me of late nights spent together in this sacred space, exploring each other's dreams and fears through the lens of creativity. But today, the atmosphere feels charged, taut with tension, as if the very walls are holding their breath, waiting for the inevitable confrontation.

Ethan is perched on a stool, his hands buried in the depths of his hair, the tousled locks falling haphazardly over his forehead. He seems smaller, the vibrant energy that usually radiates from him dimmed, casting a shadow that echoes my own turmoil. The gallery, once a sanctuary, now mirrors our emotional landscape—a cacophony of color, a swirl of doubt. Our eyes lock, and for a moment, time suspends. The silence between us is deafening, a reminder of the distance we've allowed to creep in since that fateful day, when anger and hurt spilled over like paint splattering across a pristine canvas.

I take a tentative step forward, the polished wooden floor creaking beneath my weight, and the sound seems to break the spell. "Ethan," I whisper, my voice barely carrying over the silence. It's both a question and a plea, a fragile thread reaching out to bridge the chasm that has formed between us.

He looks up, his gaze piercing yet softening as he processes my presence. I see the flicker of recognition in his eyes, a momentary spark that mirrors my own yearning. "I didn't think you'd come back," he admits, his voice a rough whisper, laden with regret and vulnerability.

"Neither did I," I confess, crossing the gallery floor until I stand before him. The pieces on the walls—abstract landscapes bursting with color—suddenly seem irrelevant in the face of the reality between us. "But I needed to see you. I missed this... us."

As if drawn by an invisible force, he stands, and we share a heartbeat of stillness before the floodgates open. The words spill out, raw and unfiltered, tumbling over one another as we lay bare our insecurities and dreams. I tell him of my fears—how I've felt lost in the shadows of expectations, of art that never seems to capture the chaos within me. I share the nagging worry that I'm not enough, that my creative voice is a whisper among roaring giants.

His gaze softens, and I can almost see the wheels turning in his mind. "I've been scared too," he admits, rubbing the back of his neck, a telltale sign of his discomfort. "Scared that I'm losing you, that I've pushed you away. The fight... it felt like a nightmare I couldn't wake from."

The truth in his words resonates within me, stirring something deep and longing. I step closer, the gap between us narrowing until the heat radiating from his body envelops me like a summer night. "You didn't lose me, Ethan. We just... lost sight of what mattered."

We stand there, words hanging in the air like unfinished strokes on a canvas, both vulnerable yet yearning for connection. In this moment of raw honesty, I can feel the remnants of our fight fading into the background, replaced by the electric pulse of unspoken feelings simmering beneath the surface.

His hands find their way to my waist, drawing me into an embrace that feels both familiar and foreign. The warmth of his body against mine ignites a spark, a flicker of hope that dances in the darkness. I close my eyes, losing myself in the rhythm of our heartbeats—his steady, mine a chaotic symphony. It feels like home, yet there's an undercurrent of uncertainty that we both can't ignore.

"Do you remember the first time we came here?" he asks, his breath warm against my ear, coaxing a memory long tucked away. "You were so excited about the new exhibit. I thought you'd burst from joy."

I laugh softly, recalling the way I had dragged him through the gallery, pointing out every piece with a passion that lit up my soul. "And you pretended to be bored," I tease, pulling back slightly to look into his eyes, their depth drawing me in like an endless ocean.

"Maybe I was just trying to play it cool," he quips, a smirk breaking through the heaviness. "But honestly, I loved seeing you like that. It was contagious."

The laughter between us is a balm, soothing the scars of our conflict. Yet, as I pull away, the shadows from our past loom ominously on the edges of our fragile reconnection. "Ethan, we can't ignore what happened. We need to talk about it."

He nods, the playful glint in his eyes fading as the weight of reality settles back over us. "I know. I'm just scared that if we dig too deep, we might unearth something we can't handle."

"Maybe we can tackle it together," I suggest, my heart racing at the thought. The prospect of vulnerability is daunting, yet it feels like the only way forward.

He meets my gaze, the intensity of his expression sending shivers down my spine. "Together," he echoes, and the promise in his voice hangs in the air, mingling with the scent of paint and hope. As we lean into each other, the barriers begin to crumble, and in that sacred space between us, I sense a flicker of light—an ember ready to be fanned into a flame, if only we dare to breathe life into it.

The silence wraps around us, heavy and suffocating, yet within it lies a peculiar comfort—a cocoon woven from our shared history, the laughter and tears that defined us. The gallery, once a vibrant playground of creativity, transforms into a theater of intimacy, where each painting whispers secrets of our past. I can almost hear the echoes of our laughter bouncing off the walls, the way we once flitted from canvas to canvas, each brushstroke a new adventure, a new possibility. Today, however, every stroke feels like an echo of our unresolved tension.

Ethan steps back, allowing the space between us to breathe. The faint light filters through the tall windows, casting elongated shadows that dance along the polished floor, their movements mirroring the uncertainty between us. "What if we tried to paint again?" he suggests, a hint of a challenge sparking in his eyes. "You know, like we used to."

The idea strikes a chord within me, vibrating through my veins like an electric current. There's something alluring about recapturing that connection through our art, something that could anchor us amidst the chaos. "You mean like our little painting sessions?" I ask, my heart racing at the thought.

"Exactly. Just you and me, no expectations," he replies, a tentative smile breaking through the remnants of our heaviness. "Just paint. Let's create without boundaries, like we did when we first started."

The prospect lights a fire in my chest, a flicker of excitement mingling with the shadows. I nod, eager yet anxious, feeling the weight of anticipation hanging in the air. We navigate the gallery toward the back room, where the sunlight spills through the windows, illuminating the clutter of paints, brushes, and canvases scattered across the wooden table. The space is a sanctuary, a testament to the creativity we once shared, now both a reminder of our estrangement and a canvas for our reunion.

Ethan reaches for the brushes, his fingers grazing mine, sending a shiver of electricity through the air. "What color do you want?" he asks, eyes sparkling with mischief. I can see the boy I fell for hidden behind the man who carries the weight of our arguments, a reminder of the joy that still lingers beneath the surface.

"Something vibrant," I reply, my voice gaining strength as I delve into the memories of our past. "Let's use the brightest colors we can find. Something that feels like a celebration."

He grins, the expression lighting up his face, and for a moment, it feels as if the past few days of silence have melted away. We dive into the task, our movements fluid and instinctual, mixing paints on the palette and laughing at the splatters that adorn our hands and clothes. I watch as he swipes a generous brush of cobalt blue across the canvas, the boldness of the stroke matching the intensity of his spirit. I follow suit, splashing fiery reds and yellows, creating a vivid explosion that reflects the turbulence of our emotions.

As we paint, the walls around us fade, and I can almost forget the shadows lurking in the corners of our minds. The rhythmic sound of the brushes gliding over canvas drowns out the noise of our worries, transforming the gallery into a sanctuary of expression. Our conversation flows freely, the words punctuated by laughter, teasing, and the occasional playful shove. Each color becomes a thread that weaves our narratives back together, the unspoken bond between us tightening with every brushstroke.

"What if we painted our emotions?" I suggest, my voice light and teasing. "Like, I'll do happiness, and you can tackle anger."

Ethan raises an eyebrow, a playful smirk tugging at his lips. "I think I can manage anger pretty well." He pauses, leaning closer to me, the warmth of his body radiating against mine. "But you better prepare yourself for the chaos I'm about to unleash."

I laugh, feeling the tension ebb away, replaced by a familiarity that feels like coming home after a long journey. The gallery hums with life, as if responding to our playful banter. In those moments, the pain of our recent arguments begins to dissipate, replaced by a sense of belonging.

Yet, beneath the surface of our playful interactions, the specter of our past lingers like a shadow, reminding us of the fragility of our reconciliation. As I step back to assess my work, I catch Ethan's gaze drifting toward the unfinished canvas, his expression turning serious. "You know, I've always admired your ability to put your feelings into your art," he says, the weight of his words anchoring us in the moment. "It's something I've struggled with."

The honesty in his voice tugs at my heart. "We all have our struggles, Ethan. It's part of being human."

"Yeah, but I don't want to hold you back," he murmurs, running a hand through his hair, the familiar gesture revealing his vulnerability. "I don't want my fears to stifle your creativity."

His admission resonates deeply within me. "But it's not just about you, Ethan. We're in this together. I want us to lift each other up, not pull each other down."

For a moment, he is quiet, contemplating my words. The silence stretches between us, thick and palpable, until finally, he nods, a flicker of understanding igniting in his eyes. "Together," he agrees softly, the promise of it hanging in the air, warm and heavy.

As we continue to paint, a new rhythm settles between us, each stroke a reaffirmation of our commitment to not just our art, but to each other. The colors swirl together, a chaotic harmony of reds and blues, blending to create something uniquely ours. I can feel the past gradually losing its grip, replaced by the vibrant possibilities of the present.

The hours slip by, our laughter echoing through the gallery as we create a masterpiece that feels like a celebration of our journey—a testament to our resilience, our ability to rise from the ashes of misunderstandings. Each brushstroke solidifies our bond, reminding me of why I fell for him in the first place.

As the last rays of sunlight filter through the windows, casting a golden glow on our creation, I realize that this moment is not merely about the art we've produced but about the healing that has begun to unfold between us. The shadows may linger, but together, we are learning to illuminate the darkness, step by tentative step, one stroke at a time. In this sanctuary of color and emotion, the flames of our love begin to flicker back to life, promising warmth, hope, and the beauty of what lies ahead.

The vibrant strokes of our newly crafted masterpiece lay before us, a testament to our efforts, yet the air is still thick with questions. As the last rays of sunlight dip beneath the horizon, they cast a warm amber glow over the gallery, making the colors dance with a vitality that almost feels surreal. I glance at Ethan, whose eyes reflect a mixture of exhilaration and apprehension. The laughter we shared feels fragile, suspended in time, as if we are balancing on the precipice of a cliff, teetering between the exhilaration of creativity and the uncertainty of our relationship.

"Do you ever think about what we were before?" I ask, my voice barely above a whisper, the weight of the question pressing heavily on my chest. The gallery, with its comforting chaos of paint and canvases, feels like the perfect backdrop for this delicate moment—a cocoon wrapped in nostalgia.

Ethan shifts, the tension in his shoulders visibly easing. "All the time," he replies, his expression shifting to one of contemplation. "It feels like a lifetime ago, doesn't it? The way we lost ourselves in art, in each other. It was as if nothing else mattered."

A smile tugs at the corners of my lips as I recall those carefree days, when the world outside felt like a distant echo, and the only reality that existed was the one we painted together. "I remember the way we'd sit for hours, dreaming up stories for each painting," I say, feeling warmth blossom in my chest. "Every piece had a narrative, a heartbeat. It made everything feel more alive."

"Yeah," he chuckles, running a hand through his hair, the familiar gesture igniting a spark of affection. "Even the absurd ones, like that giant chicken we painted."

"Don't underestimate the artistic depth of poultry," I retort, laughter spilling from my lips, momentarily dispelling the lingering shadows. But beneath the humor, there's a seriousness threading through our conversation, a desire to reclaim what was lost.

Ethan's gaze grows intense, the light in his eyes flickering with an emotion that feels both foreign and familiar. "But it's not just about the art, is it? It's about us—the connection we had, the way we inspired each other."

The honesty in his words hangs in the air, wrapping around us like an embrace. I nod, the truth resonating deep within me. "Exactly. I think that's what I've missed the most. Not just the painting, but the way we shared everything—our hopes, our fears, our dreams."

A moment of silence stretches between us, heavy with unspoken thoughts. The gallery, once a space for exploration and joy, transforms into a chamber of revelations. We're navigating the landscape of our shared memories, trying to stitch together the frayed edges of our relationship.

Ethan steps closer, the distance shrinking until his presence envelops me in warmth. "We can't ignore what happened," he murmurs, the weight of his admission settling like a stone in my gut. "But I want to try. I want to figure this out."

His sincerity washes over me, calming the storm of anxiety brewing in my chest. "I want that too," I say, my voice steadier than I feel. "But we need to be honest about everything—the good and the bad. We can't let the past define us."

"Then let's start fresh," he suggests, a spark of determination igniting in his eyes. "We can create a new narrative, one where we don't let fear drive us apart."

The idea blooms within me, a fragile seed of hope taking root. "A new narrative," I repeat, testing the words like a promise. "Together."

With a shared smile, we move back to our canvas, the world outside fading into insignificance as we begin to paint again. Each stroke is deliberate, each color an echo of our resolve. The vibrant hues blend together, creating a tapestry that speaks to our journey—one filled with shadows and light, chaos and clarity.

As we work, the atmosphere shifts, infused with the tangible energy of collaboration. I watch as Ethan dips his brush into a brilliant gold, the color radiant against the blues and reds we've layered beneath. "This is like our relationship, isn't it?" he says, his voice filled with conviction. "It takes all the colors, even the dark ones, to create something beautiful."

I pause, captivated by his analogy. "Yes! Without the darkness, the light wouldn't shine nearly as bright."

Our laughter fills the space again, light and unguarded. The walls seem to pulse with life as we continue to layer our creation, each brushstroke further unraveling the knot of tension that had once held us captive.

Yet, even amidst the blossoming connection, I can't shake the feeling that the shadows are merely lying in wait. I catch glimpses of doubt in Ethan's eyes, the flicker of concern that reflects my own uncertainties. "What if we don't succeed?" I ask, my voice wavering, the weight of reality pressing down on me.

He pauses, meeting my gaze with an intensity that makes my heart race. "What if we do? What if we find a way to not only rekindle what we had but build something even stronger?"

The thought hangs in the air, a tantalizing promise of possibility. I lean closer, emboldened by his conviction, ready to step into the unknown with him. "I want that, Ethan. I want us to be something more than we were before."

As the last strokes of our painting come together, the colors merge into a vivid symphony of hope, illuminating the room with a vibrancy that feels almost magical. The canvas now captures the essence of our journey—a reflection of not only our struggles but also our resilience, a reminder that beauty can emerge from chaos.

In that moment, surrounded by the warmth of his presence and the colors of our creation, I realize that this is more than just a painting; it's a new beginning, a promise that even amidst the shadows, we can find a way to shine. As the light dims outside, I feel the embers of our rekindled flame flickering to life, and for the first time in days, I believe in the magic of what we can create together.

The gallery, once a stage for our struggles, now transforms into a sanctuary of hope, a space where we can continue to explore not just our artistry but the depths of our hearts. The warmth of our shared laughter mingles with the scent of paint and promise, and as we step back to admire our work, I know we are on the cusp of something extraordinary—a journey that we will navigate together, hand in hand, heart to heart.

Chapter 8: A Bitter Truth

The night air clung to my skin like a forgotten promise as I raced through the dimly lit streets of Chicago, each red light blurring into a crimson haze. I had just settled into the fragile sense of peace that comes with mending a rift—my laughter echoing in my mind from the earlier phone call with Sarah, filled with inside jokes and plans to paint the town red. Yet, within moments, that laughter shattered like glass against the unforgiving truth of the universe. A phone call had shattered my world.

"Accident," the voice on the other end had said, each syllable slicing through the remnants of joy I'd held onto just moments before. I could barely digest the information, my heart racing, pounding a relentless rhythm in my chest. My grip tightened around the steering wheel, knuckles white against the worn leather, as I sped toward the hospital, a place that loomed ahead like a monster hiding behind darkened windows, waiting to devour me whole.

Arriving at the hospital, a sterile fortress, I stumbled into the fluorescent lights, each flickering bulb a reminder of my stark reality. The antiseptic smell wrapped around me, stinging my nostrils and pulling me deeper into dread. The sounds of distant beeping machines and hushed conversations formed a symphony of anxiety that reverberated through the sterile halls. My heart pounded a steady beat of panic as I searched the waiting room, my eyes locking onto Sarah's parents. They were the embodiment of fear and heartbreak, their bodies rigid with an unspoken weight.

I approached them, feeling as if I were encased in glass, a distant observer of a reality too harsh to bear. Sarah's mother, her eyes puffy and red, grasped my hand with a force that spoke volumes. "She's in surgery," she whispered, her voice trembling like a fragile leaf in a storm. I nodded, my throat tightening, unsure of how to offer comfort when I was the one who felt utterly shattered.

Hours felt like years as we waited, the ticking clock mocking our anxiety, the silence punctuated only by the occasional footstep echoing in the sterile hallways. I tried to distract myself by recalling memories of Sarah—her laughter, bright and infectious, her penchant for making even the dullest days sparkle. I remembered the time she convinced me to sneak into a carnival under the stars, our feet pounding against the cracked pavement as we devoured cotton candy and rode the Ferris wheel, the city sprawling beneath us, a glittering tapestry of life. How could she have been reduced to this?

A doctor finally emerged, his face solemn, each line etched deeply with the gravity of his words. "She's stable," he said, but the way his gaze drifted told a different story, a hidden weight that sank deep into my gut. I found myself grappling with emotions I didn't want to acknowledge, the bitter tang of fear mingling with the sweetness of relief. "You can see her, but just for a moment," he added, his voice steady, as if trying to keep me tethered to hope.

I walked into the dimly lit room, where Sarah lay motionless, a delicate flower crushed under a heavy boot. The steady rhythm of the machines seemed to fill the void of silence, a reminder of the battle she was fighting. I hesitated at the threshold, tears welling in my eyes, threatening to spill over like rain on a fragile petal. She looked so small, swallowed by the hospital bed, the tubes snaking around her as if holding her hostage. I wanted to scream, to shake her awake and demand she return to our vibrant lives, filled with laughter and late-night confessions over cups of lukewarm coffee.

As I sat beside her, the sterile smell of antiseptic suffocating my senses, my phone buzzed insistently in my pocket. I fished it out, my heart racing as I saw Ethan's name flash on the screen. In the chaos swirling around me, his existence felt like a puzzle piece that had suddenly fallen out of place. I pressed my lips together, fighting the urge to answer. The memories of our last conversation flashed before me, his teasing laughter, the warmth in his eyes that had made me question everything I thought I knew about love.

But then, a wave of doubt crashed over me. Why was I thinking about him when Sarah needed me? The frantic memories of Ethan and Sarah's friendship bubbled to the surface, each fragment tainted by uncertainty. I recalled the times they'd shared together, the inside jokes, the late-night conversations. Did they share a bond deeper than I had realized? The nagging thought wrapped around my heart, squeezing tight, a silent accusation.

I felt torn between the love I had begun to nurture for Ethan and the loyalty I owed to Sarah. The longer I sat there, the more I grappled with the idea that perhaps I was not the only one who cared for her. But with every tick of the clock, I felt a growing dread. What if there was a complicated history I had yet to uncover, lurking beneath the surface like an undiscovered abyss?

My resolve to protect my heart began to crack as the weight of the situation bore down on me. I could either confront Ethan and demand answers or bury my fears deep within, hoping they would fade away like the dying light outside the window. As the shadows lengthened, I knew a reckoning was approaching, and with it, the bittersweet truth that would either bind us closer together or tear us apart forever.

The sterile hospital room, once a refuge for hope, felt more like a cell, its walls closing in as I watched Sarah, fragile and still, beneath the harsh glare of fluorescent lights. The rhythmic beeping of the machines created a haunting lullaby, lulling me into a false sense of calm even as my heart raced in confusion. I reached for her hand, feeling the coolness of her skin against mine, and whispered stories about the adventures we would have once she woke up—tales of road trips through the Midwest, nights spent painting our nails under the stars, and our dream of launching a podcast that would take the world by storm. Each word was an act of defiance against the bleak reality that loomed like a storm cloud over my head.

Suddenly, my phone vibrated again, its insistence a stark reminder that life outside this room continued, oblivious to the chaos swirling within me. Ethan's name lit up the screen, and for a fleeting moment, I felt a rush of warmth. The warmth quickly dissipated, replaced by a biting chill of doubt and frustration. Would I really let the ghost of our romantic misadventures haunt me in this moment of anguish? With a quick decision, I silenced the phone, slipping it back into my pocket like a rebellious secret. The last thing I needed right now was to be swept into another storm.

Hours blurred into an indistinct haze, each minute dragging like a weight around my neck. Eventually, the comforting presence of Sarah's parents began to feel heavier. Their silent grief pressed against me, an unbearable pressure that stifled the air in the room. I watched as her mother sat with her head in her hands, shoulders trembling with silent sobs, while her father stared vacantly at the floor, his eyes hollow and searching, as if hoping to find solace in the scuffed linoleum.

In that moment, I felt the urge to reach out, to comfort them, yet I hesitated. What words could possibly mend the fabric of their broken hearts? I was a mere spectator, a reluctant bystander in this tragedy, a role I hadn't chosen. As I looked at Sarah, my mind began to wander through the tangled vines of memories, desperately searching for answers, for clarity amid the chaos. What did I truly know about the lives intertwined with my own? The threads connecting Sarah and Ethan began to unravel, revealing a tapestry that I was not fully a part of.

As the hours dragged on, I felt the grip of anxiety tighten around my chest. With every passing moment, I was forced to confront the undeniable truth: I had to face Ethan. How could I expect to navigate my relationship with him while knowing there was a shadow lurking just beyond my perception? The thought of confronting him sent shivers down my spine, an icy chill that made my heart race. Still, it felt inevitable, the confrontation hanging over me like a thunderstorm waiting to burst.

When I finally decided to leave the hospital, the city outside felt alien. The sun had dipped below the horizon, casting a twilight glow over the streets. Neon lights flickered to life, vibrant hues illuminating the weary faces of passersby. I walked aimlessly, lost in a maze of thoughts. The laughter of friends echoed from nearby bars, a stark contrast to the somber reality I had just escaped. I longed to lose myself in that laughter, to drown out the worry and fear that clung to me like a shadow. Yet, I also felt an overwhelming need to confront the truth, to piece together the fragments of Sarah's and Ethan's connection before it threatened to consume me.

As I made my way toward the little café that served the best espresso in the city, I felt the familiar weight of uncertainty settle on my shoulders. I pushed the door open, the rich aroma of freshly ground coffee enveloping me like a warm hug. The barista, a kind-faced woman with an apron speckled with flour, greeted me with a knowing smile, as if she could sense my turmoil. I ordered a latte, its warmth soothing my frayed nerves.

In a corner, I spotted Ethan, his head bent over a table, the faint flicker of his phone screen illuminating his handsome features. My heart fluttered erratically, caught in a web of conflicting emotions. Was he waiting for me? Did he know? I took a deep breath, steeling myself for the conversation I had avoided for too long.

"Hey," I said, my voice breaking slightly as I approached him. He looked up, surprise etched across his face, swiftly replaced by a mask of concern.

"Hey," he replied softly, pushing his phone aside as if it held no importance anymore. "I heard about Sarah. I—"

"I need to talk," I interrupted, the words tumbling out like a torrent. "I need to know what you two were hiding from me."

His expression shifted, a shadow crossing his features. "It's not what you think."

A bitter laugh escaped my lips, a mixture of disbelief and pain. "Then what is it, Ethan? Because I feel like I've been living in a sitcom without a script, and it's getting a little ridiculous."

He ran a hand through his hair, frustration flickering in his eyes. "Sarah and I had a thing a long time ago. It was... complicated. But that was before you."

"Before me," I echoed, the words heavy with unspoken implications. "And yet, you never thought to mention it? Why keep it a secret?"

"I didn't want to hurt you," he said, his voice steady but laced with vulnerability. "I thought we were past it."

"Past it?" I repeated incredulously. "You think I can just forget that you had a history together? How am I supposed to feel secure with you when there's a whole chapter of your life that I know nothing about?"

Ethan leaned forward, his gaze locking onto mine with an intensity that made my heart flutter against my will. "Because what we have is real. I care about you, and I thought that was enough."

"Enough for what?" I snapped, my emotions boiling over. "For me to just accept it and move on like it's nothing? This isn't just a side note in a love story, Ethan; it's the whole plot twist."

The weight of my words hung in the air between us, a chasm that threatened to swallow us whole. For a moment, the world outside faded away, leaving only the two of us trapped in a moment that felt like an eternity.

Ethan's eyes held a depth I had never seen before, a swirling storm of emotions mirrored in their amber hue. The café, with its warm lighting and the rich scent of espresso hanging in the air, felt like a world away from the chaos swirling around us. Yet, here we were, two souls caught in an emotional tempest, tethered by the unresolved threads of our lives. The lively chatter and laughter of patrons became a distant murmur, fading into the background as our confrontation loomed large.

"You think what we have is real?" I asked, my voice steady despite the tumult within. "But can it be real when it's built on secrets? On things left unsaid?" Each word dripped with the weight of my insecurities, and I felt raw, exposed. It was as if I were peeling away layers of myself, revealing the tender flesh beneath.

Ethan opened his mouth, but I pressed on, feeling the momentum of my emotions propel me forward. "You think I'm just supposed to overlook the past? To believe that you and Sarah were just a blip on the radar? Because it feels like a lot more than that to me." My voice trembled, caught between accusation and a desperate plea for understanding.

He shifted in his seat, the tension palpable. "It wasn't just a blip, okay? It was complicated, and I didn't know how to tell you. I thought it was behind me, and I wanted to focus on us. I thought you'd be safe. I—" He paused, the frustration boiling beneath the surface as he struggled for words. "I wanted to protect you."

"Protect me?" I scoffed, the laughter that escaped my lips was brittle, a fragile shield against the flood of hurt threatening to engulf me. "By hiding the truth? You think that's protection? That's deception."

The words hung heavy between us, each syllable a reminder of the cracks forming in our once solid foundation. Ethan's expression shifted from determination to a desperate plea, his eyes searching mine for a flicker of understanding. "I never meant to hurt you. I swear, when I met you, I thought it was different. With you, everything felt real. I was falling for you, and it scared me."

The admission caught me off guard, and I felt my heart flutter against the weight of my defenses. "Falling for me? You mean while you were still carrying the weight of what happened with Sarah?" The bitterness in my voice tasted like ashes, bitter and acrid.

"I didn't carry it with me, not like that. Sarah and I—" he hesitated, pain etched in his brow. "It was a mess. We were young and foolish. I was looking for something that wasn't there, and when I found it with you, I thought it was worth the risk."

"You can't erase the past, Ethan. It doesn't just disappear because you want it to." The words tumbled out, driven by a mixture of anger and desperation. I searched his face for any sign of clarity, any hint that he understood the labyrinth of emotions I was navigating.

As silence enveloped us, I was struck by the enormity of the moment. I had stepped into the path of a truth I was ill-prepared to confront, a truth that could shatter the delicate web of our connection. And there, behind the tension, I felt a flicker of empathy for Ethan—a fellow traveler on this rocky road of love, guilt, and unresolved history.

"Did you ever love her?" I whispered, the vulnerability of my question sending a tremor through the air. The question hung between us like a heavy cloud, thick with anticipation.

His gaze faltered, and I could see the weight of the past settling on his shoulders. "I thought I did," he admitted, his voice barely above a whisper. "But it was a different kind of love. One that felt like a chase, a thrill, but never a home. With you, it feels like... like coming home."

I wanted to believe him. My heart ached for the kind of clarity that love often promised but rarely delivered. I took a deep breath, the warm aroma of coffee mingling with the cool air wafting through the open door, grounding me. "What if Sarah wakes up?"

He flinched, the question striking at the heart of our situation. "What do you mean?"

"What if she remembers? What if she wants to talk about the past? What if she tries to come back?"

"Don't," Ethan said, his voice laced with urgency. "I can't think about that right now. I can only think about you and how much I care about you. You're my present, not my past."

But the truth loomed over us, an undeniable specter. I felt as if I were standing at the edge of a precipice, staring down into the depths of uncertainty, wondering if I would find the courage to jump or the wisdom to turn back.

"I don't want to be your second choice," I confessed, tears pricking at the corners of my eyes. "And I don't want to be a chapter in your book that you can flip back to whenever you feel nostalgic. I want to be your story."

The vulnerability of my confession hung in the air, raw and aching. Ethan reached across the table, his fingers brushing against mine, igniting a spark of warmth that cut through the chill of our conversation. "You are my story, and I'll do whatever it takes to prove it to you. Just give me a chance. Let me show you that I'm not the same person I was then."

I looked into his eyes, searching for the truth behind the promise. The hope flickered like a candle, fragile yet insistent. "But can we survive this? Can we navigate what comes next?"

His grip tightened around my hand, the warmth radiating from him providing a momentary solace. "We can. I'll fight for you. I just need you to trust me."

As the words settled between us, I felt a shift in the air, a movement that whispered of possibility. It was not a guarantee, but a fragile promise that could weather the storms of our past. The world outside continued to bustle, the laughter of strangers a haunting melody that contrasted with our heavy hearts. But here, in this small café filled with the aroma of fresh coffee and the echoes of quiet conversations, I allowed myself to consider the threads of hope that could be woven into our story.

With a deep breath, I nodded, a tentative acceptance blooming within me. "Then let's start fresh. No more secrets, no more shadows."

"Agreed," he said, a flicker of relief washing over his face.

But even as the words left my mouth, a small voice in the back of my mind whispered doubts. The ghosts of our pasts were never far behind, lurking in the corners of our lives, waiting for the opportune moment to strike. As I sat across from Ethan, my heart intertwined with his, I felt the weight of that truth—a truth that would shape our future, as uncertain as it was exhilarating.

And somewhere, in a sterile room filled with the sound of machines and hushed voices, Sarah lay asleep, unaware of the tumult her life had set in motion. The threads of our stories were woven together, tangled yet vibrant, each pulling us toward a destiny yet unwritten, filled with potential and peril. The only question left was whether we would find our way through the labyrinth of love, loss, and forgiveness together, or if we would ultimately become lost in the shadows of our pasts.

Chapter 9: The Choice Between Love and Loyalty

The gallery buzzed with an electric energy, a blend of art and emotion swirling in the air, much like the vibrant colors splashed across the canvases that hung on the walls. I could feel the whispers of paintbrushes, the laughter of patrons sipping wine, and the soft jazz playing in the background—a symphony of chaos that both invigorated and unsettled me. Each painting seemed to pulse with life, vivid strokes capturing fleeting moments, lost loves, and dreams untold. But none of that mattered. I was there for Ethan.

His tall figure leaned against a wall, silhouetted by the soft glow of the track lighting. He looked both at home and out of place, like a wildflower sprouting in a manicured garden. His dark hair fell into his eyes, which flickered with uncertainty as I approached. I'd spent countless nights tossing and turning, grappling with the secret he held and its implications for Sarah, my best friend. She lay in her hospital bed, fragile but fierce, battling through the aftershocks of her accident while I prepared to face a different kind of battle.

Ethan's gaze flickered toward me, and for a moment, the world around us faded. His features softened, and I could see the shadows of regret etched in his handsome face. I hated how much I wanted to reach out and touch him, to feel the warmth of his skin, but the thought of Sarah loomed larger than my own desires. The unspoken tension between us crackled in the air, a tangible force that made it hard to breathe.

"Thank you for coming," he said, his voice low, almost drowned out by the distant clinking of glasses and the murmurs of art aficionados.

"I had to," I replied, my heart pounding. "We need to talk about Sarah."

The moment those words left my mouth, a silence settled between us, heavy and thick. He pushed off the wall, and we stepped aside, into a corner where the shadows felt a bit more forgiving. I could see the conflict in his eyes—a tempest of guilt and longing that mirrored my own confusion.

"She's my best friend, Ethan," I continued, my voice steadier than I felt. "You can't just brush this off as nothing. I need to understand what happened between you two."

His jaw tightened, and I caught the flicker of anguish as he ran a hand through his hair. "It was a mistake, that's all it was—a moment of weakness. I never meant to hurt her, and I never thought it would come to this."

His words danced around the truth, a clever choreography designed to evade the sharp edges of reality. My mind raced back to the moments when Sarah had first mentioned him—the gleam in her eyes, the way her laughter spilled into the room like sunlight. I could almost hear her soft voice, recounting tales of their encounters, her dreams blooming like flowers in spring. To think that one fleeting moment could unravel everything between us felt like a cruel twist of fate.

"Then why didn't you tell me?" I pressed, the sting of betrayal cutting deeper. "Why keep it a secret?"

Ethan sighed, his shoulders sagging under the weight of his choices. "I thought I could protect both of you. I never wanted you to find out like this, especially not now."

My heart ached for him, but it was impossible to overlook the betrayal woven into his words. Here we were, two people caught in a web of emotions, each thread tugging at my loyalty to Sarah while drawing me closer to Ethan. I wanted to be angry, to lash out and demand more, but the undeniable connection we shared—the late-night conversations, the stolen glances—wrapped around me like a vine, stifling my resolve.

"I can't just ignore this, Ethan," I said, my voice barely above a whisper. "I won't betray Sarah. She deserves better than this."

His expression shifted, the anguish in his eyes turning to desperation. "And what about you? What about what you feel? You can't pretend this connection isn't real. I see it in the way you look at me."

I opened my mouth to respond, but no words came. The air thickened, charged with the weight of unspoken truths. My heart raced as I wrestled with my feelings, with the tantalizing pull of what could be against the steadfast loyalty I had sworn to uphold. It was an impossible choice, one that felt like a game of chess where every move had dire consequences.

"I don't want to lose you," he added, stepping closer, the warmth of his body seeping into the chilly air between us.

Those words hung like a spell, wrapping around my heart and squeezing it tight. I could almost taste the bitterness of betrayal in the back of my throat. I wanted to scream, to run away from this beautiful disaster unfolding before me. But the truth was, every time I looked at him, I felt alive in ways I hadn't in years. Each heartbeat echoed with the thrilling promise of what might lie ahead.

Just then, a couple passed by, laughing and sipping their wine, their carefree joy a stark contrast to the turmoil roiling within me. I wanted that—the ease, the laughter, the blissful ignorance of complicated entanglements. But life was not that simple, was it? Choices loomed before me, and each one was laced with the potential for heartbreak, not just for myself but for the people I cared about.

"I need to go," I said finally, pulling away from the heat of his gaze. The choice before me was stark, a fork in the road that could lead to love or loyalty. As I turned to leave, a part of me shattered, the weight of the moment pressing down on my chest. I stepped out into the cool evening air, letting the chill wash over me, hoping it would numb the ache inside. The world outside felt vibrant and alive, yet all I could see were the shadows of my decision looming ahead, a reminder of what I had to confront, both with Ethan and within myself.

The crisp evening air wrapped around me like a gentle embrace as I stepped away from the gallery, each breath mingling with the distant sounds of laughter and music, fading into the backdrop of the city. The sidewalks shimmered under the glow of streetlights, casting playful reflections on the damp pavement, while a light breeze carried the mingled scents of fresh rain and the warmth of roasted chestnuts from a nearby vendor. I could hear the city breathing, alive with stories waiting to be told, yet my heart felt anchored in an unsettling heaviness.

Every step I took felt like a defiance of gravity, as if the weight of my choices threatened to pull me back toward Ethan. I could still see him standing there, the conflicted lines etched across his face, the heat of our exchange lingering like the taste of a forbidden fruit. It wasn't just guilt that held me captive; it was the promise of a different life, one that sparkled enticingly on the horizon, a life intertwined with his. But the specter of Sarah haunted me like a shadow, a constant reminder that I was teetering on the edge of a chasm, and one misstep could send me spiraling into chaos.

I navigated through the throngs of people, my thoughts swirling like the autumn leaves dancing in the wind. The bustling streets of the city felt alive with color and warmth, a stark contrast to the chill gnawing at my insides. I thought about Sarah, her laughter, the way her eyes sparkled with joy as she shared her dreams of the future. She had always been the sun in my life, brightening even the darkest days, and now she lay vulnerable and fragile, needing my unwavering loyalty.

As I reached the edge of a small park, I paused to collect my thoughts. The trees, their branches swaying gently in the breeze, stood like silent witnesses to my turmoil. I closed my eyes for a moment, letting the sounds of the city wash over me—laughter, distant music, the rhythmic honk of a taxi. But it was the echo of Ethan's voice that played in my mind, a haunting melody of longing and regret.

"Why can't you just let it go?" I whispered to the wind, but it carried my words away, leaving me in solitude with my thoughts.

In that moment, I imagined a world where choices didn't bind us, where love didn't come at the cost of loyalty. Perhaps if I could just lift the veil of uncertainty, everything would fall into place like the final piece of a puzzle. But reality had a way of crashing down on our dreams, shattering them into a million fragments, each one reflecting a different truth.

I decided to walk a bit further, seeking solace in the gentle rustle of leaves overhead. A flicker of movement caught my eye, and I glanced toward a nearby bench, where an elderly couple sat, their hands intertwined, whispering sweet nothings to each other. The sight warmed my heart, yet it also deepened my internal conflict. Their love was effortless, a bond forged through years of shared memories and unspoken understanding. I longed for that, to have a connection so profound that it transcended the fleeting moments of doubt and betrayal.

Yet, was I willing to gamble my friendship with Sarah for a chance at that kind of love? The question gnawed at me like an insistent pest.

With a sigh, I turned and headed back toward the gallery, the very place where it all began. The night had deepened, and the lights twinkled like stars against the velvet sky, their radiance a stark contrast to the shadows of my heart. I knew I had to face Ethan again, to confront not only him but the tangled mess of my emotions.

As I re-entered the gallery, the atmosphere felt charged, each whisper and laughter echoing like a heartbeat, a reminder that life continued to unfold regardless of my inner turmoil. I spotted Ethan across the room, surrounded by a cluster of admirers who admired his artwork, unaware of the storm brewing beneath the surface. He glanced up, his eyes locking onto mine, and the air between us seemed to crackle with energy, drawing me toward him like a moth to a flame.

"Can we talk?" I asked, cutting through the buzz of conversation with a voice that felt steadier than I imagined.

He nodded, his expression shifting from surprise to concern as he led me toward a quieter corner, away from the prying eyes and ears. I could feel the tension wrapping around us, thick and suffocating, as I prepared to lay bare my thoughts, my fears.

"I can't just forget what you said," I began, my heart pounding against my ribcage. "It feels like there's a storm brewing between us, and I don't know how to navigate it."

Ethan shifted, running a hand through his hair in that familiar gesture that signaled his inner turmoil. "I never wanted this to happen, you know. I was a fool to think I could keep it from you forever."

The truth hung heavy in the air, raw and unfiltered. "But you did," I replied, my voice sharper than intended. "You chose to keep me in the dark. You made decisions that affect me and Sarah without considering our feelings."

He stepped closer, his eyes searching mine for understanding. "I know I messed up. But what I feel for you is real, and I thought we could have something incredible."

"I want to believe that, but how can I? Everything is so tangled."

His gaze held mine, the weight of our emotions palpable in the charged space between us. "You have to decide what matters more. Is it the loyalty you owe to Sarah or the love we share?"

Those words hung in the air, a haunting echo that threatened to drown me. The choice felt insurmountable, as if the walls of the gallery were closing in around us, the vibrant art becoming a blur of colors and shapes. I could almost hear Sarah's laughter ringing in my ears, a reminder of what was at stake.

The world around us faded as I considered the two paths laid out before me—one illuminated by the warmth of potential love, the other cloaked in the shadows of loyalty and friendship. I took a deep breath, steeling myself for the choice that would shape not only my future but the very fabric of the relationships I cherished most. The weight of that decision pressed down on my chest, and I knew that whatever path I chose would resonate far beyond this moment, rippling through the lives of those I cared about, including my own.

The moment hung in the air, shimmering with the weight of my choices, as Ethan's gaze bore into mine. Each second stretched like the tightrope of a circus performer, ready to snap under the pressure of uncertainty. I could sense the pulse of the gallery around us, the murmurs of art enthusiasts mingling with the clinking of glasses, but within our private sphere, it was only silence, thick and suffocating.

"Do you think I'm just a mistake?" he asked, his voice barely above a whisper. The question lingered, unspoken fears lurking in the corners of his expression, shadows casting doubt on our fragile connection.

"Ethan, it's not that simple," I replied, grappling with my emotions. I could feel my heart flutter, a wild bird trapped in a cage of confusion. "You were a mistake for Sarah, but..." I hesitated, feeling the weight of the world pressing down on my shoulders. "But it feels different with us."

His eyes flickered with hope, and for a fleeting moment, I imagined what it would be like to surrender to that hope, to let go of my doubts and embrace the fiery connection that crackled between us. But the image of Sarah's face, pale and fragile in her hospital bed, flooded my mind. Her laughter echoed in my ears, a reminder of the loyalty that felt like an anchor, heavy yet grounding.

"I can't betray her, Ethan," I said, shaking my head, my resolve hardening. "She needs me now more than ever."

He stepped back, his face falling, the light in his eyes dimming like the flickering candles lining the gallery walls. "What if she never finds out? What if we could keep this between us?"

The suggestion curled around my heart like smoke, tantalizing and dangerous. "That's not fair to either of us. You know it. I want to be happy, but I can't do that at her expense."

He clenched his jaw, frustration boiling beneath the surface. "What if she's not the same person when she wakes up? What if she doesn't want what you want?"

The challenge hung heavy in the air, and my heart plummeted at the thought. What if she returned, a shell of her former self? The idea sent shivers down my spine, a cold whisper of dread creeping into my thoughts. Would I still be the same person if she didn't bounce back, if our friendship crumbled under the weight of her trauma?

"I won't make a choice based on 'what ifs,'" I asserted, fighting against the tempest within. "I need to be here for her, to help her heal."

Ethan sighed, rubbing the back of his neck in frustration, his posture a portrait of defeat. "I never wanted this to come between us. I thought we had something special."

As the words left his lips, I realized he wasn't just talking about us; he was speaking to the void that was opening up between our intertwined lives. A chasm formed, and I could see the dark abyss stretching out, threatening to swallow the love that had blossomed in the shadows. I wanted to reach across the space that separated us, to bridge the gap, but the weight of Sarah's friendship anchored me in place.

"I feel it too," I admitted, my voice softer, tinged with sorrow. "But love shouldn't come at the cost of loyalty. I can't have both, not without losing part of myself."

The gallery's vibrant colors faded into a blur, drowning in a sea of emotions. I stepped back, needing space to breathe, to think. The bustling art scene that once filled me with excitement now felt like a stage for my personal tragedy, each vibrant piece a reminder of what could be lost.

Just then, my phone buzzed, its harsh vibration cutting through the tension like a knife. I pulled it out, my heart racing at the sight of Sarah's name lighting up the screen. A message from her, a lifeline tossed into the storm of my uncertainty.

Hey! I'm feeling a bit better today. Can you come by later?

My breath caught in my throat, a wave of relief washing over me. "I have to go," I said, my voice a mere whisper, the realization hitting me like a wave. "I need to be with her."

Ethan stepped forward, a mixture of understanding and desperation etched into his features. "Will you at least think about us? About what could happen?"

I nodded, my heart aching for the connection we shared, the love that was just within reach yet felt so impossible. "I will. But right now, Sarah needs me."

I turned, walking away with a heaviness in my chest, leaving behind the warmth of his presence. The outside world felt like a cold reality check as I stepped into the bustling city streets. I could hear the distant laughter of children playing in a nearby park, the sounds of life echoing all around me, and I felt momentarily disconnected from it all.

When I arrived at the hospital, the antiseptic scent filled my nostrils, a stark reminder of where I was headed. The fluorescent lights buzzed overhead, casting a harsh glare on the walls painted a dull beige. Each step toward Sarah's room felt like a march into the unknown, my heart pounding with anticipation and dread.

As I entered, I found her propped up against the pillows, her face pale but serene, a soft smile gracing her lips as she spotted me. "You came," she said, her voice a fragile whisper, yet it resonated with warmth that melted away the icy grip of guilt I had been holding.

"Of course," I replied, rushing to her side, feeling the love swell within me. "How are you feeling?"

"I'm getting there," she replied, her eyes shimmering with determination. "The doctors say I'm on the mend. It's just going to take time."

As we talked, I could feel the space between us fill with the familiar comfort of our friendship, the laughter and the shared memories weaving a protective barrier against the uncertainty that loomed outside. I told her stories, recounting moments from our adventures, all while keeping the truth about Ethan hidden, locked away in a compartment of my heart that felt both heavy and necessary.

Her laughter rang out, a melody that brought life back into the sterile room, reminding me of everything we had built together. I couldn't let my fear for her recovery compromise what we had.

"Promise me something," Sarah said suddenly, her eyes locking onto mine, piercing through the veil of my thoughts. "Promise you won't let this change us. I can't bear the thought of losing you too."

The weight of her words settled over me, heavy and transformative. I nodded, feeling a surge of determination. "I promise."

In that moment, I realized that loyalty didn't mean sacrificing my happiness, nor did it mean choosing one person over another. It was about balancing love and friendship, finding a way to honor both. I could be there for Sarah while navigating the complexities of my feelings for Ethan.

As I sat by her side, the weight of my choices shifted, no longer a burden but a spectrum of love that stretched across the horizon. Whatever came next, I would face it with courage, weaving the threads of my heart together, crafting a tapestry rich with love, loyalty, and the beautiful chaos of life.

Chapter 10: A Recipe for Healing

Sitting at Sarah's bedside, I find myself enveloped in a world painted in shades of muted gray and clinical white. The fluorescent lights overhead cast an unflattering glow, making everything feel slightly surreal, as if I'm peering through a foggy window into a dream where time drips like melting wax. I clutch Sarah's hand, a fragile connection between us, her fingers cool and delicate, reminiscent of a butterfly perched on the brink of flight. I trace the contours of her palm, a well-worn map of our shared memories, and I can't help but recall the countless moments that have woven our lives together—our laughter echoing in sun-drenched parks, the whispered secrets exchanged under the twinkling stars, and the endless cups of coffee shared in cozy corners of our favorite café. Each memory is a thread in a tapestry, vibrant yet fraying at the edges, reminding me of the fragility of life itself.

The antiseptic aroma fills my lungs, sterile and sharp, a constant reminder of the precarious situation we find ourselves in. I glance at the machines beeping rhythmically beside her, their sterile hum underscoring the tension in the air. The beeping feels almost mocking, a reminder of how time refuses to stand still, even when we wish it would. As I gaze at Sarah's serene face, the soft rise and fall of her chest are the only signs of life, and my heart aches with the knowledge that she is fighting a battle I can only observe from the sidelines. In this moment of vulnerability, enveloped in uncertainty, I am struck by the weight of my own feelings—fear, guilt, and a deep-rooted longing to make things right, not just for her, but for me too.

I take a deep breath, attempting to steady the whirlwind of emotions threatening to spill over. What would she want? What would bring her back to the vibrant life she lived? A quiet resolve begins to bubble within me, igniting a flicker of hope amidst the shadows. I recall how Sarah always believed in the healing power of baking. How the warm aroma of vanilla and sugar could transform a dull day into a symphony of comfort. She often spoke of baking as an act of love, a tangible expression of care that could bring people together, bridging gaps and mending hearts. In her absence, I realize that I have neglected my own passion, allowing the weight of adult responsibilities to crush my creativity like a fallen soufflé.

As I leave the hospital, the cool evening air greets me like an old friend. The sun has dipped below the horizon, and the world is wrapped in a blanket of indigo twilight. I pull my jacket tighter around me, the soft fabric offering a semblance of warmth and protection against the encroaching darkness. My footsteps echo against the pavement, each step a reminder of my determination. I will bake again, and this time, it won't just be for the sake of baking; it will be a tribute to my friendship with Sarah, a way to summon her spirit back into my life.

The city is alive, the streets buzzing with activity. I pass the familiar storefronts, their windows glinting with reflections of the bustling world outside. Each shop has its own personality, like characters in a beloved novel, and I smile as I recall the hours spent exploring each one with Sarah, our laughter mingling with the sounds of the city. I make my way to the corner bakery we used to frequent—a quaint little spot that smells of freshly baked bread and sweet confections. The door chimes softly as I enter, and the warmth envelops me like a hug, making my heart swell with nostalgia.

The bakery is a riot of colors, the shelves laden with pastries that seem to whisper promises of comfort. Croissants golden and flaky, éclairs oozing with rich chocolate, and cakes decorated with delicate frosting flowers—each creation a masterpiece that beckons for attention. My heart races as I absorb the vibrant scene, the sight igniting a spark of inspiration deep within me. I approach the counter, where the baker—a stout man with flour-dusted hands and a welcoming smile—greets me like an old friend.

"Back for more, are we?" he asks, his eyes twinkling with mischief.

I chuckle, my spirits lifting. "You could say I'm looking for a bit of a creative revival."

"Ah, the best kind. What are you thinking?"

My mind races with possibilities, a flurry of flavors and textures dancing before me like a sweet ballet. "Something comforting yet bold. A recipe that embodies friendship." I pause, the words rolling off my tongue as if they've been waiting to be spoken. "How about a twist on the classic carrot cake? Warm spices, a hint of orange zest, and cream cheese frosting?"

The baker nods approvingly, a grin spreading across his face. "You've got a good sense for flavor. Let's make it memorable."

I can almost see Sarah's approving nod, her smile lighting up her face as she would always do when I shared my culinary ideas. The idea of this cake becomes a lifeline, pulling me from the depths of despair and into a world of possibility. We begin gathering the ingredients, the scent of cinnamon and nutmeg filling the air like an embrace, igniting a wave of warmth in my chest.

As I sift the flour and fold in the grated carrots, I feel the worries that had clung to me like a heavy cloak start to peel away. The act of creating is therapeutic, a form of meditation that quiets my mind and nourishes my spirit. I mix the batter with a fervor, pouring my heart into each stir, envisioning the moment Sarah would take a bite, her eyes widening in delight. With each ingredient added, I find myself more alive, reconnected with a part of me that had lain dormant for far too long. This cake would be my offering, a recipe for healing—not just for Sarah, but for the both of us.

The oven hums with a quiet confidence as I watch the carrot cake rise, its golden surface puffing up like a promise kept. I lean against the counter, a small smile creeping onto my face as the sweet aroma envelops the kitchen. The air is warm and inviting, heavy with the scent of spices that evoke memories of family gatherings and laughter echoing around the dining table. In this cozy haven, I find solace, my thoughts drifting like flour dust in the gentle sunlight streaming through the window.

As the timer ticks down, I decide to distract myself with a bit of tidying up. The kitchen, usually a battleground of flour and sugar, now feels like a sanctuary. I run my fingers along the wooden countertops, catching a glimpse of my reflection in the shiny surface—a face marked with both worry and hope, an expression I hadn't seen in a long time. I catch a glimpse of the mismatched mugs on the shelf, remnants of countless coffee dates with Sarah, each one holding a story, a secret shared over steaming cups of brew.

The kettle begins to whistle, a sharp reminder of my own needs, and I pour myself a cup, the steam curling up into the air, as I allow myself a moment of reflection. This kitchen is a canvas, and today, I'm an artist reclaiming my brush after years of putting it aside. The vibrant hues of the ingredients remind me of the joy that once flowed so freely from my fingertips. Baking had always been my therapy, a way to transform chaos into something beautiful and delicious. Today feels different, though; it feels like a rebirth, a chance to turn the page and write a new chapter.

With the cake cooling on the rack, I turn my attention to the cream cheese frosting. I whip the softened cheese with butter until it's light and airy, the rich, tangy sweetness sending my taste buds into a dance. I can already imagine how it will pair with the spiced cake—a perfect balance of flavors, just like the friendship Sarah and I had built over the years. Each swirl of frosting feels like a word in a poem, each layer an affirmation of my commitment to her, and to myself.

Once the cake is frosted, I step back to admire my work. The layers, slightly uneven yet charming in their own right, are adorned with a generous swirl of frosting, a final touch of love that ties it all together. I pause, soaking in the sight of it—a reflection of my heart laid bare. I'm not just baking for Sarah; I'm crafting a piece of my soul, a declaration that I will not let fear dictate my life any longer.

With the cake in its box, I head out, the weight of it in my hands a comforting reminder of my purpose. The sun has dipped lower in the sky, painting everything in soft pastels, casting a golden glow that makes the city feel alive. I navigate the streets with a sense of determination, each step fueling my resolve. The cool breeze whispers secrets of renewal, wrapping around me like a warm embrace.

As I approach the hospital, a surge of anxiety rushes through me, but I push it aside, reminding myself of the love and care infused in every bite of the cake. I take a deep breath, steadying myself before stepping into the sterile environment that holds my dear friend. The moment I enter her room, the familiar sounds of beeping machines and soft voices greet me. Sarah lies there, peaceful yet still, as if she is merely sleeping.

"Hey, you," I say softly, placing the cake gently on the table beside her. "I brought you something."

I move closer, my heart racing. As I unwrap the cake, the sweet aroma fills the air, mingling with the hospital's sterile scent, creating a strangely comforting concoction. I can almost see her smile, the one that lights up her entire face and transforms her into a beacon of joy. "It's carrot cake," I explain, carefully slicing a generous piece and placing it on a plate. "Your favorite. I thought we could celebrate your recovery, you know, when you wake up."

I can't help but reminisce about our last baking adventure—the way flour had danced in the air like confetti, and how we'd ended up with more batter on ourselves than in the bowl. It was a chaotic, wonderful mess, and laughter had echoed off the walls, creating a warmth that made everything feel right in the world. I lean over her, whispering, "You have to come back soon, so we can make a mess together again."

After a moment of silence, I take a small bite of the cake, letting the flavors swirl around my mouth. "It's delicious," I say with a grin, hoping she can hear me. "And once you're back, we'll perfect it together." I'm met with silence, the machines continuing their rhythmic beeping, but somehow, I feel her presence. It's almost as if she's there, nudging me to keep talking, to keep our connection alive even in the stillness of this room.

As I sit, I find myself sharing stories, recounting the little moments that pepper my days—the barista at our favorite café who always knows our order, the new book I've been reading, and the curious little cat that has taken up residence in my backyard. Each tale is a thread woven into the fabric of our friendship, a reminder that even in her absence, I carry her with me. The cake becomes more than just a dessert; it transforms into a bridge, a way for me to express the love and hope I have for her recovery.

Time slips away unnoticed, and before long, the room is bathed in the soft light of dusk. I pause, glancing at the untouched slice of cake on the plate. I want so desperately for her to taste it, to feel the comfort it brings. "I'll save you a slice, I promise," I murmur, my voice barely above a whisper. The silence that follows is heavy, yet filled with an unspoken understanding.

With a heart full of hope, I take a moment to appreciate this space between us—this beautiful, fragile moment where love transcends the physical realm. It's not just about the cake or the memories; it's about the bond we share, the resilience that life demands, and the unwavering belief that healing is possible. I know that, like the layers of this cake, our friendship has depth, complexity, and sweetness, and it will rise again, stronger and more vibrant than before.

The cake, with its sumptuous layers and billowy frosting, has become my talisman—a physical embodiment of my hopes for Sarah. I carefully pack it up and transport it through the bustling streets, feeling an electric pulse of life around me. The sunset casts an amber glow over the city, bathing everything in warmth. Each step feels purposeful, resonating with the rhythm of my heartbeat as I traverse the familiar sidewalks where Sarah and I had once walked side by side, sharing dreams and whispers.

I stop by the park, a sanctuary where we used to escape from the chaos of life, a slice of nature in the heart of the urban sprawl. The trees stand tall, their leaves rustling gently in the evening breeze, each whispering a secret. I can almost hear Sarah's laughter weaving through the branches, inviting me to linger a little longer. I take a moment to sit on a weathered bench, the wood cool against the warmth of my hands, and close my eyes. In the distance, children's laughter echoes, their joyful shouts punctuating the air with innocent exuberance. This park has always been a backdrop to our lives, a canvas for our memories—sun-drenched afternoons spent picnicking on the grass, late-night heart-to-heart talks illuminated by the silvery glow of the moon.

With a deep breath, I ground myself in the present. My thoughts drift back to the cake, a sweet reminder of everything we've shared. The past few weeks have felt like a whirlpool of emotions, a blend of fear and determination, and now, standing in this moment, I can feel the resolve hardening within me. I must channel this energy, this creative force, not only into baking but into every facet of my life.

As twilight deepens, I rise from the bench, adjusting my jacket against the cool evening air. The hospital looms ahead like a modern fortress, its stark lines softened by the glow of the lights within. My heart quickens as I step inside, the familiar antiseptic scent washing over me like a tidal wave. The nurses greet me with nods, their expressions warm yet tinged with concern, reminding me of the reality that waits beyond the walls.

Entering Sarah's room, the quiet hum of the machines fills the air. I set the cake on the table beside her, the sight of it bringing a smile to my face even in this sterile environment. "Look what I brought you," I whisper, gently brushing a stray hair from her forehead. "I made it just for you. It's our recipe, you know—just like the ones we used to make together." The silence settles around us, thick and palpable, yet in my heart, I feel her presence.

I slice a piece, the knife gliding through the tender cake with ease. As I bring the fork to her lips, a spark of hope ignites within me. I imagine the taste, the sweetness melting away the bitterness of our circumstances. "Just a little taste, Sarah. You've got to come back for more," I coax softly, the words laced with both humor and longing.

The hours pass like fleeting shadows, each moment an echo of the life we've shared. I recount our adventures, painting pictures with my words, as if to conjure her spirit from the depths of sleep. I speak of the absurdity of the barista's latest attempt at latte art, of the way he claimed he could create a perfect heart shape. "It looked more like a potato," I laugh, hoping to invoke a reaction from her, even if it's just a flicker of an eyelid.

In the midst of my stories, a low beep from the machines pulls my attention. I watch the rhythm of the monitors, feeling an odd sense of calm wash over me. I talk on, weaving memories into the fabric of our shared past, letting each tale breathe life into the room.

As the night drags on, a quietness envelops the hospital, the kind that seeps into your bones. I sip the lukewarm coffee a nurse had brought me hours earlier, its bitter taste now unappealing. Just as I consider leaving for a fresh cup, I catch a glimmer of movement from the corner of my eye. My heart skips a beat. Sarah's fingers twitch, a slight flutter that sends a jolt of energy through me. I lean closer, willing her to hear me. "You're still here with me, right? Just hang on a little longer."

In that instant, the air shifts. The weight of uncertainty hangs heavy, yet hope dances like fireflies in the dark. My heart races, pounding in tandem with the pulse of the machines. I reach for her hand, intertwining my fingers with hers, feeling a warmth begin to bloom once more. "You have to wake up. We have more cakes to bake, more laughter to share. I need you, Sarah."

As if summoned by my words, her eyes flutter open, revealing the rich depths of her brown irises. Confusion etches her features, but then recognition dawns, and her lips curl into a faint smile, one that tugs at my heart. "Caitlyn?" she whispers, her voice barely more than a breath, yet it rings like a bell in the stillness of the room.

"Yeah, it's me!" I exclaim, unable to contain my joy. "You scared me for a moment there. I brought you cake!" My laughter bubbles up, almost hysterical, a release of the tension that had been coiling inside me.

"I—cake?" she murmurs, blinking slowly as if the world is coming back into focus.

"Yep! Your favorite carrot cake," I reply, the words tumbling out with unrestrained excitement. "I knew you'd want to celebrate your return to the land of the living."

As I lift the fork to her lips, I feel the warmth of her hand tighten around mine. She takes a small bite, her expression shifting from confusion to bliss as the flavors dance across her palate. "It's so good," she whispers, a hint of her old spark returning to her eyes.

"Just wait until you have more," I tease, holding the cake as though it were the most precious thing in the world. And in a way, it is—a testament to our friendship and the promise of new beginnings. The room brightens with her smile, a beacon of hope in the dim light.

With every bite she takes, my heart swells with gratitude. The healing I had sought for her is unfolding right before my eyes. I can feel the shadows lifting, the heaviness of the past few weeks dissipating like fog under the morning sun. We sit together, lost in our own little world, savoring the simple pleasure of being alive and connected.

In that moment, I know that whatever challenges lie ahead, we will face them together, hand in hand, armed with laughter, love, and the knowledge that healing takes time but is always possible. The world outside may be chaotic, but within these four walls, we have created our own sanctuary, a haven where friendship and resilience reign supreme. And as we share the last bites of cake, I realize that this is just the beginning—of healing, of growth, and of the unbreakable bond that will carry us through whatever life throws our way.

Chapter 11: Whispers in the Wind

The sun dipped low in the sky, casting a warm golden hue over the streets of our quaint little town, where the scent of fresh-baked bread and the whisper of sweet pastries mingled with the brisk autumn air. Luna's Sweet Retreat stood proudly at the corner, its window displays adorned with an array of colorful confections that seemed to dance in the light, each one a beacon calling to those who craved something extraordinary. As I stepped inside, the familiar jingle of the bell above the door rang like an invitation to a world where worries melted away with each bite of dessert.

I threw my apron over my head, the soft cotton fabric still faintly scented with flour and vanilla from the day before. My heart raced with anticipation, not just for the sweet creations I was about to craft, but also for the memories I would weave into each pastry. The kitchen was a canvas, and I was an artist determined to create a masterpiece born from friendship. Memories of Sarah enveloped me like a warm embrace, her laughter a sweet melody that echoed through my mind as I gathered the ingredients: plump raspberries, juicy peaches, and tart lemons, each one a thread in the tapestry of our shared experiences.

My hands moved deftly as I combined the flour and butter, the chill of the ingredients a stark contrast to the warmth in my heart. I could almost hear Sarah's voice, her playful banter about my baking quirks, as I meticulously measured each component. This new collection was my way of honoring our friendship, of turning every worry into something delightful and edible. A dash of cinnamon here, a splash of cream there—each decision carried the weight of our shared past, a celebration of moments spent in laughter and camaraderie.

As I began to roll out the dough, my thoughts wandered to the last time we had been together, standing in this very kitchen. We had laughed over failed recipes and celebrated small victories, each one a testament to our resilience and creativity. I could picture her, her dark hair tied back in a messy bun, flour dusting her cheeks as she leaned over the counter, her eyes sparkling with mischief. It was those memories that pushed me forward, igniting a fire within me to create something that would not only be a feast for the palate but also a feast for the soul.

Lost in my culinary reverie, I barely noticed when Ethan stepped into the bakery. The moment he crossed the threshold, the atmosphere shifted, a gentle breeze bringing in the scent of the crisp fall air mixed with the aroma of fresh pastries. I turned, a smudge of flour dusting my nose, and found him standing there, concern etched on his handsome face. His brows knitted together as he scanned the room, but the moment our eyes met, I could see a flicker of something else—hope? Perhaps.

"Hey," he said, his voice low but warm, breaking the comfortable silence that had settled between us. "You look like you're in deep trouble."

I chuckled softly, the sound a balm against the tension. "Just experimenting. It's either going to be brilliant or a complete disaster."

He stepped closer, hands tucked into the pockets of his jeans, his posture relaxed yet attentive. "Can I help?"

The invitation hung in the air like a tantalizing aroma, filling the space with possibility. I hesitated, the weight of my doubts pressing against me, but then I nodded, unable to resist the chance to work alongside him again. We had shared so many moments in this kitchen, and though the air was still thick with unsaid words, there was a warmth in the way he looked at me, a connection that made my heart flutter.

Together, we set to work, the rhythm of our movements creating a harmony that felt both familiar and new. Ethan grabbed a mixing bowl, and I handed him the raspberries, their vibrant red color bursting with life. As we prepared the vibrant fruit tarts, our conversations flowed effortlessly, each laugh punctuating the air like confetti, lifting the weight of uncertainty that had settled between us since that last encounter.

He was surprisingly adept, tossing the fruits with a deftness that belied his initial hesitance in the kitchen. "Who knew you had a secret pastry chef in you?" I teased, a smile breaking across my face. The tension of earlier moments began to dissolve, replaced by the easy banter we had once shared so effortlessly.

"Let's just say I'm a quick learner," he shot back, a playful grin tugging at his lips. The lightness between us was palpable, and with each tart we crafted, I could feel the distance that had kept us apart shrinking, the invisible barriers dissolving with the heat of the oven.

The kitchen became our sanctuary, each pastry we created echoing our laughter and shared stories. I poured my heart into the tarts, each layer a reflection of my feelings, my hopes, and the memories that wrapped around us like a warm blanket. It felt like a dance, a push and pull of emotion that flowed seamlessly between us. I couldn't help but steal glances at him, his focused expression juxtaposed against the lightheartedness we shared. The flickering of something more danced at the edges of my mind, like the last rays of sun slipping away at dusk.

As we placed the last tart in the oven, I let out a contented sigh, a sense of accomplishment washing over me. The kitchen smelled heavenly, the sweet and tart aromas swirling together, promising something extraordinary. Ethan leaned against the counter, arms crossed, watching me with an intensity that made my heart race. The glimmer in his eyes suggested he understood the weight behind my creations, the love I poured into them, and perhaps, just perhaps, the love that was beginning to blossom between us once more.

I felt a rush of warmth spread through me, a delicate reminder that in the midst of my worries and uncertainties, there was still beauty to be found, not just in the pastries but in the connections we forged. In that moment, surrounded by the sweet scent of success, I realized that maybe, just maybe, the echoes of my doubts were simply whispers in the wind, overshadowed by the vibrant energy that pulsed between us.

The oven hummed softly in the background, its warmth wrapping around us like a comforting shawl, as we patiently awaited the fruits of our labor. The sweet scent of sugar mingled with the vibrant notes of citrus and berry, creating an atmosphere that felt both alive and electric. I caught Ethan glancing my way, a soft smile playing at the corners of his lips. The way he watched me, not with scrutiny but with genuine appreciation, ignited a warmth in my chest, a flicker of something that reminded me how easily we had once connected.

"Have you ever thought about doing this on a larger scale?" he asked, breaking the comfortable silence as we leaned against the counter, the stillness punctuated only by the gentle ticking of the clock on the wall. "I mean, your pastries are incredible. You could turn this place into something really special."

His words wrapped around me, lifting me like the dough rising in the bowl. A world of possibility unfolded in my mind. I had never considered expanding Luna's Sweet Retreat beyond its quaint walls, but now, the idea spun through my thoughts like sugar spun into candy. I glanced around the cozy bakery, its rustic charm and warm atmosphere an extension of myself, a little haven where I had poured my heart into every cupcake and cookie. What would it look like to share that joy on a grander scale?

"Maybe," I replied slowly, the notion swirling in the air between us, a sweet aroma just waiting to bloom. "But it feels so personal here. I like that every pastry tells a story, you know? Each one has a piece of my heart baked into it."

Ethan's expression softened as he nodded, as if he understood the weight of those words better than I did myself. "And you're doing something right. People love coming here. Your pastries make them happy."

A sudden burst of laughter erupted from the oven as the timer dinged, breaking the moment's intensity. I rushed to pull out the trays, the delightful sight of the golden-brown tarts almost too beautiful to touch. They gleamed with a glossy fruit glaze, the vibrant colors inviting and cheerful, a true reflection of the emotions we had poured into them. "These are incredible!" I exclaimed, a sense of pride swelling in my chest. "I think we've created a masterpiece."

Ethan leaned closer, his breath warm against my cheek as he peered at the tarts. "You know, I'm pretty sure you could win some kind of baking award for these."

I could feel my cheeks warming under his gaze, the compliment settling around me like a soft blanket. "I don't know about that. I think I'm just doing what feels right." My laughter mingled with his, the lightness between us palpable. It was in moments like these that I felt the weight of my worries lift, even if just for a fleeting second.

As we began plating the tarts, the sunlight streaming through the bakery windows painted golden patches on the countertop. I glanced out at the world beyond, where leaves danced in the wind, their colors transitioning into fiery hues of orange and red. Autumn was in full swing, and it brought with it a sense of change that echoed through my own life. I inhaled deeply, letting the sweet scent of success fill my lungs.

"Want to try one?" I asked, lifting a fork and playfully nudging it in his direction. "You can be my official taste tester."

Ethan chuckled, his eyes sparkling with mischief. "Only if you promise to share the recipe with me."

"Deal," I said, the words spilling out before I could think. In truth, I had never shared my recipes—each one was a sacred part of my craft. But something about the way he looked at me made it feel right. As we indulged in the first bite, the flavor exploded on my tongue—tangy, sweet, and buttery all at once. I couldn't help but close my eyes, letting the moment envelop me.

"Wow," he said, his voice a low rumble, breaking my reverie. "This is amazing. You really have a gift."

There was something electrifying about standing there with him, our shoulders brushing as we savored the tarts, our laughter punctuating the air like the notes of a favorite song. I felt a surge of courage, a gentle nudge from the universe reminding me that perhaps I didn't have to navigate my fears alone. There was beauty in sharing, and in that moment, it felt like we were building a bridge over the chasm of doubt that had separated us.

As the afternoon sun began to sink, casting elongated shadows across the bakery floor, our playful banter turned into something deeper. We spoke about dreams, desires, and the fear of pursuing them, the conversation flowing like melted chocolate—rich, dark, and utterly addictive. I shared my aspirations for Luna's Sweet Retreat, my hopes to transform it into a gathering place for the community, where people could come together over pastries and connect through shared experiences.

Ethan listened intently, nodding with encouragement, and as I spoke, I could see a flicker of admiration in his eyes. "I think you're onto something special," he said thoughtfully. "A place where people feel at home, where they can enjoy good food and good company. That's what life is about, right?"

His words hung in the air, a soft promise of possibility that warmed my heart. Suddenly, I felt bold, like the dough that had risen to new heights. "You could help me," I blurted out, the suggestion slipping out before I could reel it back in. "If you wanted to, of course. You're great with people, and I could use an extra set of hands."

He raised an eyebrow, a playful smirk tugging at his lips. "Are you sure you want me around in your kitchen? I might eat all your profits."

I laughed, the sound bright and genuine, and I couldn't shake the feeling that I wanted him around—beyond the kitchen, beyond the pastries. "I guess I'll just have to keep the snacks hidden then."

His smile widened, a glimmer of enthusiasm lighting up his face. "Count me in. I'd love to help."

In that moment, the uncertainty of our past began to fade, replaced by the promise of a shared future. As we continued to talk and laugh, I felt the walls I had built around my heart begin to crumble. I was reminded that, while the echoes of doubt may linger in the corners of my mind, they could never overshadow the joy of shared experiences and the warmth of companionship. Life, like a perfectly baked tart, was meant to be savored—each layer revealing a new surprise, a delightful burst of flavor that left you yearning for more. And standing there, in the heart of Luna's Sweet Retreat, I felt ready to embrace whatever came next, with Ethan by my side, the winds of change carrying us forward into a brighter, sweeter tomorrow.

As twilight settled around Luna's Sweet Retreat, the soft glow of fairy lights twinkled against the dusky sky, casting a warm ambiance that wrapped around us like a comforting embrace. The bakery, with its rustic wooden beams and flour-dusted counters, felt like a cocoon, a safe haven where the outside world's chaos faded away. Ethan and I stood side by side, savoring the last of our tarts, the delightful sweetness lingering on our lips.

With the oven cooling and the last rays of sun filtering through the windows, I turned to Ethan, emboldened by the camaraderie we had fostered. "What do you think about hosting a little tasting event?" The idea burst forth, as spontaneous as the first drop of rain on a parched day. "We could invite our friends, maybe even some locals. Showcase the new collection and get feedback. It could be fun!"

Ethan's eyes lit up, a spark igniting in the depths of his gaze. "I love that! It's a great way to get people involved, and who wouldn't want to sample your creations?" His enthusiasm was contagious, and I felt my heart lift, buoyed by the potential of what we could create together.

The more I envisioned the event, the more I realized it wasn't merely about the pastries; it was about connection, community, and sharing my heart with others. I could picture the bakery filled with laughter, the walls echoing with joy, the air thick with the scent of freshly baked goods. It would be a celebration of friendship, a tribute to Sarah, and perhaps even a step toward a brighter future.

"Let's do it!" I declared, a giddy rush surging through me. "I can start preparing invitations tomorrow, and we can plan the menu together. It'll be a collaboration." The thought of creating something with Ethan sparked a fire within me, illuminating a path forward that felt both thrilling and terrifying.

With newfound determination, I began outlining the details in my mind, the bakery transforming into a vibrant space filled with people sampling pastries and sharing stories. I imagined an inviting display, an array of colorful tarts and delicate pastries, each one telling a story of its own—a piece of my heart on a plate. I could envision friends gathering around the tables, laughter spilling from their lips, the clinking of glasses as they toasted to friendship and new beginnings.

Ethan's laughter snapped me back to the present, the sound warm and genuine. "Okay, let's take it one step at a time. We'll need a solid plan." His practical nature grounded me, and together, we began to draft our vision for the event.

As the evening wore on, we transitioned from planning to a comfortable rhythm, our conversations effortlessly weaving from serious to playful. I found myself reveling in the lightness of our banter, the way our laughter intermingled like the flavors in the pastries we had created. Each moment felt precious, and I cherished the way he leaned closer when he spoke, the subtle spark between us igniting with every shared glance.

Time slipped by unnoticed, the world outside fading into the backdrop as we worked side by side, filling the bakery with an infectious energy. With each passing hour, I could feel the weight of my doubts dissipating, replaced by an exhilarating sense of possibility. Ethan became a part of my creative process, not just as an assistant but as a collaborator, breathing new life into my ideas and challenging me to think outside the confines of my cozy little bakery.

Finally, as we finished drafting our plans, Ethan stretched and let out a contented sigh. "I think we've done well for one night. It's late, and I should probably head home." His eyes held a hint of reluctance, and I felt a twinge of disappointment at the prospect of him leaving.

"Wait," I said impulsively, my voice a blend of hope and nervousness. "How about we celebrate this new venture with a slice of pie?"

"Pie?" he echoed, eyebrows raised in playful surprise. "Are we moving into the realm of savory? I thought we were just about sweets."

"Only if I can make it sweet," I replied, grinning. "I have a fantastic recipe for a spiced apple pie. It's one of my favorites."

The smile that spread across his face sent warmth flooding through me. "I'm in," he said, his voice low and inviting.

The kitchen sprang to life again as I pulled out ingredients, the familiar dance of flour and sugar invigorating me. With Ethan by my side, we navigated the process, our movements fluid and in sync, as if we were performing an intricate ballet. I tossed a handful of spices into the bowl, and the warm scent of cinnamon and nutmeg filled the air, wrapping around us like a cozy blanket.

As the pie baked, we settled into a comfortable silence, the warm glow of the oven casting flickering shadows across the room. I caught Ethan stealing glances at me, and each time, my heart skipped a beat. There was something magnetic about him, a pull that made it impossible to look away. I felt the words I wanted to say hovering just at the edge of my lips, but fear held me back, like a child clutching a fragile dream.

"What about you, Ethan? What's your dream?" I asked suddenly, my voice breaking the stillness. The question hung in the air, and I watched as his expression shifted, a flicker of surprise followed by thoughtfulness.

He leaned back against the counter, arms crossed over his chest, contemplating. "Honestly? I've always wanted to travel, see the world beyond our little town. I've dreamed of experiencing different cultures, trying foods I've only read about." His eyes sparkled with passion, and I felt a pang of longing for him, for the adventures he yearned for, the places he dreamed of exploring.

I wanted to tell him that it was possible, that he didn't have to settle for the confines of our little bakery, but the words tangled in my throat. Instead, I reached out and brushed a stray flour speck from his cheek, my fingers lingering longer than necessary. "You should go," I whispered, the urgency of my words catching us both off guard.

Ethan's gaze met mine, his eyes deep pools of emotion, and for a moment, the world outside faded into nothingness. "Maybe someday," he replied, his voice low, laced with an intensity that sent shivers down my spine.

The oven timer chimed, pulling us back into the moment, and I jumped to retrieve the pie. As I opened the door, the scent wafted out, enveloping us in a warm embrace. I couldn't help but beam with pride at the golden crust, perfectly baked, its surface glistening with the promise of sweet indulgence.

With a flourish, I cut us generous slices, and as we sank our forks into the warm pie, the mingling flavors burst forth, a delightful symphony of sweet apples and spices dancing across our tongues. Each bite was a celebration, a testament to the journey we were embarking on together.

"I think we've outdone ourselves," I said, savoring the moment, the richness of the pie echoing the richness of our connection.

Ethan chuckled, his eyes crinkling with delight. "I have to admit, this might just be the best way to end the night."

The kitchen hummed with warmth and laughter, and in that moment, I knew that this wasn't just a pastry or a pie; it was the beginning of something extraordinary. As the flavors melded on our tongues, the uncertainty of the future transformed into a canvas waiting to be painted with new memories. I felt ready to embrace whatever came next, the winds of change swirling around us, promising adventure, connection, and the sweet thrill of possibility.

Chapter 12: Tides of Change

The air inside the bakery is alive with the comforting warmth of freshly baked goods, a symphony of sugary scents swirling around like a delightful melody. Each day, I stand behind the counter, draped in my flour-dusted apron, the gentle hum of the ovens a constant companion. Today, however, a thunderstorm grumbles outside, casting a dramatic shadow over the quaint storefront. Raindrops patter against the windowpanes, creating a rhythmic backdrop that feels almost theatrical. I watch the world beyond, where umbrellas bloom like flowers and the streets shimmer with the sheen of rain, and it strikes me how my bakery is a refuge in this tumultuous weather—a place where worries can melt away like the chocolate in my signature éclairs.

As the door swings open, the little bell above jingles cheerfully, momentarily cutting through the sound of the rain. A couple enters, shaking off droplets like dogs after a swim. They pause, taking in the scene with wide-eyed wonder, as if they've stumbled into a dream. My heart skips at the sight of their smiles, so bright against the dim light of the bakery. The man, tall with tousled hair and a lopsided grin, immediately gravitates toward the display case, eyes glistening with anticipation. Beside him, a woman with an infectious laugh catches my eye. Her vibrant scarf—an explosion of reds and oranges—frames her face, echoing the autumn leaves that flutter just beyond the glass.

"Wow," the man says, leaning closer, a childlike curiosity illuminating his features. "This is incredible! I think I can actually feel my taste buds quivering with excitement."

I can't help but laugh, a sound that feels as light as the macaron shells I've painstakingly crafted. "That's the goal! Each pastry is meant to spark a little joy."

As they introduce themselves as food critics for a prominent magazine, my heart leaps. I've dreamt of moments like this, when my creations would earn recognition beyond my small town, carried by the hands of those who understand the artistry behind baking. It's a bittersweet moment, though; I can feel Ethan, standing a few steps behind me, retreating into his shell, a faint shadow amidst the bright colors of the room. He's been a constant presence since I opened the bakery, the quiet artist to my loud pastry chef, his talents in the kitchen almost a whisper compared to my vibrant shout.

"What do you recommend?" the woman asks, her eyes sparkling with the thrill of discovery.

I step forward, a swirl of excitement coursing through me. "The raspberry croissants are a must-try, and the dark chocolate tarts—" I pause, catching Ethan's eye. His expression is inscrutable, a mask of quiet contemplation, which makes my heart twist in a way I can't quite articulate. "—they're rich, with a hint of sea salt to balance the sweetness."

The critics nod eagerly, their attention still riveted on me as they survey the counter. It's in moments like this that I feel invincible, as if the bakery itself is an extension of my spirit, filled with hope and sweet dreams. I tell them the stories behind my recipes—how the croissant dough is layered and folded, kissed by the breeze of nostalgia from my grandmother's kitchen. The words spill from me like the batter from my mixing bowl, thick with passion and buoyed by the warmth of their interest.

But as I talk, I can sense Ethan's retreat, his body language shifting as he stands at the edge of the scene, arms crossed, an expression of uncertainty clouding his features. I want to reach out, to pull him into this whirlwind of excitement, but I hesitate. Is this what he wants? I've never known someone so talented yet so reluctant to embrace the spotlight. He's the kind of guy who finds solace in the corners of a crowded room, observing rather than engaging, and I worry that I've pulled him too far into my world.

The couple orders several pastries, and I watch them savor each bite, their delight palpable. My heart swells with pride as they rave about the flavors. But the jubilance feels muted, like a song playing in a distant room. I steal glances at Ethan, who has retreated to the back, washing his hands with the same meticulous care he uses when crafting his own dishes. The distance between us grows, and with it, a storm of insecurities brews. Is it selfish of me to revel in my moment of recognition when he seems to struggle with his own?

"Your pastries are magical!" the woman exclaims, breaking me from my reverie. "I can see why people rave about this place. It's a little slice of heaven."

Her words swirl around me, yet they can't touch the turmoil brewing beneath my surface. "Thank you," I manage, my voice a soft whisper. I glance back toward the kitchen, catching Ethan's eye for just a moment before he looks away. It's as if he's retreated behind a veil, and I'm left on this side, grappling with the weight of my burgeoning success.

As the couple leaves, their laughter trailing like a warm breeze behind them, I can't shake the unease settling in my chest. I turn to find Ethan, but he's already slipping into the back, his footsteps quiet against the tiled floor. The weight of the day presses down, and I'm left alone in the bakery, surrounded by the remnants of joy and the ghosts of my worries. I can't help but wonder if our paths are meant to intertwine or if fate is leading us apart, like the shifting tides outside my door, always moving, always changing.

The raindrops continue to dance against the window, and I'm left standing in the dim glow of the bakery, a whirlwind of emotions threatening to sweep me away. The joyful chatter from the critics lingers in the air, but the warmth of their praise feels like a distant echo, fading as I turn toward the kitchen. The space feels heavier now, like the calm before a storm, and my heart beats a little faster as I approach the door that separates us.

Inside, Ethan is busy tidying up, wiping down surfaces with a meticulousness that's almost meditative. There's something soothing about the way he moves, each gesture purposeful, yet I sense an uncharacteristic tension in the air. As I step in, the kitchen envelops me like a comforting embrace, but I can't shake the feeling that something deeper lies beneath the surface. I want to break through, to offer him the same sense of buoyancy the critics have given me, but every word feels like it might shatter the fragile atmosphere we've built together.

"Hey," I say softly, my voice almost swallowed by the clatter of pans and the whir of the mixer. "Did you try any of the pastries?"

Ethan glances up, his eyes momentarily sparkling with a hint of mischief, but it quickly dissipates. "I caught a whiff of the raspberry croissants. They smell incredible," he replies, his tone light but lacking the usual enthusiasm. He leans against the counter, arms folded, a wall of uncertainty between us.

"Did you want to taste one?" I step closer, determined to bridge the gap that feels like it has stretched into an abyss. "They're even better fresh out of the oven."

"I'm good." The refusal slips from his lips too quickly, a reflex rather than a decision. He glances back at the sink, as if the dishes hold more interest than our conversation. A twinge of disappointment stings.

I watch him, the way his fingers toy with the edge of a towel, and I wonder what thoughts are swirling behind those quiet eyes. How could I ever be so bold as to uncover the layers of his insecurities when I can barely unearth my own? It's as if we're two ships passing in the night, anchored in our own harbors, afraid to reach out and tether ourselves to the other.

"Ethan, can we talk?" The words escape me before I can reconsider, and I instantly feel vulnerable, exposed in a way I haven't allowed myself to be since opening the bakery.

He straightens, the lines of his shoulders tightening. "Sure."

I take a deep breath, gathering courage like dough rising in a warm oven. "I can't shake the feeling that you've been distant since the critics came in. I want you to share in this excitement with me."

A shadow crosses his face, and I can see the wheels turning, a battle waged between his desire to open up and the familiar urge to retreat into the safety of silence. "It's just... I've always been in the background. I'm not the one people come to see."

"But your creations are incredible! I couldn't have done any of this without you," I counter, urgency coloring my voice. "You have this amazing talent, Ethan. Don't you want to share that with others?"

He sighs, a sound that seems to echo against the walls, and I can feel the weight of his uncertainty pressing down like an anvil. "It's easier for me to stay behind the scenes. I like it that way. This is your bakery, your spotlight. I don't want to take that away from you."

A small part of me aches at the thought of him dimming his light for my sake. "You're not taking anything away from me. If anything, I feel like I'm missing a piece of the puzzle when you don't let your voice be heard."

Ethan looks away, gaze drifting to the window, where the rain continues to patter softly, a backdrop to our brewing storm. "What if no one cares? What if they don't like what I have to offer?"

His vulnerability is palpable, and my heart swells with a need to protect him. "Then we'll figure it out together," I say gently, stepping closer, the distance between us narrowing. "I'm not going to let you fade into the background. You have so much to offer, and it deserves to be celebrated."

For a moment, his eyes flicker with something—hope, perhaps?—before the shadow of doubt reclaims its space. "You really think so?"

"I know so," I insist, my voice steadier than I feel. "You're a brilliant chef, Ethan. The world needs to see that."

He finally meets my gaze, and the tension in his expression begins to soften, like butter melting on warm toast. "Okay," he says slowly, as if testing the word on his tongue. "I'll think about it."

My heart lifts at his willingness to entertain the idea, but a tiny voice in the back of my mind warns me not to hold my breath. "That's all I ask. Just consider it. You have a talent that deserves to shine."

The kitchen, once heavy with uncertainty, begins to feel lighter. A tentative smile breaks across his face, a crack in the armor he often wears, and I can't help but mirror it. It's in these fleeting moments, filled with unspoken possibilities, that I realize how much I want him by my side, not just as my partner in the kitchen but in this beautiful chaos we've created together.

We spend the rest of the afternoon preparing for the weekend rush, laughter weaving through the air as we bake side by side. Each whisk of the mixer, every roll of dough becomes a conversation, a shared experience that strengthens the bond we've begun to forge. The rain slows outside, and a ray of sunlight breaks through the clouds, illuminating the kitchen like a spotlight on our unfolding story.

As we package the pastries together, I can't help but feel that change is on the horizon, a tide gently nudging us toward something new. Ethan may not be ready to step fully into the light just yet, but the warmth in his eyes speaks of a spark ignited, and I'm willing to wait, to nurture that flame until it burns bright enough to light the way for both of us.

The aroma of butter and sugar clings to the air, weaving through the bakery like an old friend's laughter, warm and inviting. The critics, buoyed by the exquisite pastries, drifted out of the shop, their words of praise hanging in the air like the last notes of a symphony. I feel a giddy flutter of excitement as I clean up, an adrenaline rush washing over me, yet a disquieting pang lingers, anchored to Ethan's retreating figure. He moves with a quiet grace, focused on his tasks, but I notice the way his fingers linger on the edges of flour-dusted surfaces, almost as if he's anchoring himself to the familiar instead of embracing the bold unknown.

With each clatter of pans and the whir of mixers, I sense that change is looming, yet an unshakable uncertainty surrounds us. My gaze falls upon the empty corner where I envision a new display, one that would feature not just my creations but also a spotlight for Ethan's culinary artistry. What would it look like, I wonder, to see his name shining alongside mine? The thought ignites a spark in my chest, a promise of possibility, yet I'm acutely aware of the delicate balance we must navigate.

As the afternoon sun begins to dip below the horizon, casting a golden hue over the bakery, the familiar sound of the bell jingles again. This time, it's not the couple from earlier, but a small group of locals who wander in, bringing with them the scent of damp earth and the lightness of post-rain chatter. I greet them with a smile, ready to share the new treats inspired by the earlier excitement.

"Just in time for a little taste of heaven," I say, gesturing toward the display. "The raspberry croissants are still warm."

They crowd around the case, eyes wide with wonder, and for a moment, I feel the weight of my dreams, the vision I've fought to bring to life, crystallizing into reality. As I chat with the customers, offering samples and anecdotes behind each pastry, I can't help but glance back toward the kitchen where Ethan is working. He seems to be absorbed in his tasks, but his posture is more relaxed now, shoulders unknotted as he rolls out dough with a sense of purpose. I catch a glimpse of a smile tugging at the corners of his lips—a small victory in a long journey.

With the last of the customers satisfied and on their way, I wipe my hands on my apron, determination burning in my chest. I step into the kitchen, a place that has become a sanctuary, filled with the warmth of our shared efforts. "Ethan, can we talk about that new display?" I ask, my heart racing.

He looks up, a hint of curiosity sparking in his eyes. "What do you have in mind?"

I gesture to the empty corner. "What if we create a special feature for your desserts? Something to highlight your work, maybe a weekly special?"

He blinks, processing the idea. "You really think people would want to try my stuff?"

"Absolutely!" I say, enthusiasm bubbling within me. "You have a gift that deserves to be celebrated, and I want to help you share that."

A hesitant smile crosses his face, but I can still see the lingering doubt in his eyes. "What if they don't like it? What if it's not good enough?"

"Then we'll learn and adapt. That's what this place is all about—exploration and growth." My voice is firm, infused with the hope that has fueled my own journey. "But I can't do this without you. Your input, your creativity—they matter to me."

He takes a moment, glancing at the empty space, the air around us thick with potential. "Okay," he says finally, a cautious excitement threading through his voice. "Let's do it."

The thrill of his acceptance sends a rush through me. Together, we can build something that showcases both our talents, creating a fusion of flavors and ideas that could attract even more patrons to our little sanctuary.

As the week unfolds, the bakery transforms into a hive of activity, each day marked by our collaboration and shared laughter. Ethan becomes increasingly involved, offering suggestions for flavor pairings and presentation, his creativity unfurling like the petals of a flower kissed by the sun. We create a new special each week, each one telling a story of inspiration drawn from our local surroundings, whether it's the luscious peaches from the nearby orchard or the tart blackberries that grow wild along the back roads.

One morning, as the light spills through the windows, illuminating the dust motes dancing in the air, we gather around the wooden table to brainstorm. "What if we did a fall-themed special?" I suggest, pulling a stack of recipe cards toward me. "Pumpkin spice muffins with a maple glaze?"

Ethan raises an eyebrow, a teasing smile forming. "You mean, the basic pumpkin spice?"

"Hey, don't knock the classics! They're classics for a reason." I shoot back, laughter bubbling up between us like a fizzy soda.

"Well, maybe we can do something unexpected, like adding a ginger snap crumble on top," he counters, and as he speaks, I can see the enthusiasm growing in his voice.

"Yes! That's perfect!" I exclaim, feeling the energy in the room shift, morphing into something electric.

The rest of the day flies by in a blur of mixing, pouring, and tasting, the rhythm of our collaboration infusing every moment with joy. Each new creation pulls us closer together, our shared passion knitting a bond that feels both exhilarating and terrifying. As the sun dips low, casting a warm glow across the kitchen, I feel a sense of belonging blooming in my chest—a feeling that Ethan and I are creating something greater than ourselves.

The following week, we unveil our new fall special, and the response is immediate. Customers flock to the bakery, eager to taste the fusion of flavors, and I can hardly contain my excitement as they rave about our creations. Ethan stands by my side, a mix of pride and disbelief playing across his features, and I can see the joy blooming in his heart, just as it has in mine.

Yet, amidst the whirlwind of success, I can't shake the feeling that this newfound connection is also opening the door to uncharted territories—territories that spark both hope and fear. The line between friendship and something deeper begins to blur, and with each shared laugh, every lingering glance, the tension shifts, electrifying the air between us.

As night falls, the bakery glows warmly against the backdrop of a starry sky, and I can't help but wonder what the tides of change will bring next. In this cozy haven, filled with the sweet aromas of our labor, I feel the boundaries of our lives intertwining, our stories merging into a singular narrative that beckons us to dive deeper into the unknown. With the promise of new beginnings shimmering on the horizon, I can't help but embrace the uncertainty ahead, ready to face whatever waves may come.

Chapter 13: The Sweetest Victory

The aroma of freshly baked pastries wafted through the air, wrapping around me like a warm embrace as I stood behind the counter of my bakery, "Sweet Serenity." The sun filtered through the large windows, casting a golden hue on the flour-dusted surfaces, and the soft chime of the doorbell heralded the arrival of the critics. My heart raced in anticipation, each beat echoing the hope I clutched tightly. Today wasn't just any day; it was the day my creations would be scrutinized under the discerning eyes of culinary experts.

As I arranged the delicate pastries on the pristine white plates, I couldn't help but reminisce about the countless hours spent perfecting each recipe, the frenzied trials and sweet failures that had brought me to this moment. My hands trembled slightly, a mix of excitement and nerves dancing in my veins. The luscious chocolate éclairs glistened under the bakery lights, while the fragrant fruit tarts beckoned with their vibrant hues of strawberries and kiwi. Each dish was a small piece of my soul, a tangible manifestation of my dreams and aspirations.

The critics arrived with an air of authority, their laughter echoing in the cozy space, which had often served as a sanctuary for my thoughts and dreams. They were a formidable trio, well-known in the culinary world, their reputations resting on the sharpness of their tongues. Yet, beneath their stern exteriors, I hoped for a hint of appreciation, a glimmer of joy amidst their professionalism. I had prepared an array of flavors that spoke not just of technique but of the passion that had driven me to open this place.

As the first fork clinked against the plate, I felt the rush of adrenaline. It was as if time suspended for a heartbeat, each critic pausing to savor the delicate balance of sweetness and acidity in the lemon tart I had perfected. Their eyes widened, reflecting the sheer delight I yearned to see. A murmur of approval swept through the room, a sound so sweet it danced in the air like music. I moved from table to table, each smile and nod igniting a fire within me.

"Exceptional! The crust is beautifully flaky!" one critic exclaimed, her voice tinged with genuine surprise. I soaked in every compliment, each word a salve to the doubts that had plagued me during the countless sleepless nights. This was what I had envisioned, a place where my love for baking could blossom and where my flavors could create connections, even if they were temporary.

As the tasting progressed, my heart soared. The highlights were numerous: the espresso cake was rich yet balanced, the raspberry macarons were delicate and just the right amount of tartness. I poured my heart into each dish, a tiny universe of flavor and emotion within every bite. I felt a rush of satisfaction when the critics shared approving glances, and for a fleeting moment, the bakery felt like a world where everything was possible, where dreams could indeed rise like the yeast in my dough.

When the tasting concluded, the critics exchanged pleasantries, their faces flushed with delight. As they prepared to leave, I felt a lump in my throat, overwhelmed by their kind words. "Expect a glowing review," one of them promised, his eyes glinting with genuine warmth. My heart soared, and I could hardly breathe. This wasn't just validation; it was a beacon of hope, a promise of brighter days ahead.

But just as the euphoria began to settle, a familiar face pierced the air like a shard of ice. Emma stood in the doorway, her presence drawing an invisible line across the warm, jubilant atmosphere. She wore a tight smile, but the glint in her eyes hinted at a tempest brewing beneath the surface. I felt the color drain from my cheeks as she stepped into my sanctuary, each step purposeful and heavy, as if she were walking on a battlefield.

I had never expected to see her again—not here, not after the way our last encounter had unraveled. The air thickened with tension as I tried to read her expression, the gleam of satisfaction from my recent triumph quickly dimming. My heart sank; the thrill of victory was now clouded by her looming presence.

"Congratulations, Maya," she said, her voice smooth yet laced with a hint of sarcasm that twisted the knot in my stomach tighter. "I heard you had quite the tasting today."

"Thanks," I managed, forcing a smile that felt more like a grimace. Her eyes roamed the bakery, taking in the decorations and the assortment of treats. I could practically hear the gears in her mind turning as she calculated her next move.

I braced myself for the inevitable onslaught of criticism, the biting words that seemed to be her specialty. "You know, it's so quaint here," she continued, her tone dripping with insincerity. "It's adorable how you've created your little corner of the world."

"Emma, I—" I began, but she waved her hand dismissively, cutting me off like a sharp knife slicing through warm bread. I could feel Ethan's presence lingering at the back of the bakery, his comforting aura juxtaposed against Emma's biting remarks. I shot him a glance, seeking solace in his steady gaze, and he nodded imperceptibly, grounding me in the moment.

"I just wanted to see how the competition was faring," she added, her lips curving into a smile that didn't quite reach her eyes. "You know, being in this business, it's important to know what others are up to."

Each word dripped with condescension, each syllable a reminder of the rivalry I had tried so hard to push aside. Emma thrived on the tension, on the unspoken challenge that hung in the air. I took a deep breath, reminding myself that today was about celebration, about the successes I had worked tirelessly to achieve.

"Glad you could stop by," I replied, summoning all my strength to keep my tone steady. "Perhaps you'll find some inspiration here?"

The exchange was a dance of sharp words and thinly veiled jabs, but in that moment, I realized that I wouldn't let her dark cloud extinguish the flickering flame of my triumph. As she lingered, I focused on the warmth of the bakery, the sweetness of the pastries that had just won accolades, and the knowledge that no matter what she threw my way, I was not just surviving but thriving.

The air grew thick with unspoken tension as Emma surveyed the bakery, her eyes flickering from the colorful pastries to the flour-dusted countertops, as if assessing the quality of my work with every lingering glance. I stood my ground, the warmth from Ethan still enveloping me, a reminder that even in the face of adversity, I wasn't entirely alone. Emma leaned against the counter, her posture casual but her gaze sharp, like a hawk poised to swoop down on its unsuspecting prey.

"I didn't realize a little place like this could gain such traction," she said, her tone a careful blend of faux admiration and barely concealed disdain. "It must be nice to have such... dedicated clientele." The way she emphasized the word "dedicated" made it sound more like a jab than a compliment, but I refused to let her bait me into a petty exchange.

"Thank you, Emma. I've worked hard to create a space that resonates with my customers," I replied, my voice steady, though my insides churned. The last thing I wanted was to let her derail the joyful momentum I'd just built with the critics. Each success in the bakery had been a small victory against the insecurities that had haunted me since I first opened the doors.

"Right," she said, arching an eyebrow, "it seems your little victories have attracted quite the buzz. But can they last? That's always the question in this business."

I felt a spark ignite in my chest, a flaring of determination that demanded I stand up to her. "Sustaining success requires passion and authenticity, Emma. It's not just about the buzz; it's about the heart behind the pastries. My customers know that."

Her laughter rang out, sharp and brittle. "Ah, the heart. Isn't that what we all say when we can't rely on numbers? I wonder how long you can charm your way through a culinary landscape that's ever-changing."

Each word dripped with poison, but I refused to let it seep into my spirit. I forced a smile, striving to maintain the cheerful facade of my bakery, the one I had built on sweet dreams and hard work. "The only number I care about right now is one: the number of people who leave with smiles after tasting my desserts."

Just then, the bell above the door chimed again, drawing my attention. A couple strolled in, eyes lighting up at the sight of the displays, and I seized the moment. "Would you like to try a sample?" I offered, gesturing to a plate of freshly baked madeleines, their golden edges still warm from the oven. The couple approached eagerly, their expressions full of curiosity.

Emma watched, her face a mask of frustration as the couple savored the buttery, delicate morsels. I could feel her annoyance radiating through the room, but I was determined to let my work speak for itself. With every delighted reaction, I could sense her confidence waning, and a small part of me relished the triumph.

As I chatted with my customers, offering snippets of my inspiration for each pastry, I glanced back at Emma. She stood a little straighter now, her arms crossed, but I detected a flicker of something—maybe respect or annoyance; it was hard to tell. But I wasn't interested in her approval. All that mattered was the connection I was forging with the people who walked through my doors, the relationships that blossomed over shared love for sweets and community.

The couple, now thoroughly enchanted, placed their orders and promised to return with friends. Their laughter lingered like the faint scent of vanilla in the air as they left, leaving me with a renewed sense of purpose. I turned back to find Emma staring at me, an unreadable expression flickering across her features.

"You know, Maya," she said slowly, "it takes more than just charm to thrive in this business. It requires grit and resilience. I hope you have enough of both."

"Grit and resilience are two things I've learned along the way," I replied, keeping my voice steady. "But they're best cultivated in a supportive environment. Something that this bakery thrives on."

The challenge in my tone was not lost on her. For a moment, we stood locked in a silent duel, the energy crackling between us like a live wire. Yet amidst the clash of wills, I couldn't help but see the underlying fear in her eyes—fear of being overshadowed, fear of failure. It was a feeling I knew all too well, one that had driven me to the brink of giving up on more than one occasion.

Emma's expression softened for the briefest of moments, revealing a glimpse of vulnerability before she masked it with that familiar air of superiority. "Just remember, everyone loves a new flavor until they find something they like better," she remarked, the barbs hidden beneath her words. "You might want to keep your eyes peeled."

With that, she turned and sauntered out of the bakery, the door closing behind her with a definitive click that resonated in the otherwise vibrant space. I took a deep breath, feeling the weight of her presence lift, leaving behind a refreshing sense of clarity. The sunlight streamed in once again, bathing the bakery in a golden glow as I refocused on the task at hand—building connections, creating memories, and, above all, baking from the heart.

Ethan stepped forward, a reassuring smile spreading across his face. "You handled that beautifully," he said, his voice low and comforting. "Don't let her get to you. You've already proved yourself today."

I leaned against the counter, the adrenaline from the encounter still coursing through my veins. "It's just hard, you know? Every time I think I'm making progress, she shows up like a ghost from my past."

Ethan nodded, his eyes warm with understanding. "You're building something incredible here, Maya. Don't let anyone dim your light. Remember why you started this in the first place."

His words sank deep, resonating with the core of my ambition. I turned to the gleaming display of pastries, each one a testament to the long nights, the trials, and the passion that had fueled my journey. This was my dream—my sweet sanctuary where I could create and connect, and I wasn't about to let anyone overshadow that.

With renewed vigor, I dove back into my work, my mind a whirl of ideas for the next batch of delights. Flour danced in the air as I prepared the dough for croissants, envisioning the flaky layers that would soon emerge from the oven. The scent of butter and sugar filled the space, mingling with the lingering sweetness of success.

As I kneaded and shaped, I felt the rhythm of the bakery pulse around me, a symphony of laughter, warmth, and camaraderie. Each pastry was not just a treat; it was a story, an invitation to share in the joy of life's simplest pleasures. I looked around, the cozy shop filled with the soft chatter of patrons and the clinking of coffee cups, and I knew I was where I belonged.

And with that realization, the sweet victory felt all the more satisfying, like the first bite of a perfectly crafted pastry—full of promise, warmth, and the undeniable magic of hard-won success.

The gentle clink of glass jars filled with colorful sprinkles and vibrant icing decorated the bakery's shelves, creating a kaleidoscope of colors that contrasted sharply with the tension that lingered after Emma's visit. Each corner of "Sweet Serenity" radiated warmth, yet my heart remained a touch colder, weighed down by the interaction. I watched as the last of the patrons filtered out, their laughter fading into the crisp afternoon air, leaving only the scent of warm pastries and my lingering anxiety.

With Ethan busy behind the counter, preparing for the evening rush, I took a moment to gather my thoughts. I moved toward the large window that framed the street outside, where leaves danced on a gentle breeze, their colors ablaze in the golden light. As I leaned against the cool glass, the world outside buzzed with life—children chased each other in the park across the street, while couples strolled hand in hand, blissfully unaware of the quiet storm brewing in my heart.

Emma's words echoed in my mind, taunting yet oddly empowering. Was I really ready for the competitive landscape that lay ahead? Could I sustain the momentum I had finally built? I could feel the determination bubbling inside me, a fire igniting with the thought of proving her wrong. After all, Sweet Serenity wasn't merely a bakery; it was a reflection of everything I had fought for—the late nights, the failures, the countless recipes thrown into the trash.

"Hey, Earth to Maya," Ethan's voice broke through my reverie, pulling me back into the cozy cocoon of our bakery. He was leaning against the counter, wiping his hands on a dish towel, his expression a mixture of concern and encouragement. "You okay? You've been staring out that window like it holds the answers to the universe."

"Just lost in thought," I replied, a half-hearted smile curling my lips. "I suppose I'm just processing Emma's visit. You know how it is."

Ethan nodded, his eyes filled with empathy. "She has a knack for raining on parades. But you've got something special here, Maya. Don't let her get in your head."

His words washed over me like a soothing balm, and I appreciated how he always seemed to know exactly what to say. "I just feel like I need to step it up, you know? This isn't just about me anymore. It's about everyone who walks through these doors."

Ethan's brow furrowed, and he crossed his arms, leaning closer. "Then let's do it together. What do you have in mind?"

A spark ignited in my chest, and I began to outline a vision that had taken root in my mind—a series of baking workshops, where I could invite the community to share in the joy of creating pastries. "Imagine it," I said, my excitement bubbling over. "A space where people can learn to bake from scratch, share stories, and just... connect. We could offer themed classes, maybe even host competitions."

Ethan's eyes lit up with enthusiasm. "That sounds incredible! It would not only showcase your skills but also create a stronger bond within the community. People love to learn, and everyone enjoys a little friendly competition."

"Yes!" I exclaimed, unable to contain my excitement. "It would add an interactive layer to the bakery, make it feel even more like home. Plus, it could bring in new customers, families looking for something fun to do."

The idea cascaded like the frosting I so lovingly whipped—each detail rich with possibility. We brainstormed together, bouncing ideas back and forth until the bakery buzzed with inspiration. I envisioned evenings filled with laughter, the scent of warm butter filling the air as families decorated cupcakes or crafted their own loaves of bread.

"Let's do it," I said, a determined glint in my eye. "Let's launch the first workshop next week. We can start small and build from there."

Ethan grinned, his excitement infectious. "I'll help with the promotions—social media, flyers, whatever it takes to get the word out. We can even feature a few of your best recipes!"

As we began laying the groundwork, the bakery seemed to take on a life of its own. I envisioned tables covered in flour and laughter, children giggling as they clumsily attempted to pipe icing onto cupcakes. I could picture the joy of sharing secrets of the trade, of creating a little community within these walls—a sanctuary for budding bakers and seasoned pros alike.

The following days blurred together in a whirlwind of flour and frosting. I found myself more energized than I had been in weeks, the doubts I had harbored about Emma's visit melting away like sugar in the heat of the oven. Each day, as I crafted new recipes and finalized plans for the workshop, I felt the exhilarating rush of possibility wash over me.

The first workshop arrived before I knew it, and the bakery was abuzz with anticipation. The tables were adorned with cheerful tablecloths, and I had prepared a selection of ingredients that gleamed under the soft glow of the lights. My heart raced as I set up, knowing this was my chance to connect with the community in a way I had always envisioned.

As the clock ticked down to the start time, I glanced around the bakery, taking in the warm ambiance. Familiar faces appeared, mingling with new ones, a delightful blend of laughter and chatter filling the air. Ethan moved gracefully among the guests, welcoming them with his natural charm, offering samples of pastries while setting the tone for a joyful evening.

When I finally stepped forward to introduce myself, the room fell silent, eager eyes fixed upon me. "Thank you all for being here today. I'm thrilled to welcome you to our very first baking workshop! Today, we're going to create the perfect vanilla cupcakes, and I can't wait to see what we come up with together!"

Cheers erupted, and as I began to share my passion, I could feel the atmosphere shift. This was what I had dreamed of—a space where everyone could come together, share experiences, and learn something new. I guided them through each step, my heart swelling with pride as I watched novice bakers transform into creators, each one adding their personal touch to the recipe.

As we measured, mixed, and baked, stories flowed as easily as the batter. I heard laughter echo off the walls, punctuated by the clinking of spatulas and the faint beeping of timers. It was a celebration of creativity and camaraderie that made the challenges of the past few weeks fade into the background.

The smell of freshly baked cupcakes wafted through the air, enveloping us like a warm hug. When we finally gathered around the table to taste our creations, it felt as though we were not just sharing treats but also a part of something much larger—a shared joy that transcended mere baking.

As the evening unfolded, I couldn't help but glance around at the faces lit up with happiness, the sweet rewards of our labor in front of us. Ethan caught my eye from across the table, a knowing smile on his face, and I realized that this was just the beginning. The potential for growth, for community, and for connection stretched out before us like a well-risen loaf of bread, warm and promising.

And in that moment, I knew that no matter how many storm clouds tried to gather, the sun would always shine through as long as I had my passion, my community, and my determination to keep Sweet Serenity a sanctuary of joy and love. Together, we would bake not just pastries but memories, flavors that would linger long after the last crumb had been savored.

Chapter 14: Eclipsed by Doubt

The warm scent of vanilla and freshly baked bread enveloped me as I stood in the bustling kitchen, my safe haven amidst the swirling uncertainties of the world outside. The soft hum of the mixer filled the air, harmonizing with the distant laughter echoing from the main room where the event was unfolding. My fingers worked methodically, kneading dough with a rhythm that felt both therapeutic and familiar, each press and fold a distraction from the prickle of tension simmering just beyond the threshold of my focus.

The light filtering through the old, stained glass windows danced across the countertops, casting vibrant patterns that felt almost like a celebration of the moment. The kitchen had always been a canvas for my creativity, a place where flour dust motes floated like tiny stars, each ingredient a possibility waiting to be transformed. Yet, today, that sanctuary felt tainted by an uninvited sense of dread. I could hear Emma's voice, bright and effervescent, cutting through the sounds of clinking glasses and cheerful chatter.

I glanced up from the dough, my heart quickening as I caught a glimpse of her laughter lighting up the room like the flickering flame of a candle. Emma, with her effortlessly perfect hair and that smile—so dazzling, so infectious—had always been an enigma to me. She was the kind of woman whose presence commanded attention, yet, I knew she was far more than just an attractive face. She was clever, ambitious, and far too comfortable in Ethan's orbit. I chided myself for feeling threatened; it was just a charity event after all. But my instincts whispered a different tale, one woven from threads of jealousy and insecurity.

"Emma! You should totally ask Ethan to collaborate with you on that charity gala! It's such a great opportunity for both of you!" The words slipped from my lips with a force that surprised even me. I spun around, my heart racing as I caught sight of my friend

Claire, her eyes gleaming with encouragement. She was always the first to advocate for taking chances, for diving headfirst into the unpredictable waters of opportunity.

"Right?" Emma chimed in, her enthusiasm palpable as she leaned closer to Ethan, their shoulders brushing lightly as they plotted ideas. I should have felt happy for them, for this chance to make a difference together. Instead, the walls of the kitchen seemed to close in, my breath catching in my throat as I felt increasingly isolated. The rhythmic pulse of the mixer faded into the background, leaving only the frantic drumming of my heart as I retreated deeper into my baking cocoon.

As I kneaded the dough, each fold mirrored my own turmoil. My fingers worked harder, pressing and rolling as if I could smooth out the creases of my doubts, my insecurities. A sprinkle of flour here, a dash of salt there, I focused on transforming raw ingredients into something beautiful. Yet, every time I caught a fleeting glance of Ethan's radiant smile directed at Emma, the chill of anxiety seeped into my bones. They spoke with an ease that was both endearing and infuriating, as if they had long since woven their connection into the fabric of their lives.

The clock on the wall ticked away, each second stretching into an eternity. The distant sounds of the event—the clinking of glasses, the chorus of laughter—morphed into a cacophony that drowned out my thoughts. I fought against the rising tide of doubt, desperately trying to regain control over my spiraling emotions. In the sanctuary of my kitchen, the world faded, leaving just me and the warm dough cradled in my hands.

"Why don't you join them?" Claire's voice broke through the haze, gentle yet insistent. She peeked through the doorway, her brow furrowed with concern. "You're missing out on a great opportunity too."

"Right, because what could I possibly add to a discussion about charity events? I'm just the baker," I replied, my voice laced with sarcasm, but the weight of her words lingered. Perhaps I had always been too comfortable in the role of the background character, more at home in the safety of my kitchen than the spotlight of social interactions.

Claire stepped into the kitchen, her presence a balm for my frayed nerves. "Emma may be charming, but you have something she doesn't—a unique perspective and talent. Your baking has a way of bringing people together, of making them feel cherished. Don't underestimate that."

Her encouragement simmered within me, battling against the insecurities that clung like a shadow. I had poured my heart into every cake and pastry, every batch of cookies crafted with love and care. But in that moment, standing in the kitchen that had always welcomed me, I felt like an imposter. The feeling gnawed at me like a persistent hunger, a reminder of the self-doubt I had tried so hard to silence.

I released the dough onto the floured surface, my fingers moving instinctively as I shaped it into rounds, the edges crisping slightly under my touch. Baking was more than just a task; it was an art form that required patience, precision, and an understanding of how ingredients danced together. Yet, I couldn't shake the feeling that I was merely a spectator in my own life, watching as the vibrant colors of the event played out without me.

With each breath, the comforting scent of baking filled the air, mingling with the distant melodies of the gathering. I inhaled deeply, allowing the warmth of the kitchen to embrace me, a momentary refuge from the encroaching shadows of doubt. The world outside thrived with possibilities, yet here, surrounded by the comforting chaos of my craft, I was reminded of my worth. I was more than just a baker; I was a creator of experiences, a conjurer of joy. But would that ever be enough to stand alongside Emma?

The echo of laughter reached me again, and I turned my gaze toward the door, my heart lurching as I caught Ethan's eye, sparkling with warmth and a touch of mischief. In that fleeting moment, a flicker of hope ignited within me, daring me to step out from behind the wall of flour and sugar, to reclaim my place not just as a baker but as a participant in this vibrant tapestry of life.

The minutes slipped away, each one filled with the sounds of laughter and conversation that drifted like a bittersweet melody through the kitchen door. I focused on the dough, my fingers coated in flour, as I shaped it with a sense of purpose, trying to keep my mind tethered to the present and away from the tempest of emotions swirling just outside. With every swirl of the wooden spoon, I imagined weaving together not just ingredients, but my fractured confidence, hoping to create something whole, something beautiful.

Just as I pressed the last round of dough into place, Claire's soft voice broke through the clutter of my thoughts again. "You know, if you really want to impress Ethan, you should showcase that new raspberry tart you've been experimenting with. It's a showstopper." The idea of my tart, its bright red berries gleaming against the buttery crust, filled me with a sudden surge of inspiration. Maybe that was it—the secret ingredient I needed to step back into the spotlight.

"Good idea," I replied, a flicker of determination igniting within me. I quickly gathered the ingredients, each one a friend in this familiar dance. The chilled butter crumbled effortlessly as I cut it into the flour, the sharpness of the knife giving me a sense of control. The tart was a piece of art, each layer a reflection of my journey—sweet yet tangy, just like the fleeting moments of joy and insecurity that intertwined my life.

The vibrant raspberries, plump and inviting, begged to be cradled in my buttery crust. I could picture Ethan's face lighting up as he took the first bite, his eyes sparkling with delight. The thought made my heart skip, a gentle reminder that maybe I wasn't just a background character in this story. The laughter outside faded, replaced by the rhythmic sound of my mixing, the occasional clang of a utensil grounding me further in my craft.

Claire leaned against the counter, watching with an appreciative smile. "See? This is where you shine. Just remember to let him in on your creative process, not just the end product. He'll love that." I glanced up, catching her encouraging gaze, and for the first time that evening, I felt a sense of clarity. It wasn't just about baking; it was about sharing my passion, about inviting someone else into my world. I had always kept my kitchen as my sanctuary, a place where I could retreat and create in solitude. Maybe it was time to allow someone else to step inside.

With renewed energy, I set to work on the raspberry filling, combining sugar and cornstarch, watching as the mixture transformed into a glossy, vibrant concoction. The fruit folded into it like a promise, each berry a burst of color, reminding me of the possibility that existed in every moment. As I carefully poured the mixture into the crust, the warm aroma of sugar and berries filled the air, wrapping around me like a comforting hug.

I could hear the hum of conversation filtering in from the event—a chorus of voices rising and falling like waves crashing against a shore. The sweetness of my tart mingled with the salty tang of my insecurities, creating an unintentional blend that left me dizzy. I wiped my hands on my apron, a ritualistic gesture that settled my nerves, and took a deep breath. This was it—the moment to emerge from my self-imposed cocoon, to stop letting doubt dictate my actions.

With a sense of purpose, I carried the tart, still warm from the oven, toward the living room, its golden crust glistening under the soft glow of the overhead lights. As I stepped through the doorway, the vibrant scene unfolded before me—a tapestry of laughter, clinking glasses, and animated discussions. Ethan stood at the center, his laughter booming, a gravitational pull drawing everyone toward him. Emma hovered nearby, her smile bright, yet there was an underlying tension in her posture that I couldn't quite place.

My heart raced as I approached, my nerves tangling with the sweet scent of the tart, making me feel light yet grounded. I caught Ethan's eye, and his face lit up with genuine warmth, the kind that could ignite even the faintest flicker of hope. "There she is! Just in time for the main event!" He gestured toward me, his enthusiasm infectious.

Emma glanced over, her expression shifting slightly. The brightness of her smile faltered, and I could almost see the gears turning in her mind, an unmistakable competition crackling between us, subtle yet sharp. I felt an unwelcome wave of trepidation, the kind that crept in when I least expected it. But I wouldn't let her see me falter. With a confidence I hadn't anticipated, I set the tart down on the table, its presence demanding attention.

"I brought a little something special," I announced, my voice steady despite the tumult swirling within. The moment stretched as eyes turned toward the tart, the vibrant raspberries glistening like rubies. Ethan stepped forward, his gaze fixed on the creation with childlike wonder.

"Wow! That looks incredible!" he exclaimed, leaning in closer. I felt a rush of warmth, knowing that my effort had found its way to the right audience. As I watched him slice into the tart, the flaky crust giving way to the luscious filling, I couldn't help but smile.

Emma stepped forward, her eyes narrowing slightly as she took a piece for herself. "Impressive, really. I didn't know you had it in you," she remarked, a hint of challenge lacing her tone. There it was again—the unspoken rivalry. I swallowed hard, determined not to let her words cut deeper than they needed to.

"Baking is kind of my thing," I replied lightly, infusing my voice with the same charm I'd poured into the tart. "Just like charity is yours, I suppose."

Ethan chuckled, taking a bite and closing his eyes in delight. "Seriously, this is amazing. You have to teach me how to make this!" The way he savored each bite ignited something in me—a flicker of pride that drowned out the doubts threatening to resurface.

The atmosphere shifted slightly, and I found myself standing taller. It wasn't just about baking; it was about connection. About sharing pieces of myself—my passion, my dreams—while navigating the complexity of relationships that seemed to intertwine and weave around me like the very dough I had kneaded just hours before.

As the evening unfolded, the tart became a catalyst for conversation. People gathered, drawn to the table like moths to a flame, each piece of raspberry treasure igniting stories, laughter, and shared experiences. I found myself slipping into the rhythm of the gathering, my nerves settling as I shared not just the story of the tart, but of my journey—how every recipe held a memory, every bake a lesson.

Ethan listened, his attention unwavering, and Emma, despite her initial apprehension, began to engage with the group, her competitive edge softening just enough for me to see glimpses of sincerity. The laughter mingled with the sweetness of the evening, wrapping us all in a cocoon of shared humanity. I felt myself emerge, no longer eclipsed by doubt but illuminated by the connections forming around me.

As the night wore on, the kitchen buzzed with excitement, the air filled with the scent of camaraderie and joy. I had stepped out of the shadows, finding my place not only in the kitchen but in this vibrant, imperfect tapestry of life. With every shared smile and every slice of tart, I realized that I was not just a spectator in my own story; I was the author, pen in hand, ready to write the next chapter, no matter how uncertain it might seem.

The evening's energy pulsed around me, vibrant and intoxicating, each laugh and clink of glasses a reminder of the joy I had been missing. As the last crumbs of the tart vanished from eager hands, I felt an unfamiliar sense of belonging, a warmth spreading from my fingertips to the very tips of my toes. The initial pang of insecurity began to ebb, replaced by a growing sense of camaraderie that wrapped itself around my heart like a favorite scarf, soft and reassuring.

"Can you believe how good that was?" Claire leaned in, her voice just above the din, her eyes sparkling with delight. "You've got a gift, Emma. Seriously, you need to do this more often." Her praise wrapped around me like a hug, bolstering my confidence even further. I shrugged, feigning modesty, but inside, I could feel my spirit fluttering.

The conversations had morphed from polite chit-chat to something deeper, the fabric of our shared experiences weaving us closer together. As Ethan moved through the crowd, sharing laughter and stories, I couldn't help but watch him, that magnetic pull drawing me into his orbit. His easy charm captivated not just me but everyone around him. In that moment, I decided to embrace the challenge rather than shy away from it. After all, I had just poured my heart into something delicious, and if that could bridge the gap between us, then perhaps I wasn't so eclipsed after all.

"Next time, you should let me help," Emma interjected as she approached, her voice smooth yet edged with an unspoken rivalry. "I could bring some of my event planning skills to the table. We could really elevate things together." Her suggestion hung in the air like a storm cloud, and I caught myself biting the inside of my cheek. The urge to dismiss her proposition flared in me, but I quelled it, focusing instead on the opportunity this presented.

"Sure! I think it could be a fantastic collaboration." The words flowed from my mouth before I had a chance to think through the implications. Claire shot me a sideways glance, a mixture of surprise and admiration. I knew Emma's reputation—sharp, driven, and relentlessly ambitious—but perhaps we could harness that energy for something constructive.

Ethan, standing beside us, looked from me to Emma, a curious expression crossing his features. "That would be incredible. You two would make a great team." His enthusiasm sent a pleasant warmth coursing through me, a reassurance that even in the presence of Emma, I was not diminished. Instead, I felt emboldened to assert my place alongside her, ready to make my voice heard.

The night unfolded like the petals of a blooming flower, vibrant and rich, filled with the kind of laughter that feels both ephemeral and eternal. We discussed ideas for the charity gala, sketching plans and dreams on napkins, the ink barely keeping up with the excitement bubbling in the room. Ideas flowed like the wine, and with every passing moment, the trepidation I had felt earlier began to fade, like a fog lifting in the morning light.

As the conversations turned to logistics, I let myself dive deeper into the whirlpool of possibilities, envisioning tables draped in rich, emerald cloth, candlelit centerpieces illuminating the room with a soft, warm glow. My mind swirled with images of a stage where local musicians would play, their melodies mingling with the chatter and laughter, creating an atmosphere of celebration and community. I could see it so clearly—the essence of what I wanted to create, something that would leave an imprint on the hearts of those who attended.

The details mattered, and for the first time, I felt like I could contribute to something larger than myself. I could be more than just the baker; I could be a curator of experiences, a weaver of connections. Emma's initial challenge morphed into a partnership, our contrasting styles bringing balance and depth to the project.

"Let's make it unforgettable," Emma suggested, her eyes sparkling with enthusiasm that was hard to resist. "What if we featured local artists? Their stories could be woven into the theme of the event." I could see the gears turning in her mind, each idea leading to another, and I found myself nodding along, feeling the infectious energy of her ambition.

As the night wore on, my initial apprehension transformed into excitement. I could feel the tension between Emma and me begin to shift, like the air before a summer storm, charged with electricity. We both wanted to make this event a success, and despite the flickering rivalry, I sensed a budding respect forming—a realization that we each had something valuable to bring to the table.

As the party began to wind down, the lingering warmth of camaraderie filled the room, settling over us like a soft blanket. I glanced at Ethan, who was deep in conversation with a couple of guests. His laugh rang out, bright and genuine, and in that moment, I was struck by a wave of gratitude. This night had become a tapestry of connection and creativity, an opportunity to grow not just as a baker but as a person.

Emma turned to me, her expression softening. "You know, I admire your passion. It's contagious." There was a sincerity in her tone that caught me off guard, the rivalry fading into the background as we forged a new understanding. "We might actually make a great team."

I returned her smile, warmth flooding my chest. "I think we can do something really special together."

The journey we were embarking on felt thrilling, the unknown stretching out before us like a blank canvas. I could almost see the colors of our collaboration—emerald green, ruby red, and hints of gold—each one a testament to our combined efforts.

As I stepped outside for a breath of fresh air, the crisp night enveloped me, stars twinkling against the deep velvet sky. The moon hung low, casting a silver glow over the world, and for a moment, I stood there, absorbing the beauty of the night. This was a new beginning, a chance to step out from the shadows of doubt and into the vibrant light of possibility. I inhaled deeply, the cool air filling my lungs, carrying away the remnants of my insecurities.

The soft murmur of voices floated from inside, and I could hear laughter punctuating the night. I felt a renewed sense of purpose, a burgeoning excitement that surged through my veins. There was a world of opportunities waiting for me, and with each heartbeat, I felt more prepared to seize them.

Ethan stepped outside, his presence a comforting anchor against the backdrop of the starry night. "Hey," he said, leaning against the doorframe, the warmth of his smile sending a flutter through my stomach. "You were incredible tonight. Seriously."

"Thanks," I replied, trying to suppress the blush that crept up my cheeks. "It felt good to share something I love."

"You have so much talent. I'm really glad you decided to get involved with Emma." His words wrapped around me, and I felt a sense of gratitude swell within. This was the validation I had yearned for, the acknowledgment that my craft mattered.

As we stood there, the energy of the night enveloping us, I couldn't help but feel that this was just the beginning. The budding partnership with Emma, the burgeoning friendship with Ethan, and the dreams swirling in my heart all converged into a singular moment of clarity. I was ready to embrace the challenges ahead, to weave my story into the fabric of our community, and to create something extraordinary—one delicious moment at a time.

Chapter 15: Bitter Sweetness

The grand hall shimmered like a jewel under a canopy of fairy lights, each flickering point twinkling with the promise of the night ahead. The scent of gourmet hors d'oeuvres wafted through the air, a tantalizing blend of roasted garlic and fresh herbs, punctuated by the sweet, decadent aroma of my desserts waiting to be unveiled. My heart raced with the rhythm of the laughter and chatter enveloping me as I navigated through the crowd, careful to balance the delicate trays stacked high with my creations. The glimmering chandeliers overhead caught the glints of sparkling champagne flutes, and each clang of laughter felt like a discordant note against my growing unease.

Ethan was everywhere, a magnetic force drawing people into his orbit. His easy smile, framed by that unruly tuft of dark hair, illuminated the room, but I felt like a wisp of a ghost drifting in the periphery, hidden behind layers of frosting and fondant. I had spent hours perfecting each bite-sized piece of art, pouring my soul into the intricate designs that danced across the platter. There were dark chocolate ganache tarts, delicate fruit tarts with glistening raspberry coulis, and my signature miniature red velvet cupcakes, their rich crimson color like a soft whisper against the vibrant hues of the evening.

As I set up my dessert station, arranging everything with the precision of a seasoned artist, a wave of pride washed over me, momentarily pushing away the gnawing sensation in my gut. This was my passion, my solace in a world that often felt too chaotic. I had always found comfort in baking, each whisk of the egg, each fold of the batter a silent meditation, a moment to pause and breathe amidst the whirlwind of life. But as I turned to greet the first eager guests, the corners of my joy curled into something bittersweet.

Every burst of laughter from across the room felt like a gentle prod to my heart. I caught sight of Ethan, his face alight with animated conversation, as he leaned closer to Emma, the local celebrity who had somehow weaved herself into every corner of his world. I watched her toss her hair back, her laughter ringing like a chime, melodious and effortlessly charming. In that moment, I could feel the jealousy begin to coil tightly around my heart like an insidious vine. It slithered deeper, feeding off the insecurity that had long taken root within me.

"Your desserts look incredible!" a voice exclaimed, breaking my reverie. I turned to find a woman with kind eyes and an enthusiastic smile. Her presence was a balm, a brief reprieve from the sting of envy. I returned her smile, albeit somewhat wanly, and nodded. "Thank you! I hope they taste as good as they look."

The woman took a small bite of one of the tarts, her eyes widening in delight. "Oh my goodness, this is divine!" Her words hung in the air, sweet and buoyant. I felt a small flicker of pride ignite within me, only to be smothered as I glanced back at Ethan, who was still lost in conversation with Emma, their hands brushing with an intimacy that made my heart ache.

The night wore on, the atmosphere thick with mingling voices and clinking glasses, but I couldn't shake the feeling of being an outsider in my own world. I watched as groups formed around Ethan, each one eager to bask in his charm, while I stood behind my dessert station, trying to appear welcoming even as my heart sank further into a pit of longing and resentment.

The cacophony of joy blurred into a murmur, and suddenly the air felt stifling. Seeking solace, I slipped away from the buzzing hall and onto the balcony. The night air hit me like a refreshing wave, cool and invigorating, a stark contrast to the warmth of the room I had left behind. I leaned against the railing, letting the soft breeze tousle my hair as I gazed out at the twinkling city lights below, each one a reminder of the world that existed outside the confines of this glittering cage.

But even here, the weight of uncertainty lingered, settling over my shoulders like an unwelcome shawl. What was I doing? Why did it feel like I was fighting a battle I didn't even want to be a part of? My heart raced as I considered the possibility that Ethan's laughter might not just be a fleeting moment but a glimpse into a future I wasn't a part of.

As I inhaled the crisp night air, a mix of emotions spiraled within me. I longed to be the one making him laugh, to feel his warmth radiate towards me rather than away, but the thought of stepping into the light of that affection made my insides twist with uncertainty. The breeze whispered sweet nothings of encouragement, urging me to be bold, yet the specter of jealousy crept back in, muddying my thoughts.

The door to the hall creaked open, and I turned, half-expecting to see Ethan emerging, searching for me. Instead, it was a flood of guests spilling onto the balcony, their laughter spilling like champagne, effervescent and bright. I stepped back, fading once again into the background, a mere spectator to the scene unfolding before me. I could feel the walls of my heart closing in, a bittersweet echo of longing entwined with the sweet fragrance of my desserts wafting from the hall. I felt both anchored by the joy around me and adrift in my turbulent thoughts, torn between the sweetness of the night and the bitterness clawing at my heart.

The laughter and chatter from inside the hall faded into a distant hum as I leaned against the cool railing of the balcony, feeling the crisp air envelop me like a refreshing embrace. The city sprawled beneath me, a shimmering tapestry of lights that twinkled like stars fallen to earth. I took a deep breath, inhaling the mingled scents of the evening—fried calamari, floral arrangements, and the sweet hint of caramel from my desserts, all of which clung to me like a second skin. Each breath I took felt like a reminder of my own existence, yet I still felt trapped within a fog of my own insecurities.

As I stared out over the city, I couldn't help but think of how my heart had danced with hope at the prospect of tonight. I had envisioned laughter shared with Ethan, our fingers brushing over a shared dessert, the world fading away as we got lost in each other's company. But reality had woven a different tale—one that felt like a cruel twist of fate. The sound of Emma's laughter echoed in my mind, bright and carefree, a melody I couldn't shake. It made me wonder if I'd ever be more than a mere footnote in the story he was writing.

I closed my eyes, letting the cool breeze ruffle my hair, desperate for clarity. "Get a grip," I whispered to myself, attempting to dispel the storm brewing within. I couldn't let jealousy consume me. I had worked hard for this moment, pouring my heart into every dessert I created, not just for the sake of the event, but because it brought me joy. So why was I allowing a fleeting moment of doubt to overshadow everything I had accomplished?

As I stood there, lost in thought, the door creaked open once more, and a figure stepped onto the balcony. It was Ethan, his face illuminated by the gentle glow of the fairy lights, a welcome sight amidst the chaos of my emotions. He leaned against the railing beside me, casually running a hand through his hair, a gesture that seemed to reveal more than he intended. "Hey," he said, his voice a soft rumble against the backdrop of the night.

"Hey," I replied, trying to keep my tone light. But my heart raced, a wild drumbeat that betrayed my calm facade.

"What do you think?" he asked, gesturing toward the party inside. His smile, warm and inviting, sent a flutter through my chest. I forced a grin, nodding. "It looks amazing. You've really brought the energy tonight."

"Thanks," he said, his gaze drifting back inside, where laughter erupted like fireworks. "I just hope we can raise a lot of money for the charity. That's what it's all about, right?"

I nodded again, my mind racing. Here was the man I admired, standing beside me under the starlit sky, yet my heart ached at the thought of Emma, the laughter still echoing in my ears. "Definitely," I managed, my voice steadier than I felt. "It's such a worthy cause."

He turned to me, his eyes searching mine, and for a moment, I felt as though the world had narrowed to just the two of us. "You know, I've seen your desserts. They're incredible. You've really outdone yourself this time," he said, his voice low and sincere.

The compliment warmed me, melting some of the icy tendrils of jealousy that had wrapped around my heart. "Thank you. I really put my heart into them," I admitted, a hint of vulnerability creeping into my tone. It felt good to share a piece of myself, even if the weight of my insecurities still lingered.

"Is that what you do with everything you make?" he asked, a playful spark lighting his eyes. "Pour your heart into it?"

I couldn't help but chuckle at the question. "Maybe. Or at least, I try to."

"Good," he said, that charming grin making an appearance. "Because I think the world needs more of that. More people who put their hearts into what they do."

His words were a balm, soothing the restless turmoil inside me, but the specter of Emma loomed large in my mind, a dark cloud over the silver lining of our conversation. "And what about you? Do you pour your heart into everything?" I asked, attempting to steer the focus away from myself, fearing the crack in my facade might widen.

He chuckled softly, shaking his head. "Honestly? Sometimes I feel like I'm just going through the motions. But tonight feels different. It feels special."

The sincerity in his voice sent another shiver down my spine. Was he hinting at something more? My heart thudded heavily in my chest, caught between the hope that bloomed like wildflowers in spring and the dread of what I'd seen inside the hall.

Just then, the night air shifted, bringing with it a burst of laughter from the party, a reminder of the world we'd momentarily stepped away from. I glanced back inside, catching a glimpse of Emma's radiant smile directed toward Ethan. My stomach twisted painfully, the jealousy rearing its ugly head once more.

"Hey, would you like to get a drink?" Ethan asked, breaking the tension. "I could use a break from all the mingling. I'm sure you're not a big fan of it either."

The idea of stepping back into that vibrant world felt daunting, but there was something reassuring in his tone, a sense of camaraderie that beckoned me closer. "Sure," I replied, forcing a smile as I took a deep breath, determined to push aside the creeping shadows.

As we walked back inside, I felt a flutter of excitement and trepidation blend together, a concoction of hope and anxiety swirling within me. The party bustled with energy, and for a moment, I forgot about the hurt and jealousy that had threatened to consume me. With Ethan by my side, I stepped back into the lively atmosphere, ready to embrace the night—whatever it might hold.

The energy in the hall crackled with anticipation, a palpable force that tugged at my spirit as Ethan and I returned to the party. I noticed how the fairy lights, draped like delicate strands of starlit silk across the ceiling, flickered in rhythm with the laughter and music. Each step we took felt like a dance between the hope of connection and the shadow of doubt clinging to me. The room swelled with the mingling of elegant voices, the clinking of champagne flutes like tiny bells chiming in celebration.

Ethan guided me through the crowd, his presence a buoy in the sea of unfamiliar faces. I could feel the warmth radiating from him, a safe harbor amidst the swirling emotions threatening to capsize me. He introduced me to various guests, his hand resting casually on my lower back, an innocent gesture that ignited butterflies in my stomach. Each introduction was like a small leap into the unknown, where I smiled and engaged, yet my mind often drifted back to Emma, whose laughter floated like perfume on the air, sweet and intoxicating.

As we navigated the throngs of attendees, I caught fleeting glimpses of Emma, her confident strides and radiant smile lighting up the room. It was hard not to feel overshadowed by her, with her effortless charm that drew people in like moths to a flame. I tucked a stray hair behind my ear, willing my insecurities to evaporate into the ether, and turned my focus to the conversations around me.

A few guests marveled at the dessert station, their eyes wide with delight. "The chocolate tarts are to die for!" one exclaimed, her voice laced with enthusiasm. A wave of pride washed over me, soothing the sharp edges of my jealousy. It was a small victory, yet it felt significant, as if I were carving out a space for myself amidst the evening's grandeur.

Ethan caught my eye as we approached my dessert table. "I think you've officially stolen the show," he teased, his voice low and playful.

"Only until Emma arrives with her next dazzling outfit," I retorted, trying to infuse humor into my words, even as the truth behind them gnawed at me. He laughed, a sound so genuine that it momentarily banished my darker thoughts. I felt lighter, as if for a brief moment, the weight of my jealousy had been lifted.

"Come on, she's great and all, but have you tasted your own desserts? They're exquisite," he said, gesturing to the tarts, cupcakes, and tiny pastries that sparkled like jewels on my table.

I smiled, a genuine warmth spreading through me. "Thanks, but I'm not the one charming the crowd."

He leaned in slightly, his eyes gleaming with mischief. "Well, I think you're doing just fine. Just look at all these people lining up for your sweets. You've created a haven for them."

As if on cue, a small group gathered at my station, eagerly sampling my creations. Their faces lit up with joy, and I felt a swell of fulfillment that mingled with the remnants of my insecurity. The sight of people genuinely enjoying something I had crafted brought clarity; perhaps this was my niche, my space to shine in a world that often felt overshadowed by others.

"Will you save one of those cupcakes for me?" Ethan asked, his eyes sparkling with a playful challenge. "I want to be able to say I had the best dessert at this charity gala."

"Only if you promise to take a bite in front of everyone," I countered, the words tumbling out before I could second-guess myself.

He laughed, a deep, rumbling sound that sent warmth cascading through me. "Deal. But you have to join me. I can't be the only one making a spectacle of myself."

With a shared sense of mischief igniting between us, I nodded, and we fell into an easy rhythm, discussing flavors and ingredients as we served the eager guests. I caught myself stealing glances at Ethan, his charisma pulling people in like a magnet. He had a way of making everyone feel special, and the laughter that flowed around him felt like a symphony, inviting and infectious.

But just as I began to revel in this moment, I caught sight of Emma again, her arm linked with Ethan's, a seemingly innocent gesture that sent a wave of bitterness crashing over me. I forced myself to look away, focusing instead on the guests who were now raving about the chocolate tarts, their excitement a welcome distraction.

Suddenly, a flash of movement caught my eye. Emma was approaching, her smile wide, the kind that could light up a darkened room. I felt my heart race as I prepared for the inevitable confrontation, a battle between my instincts to be gracious and the rising tide of jealousy.

"Ethan!" she called, her voice like music, laced with sweet mischief. "I hear you've been raving about these desserts. I need to taste them."

As she approached, I could see the glimmer in her eye, a spark of confidence that seemed to heighten the stakes. The air around us crackled with tension as I fought the urge to shrink into the background.

"Absolutely, you'll love them," Ethan said, his gaze flickering between us. "This is where the magic happens."

Emma stepped closer, her attention suddenly fixed on me. "Oh, I've heard so much about you! You're the dessert queen tonight, aren't you?"

I forced a smile, my insides twisting as I acknowledged her. "Just trying to add a little sweetness to the evening," I replied, striving for lightness, but my voice felt like an anchor dragging me down.

"Sweetness indeed! I can't wait to dive in." She glanced back at Ethan, a conspiratorial grin spreading across her face. "You have to let me know what you think once you taste these creations, Ethan. You are quite the connoisseur, after all."

The conversation flowed, a current of playful banter mixed with an undercurrent of tension. I forced myself to engage, to participate, even as every word exchanged felt like a silent competition. I offered Emma a plate, and as she took a cupcake, our hands brushed together—a fleeting touch that ignited a spark of something I couldn't quite define.

Ethan's gaze flicked between us, a flicker of curiosity and confusion dancing in his eyes. "I think I'm about to witness a cupcake duel," he remarked, trying to lighten the mood.

The moment stretched, and I could feel the weight of unspoken words hanging in the air. In the middle of this chaotic swirl of emotions and laughter, I found myself at a crossroads. I could either let the envy consume me, or I could stand firm in my own worth.

"Why don't we all try a bite at the same time?" I suggested, my heart racing. "A taste test, if you will. That way, we can settle who's truly the best judge of desserts here."

The suggestion caught Emma off guard, and for a moment, I could see a flicker of surprise cross her features. "You're on!" she replied, her competitive spirit flaring as she eagerly bit into the cupcake, the frosting smearing across her lips in a way that somehow made her appear even more charming.

I took a deep breath, stealing a glance at Ethan, who seemed both entertained and intrigued by the spontaneous challenge. "Okay, let's see what you think!" I exclaimed, mirroring Emma's enthusiasm as I took a bite of my own creation.

The sweetness exploded on my tongue, the rich chocolate melding perfectly with the cream cheese frosting, a flavor I had perfected over countless late-night experiments in my kitchen. I watched as Emma's eyes widened in delight, her laughter ringing like a bell.

"This is incredible!" she exclaimed, and for a moment, her enthusiasm eclipsed the insecurities swirling within me.

Ethan grinned, clearly enjoying the moment. "See? You both are killing it tonight. This is exactly what we need—friendly competition and delicious desserts!"

In that whirlwind of flavors and laughter, I realized that maybe, just maybe, I could carve out my own place in this world. Standing there, surrounded by the glow of fairy lights and the warmth of camaraderie, I began to feel a shift—a spark of resilience igniting within me.

The rest of the night passed in a blur of laughter and shared stories, each moment layering a rich tapestry of connection. Ethan and Emma's laughter intertwined with mine, creating a vibrant melody that filled the room. I let go of the bitterness that had threatened to cloud my joy, allowing myself to revel in the moment. I could taste the sweetness not only in the cupcakes but in the fleeting yet beautiful interactions that unfolded before me.

As the evening wore on, I felt a renewed sense of self. I was no longer just a shadow in Ethan's world; I was a vibrant presence, an artist weaving my own narrative amidst the chaos. And as I shared in the joy of that night, I knew that while life was often bittersweet, it was also rich and layered, filled with the promise of possibility.

Chapter 16: Shattered Facades

The sky sprawled above us, a canvas of indigo and silver, speckled with stars that twinkled like distant promises. The warm, salty breeze from the ocean flirted with my hair, tangling it like a playful child's fingers. Ethan stood at the edge of the balcony, his silhouette framed against the night, the city lights beneath us flickering like fireflies caught in an electric dance. It was one of those nights in San Diego where the atmosphere hummed with a certain kind of magic, as if the universe itself was leaning in to listen.

I took a deep breath, savoring the mingled scents of blooming jasmine and the ocean's brine. Each step toward him felt heavy, laden with unspoken words that had been swirling between us for weeks. The sight of him, so serene and yet so distant, tugged at my heart. There was a vulnerability in his posture, an echo of something deeper—something that resonated with the fears I tried so hard to suppress. I could almost feel the weight of his thoughts, pressing down on him like the heat of the day lingering stubbornly into the cool of the night.

"Ethan?" My voice came out softer than I intended, a tentative whisper as if the night itself might shatter at any loud sound. He turned slowly, his expression unreadable. The twinkle of the stars reflected in his eyes, but there was a shadow lurking just beneath the surface, a tempest I wasn't sure I could navigate.

"Hey," he replied, his tone clipped. He looked back at the horizon, the waves crashing below, the rhythmic pulse of the ocean mirroring the beat of my heart. I stepped closer, the wooden floorboards creaking softly beneath my weight, and for a brief moment, I considered retreating, leaving him to his thoughts. But something inside me urged me to stay, to push past the discomfort and reach for whatever connection still lingered between us.

"Are you okay?" I ventured, my voice laced with concern, knowing full well that the answer would be buried beneath layers of his carefully constructed façade. Ethan's brow furrowed as he sighed, the sound heavy with unshed frustration.

"Do I look okay?" His response was sharp, like glass shattering in the stillness. I felt the sting of his words, but I understood—this was the storm brewing in him, the clash of what he felt and what he believed he should feel.

"I didn't mean—" I began, but he interrupted me, his eyes narrowing as if trying to pierce through the fabric of my own insecurities.

"No, really. Do I look okay? Because I feel like I'm losing my grip on everything." The vulnerability in his voice made my heart ache. I had seen this side of him before, the haunted look when the past clawed its way back into the present, but I never realized how deeply it affected him.

"Ethan," I said softly, "you don't have to pretend with me. I know it's hard, and I know you feel pressure—"

"Pressure?" He laughed, but there was no humor in it, just a bitter edge. "You have no idea. I'm suffocating under the weight of it. My family expects so much, and I keep failing. It feels like I'm stuck in this cycle of disappointment. And then there's you." His voice dropped to a murmur, as if he were afraid of saying my name too loudly, afraid it might summon the specter of my own expectations.

"What about me?" I asked, stepping closer, my heart racing with an unfamiliar mix of dread and hope. The air crackled between us, thick with unexpressed emotions that longed to break free.

"You think I can't see it? You're perfect, and here I am—" He gestured wildly, frustration bubbling just beneath the surface. "I'm a mess, and I don't know how to be the person you need me to be."

I felt a wave of warmth wash over me, a deep sense of empathy that cut through the tension. "Ethan, you're not a mess. You're human, and it's okay to struggle. I'm not looking for perfection. I just want you." The sincerity in my words hung in the air, shimmering like the stars above us, illuminating the darkness.

But his gaze faltered, turning inward as if he were caught in a whirlpool of his own making. "You say that, but I can't help but feel like I'm dragging you down with me. You deserve someone who's... whole, someone who doesn't come with all this baggage."

The accusation hung between us, raw and heavy. I felt the sharpness of his words, the way they dug into the soft spaces of my heart. He was projecting his fears, his sense of inadequacy, onto me, and suddenly, clarity dawned. I had been doing the same, hadn't I? Expecting him to fill the voids in my own soul, hoping that love could somehow solve everything.

"Ethan, we're both trying to figure it out," I said, my voice steadying, confidence blooming like the moonflowers that lined the balcony. "You're not dragging me down; you're allowing me to walk alongside you. We're stronger together."

For a heartbeat, the world around us faded, and I could almost see the walls we'd both built around ourselves begin to crack. His features softened, the tension in his shoulders dissipating as if my words had somehow woven a fragile bridge between our tumultuous hearts.

"Maybe I've been looking at this all wrong," he admitted, a hesitant smile breaking through the storm cloud in his eyes. I stepped forward, the distance between us narrowing, feeling the warmth radiating from him like a lifeline. We were two flawed souls searching for solace in each other's brokenness, and perhaps that was enough.

His hesitant smile ignited a flicker of hope within me, igniting the small embers of connection we had been stoking amidst the chaos. I could see the gears turning behind his eyes, a mixture of confusion and longing that resonated deep within my own chest.

As the soft moonlight bathed us in a silvery glow, I stepped closer, feeling the magnetic pull between us as palpable as the salty air.

"Maybe we don't need to have it all figured out," I said softly, my voice almost lost to the sound of the waves crashing against the rocks below. "Maybe we can just... be, without the weight of expectations hanging over us."

His gaze remained locked on mine, searching for something—an affirmation, perhaps, or the reassurance that vulnerability didn't equate to weakness. The warm breeze tousled his hair, making him look boyish and vulnerable in a way that struck me deeply. I wanted to reach out, to touch his cheek and anchor him in this moment, but I held back, letting the silence weave its own magic.

"I guess I've always been the type to overthink everything," he admitted, the words tumbling out as if they had been trapped for far too long. "It's like my brain is wired to run a thousand miles a minute, and it's exhausting." He ran a hand through his hair, the gesture both endearing and disarming. "I thought that if I just achieved a certain level of success, then maybe I'd feel whole. But every time I get close, it feels like I'm just chasing shadows."

"Success doesn't define us," I said, my heart aching for the boy who had spent so much of his life tethered to that elusive concept. "What if we found worth in each other, instead? What if we let go of the pressure to be perfect and just embraced the messy parts?"

He paused, the air around us thickening with the weight of our conversation. I could see the flicker of doubt in his eyes, a hesitant dance that echoed my own fears. But there was something about the honesty we shared in this moment that made me believe we could forge a new path together, one that didn't involve masks or pretenses.

"Maybe you're right," he murmured, the corners of his mouth lifting slightly. "It's just hard to shake off everything that's been drilled into my head. I want to be the man you deserve." There was a vulnerability in his confession that felt like an open wound, raw and beautiful in its honesty.

"You don't have to be anything other than yourself, Ethan. That's all I've ever wanted," I replied, my voice firm yet tender, grounding him as the night wrapped around us like a familiar blanket. The vulnerability radiating between us was electric, igniting a spark I hadn't realized had been dormant for so long.

He shifted closer, the distance between us now filled with an intimate tension that thrummed with possibility. "You have this way of making everything feel lighter. Like, somehow, I'm not just a collection of my failures." The sincerity in his words washed over me, a gentle tide that sought to erode the barriers I had built around my own heart.

"It's because you let me in," I replied, emboldened by his openness. "You have to understand that we're all just figuring it out as we go. Life is messy, and love—love is even messier. But it's the chaos that makes it beautiful."

The city below us sparkled like a treasure chest, each light a flicker of hope, a testament to lives intertwined in a tapestry of dreams and disappointments. I couldn't help but think of how many stories played out beneath that vast sky, each one rich with complexity, just like ours. The thought filled me with a sense of purpose; if we could face our fears together, perhaps we could also help each other heal.

Ethan took a step closer, our arms nearly brushing against one another, and for a fleeting moment, I thought he might close the gap entirely. "I just... I want to be brave enough to let you see all of me," he confessed, vulnerability glistening in his eyes. "It terrifies me, but I want to try. I want to be honest."

"Then let's be honest together," I whispered, my heart pounding as I stepped into the unknown with him, my breath catching at the intimacy of the moment. "No more facades, just us. We can be vulnerable without judgment."

The smile that spread across his face lit up the darkness around us, illuminating the edges of the uncertainty that had clouded our relationship for far too long. "Okay," he said, the word a promise, a commitment to vulnerability that felt like a shared secret in the stillness of the night.

As the waves crashed rhythmically against the rocks, I felt the weight of the world lifting from my shoulders. The night air was sweet with the scent of blooming flowers and sea salt, a reminder that even amidst chaos, beauty thrived. I reached out, brushing my fingers against his, a silent invitation to bridge the gap that had kept us apart for so long.

Ethan's hand found mine, the warmth of his skin sending a jolt of electricity through me. It was as if the universe had conspired to bring us to this moment, and I couldn't help but marvel at the wonder of it all. We stood there, hands intertwined, bathed in moonlight, two souls entwined in a dance of vulnerability and trust.

"I'm scared," he admitted, his voice barely above a whisper, yet the truth in his words resonated deeply within me.

"Me too," I confessed, squeezing his hand gently. "But fear can be a catalyst for change. We don't have to face it alone. Let's face it together."

In that instant, I felt a sense of clarity wash over me, a burgeoning understanding that this was only the beginning. With each moment spent unraveling our fears and insecurities, we were crafting a story that was uniquely ours. No longer would we allow the specters of our pasts to dictate our future. Together, we would write a new narrative, one where our broken pieces could fit together to create something whole and beautiful.

The stars above us seemed to shine even brighter as we stood on that balcony, our hearts finally aligned in a shared understanding that, despite the imperfections, we were exactly where we were meant to be. And in that shimmering expanse of possibility, the shattered facades began to mend, revealing the true selves that had long been waiting to be seen.

The gentle pressure of Ethan's hand in mine felt like a lifeline in the vast sea of uncertainty. His gaze held a mixture of apprehension and determination as if we were standing at the precipice of something monumental. The city stretched out below us, a tapestry of lives intertwined with dreams and secrets, and somehow, in that moment, our fragile honesty felt like a beacon against the backdrop of it all.

"Do you think we're ready for this?" he asked, the vulnerability in his voice tugging at my heart. "To let go of everything we've held on to for so long?"

I took a deep breath, inhaling the salty air mixed with the sweetness of the jasmine blooming nearby. "I think we're ready to be honest with ourselves first," I replied, letting the words linger like the last rays of sun before twilight. "And if we can do that, maybe we can be honest with each other."

Ethan looked thoughtful, his brow furrowing as he turned his gaze back to the ocean, where the waves crashed rhythmically against the shore. "I've spent so much time trying to create this perfect image, not just for others but for myself. It's exhausting." He sighed, the weight of his confession heavy yet liberating. "I thought if I could just achieve something significant, everything would fall into place."

"But what if it's not about the achievements?" I countered gently, intrigued by the vulnerability he was allowing to seep through his usually composed exterior. "What if it's about finding joy in the journey, in the people we meet along the way?"

He met my gaze again, something shifting behind his eyes, a flicker of understanding igniting the air between us. "You make it sound so easy," he murmured, almost incredulous.

"Maybe it is, in some ways," I said, my heart swelling with newfound hope. "We complicate it with our fears. What if we embraced the messiness of our lives instead of trying to curate some flawless version?"

The laughter that erupted from him was unexpected, a rich sound that danced on the warm breeze, chasing away the shadows that had lingered too long. "You're right, you know. I've been so focused on trying to be perfect that I've missed out on what really matters."

"Then let's promise to be messy together," I suggested, a teasing lilt in my voice. "We can navigate the chaos side by side."

"Deal," he agreed, and in that moment, it felt as if the universe conspired to weave our fates together, crafting a narrative that was as beautifully unpredictable as the stars overhead.

As we stood there, hands clasped and hearts open, a sense of calm enveloped us, the kind that only comes after a storm has passed. The night deepened, wrapping us in its velvet embrace, and I could feel the warmth of possibility blooming between us, unfurling like petals under the moonlight.

"You know," I said, tilting my head to gaze up at the sky, "this reminds me of the constellations. They're not perfect; they're just clusters of stars that happened to fall into a pattern. Maybe we can find our own constellation in this mess."

Ethan chuckled softly, the sound reverberating in the cool air. "A constellation made of chaos? I like it."

The warmth in his smile ignited a spark of courage in my heart. "Let's start small. What's one thing you've always wanted to do but never had the courage to try?" I felt the thrill of the unknown coursing through me, inviting us both to leap into something new.

His eyes brightened, and for a moment, I could see the gears turning as he contemplated my question. "I've always wanted to learn to surf," he admitted, a slight blush creeping up his cheeks. "But I always thought I'd embarrass myself."

"Then let's go surfing!" I exclaimed, my enthusiasm bubbling over like champagne. "We can crash and burn together, and it'll be an adventure!"

He laughed again, genuine this time, and it sent shivers of delight down my spine. "You know what? I think I'd actually like that." There was a lightness in his voice that hadn't been there before, and it ignited a thrill in my chest.

"We can find a local surf shop tomorrow," I suggested, the thought of our next adventure causing my heart to race with excitement. "We'll rent boards and take a lesson. What do you say?"

"I say you've got yourself a surfing buddy," he replied, the mischief dancing in his eyes. The weight of our earlier conversation felt like a distant memory, replaced by the anticipation of what lay ahead.

As the stars twinkled above us, casting their gentle glow, I realized how far we had come in just a few short moments. We had opened our hearts to one another, allowing the layers of pretense to peel away, revealing the raw, beautiful truth beneath. Together, we would navigate the messy intricacies of our lives, hand in hand, embracing the uncertainty that lay ahead.

The waves roared below us, their relentless rhythm echoing the pulse of our hearts. In the depths of that night, beneath the vastness of the sky, I understood that love was not about perfection but about the willingness to be seen, to be vulnerable, and to share both the highs and lows of life with someone who mattered.

With our hands still clasped, we leaned against the railing, our laughter mingling with the sounds of the city below. It felt as if we were suspended in time, enveloped in a cocoon of possibility where anything could happen. The future stretched out before us like the endless ocean, and I couldn't help but feel that it was filled with opportunities, surprises, and, most importantly, each other.

"I think this is just the beginning for us," I said softly, leaning my head against his shoulder as we gazed out into the vastness of the night.

"Yeah," he replied, his voice filled with a warmth that wrapped around me like a blanket. "Just the beginning."

And as we stood together, watching the stars shine their eternal light upon us, I knew that whatever lay ahead, we would face it as one—two imperfect souls ready to embrace the beauty in the chaos of life, forging our own constellation in a universe that had once felt so overwhelming.

Chapter 17: Baking a New Path

The first whiff of vanilla lingered in the air, entwining itself with the warm, yeasty aroma of freshly baked bread as I stepped into the bakery. The early morning sun cast a golden hue across the wooden countertops, where flour dusted like a soft snowfall under our eager fingers. It was a typical Wednesday, or at least it had started out that way, before a spark of inspiration ignited within me and ignited Ethan's passion right beside mine. We had mended our relationship, a delicate tapestry woven from threads of shared laughter and apologies, and today marked the dawn of our collaborative journey.

Ethan stood across the counter, his brow furrowed in concentration as he kneaded a batch of dough, his muscles flexing rhythmically, each movement a dance of precision. A smudge of flour coated his cheek, and for a fleeting moment, I wanted nothing more than to reach over and wipe it away, a gentle gesture of affection that danced on the edge of my mind. He caught me staring, his lips quirking into a half-smile, that lopsided grin that could melt glaciers. My heart quickened at the sight, and suddenly, the world outside—the bustling streets of our small town, the chirping of the morning birds, the scent of spring awakening—faded into a backdrop for this vibrant scene.

"Ready to create something magical?" he asked, his voice a mix of mischief and genuine excitement, pulling me from my reverie.

"Always," I replied, feeling a rush of adrenaline course through me. Our project wasn't just a showcase of pastries; it was a celebration of our revived partnership, a chance to pour our souls into art. Together, we could transform our ordinary bakery into an extraordinary gallery of confectionery delights.

We began with sketches, pages littered with swirling designs and whimsical themes. Each line danced with possibilities, a delicate thread connecting our individual dreams into one tapestry of sugary masterpieces. I could already picture the vibrant displays: towering croquembouche adorned with spun sugar, delicate macarons boasting flavors that could tell stories, and glistening cakes dripping with ganache like they were dipped in molten chocolate rivers.

"How about a centerpiece that tells a story?" Ethan suggested, his eyes twinkling with enthusiasm. "Something that reflects both our journeys—how we started as rivals and became partners."

I nodded, inspired by his suggestion. "A pastry tree, maybe? Each branch representing a different flavor, with hidden surprises inside. We could create an adventure with every bite."

As the ideas flowed, laughter bubbled between us like the yeast in our dough. Late nights became our new rhythm, punctuated by the soft glow of fairy lights strung across the bakery. The glow reflected off the stainless-steel appliances and illuminated the shadows of our workspace, turning our humble bakery into an enchanting studio, alive with creativity.

One evening, as we dusted the countertops with powdered sugar, I glanced at Ethan, who was intently focused on a particularly intricate sugar flower. I admired the way his brow furrowed with concentration, his tongue peeking out slightly, a childlike focus that made my heart swell.

"Ethan," I began hesitantly, unsure how to voice the shadow that danced in the corners of my mind. "Do you think we should... I mean, can we talk about Emma?"

His fingers paused mid-motion, the delicate flower momentarily forgotten. I held my breath, a weight settling in the air between us, charged with unspoken words. The name hung heavy, a ghost of our past, lingering like the scent of burnt sugar.

"She's not in the picture anymore, Alex," he said softly, but I could see the tension etched in his shoulders. "I promise you, this time it's different. It's just us."

But was it? As the nights grew longer, filled with artistic fervor and whispered dreams, I couldn't shake the remnants of my insecurity. Emma had a way of haunting my thoughts, a reminder of the fragility of what we were building. I needed to confront my feelings, strip them bare and examine them like the dough we shaped each day.

"Still," I said, gathering my thoughts like ingredients, "I think we need to acknowledge it. It's not just about us now; it's about this project, too."

Ethan sighed, a breath laced with understanding. "You're right. Let's talk about it."

And so we did, pouring our fears and hopes into the warm space of our bakery, the very foundation we were crafting together. Each confession brought us closer, the emotional weight lifting, allowing our laughter to echo again. I began to feel the tension dissolve, replaced by the giddy thrill of creating.

As days turned into weeks, our collaborative spirit flourished, weaving an intricate pattern that mirrored the layers of a perfect mille-feuille. Each element of our project became a reflection of our synergy: sweet and savory, delicate yet bold. Our evenings were filled with the heady buzz of chocolate tempering, the sweet symphony of whipped cream, and the soft crackle of caramelized sugar—our senses consumed by the art of baking.

In those moments, I realized how much I cherished this partnership, this new path we were carving out together. The world outside continued to spin, oblivious to our little bubble of happiness. Our laughter echoed against the walls, mingling with the sounds of sizzling pans and the warmth of rising dough, transforming the bakery into a sanctuary where dreams took flight.

Yet, in the quiet moments, when the flour settled and the laughter faded, I could feel Emma's presence lurking at the edges of my mind. I vowed to confront her, not as a shadow to be banished but as a reminder of how far I had come. I would protect this newfound joy, this passion that ignited not just my love for baking but for the bond I was building with Ethan. My heart was a canvas, and I was ready to paint it anew.

The following morning arrived with a hint of promise, the sun spilling its light over the streets, igniting everything it touched. It was one of those rare days when the air held the scent of possibility, mingling with the sweet aroma of baking bread wafting from our bakery. I slipped into my apron, the familiar fabric comforting against my skin, and made my way to the kitchen, where Ethan was already immersed in our latest creation.

"Good morning, artist," he called out, a teasing lilt to his voice as he stood before a canvas of vibrant fruit, each piece more vivid than the last. I could barely take my eyes off the rainbow of colors: ruby-red strawberries, sun-kissed apricots, and the deep purples of ripe plums. They were the kind of hues that could make anyone's heart skip a beat.

"Looks like a masterpiece in the making," I replied, moving closer to examine his work. With careful precision, he was crafting an edible sculpture that would soon become the centerpiece of our show. Each slice of fruit was meticulously cut, forming the shape of a blooming flower that seemed ready to spring to life.

He grinned, that lopsided smile that sent my heart racing. "Just wait until you see what I have planned for the petals."

As I watched him work, I felt a pang of gratitude wash over me. How did I get so lucky to share this space, this creative energy, with someone who understood the rhythm of my heart as well as the cadence of our kitchen? We were partners in the truest sense, a duet harmonizing amidst the clatter of whisks and the hum of the mixer.

With each passing hour, our ideas blossomed. We whipped up batter infused with lavender, each fold a careful embrace, and crafted intricate pastries that promised to be both delightful and whimsical.

The kitchen transformed into our laboratory, bubbling with laughter and the occasional flour fight, which, I'd admit, felt like a throwback to childhood days of innocent play.

Yet, as the sun began to set, casting long shadows across the countertops, a familiar unease crept back in. It was in the quiet moments, like this, when the hustle of the day faded and we stood shoulder to shoulder, the chatter muted, that Emma's presence seemed to manifest in the silence. I wanted to shake it off, to immerse myself fully in our work and Ethan's laughter, but I knew I couldn't bury it any longer.

"Ethan," I began, my voice a hesitant whisper, "can we talk about what happens next?"

He paused, his hands stilling above the counter, sensing the shift in the atmosphere. "What do you mean?"

"The show is coming up, and I can't shake the feeling that we need to address the past before we move forward."

His brow furrowed, and for a moment, I feared the unspoken would hang between us like a dense fog. But then he took a deep breath, his shoulders relaxing as he turned to face me fully.

"Yeah, I guess we do," he replied, his tone more serious now, layered with sincerity. "It's easy to forget when we're wrapped up in this creative bubble, but we can't pretend that the past isn't part of us. Let's talk about it."

We shifted to a quieter corner of the bakery, the soft glow of the overhead lights casting a gentle ambiance. I felt the weight of our conversation pressing against my chest, the air thick with anticipation. It wasn't just about Emma; it was about what she represented—the choices we'd made, the paths we'd taken, and how they shaped our present.

"I know she hurt you," Ethan said softly, his gaze steady, searching mine for understanding. "But I want you to know that I'm not going anywhere. You and I, we're building something real here, and it's not overshadowed by her past."

I could feel a knot unraveling in my chest as I absorbed his words, warmth blooming where there had been apprehension. "I want that too," I admitted. "But I also need to be honest about how her actions affected me. I've spent too long worrying that she might reappear and ruin everything we've created."

Ethan nodded, his expression thoughtful. "It's natural to feel that way. But we can't let fear dictate our actions. Let's create something so vibrant that it overshadows anything that came before."

His determination was contagious, and as we shared our stories, the weight of our pasts began to dissipate, leaving behind a sense of clarity that felt refreshing. We could forge a path that was solely ours, unencumbered by what once was.

The next few days were a blur of activity, each hour rich with the scents of caramelized sugar and baked fruit. We laughed, joked, and sometimes even sang along to the radio while the bakery buzzed with life. Our project grew in scope, morphing from a simple pastry art show into a full-blown celebration of our journey—one that included not just our creations but the people who had supported us.

As we sculpted, decorated, and perfected our confections, I noticed a transformation within myself. The confidence I had once lost began to return, rekindled by the unwavering support of the man beside me. Each layer of cream, each delicate fold of pastry, became a testament to our resilience, not just as bakers but as individuals who had weathered storms and emerged stronger.

The day of the show arrived, bursting with a vibrancy that mirrored our excitement. The bakery was transformed into a gallery, each display a masterpiece waiting to be unveiled. Friends, family, and even curious locals gathered, the atmosphere charged with energy, laughter, and the intoxicating scent of sweet delights.

As I stepped back to admire our work, a sense of pride washed over me. This wasn't just a showcase; it was a celebration of our artistry, our journey, and the bond we had forged through shared passions and experiences. I turned to Ethan, his eyes sparkling with anticipation, and in that moment, I knew we had created something lasting—something that would stand the test of time, far beyond the fleeting nature of baked goods.

Hand in hand, we faced the crowd, ready to share our creations and the story behind them. This was our moment, a new path illuminated by our determination and creativity. And as the first guests approached, I felt an undeniable thrill course through me, igniting a fire of hope and excitement for everything that lay ahead.

As the day of the show unfolded, the bakery felt alive, humming with an electric energy that tingled at the edges of my consciousness. We had transformed the space into a veritable wonderland, each corner bursting with color and creativity. The soft glow of fairy lights twinkled overhead, illuminating our creations as though they were precious gems on display. Ethan and I had worked tirelessly to ensure every detail was perfect, and now, as I stood in the midst of our masterpiece, I felt a blend of exhilaration and trepidation coursing through me.

The entrance, draped with fresh greenery and whimsical ribbons, beckoned guests into our world. The scent of freshly baked goods mingled with hints of citrus and vanilla, creating an intoxicating aroma that enveloped everyone who entered. I caught glimpses of familiar faces in the crowd—friends and family who had supported us throughout this journey—each one of them radiating a warmth that soothed my nerves.

Ethan was a flurry of movement, ensuring everything was in place. His energy was contagious, and I found myself swept up in the excitement as we welcomed guests, our laughter ringing out above the gentle murmur of conversation. With each passing minute, more people filled the bakery, their faces lighting up as they caught sight of our creations. There was a sense of wonder as they wandered through the displays, their eyes widening in delight, hands reaching out to sample the tantalizing array of pastries.

We had crafted an assortment that told our story—a vibrant tapestry of flavors and textures. There were delicate lavender-infused éclairs, each one adorned with a tiny edible flower, and towering layers of chocolate cake, rich and decadent, drizzled with caramel that shimmered under the lights. A whimsical pie sat on a pedestal, its crust intricately woven to resemble a blooming garden. Each creation bore a piece of our hearts, a manifestation of the joy we had found in working together.

As the evening wore on, I felt a sense of belonging wash over me, mingling seamlessly with the sweet taste of triumph. I caught Ethan's eye across the room, and he grinned, his happiness infectious. We were in sync, our unspoken bond stronger than ever, weaving through the crowd as effortlessly as the sugar threads that adorned our creations.

Then, just as I was reveling in this moment, the door swung open with a quiet creak, drawing my gaze. A hush fell over the room as Emma entered, her presence as stark as a thundercloud on a clear day. The excitement that had buoyed my spirits moments before now felt like a lead weight in my stomach. She stood there, framed by the doorway, a silhouette of uncertainty in a dress that hugged her figure like a second skin. My heart raced, caught between the thrill of the night and the nagging unease her presence ignited.

Ethan noticed the shift in the atmosphere, and his brows furrowed as he turned to me. "You okay?" His concern was palpable, cutting through the noise of the gathering.

"Yeah, just... I didn't expect her to come," I murmured, my pulse quickening as she made her way toward us, weaving through the crowd with a practiced ease that was both enchanting and unnerving.

As she approached, a swirl of emotions hit me like a tidal wave. Memories of our tumultuous history flooded back, tainting the sweetness of the evening. I took a steadying breath, reminding myself of the strength I had found in this journey. I wasn't that uncertain baker anymore; I was a creator, an artist, and more importantly, I was no longer alone.

"Alex," she said, her voice smooth but laced with an edge of vulnerability. "I'm so glad to see you here." Her gaze flicked over to Ethan, who stood beside me, arms crossed defensively. "And you, too, Ethan."

"Emma," I replied, summoning a smile that felt more like armor than warmth. "Welcome."

Her eyes sparkled, perhaps with genuine admiration for our creations, or perhaps with something else entirely—an inkling of regret, perhaps? It was hard to tell. She stepped closer, examining a delicate tart that shimmered with a glaze that caught the light just right. "You both have really outdone yourselves. This is incredible."

"Thanks," Ethan replied, his tone cautious but polite. He had every right to be wary, yet the graciousness in his demeanor reminded me of the kindness that had blossomed between us. "We've worked hard on it."

The conversation flowed, but it felt like walking a tightrope, every word weighed with unspoken tension. I could sense the crowd swirling around us, the excitement of the evening teetering on the edge of something fragile. I needed to address this—confront Emma not only for myself but for Ethan, too.

"Emma," I began, my voice steady despite the turmoil inside me, "I want you to know that this show is really important to us. To me." I glanced at Ethan, who nodded subtly, encouragement etched in his eyes. "We've worked through a lot, and it's a new beginning."

She met my gaze, her expression shifting from surprise to something softer, perhaps even reflective. "I never meant to come between you two. I see how happy you are, and I genuinely wish you both the best."

For a fleeting moment, I felt the weight of resentment lift, replaced by a flicker of understanding. "Thank you, Emma. That means a lot."

As the evening progressed, the tension gradually began to dissolve. Emma joined the throng of guests, her demeanor shifting from observer to participant. She sampled pastries, her laughter mixing with ours, forming a delicate harmony that wrapped around the bakery like the sweet scent of vanilla.

With every interaction, I noticed the way Ethan's eyes sparkled when he talked about our work, how passionately he described the intricacies of each creation. The connection between us felt deeper than mere partnership—it was a bond forged through trust, resilience, and a shared dream. I reveled in the moment, my earlier anxieties melting away like butter on warm bread.

As the night drew to a close, the guests began to disperse, their faces illuminated with delight. They had come for pastries but left with memories of an evening that felt like a celebration of love, creativity, and new beginnings. Ethan and I stood together, surveying the remnants of our creations, the crumbs and frosting remnants telling stories of laughter and joy.

"I can't believe we did it," I said, the weight of fulfillment settling comfortably in my chest.

He chuckled, his eyes dancing with mirth. "You know what they say: great things come from a little bit of flour and a lot of heart."

We shared a laugh, the sound echoing in the now-quiet bakery, a melody of promise and possibility. I felt lighter, unburdened by the past. Emma's presence had transformed from a shadow to a gentle reminder of how far I had come. With Ethan by my side, I was ready to embrace whatever lay ahead.

As we began to clean up, I knew this was just the beginning of our journey together, a collaboration not only in baking but in life itself. We had crafted something beautiful, and with each layer we built, I felt an unwavering certainty that our story was just getting started. This new path was ours to explore, and I was more than ready to dive in.

Chapter 18: When Shadows Loom

The gallery buzzed with an intoxicating mix of excitement and anxiety, the air heavy with the scent of fresh paint and polished wood. Each canvas glowed under the soft, focused lights, their colors vibrant against the stark white walls, a riot of expression just waiting to be unveiled. My heart raced as I glanced around, taking in the throngs of elegantly dressed guests, their laughter bubbling over like the champagne flutes they clutched, glinting in the dim light. I had poured my soul into every brushstroke, and now, standing on the precipice of this grand reveal, I was caught between the thrill of anticipation and the gnawing fear of exposure.

Yet, beneath the surface of this festive façade, a knot twisted in my stomach, tightening with every second that ticked by. It was a familiar sensation, a warning that something was amiss. Perhaps it was the frantic scurrying of waitstaff, their trays laden with hors d'oeuvres that looked far too pristine to be eaten. Or maybe it was the feeling of eyes watching me, assessing me like I was a mere exhibit in my own gallery, waiting to be judged. I focused on the flurry of movement and color around me, allowing the ambiance to wash over me, yet that nagging sensation persisted like a dull throb in my chest.

As the clock crept closer to the hour, the doors swung open, and in strode Emma, her presence as striking as a thunderstorm rolling across a clear sky. She glided through the crowd with an air of confidence, her eyes darting around with a predatory gleam. My breath caught in my throat as I recalled our history—friend turned rival, a story as old as time yet uniquely our own. Emma's entrance felt almost choreographed, a deliberate performance designed to steal the spotlight. Her laughter rang out, clear and infectious, drawing the attention of everyone around her, especially Ethan.

Ethan stood a few feet away, his expression a mix of amusement and apprehension as Emma approached. I watched, frozen in place, as she swept in with a magnetic charm, her smile bright but her intentions shadowed. They shared a past that lingered like the scent of old perfume; familiar yet tainted with the bitterness of unfulfilled promises. I could see the flicker of recognition in his eyes, and with it came an unsettling sense of déjà vu. Did he realize that I was standing just a heartbeat away, the very embodiment of the art we had created together? Did he comprehend how much this night meant to me?

It took everything in me to remain composed. I reminded myself of the countless hours we had spent huddled together in the cramped corners of my studio, our laughter mingling with the strokes of our brushes, each moment woven into the fabric of our work. But that memory felt like a thin veil now, easily pierced by the sharp edges of Emma's confidence. She laughed a little too loud, touched his arm a little too long, her body language an intricate dance of flirtation and familiarity that made my skin crawl.

I could feel the frustration bubbling inside me, hot and insistent, threatening to spill over into a volcanic eruption of emotion. What was I supposed to do? Confront her? Call out her obvious attempts to undermine our hard work? No. I had to stay composed, to rise above the tide of jealousy and insecurity that threatened to sweep me away. But it was a Herculean task, especially as she leaned in closer to Ethan, whispering something that made his eyes light up.

The gallery had transformed into a theater, and I was caught in a performance I had not auditioned for, my role seemingly relegated to that of a mere spectator. I forced myself to smile as I approached them, a fragile mask of cheerfulness clinging to my features.

"Hey, Ethan! Emma! So good to see you both!" I chirped, my voice sounding strained, as if I were pulling each word from the depths of my throat. My heart thudded, louder than the music thrumming through the speakers, and for a moment, I felt utterly exposed. Emma turned to me, her smile razor-edged and unapologetic.

"Darling! I was just telling Ethan how much we used to enjoy our late-night art sessions. Remember those?" Her tone dripped with honeyed sarcasm, a barbed compliment that cut deeper than any direct insult could have. I swallowed hard, forcing my expression to remain neutral. Memories flickered in my mind—art nights filled with laughter, splattered paint, and vibrant dreams. Now they felt tainted, colored by her presence.

Ethan's gaze flickered between us, uncertainty etched across his face. I could feel the tension thickening, a storm brewing in the charged atmosphere. "Yeah, those were fun times," he replied, his voice hesitant. I could see him straddling the line between nostalgia and the present, and the moment felt precarious, like a tightrope act.

Emma's eyes sparkled with mischief as she leaned closer to him, a conspiratorial whisper escaping her lips. "You know, Ethan, I've always admired your ability to see things differently, to bring a unique perspective to art. I wonder how much you've grown since our days together." Her words dripped with insinuation, the unspoken challenge lingering in the air between us.

As I stood there, trapped in the web of this encounter, I realized I had a choice to make. I could either succumb to the shadows lurking at the edges of my heart or harness the fierce determination that had fueled my creativity all along. With every ounce of strength, I straightened my posture, refusing to let Emma's presence diminish what we had achieved. It was time to step into the light, to claim my place among the brilliance we had cultivated, and to protect the beauty we had created together.

With each passing moment, the gallery pulsed with energy, a living entity imbued with the dreams and aspirations that adorned its walls. The sound of heels clicking against polished floors echoed in my ears, mingling with the soft murmur of conversations that wove through the space like a gentle breeze. I turned my attention back to Ethan, whose brow furrowed in confusion, caught in Emma's web of nostalgia and charm. There was something about her that had the uncanny ability to draw people in, making them forget the present as they reminisced about the past.

As I stood there, rooted in place, I could feel the brush of cold air against my skin, a stark contrast to the warmth radiating from the crowd. A thin sheen of sweat broke out across my brow, not from the heat of excitement, but from the weight of the moment pressing down on me. Emma leaned closer to Ethan, her laughter ringing out like a bell, slicing through my fragile composure. I could almost hear the threads of their shared memories weaving together, a tapestry of moments I was not a part of.

"Do you remember that time we painted the sunrise on the roof of that old diner?" she asked, her voice low and conspiratorial, sending a jolt of recognition through me. I had heard the story before, how they had crept up there in the early hours, armed with a stolen bottle of wine and an insatiable need to capture the dawn. It had been a moment of reckless youth, an escape from the mundane that had bound them in ways I could only now feel echoes of.

"Yeah, that was one for the books," Ethan replied, a distant smile creeping onto his face. My stomach twisted. Was this the version of Ethan I was competing with? The one she painted with her words? A beautiful, vibrant past that left no room for the present? I felt as if I were standing on the edge of a precipice, peering down into a chasm of doubt, and I couldn't help but wonder if I would tumble over it.

Determined not to be consumed by the rising tide of envy, I cleared my throat and forced a smile that felt both heavy and hollow. "Actually," I interjected, my voice steady despite the chaos swirling within, "Ethan and I were just discussing our favorite moments from the studio last week. You know, the ones that made our artwork come alive." My gaze darted between them, the words spilling from my lips as if they were the only defense I had left. I needed to remind Ethan, and myself, of what we had built together.

Emma's expression faltered for a moment, surprise flickering in her eyes before her mask slid back into place. "Oh, I'd love to hear about that! What's been inspiring you two lately?" The challenge lingered in her tone, sharp and crystalline, demanding more than just idle chit-chat. She was testing the waters, eager to see if our connection could withstand the storm she had stirred up.

Ethan turned to me, his expression a blend of curiosity and concern. "Yeah, I'd love to hear your thoughts." The sincerity in his eyes struck me, a lifeline amid the tension. I could sense the room holding its breath, every ear pricked, every eye focused on our exchange, making the moment feel all the more monumental.

"Honestly," I began, the words tumbling out in a rush, "it's the little things. The way the light changes in the late afternoon or how a simple shadow can shift the entire mood of a piece. It's those nuances that inspire the deeper connections we're trying to convey." I watched as the tension in Ethan's shoulders eased slightly, his focus shifting back to me, grounding us both.

"Exactly," he chimed in, his voice gaining strength. "That's what I love about working together. We can bounce ideas off each other, and it feels like each piece becomes a conversation." I felt a surge of warmth radiate through me as I met his gaze, a silent understanding passing between us. For a moment, it felt like we were shielded from Emma's storm, cocooned in our own shared reality.

Yet Emma wasn't one to be easily sidelined. "Well, I've always believed that art is a reflection of our experiences. Isn't it fascinating how memories shape our work?" she said, her tone smooth, her smile deceptively sweet. "You two seem to have a lot of that, don't you?" Her eyes glittered with mischief, and I could sense the undertone of her challenge, daring us to counter her assertion.

"Absolutely," I replied, my voice steadying. "But I think it's also about what we're creating now. What we're doing together in this moment is what truly matters. This show isn't just about the past; it's about what we're building as a team." I held my breath, hoping to anchor Ethan's thoughts in the present.

"Right," he said, his voice gaining a new edge. "It's about collaboration, not just individual experiences. The beauty lies in what we're creating today." There it was, the spark I had hoped to ignite. It felt like a small victory, a reminder that we were still standing strong despite the shadows looming around us.

The gallery continued to fill with guests, laughter and music swirling around us. As I watched the vibrant mingling of colors and people, I could feel the tension in my body begin to unravel. Emma may have wielded the past like a weapon, but I had the present—and with it, the potential for a future crafted from every shared moment, every brushstroke, and every dream we had yet to realize.

Yet, in the depths of my heart, I knew this battle wasn't over. Emma's presence loomed like a storm cloud, threatening to darken our skies whenever she chose. But tonight, in this space of art and ambition, I would fight with everything I had. I would hold tight to our creation, my connection with Ethan, and the vibrant tapestry of our dreams. The night was still young, and as the voices of our guests intertwined with the rhythm of our hearts, I would not let shadows extinguish the light we had fought so hard to kindle.

The night danced around us, alive with laughter and the clinking of glasses, yet my pulse echoed in the stillness of my thoughts. I watched as guests drifted from one painting to another, captivated by the stories woven into the strokes of vibrant colors. Each piece whispered secrets of our shared dreams and painstaking efforts, the culmination of countless hours spent in the sanctuary of my studio. Yet, with every laugh that escaped Emma's lips, a shadow loomed larger, a specter haunting the very heart of my creation.

"Let's grab a drink," Ethan suggested, breaking through the haze of my thoughts. His voice was warm, a beacon in the storm that threatened to pull me under. I nodded, relief flooding through me as we made our way toward the bar, weaving through the crowd like ships navigating through a turbulent sea. The clamor of conversation enveloped us, and for a brief moment, I could forget Emma's piercing gaze and the way it seemed to cling to Ethan like a shroud.

We reached the bar, the polished wood gleaming under the dim lights, and I ordered a gin and tonic, the familiar taste a comforting reminder of carefree nights spent unwinding after long days of creation. As I sipped, I felt Ethan's presence beside me, solid and reassuring, like an anchor amid the churning waters of my emotions. He turned to me, his eyes sparkling with mischief, breaking into a grin that sent warmth blooming through my chest.

"You know, you should have seen Emma's face when I told her we were collaborating. I think it rattled her a bit," he said, a hint of laughter dancing in his tone. I couldn't help but smile at his playful demeanor, grateful for his unwavering support. Yet, a part of me wondered whether it was more of a defensive tactic than an act of solidarity. Did he sense my unease, my desire to claim my space in this artistic journey we had embarked on together?

"I'm glad to hear it," I replied, the weight of our conversation drifting momentarily. "She has a knack for twisting things to suit her narrative." As the words slipped from my lips, I felt the familiar bitterness rising within me. Why did she feel the need to pit us against each other? Why couldn't we coexist in this world we were carving out for ourselves?

"Let's not let her steal our moment, okay?" Ethan's voice pulled me back to the present. His sincerity was a balm to my fraying nerves. "Tonight is about us, about our work. The rest is just noise." I nodded, determination igniting within me as I took a deep breath. If I wanted to protect what we had built, I needed to focus on the beauty we were creating, not the shadows Emma cast.

Rejuvenated, I turned my gaze back to the gallery. The soft glow of the lights cast an ethereal sheen on the paintings, illuminating the layers of emotion captured in every brushstroke. It was as if each piece resonated with the energy of our journey—our late nights filled with laughter, our moments of frustration, and the exhilarating rush of creativity.

But as I scanned the crowd, my heart sank. Emma had found her way back to Ethan, her laughter echoing like chimes in the wind, beckoning him closer. She leaned against the wall, a vision of casual elegance, her presence a siren song that drew him back in. I watched, a quiet storm brewing in my chest, as he leaned in to hear her, the distance between them shrinking.

I felt my pulse quicken, an instinctive reaction to the invisible threads that connected them. Memories flooded my mind—moments that I had shared with Ethan, small fragments of time that felt irretrievably threatened by Emma's allure. It was an unbidden jealousy, raw and unrefined, clawing its way to the surface. Why couldn't I shake this feeling? Why couldn't I just accept that the past was the past?

In that instant, I realized I had two choices. I could succumb to the gnawing insecurity that threatened to envelop me or rise above it, take back my narrative, and reclaim the space I had carved out for myself. Gathering my resolve, I made my way across the room, each step a silent declaration of intent. The sounds of the gallery faded into the background, replaced by the steady rhythm of my heartbeat, propelling me forward.

"Ethan," I called out, injecting warmth into my voice as I approached. "There you are! I was hoping we could take a moment to talk about our next piece." I felt Emma's gaze pivot toward me, her smile faltering for just a heartbeat, and in that instant, I saw the flicker of annoyance beneath her practiced charm.

"Of course!" Ethan replied, his eyes lighting up with the same excitement I felt. "Let's definitely do that." The shift in his demeanor was immediate, and I couldn't help but feel a surge of triumph as I watched the flicker of confusion dance across Emma's face.

"Excuse us," I added, my tone polite yet firm, as I led Ethan away, away from the magnetic pull of Emma's charm. We moved deeper into the gallery, finding refuge in a quieter corner where the chatter became a distant hum. I turned to Ethan, my breath steadying as I felt the warmth of his presence envelop me.

"Thank you," I said, my voice softening. "For backing me up." I searched his eyes, seeking reassurance, a sign that he understood the invisible battle waging within me. He met my gaze with sincerity, the understanding in his eyes a comforting balm.

"Always," he replied, a smile breaking through the tension. "We're in this together, remember?" It was a reminder I needed, a tether anchoring me to the present and our shared vision.

As we stood there, the chaos of the gallery swirling around us, I felt a shift within me. The shadows cast by Emma's presence began to recede, replaced by the vibrant energy of possibility. We were creators, artists, bound by our dreams and our passion. Emma's attempts to disrupt our harmony would not prevail. With every stroke of the brush, every whispered conversation, we were writing our own story, and it was one worth fighting for.

As the night wore on, the gallery glowed like a beacon, a testament to our efforts. Guests moved from piece to piece, their appreciation palpable, and I found solace in the connection we were forging with them. The laughter and warmth that surrounded us became the backdrop to our shared journey, a celebration of our artistry and the bonds we had nurtured along the way.

Together, we would face whatever challenges lay ahead, the weight of the past becoming a mere shadow against the brilliance of our present. Emma's laughter faded into the background, replaced by the voices of friends and admirers, and as I leaned into Ethan, I knew we were destined for greatness, woven together by a tapestry of dreams, determination, and an unwavering belief in ourselves.

Chapter 19: The Fragile Balance

The vibrant hues of the art show still danced in my mind, a kaleidoscope of colors that felt too alive to belong to mere canvases. Each stroke, each piece of pottery, each shimmering glass sculpture seemed to hum with the energy of the night, drawing in admirers as they sipped wine and shared whispers of admiration. It was a world I had spent countless hours dreaming about and now, finally, it had come to life—a festival of creativity that filled the once-staid gallery with the spirit of a carnival. Laughter and clinking glasses echoed in my ears as I caught glimpses of familiar faces, but as the echoes faded and the crowd dispersed, I felt an emptiness loom behind the vibrancy.

Ethan's presence next to me was a comforting balm. His warmth radiated like the golden glow of the overhead lights that illuminated our hard work. The way he moved—his hands deftly stacking unsold artwork, brushing his hair from his forehead with a soft sigh—made my heart flutter with an inexplicable mix of pride and trepidation. We had done this together, pouring ourselves into the exhibit with the fervor of artists capturing their wildest dreams. Yet, like a tempest brewing just out of sight, Emma's specter lingered in the corners of my mind, her shadow looming over our newly forged bond. I couldn't shake the feeling that no matter how successful we were tonight, it was but a fragile façade, threatened by the complexities of Ethan's past.

"Do you remember that piece in the corner?" Ethan asked, his voice pulling me back from the brink of my spiraling thoughts. He motioned toward a vibrant canvas splattered with blues and yellows, like sunlight filtering through a stormy sea. "The one with the crashing waves?" His eyes sparkled with a hint of nostalgia, the kind that tugged at my heartstrings.

I nodded, recalling how he had stood before it earlier, lost in thought as if he were searching for something just beneath the surface of the paint. "You seemed captivated by it."

He chuckled, a sound rich and genuine, reverberating through the emptying gallery. "I used to think it looked like our lives—chaotic and beautiful, all at once." The way he looked at me then, with those deep-set eyes that held so many stories, made me feel like I was part of that tapestry he wove together with his words.

His confession hung in the air, heavy with implications I wasn't ready to untangle. There was a flicker of vulnerability in his gaze, and it beckoned me closer, inviting me to step beyond the edges of our shared successes into the murky depths of his past. I swallowed hard, the thought of Emma clawing its way back into my mind, uninvited yet insistent.

"What was it like?" I ventured, trying to keep my voice steady, my heart steady. "Your relationship with her." The question slipped out before I could retract it, a reckless dive into unknown waters.

He hesitated, his fingers stilling over a ceramic vase he was about to set down. "Complicated," he finally murmured, his tone laced with a mix of regret and resignation. "There were moments of brilliance, I'll admit, but they were often overshadowed by shadows of toxicity."

My breath caught. Ethan's vulnerability was both alluring and frightening, illuminating the darkness that hovered between us. I leaned closer, eager yet apprehensive, trying to glean what I could from the man who was slowly becoming the anchor in my stormy seas. "What do you mean by that?"

He met my gaze, a hint of sadness flickering behind his eyes. "We were both artists in our own right, but we were also both fiercely independent. The love was there, but so was jealousy, competitiveness. We fed off each other, but it often felt like we were trying to outdo one another instead of just... being."

Each word he spoke felt like a thread weaving itself into my understanding of him. I could sense the deep-rooted fears he carried—ones that mirrored my own insecurities. "So, what happened?" I pressed, desperate to untangle this web of emotions that threatened to ensnare us both.

He paused, a shadow crossing his face. "We lost ourselves in the chaos. It was like we were swimming in separate currents, always fighting against each other instead of merging into one flow." The pain in his voice struck a chord within me, reverberating through the silent gallery. "In the end, it was easier to walk away than to keep trying to make it work."

A silence enveloped us, thick and heavy, punctuated only by the distant sounds of the cleanup crew shuffling around. I could feel the weight of his words pressing against my chest, mixing with my own fears. "But now..." I dared to say, feeling bold yet frightened, "what do we do?"

He turned toward me, and in that moment, I could see the reflection of my own anxieties mirrored in his expression. The fragility of our connection loomed like a storm cloud overhead, ready to unleash its fury if we didn't navigate it carefully. "We have to trust each other," he replied, the sincerity in his voice warming me. "I want to share my dreams with you, but I need you to trust that I won't fall back into those old patterns."

His words wrapped around me, tender yet firm. The path ahead felt daunting, a labyrinth of choices that required not just passion, but faith in one another. I took a deep breath, searching for the courage to voice my own fears. "And what if I'm afraid? What if I can't let go of my jealousy?"

He stepped closer, closing the distance between us, his eyes piercing through the veil of uncertainty. "Then we work on it together. We can't let Emma or anyone else dictate our narrative." His presence enveloped me, a reminder that we were writing our own story, one brushstroke at a time, and I yearned to believe in that promise.

I found myself nodding, a quiet resolve settling over me. There would be no easy path forward, no guarantees, but together, we could navigate the storm. I could feel the bond between us strengthen, a delicate thread weaving our hearts together, holding us fast as we faced the uncertainties of the future.

The air was thick with the scent of fresh paint and lingering laughter, as if the very walls of the gallery had absorbed the joy of the night. As we meticulously packed away unsold pieces, I found myself stealing glances at Ethan, his hands deftly maneuvering framed canvases as if they were delicate treasures. His brow furrowed in concentration, and for a fleeting moment, the world outside felt suspended, allowing me to focus solely on this fragile yet electric bond that had begun to bloom between us.

"I've never done anything like this before," I admitted, breaking the comfortable silence, my voice barely above a whisper as if speaking too loudly might shatter the moment. "Not just art shows, but... this." I gestured between us, a vague but palpable energy crackling in the air. "This feels different."

Ethan paused, his gaze locking onto mine, and I could see the faint flicker of hope in his eyes. "Different can be good," he replied, his voice warm and steady, "as long as we're willing to navigate through the uncertainty together." His confidence soothed my growing anxiety, weaving a thread of reassurance through the fabric of our shared experience.

We resumed packing, but I couldn't shake the shadows of doubt lurking in the corners of my mind. Emma's name echoed like a haunting refrain, an unwelcome reminder that our newfound closeness was still precariously perched on a precipice. Every soft laugh exchanged, every gentle brush of our hands felt weighted, as if the universe itself was holding its breath, waiting for the inevitable slip.

A subtle shift in Ethan's demeanor caught my attention, a fleeting moment when his hands stilled and his eyes seemed to drift away to somewhere distant. It was in that silence that I realized how much of his past still clung to him, like an artist carrying the residue of every color they had ever used. "What if I can't meet your expectations?" I ventured, the words tumbling out before I could rein them in. "What if I'm just a passing phase?"

Ethan's expression shifted, the warmth in his eyes sharpening into something earnest. "You're not a phase. You're real, and that terrifies me as much as it excites me." He took a step closer, the intimacy of the moment wrapping around us like a cocoon. "I've spent too long fearing what could happen if I let someone in, and then I met you."

I felt my heart stutter in my chest, his admission igniting a rush of warmth that spread through me, dispelling some of the chill of uncertainty. "But what if I don't know how to navigate this world?" I pressed, my voice shaking with vulnerability. "What if I end up making the same mistakes Emma did?"

He reached out, his fingers brushing against mine in a delicate, electric touch that sent shivers up my arm. "We're not them," he said softly, the sincerity in his voice anchoring me as it wrapped around my fears like a lifeline. "You're not her, and I'm not that guy. We're different, and we can create something better if we're willing to put in the work."

The gentleness in his tone stirred something within me, a longing to believe in the possibility of us. I squeezed his hand, the warmth of his skin against mine igniting a spark of courage. "So, what do we do?" The question hung in the air between us, as heavy as the night sky outside the gallery windows, filled with endless possibilities.

Ethan tilted his head slightly, a thoughtful expression crossing his face. "We start small. Trust isn't built overnight; it's a mosaic of moments. We share our thoughts, our fears, our hopes. We don't shy away from the messy parts." His words danced in my mind like fireflies, illuminating the path we could tread together.

As we continued to tidy up, I found myself sharing bits of my life, small anecdotes and memories that had shaped me, letting the vulnerability seep into my words. I spoke of my childhood in the Midwest, where summers felt infinite, filled with fireflies and the sweet scent of freshly mown grass. I painted a picture of the warmth of family barbecues, the laughter echoing through the backyard like music that lingered long after the last guests departed.

In turn, Ethan unveiled pieces of himself, fragments of a life colored by both joy and struggle. He recounted long nights spent in dimly lit studios, pouring himself into his craft, each brushstroke a reflection of his internal battles. I could see the flicker of passion in his eyes as he spoke of his dreams, how they had been both his solace and his prison, the duality of artistry weaving through his narrative.

With each shared story, I felt the threads of our lives intertwine, binding us together in a tapestry rich with texture and depth. The weight of my jealousy began to lift, replaced by a sense of shared understanding and kinship. I could sense the shift in our dynamic, the fragile balance beginning to stabilize as we forged a bond rooted in honesty.

As the final pieces were tucked away, the gallery dimmed, leaving us alone in the hushed aftermath of our success. The soft glow of the overhead lights cast a golden hue around us, transforming the space into a sanctuary of dreams and possibilities. "This is just the beginning, isn't it?" I murmured, allowing hope to seep into my voice.

Ethan stepped closer, his presence enveloping me in warmth. "Absolutely," he said, his voice low and confident, "but we have to keep building on it. Trust is a dance, and we have to learn the steps together."

With a smile tugging at my lips, I nodded, the rhythm of his words resonating within me. As we stood side by side in the quiet gallery, I realized that the uncertainty wouldn't disappear overnight. Yet, in this moment, as the weight of our fears began to lift, I felt the delicate threads of connection weaving tighter. Together, we could learn to navigate this intricate dance, crafting our own story amidst the chaos and beauty of life.

In that sanctuary, surrounded by remnants of creativity, I knew we were embarking on a journey not just defined by the colors we would paint together but also by the trust we would build. With every step forward, we would find ourselves amidst the uncertainties, transforming our fears into brushstrokes of love and understanding. The world outside might still be a cacophony of expectations and shadows, but in our little corner of it, we were ready to carve out a new narrative, one painted with the vibrant hues of hope and possibility.

The atmosphere in the gallery hung thick with the promise of new beginnings, a heady blend of paint and anticipation swirling in the air. As I carefully placed the last of the unsold sculptures into their protective bubble wrap, I couldn't shake the exhilaration that coursed through me, mingling with a sense of vulnerability that was both thrilling and terrifying. Ethan and I had forged a connection amidst the vibrant chaos of our art show, but the shadows of his past still loomed large, leaving me to wonder how deep our bond could truly go.

Ethan stepped back to survey our work, his brow furrowing slightly as he took in the remnants of our creative endeavor. "You know, every piece tells a story," he mused, his voice low and contemplative. "They each carry the weight of our experiences, our emotions." He gestured toward a canvas splattered with bursts of red and gold, as if a sunset had decided to explode across the fabric. "That one? It's about passion, about love—"

"And heartbreak?" I interjected, unable to resist the urge to probe deeper, to peel back the layers of his soul like one would with the delicate petals of a flower.

He chuckled softly, the sound warming the space between us. "Yes, heartbreak too. It's all part of the same palette, isn't it? Each color, each stroke, a reflection of what we've been through." His eyes sparkled with an intensity that sent my heart racing, a reminder of the weight of his past relationships and the potential pitfalls that lay ahead.

"I guess that's true for all of us," I replied, leaning against a nearby easel, my heart racing as I fought the urge to close the distance between us. "We're all just a collection of our experiences, aren't we? Some beautiful, some a little... darker."

The silence that followed felt charged, the kind that hums with unspoken words and lingering glances. I could see the flicker of emotions dancing in his eyes, each one a color of its own, reflecting a story waiting to be told. "Speaking of stories," he said suddenly, breaking the tension, "I've been thinking about how we could collaborate again. Maybe we could hold another exhibition, but this time, it would be more personal. Something that really delves into our own narratives."

The thought sent a thrill through me, igniting my imagination. "What if we had a theme around vulnerability? We could each create pieces that expose our fears and desires, raw and unfiltered. It could be like peeling back layers of paint to reveal the truth beneath." The words spilled from me, buoyed by excitement, as I envisioned our work hanging together, each piece a testament to the paths we had traveled.

Ethan's face lit up at the idea, a genuine smile spreading across his lips. "I love that. It's daring, but it would be so cathartic." He paused, his expression shifting slightly. "But I want you to promise me something."

"What's that?" I asked, curious.

"That we don't hide behind our art. No masks. Just us—every flaw and fear laid bare for the world to see. It'll be a test, but it'll also be liberating." His gaze bore into mine, and I could feel the weight of his sincerity.

I swallowed hard, the prospect both exhilarating and daunting. "I promise," I replied, the words spilling forth with more conviction than I felt. It was easy to say, but the reality of baring my soul, of stripping away the protective layers I had worn for so long, loomed ahead like a vast, uncharted ocean.

As we stood amidst the remnants of our successful evening, I felt the shift in our relationship, like a tide drawing us closer together. But the thought of Emma still gnawed at me, a pesky reminder of the unresolved complexities in Ethan's life. I needed to confront that fear head-on, to understand how it could intertwine with the future I envisioned with him.

"Ethan," I began, my heart pounding as I took a deep breath, "I need to know more about Emma. What does she represent for you? How can I be sure she won't come back and disrupt what we're building?"

He shifted slightly, a shadow passing over his face. "Emma was a part of my past, yes, but I've learned a lot from that relationship. It taught me what I don't want and what I truly value. I don't want to fall into old patterns. You have to believe me."

"I want to," I said, my voice trembling slightly. "But it's hard not to feel like I'm standing on the edge of a cliff, watching you wade back into those waters."

Ethan stepped closer, his fingers brushing against my arm, grounding me in the moment. "I promise you, I'm not that person anymore. The mistakes I made with her were lessons learned the hard way." His gaze softened, and I could see the sincerity etched into every line of his face. "I want to make new memories, to build something solid and real with you."

The promise in his words resonated deep within me, sparking a flicker of hope that perhaps we could navigate this fragile balance together. The gallery, once filled with laughter and chatter, felt like a cocoon of our own making, a safe space where we could explore not just our art, but our souls.

As we stepped out into the cool night air, the streets glimmered under the soft glow of streetlights, illuminating the path ahead like a thousand tiny stars. The city hummed around us, alive with possibilities and stories waiting to unfold. The thrill of uncertainty tingled in my fingertips, and for the first time, I felt a sense of liberation wash over me, mingling with my lingering fears.

"Where to next?" I asked, glancing up at him, a smile breaking across my face.

He grinned, that same boyish charm lighting up his features. "Let's grab some late-night coffee. I think we need to keep this conversation going. We have so much to unpack."

As we walked side by side, our fingers brushing against one another, I felt a warmth blooming in my chest, the kind that promised not just connection but understanding. The journey ahead was bound to be filled with obstacles, but together, we could learn to navigate the complexities of trust and vulnerability.

The coffee shop on the corner was a cozy haven, its windows fogged with warmth and light. As we settled into a corner booth, the aroma of freshly brewed coffee enveloped us, wrapping us in a comforting embrace. We ordered our drinks, and as we waited, I found myself leaning closer to Ethan, drawn in by the magnetism that had only intensified since that first spark ignited between us.

We began to share more about our lives, the mundane details and the extraordinary dreams that colored our days. The laughter flowed easily, intertwining with our shared moments of reflection. With every sip, every glance, I felt the weight of my fears begin to dissipate, replaced by an exhilarating sense of possibility.

"I can't believe I almost let my insecurities get the best of me," I confessed, my voice barely above a whisper. "I was so focused on what could go wrong that I forgot to embrace what's right in front of me."

Ethan reached across the table, his hand enveloping mine in a reassuring grasp. "We all have those moments," he said, his gaze steady and warm. "It's part of being human, and it's okay to be afraid. What matters is how we choose to move forward."

His words resonated deep within me, reverberating like a melody that lingered long after the song had ended. I could feel the fragile threads of our connection strengthening, weaving a tapestry rich with hope, dreams, and a shared commitment to embrace whatever lay ahead.

As the night deepened around us, I realized that the path forward was not about eliminating fear but learning to dance with it, to create art from our vulnerabilities and to trust in the journey we were embarking on together. In that moment, amidst the clinking of cups and the soft murmur of conversation, I felt an unshakeable belief that we could paint our own story, vibrant and true, against the backdrop of life's complexities.

With a heart open to the possibilities, I leaned closer to Ethan, ready to embrace whatever came next, hand in hand, determined to carve out a future defined not by the shadows of the past, but by the light of our shared dreams.

Chapter 20: Confections of the Heart

The scent of freshly baked croissants fills the air, curling around me like a warm embrace, and I can't help but smile as I watch the sun stream through the bakery windows. Light spills onto the wooden countertops, illuminating the dust motes that dance like tiny fairies in a golden haze. The chatter of customers melds with the gentle clinking of mugs and the soft hum of the espresso machine, creating a symphony that feels both lively and intimate. I find joy in this bustle, a welcome distraction from the lingering uncertainty that seems to cling to my thoughts like a stubborn fog.

As I arrange a vibrant display of éclairs—each one a tiny work of art, bursting with rich chocolate ganache and bright citrus creams—I can't shake the image of the art show from my mind. The walls of the gallery, adorned with the vivid strokes of creativity, seemed to pulse with the excitement of our debut. Ethan stood beside me, his presence magnetic, as we fielded questions and basked in the admiration of our guests. I still replay the moments we shared—the laughter, the playful banter, and the gentle way he brushed his fingers against mine when he thought no one was watching. Each interaction left a sweet imprint on my heart, echoing in a way that was both thrilling and terrifying.

"Did you see how they looked at each other?" a girl's voice cuts through my reverie, drawing my attention to a small cluster of young women gathered at a table. They are bubbling over with excitement, each one holding a slice of cake like a prized possession, their eyes wide as they recount their impressions of the show.

"I know! It was like they were the only two people in the room," another chimes in, her cheeks flushed with the thrill of gossip.

My cheeks heat as I lean in slightly, pretending to wipe down the counter, my ears perked. They continue to dissect every detail, their voices rising in pitch as they relive the chemistry Ethan and I shared.

The way they giggle and nudge each other feels oddly validating, and I can't help but bask in their enthusiasm, letting it wash over me like the sweet icing I drizzled over those very cakes they're devouring.

"Do you think they're actually together?" a girl asks, her tone tinged with both hope and skepticism. My heart does a little flip at the thought. I've been so consumed with my insecurities that I hadn't paused to consider what our connection might mean to others—or to myself. The bakery, with its warm ambiance and the smell of sugar hanging thick in the air, feels like a sanctuary where anything is possible.

Then a familiar voice pulls me from my musings. "Lily! We're running low on the pistachio macarons. Can you whip up another batch?" It's Mia, my partner in baking and in life, her energy as effervescent as the bubbly icing we often use. She glides through the café like a well-loved character in a story, her smile infectious. I can always count on her to bring me back to reality, especially when I get lost in thoughts that threaten to overshadow my joy.

"Of course!" I reply, shaking off the heady daydreams that lingered just moments before. I gather my ingredients with deft movements, allowing the rhythm of the task to ground me. Each measured scoop of flour, each delicate fold of batter, feels like a step toward clarity. I pour my heart into the creation, just as I did during the show, allowing the memories of laughter and connection to sweeten my resolve.

As I work, the chatter in the bakery swells and dips like the gentle rise of dough. I catch snippets of conversations—couples planning their dates, friends sharing secrets over steaming mugs of coffee, and families celebrating milestones with our pastries. It is a tapestry of lives woven together in this small corner of the world, and I feel a part of something greater than myself. Each pastry crafted carries not just flavor but also a story, a connection made through the simple act of sharing food.

Suddenly, the door swings open with a bell's cheerful jingle, and in walks Ethan, looking every bit the charming artist I've come to admire. His tousled hair catches the light, and his eyes—a deep cerulean that always seem to hold a universe of stories—scan the room before landing on me. A smile blooms across his face, a brightening that feels like the sun breaking through clouds after a long storm. I find myself smiling back, an involuntary response that ignites warmth in my cheeks.

He approaches the counter, and the world around us fades, leaving just the two of us in this bustling bakery. "I heard the macarons are out of this world," he says, leaning against the counter with a casual confidence that somehow sends a thrill through me.

"They're not ready yet, but I'll make sure you get the first one," I reply, trying to sound casual despite the flutter of nerves in my stomach.

"Deal. But only if you promise to tell me your secret for making them so perfect." His playful challenge sends a wave of laughter bubbling up, and I can't help but feel drawn to him, like a moth to a flame. I love the way he engages with me, making me feel like I'm the only one who matters in that moment.

As he watches me work, I'm acutely aware of the way his gaze lingers, and for a moment, the sounds of the bakery fade into the background. The laughter, the chatter, even the whirring of the espresso machine become a distant hum, overshadowed by the electric connection sparking between us. But just as quickly, the shadow of Emma drifts back into my mind, a ghost from the past that makes me hesitate. The memory of her laughing at my dreams, of scoffing at my ambition, threatens to creep in, clouding the joy of this moment.

Yet, I push it away, focusing instead on the man before me. His genuine smile, the easy way he engages with the world, and the spark of creativity that seems to mirror my own. In this bakery, surrounded by sweet confections and the warmth of camaraderie, perhaps it's possible to let go of what was and embrace what could be.

The bell above the door jingles again, breaking the spell that Ethan's presence has cast over me. A couple walks in, hand in hand, their laughter mingling with the scent of freshly brewed coffee and baked goods. I turn my attention back to the macarons, folding the delicate almond flour and sugar with precision, savoring the familiar rhythm of creation. With each motion, I try to banish the nagging thoughts of Emma, the doubts that creep in like unwelcome guests at a party.

"Let me help you with that," Ethan offers, stepping closer, his eyes sparkling with mischief. He rolls up his sleeves, revealing toned forearms dusted with flour, and grabs a spatula. "What's next in this magical concoction?"

I can't help but smile, feeling a thrill at his enthusiasm. "Just folding the batter—want to give it a go?" I raise an eyebrow playfully, and he accepts the challenge with a grin. As he begins to fold, I watch the way his brow furrows in concentration, the way he bites his lip ever so slightly, and I can't help but find it endearing.

"Who knew pastry-making was so serious?" he quips, pretending to ponder the complexities of the macaron. "Maybe we should start a bakery and become the world's first artist-bakers. Think of the fame! We could call it... Artisanal Sweetness."

The laughter that escapes me feels both light and liberating, and I realize how much I've missed this kind of connection—sharing simple moments with someone who brings out the best in me. It's strange how, just weeks ago, I was shrouded in insecurity, but here I am, allowing myself to enjoy the banter without the weight of past anxieties.

"Artisanal Sweetness? Sounds like a niche market, but I'm intrigued," I reply, matching his tone with exaggerated seriousness. "Imagine the Instagram potential! BakersWithBrushes."

We share a laugh, the kind that echoes through the bakery and draws the attention of a few nearby customers. It's as if the world around us fades, and in this little bubble, nothing else matters—just us, the macarons, and the future that feels oddly bright.

But then, as I hand him a spatula to continue folding, I catch a glimpse of the reflections in the window behind him, the street bustling with life. I see couples passing, families enjoying the weekend, and I'm reminded of my own past—the missed connections and the heartbreaks that have shaped me. Emma's laughter rings in my ears, her derision at my dreams a stark contrast to the warmth blooming in my chest. It feels like a battle between the past and the present, each moment tinged with the bittersweet taste of nostalgia.

Ethan seems to notice my momentary distraction. "Hey," he says gently, his eyes narrowing slightly with concern. "You okay?"

"Just... thinking," I admit, a soft smile tugging at my lips despite the weight of the memories. "About how far I've come and how sometimes it feels like the past is just lurking in the shadows."

He nods, understanding etched across his face. "You know, I think the past has a way of trying to influence us, but it doesn't have to define us." His gaze intensifies, and I can almost see the sincerity radiating from him. "You've built something incredible here. It's not just the bakery or the art; it's you. You're the heart of it all."

His words wrap around me like a warm blanket, soothing the raw edges of my thoughts. I feel a swell of gratitude for his kindness and the way he sees me. The doubt that usually coils tightly in my chest begins to unravel, and I find myself longing to share more with him—my fears, my aspirations, and even my history.

"Thank you," I murmur, feeling the sincerity of my gratitude wash over me. "It's just that sometimes, I feel like I'm not enough, like I'm always chasing after something that's just out of reach."

Ethan places his hand on the counter, leaning closer. "You are enough, Lily. You're not just chasing; you're creating. And that's the most powerful thing anyone can do. We all have shadows, but it's how we shine our light that truly matters."

I take a deep breath, letting his words sink in, feeling the truth in them. The weight of self-doubt lifts, and I allow myself to be vulnerable for a moment, to bask in the radiance of this connection. I can almost feel the walls I've built around my heart begin to soften, crack, and let in light.

Just then, Mia pops her head into the kitchen, her curls bouncing like little springs. "Hey, lovebirds! I need a few more cupcakes for the display before the next rush. Can you handle that, or are you too busy flirting with the frosting?"

Ethan's laughter fills the air, rich and warm. "Flirting with frosting is my new favorite pastime."

As I chuckle, I realize how much I appreciate Mia's presence—she knows when to lighten the mood and how to keep things moving. We set to work, my heart lighter than before. I watch as Ethan carefully pipes frosting onto the cupcakes, the creamy swirls reflecting the artistry we had showcased at the gallery. With each cupcake adorned, it feels less like work and more like a dance, each step coordinated and fluid.

I find myself stealing glances at Ethan as we work, marveling at how he balances focus and playfulness, each smile he throws my way igniting a flicker of excitement deep within. We slip easily into a rhythm, punctuated by laughter and occasional playful jabs, our camaraderie blossoming like the sugar flowers that crown our confections.

The hours slip by unnoticed until the bakery fills with the lunchtime rush, customers spilling in with eager eyes and hungry smiles. The once-quiet ambiance transforms into a cacophony of chatter and clinking dishes, the smell of coffee and sweet pastries filling the air. It's a beautiful chaos, one that we've cultivated with love and hard work.

I watch as Ethan interacts with the customers, his charm weaving through the room like the steam rising from the coffee cups. He makes each person feel special, like they're the only one in the room, and I realize that his charisma goes beyond the bakery—he has a gift for bringing people together. It's intoxicating to witness, and I can't help but feel drawn to him even more.

"Two caramel lattes and a dozen assorted pastries!" a customer calls out, and I rush to fill the order, my heart racing with the thrill of the busy atmosphere. I feel alive, invigorated by the energy of the bakery and the people who fill it with laughter and warmth. In the midst of it all, I catch Ethan's eye, and he winks, a small gesture that sends a flutter through my chest.

This moment, this place, feels like home. The world outside may hold shadows of uncertainty, but here, amid the flour and frosting, I find clarity and purpose. With each pastry crafted, each smile shared, I'm reminded that life is a series of confections—sweet, messy, and full of surprises. And maybe, just maybe, I'm ready to embrace whatever comes next, hand in hand with the artistry that life has to offer.

The afternoon sun casts a warm glow over the bakery, the kind that invites lingering and indulging, and today, it feels as if the universe is conspiring to remind me just how much I adore this space. The comforting aroma of vanilla and fresh-brewed coffee wraps around me, stirring my senses as I pour another cup for a customer who looks lost in thought, her gaze lingering on a particularly extravagant piece of cake. I glance over at Ethan, who is now charming a group of tourists, his laughter infectious as he describes our creations like a tour guide leading an expedition through a world of sweetness.

As the line at the counter grows longer, I deftly navigate the flurry of orders, my heart racing with the delightful chaos of the moment. Each interaction feels like a brushstroke on a canvas, and I am both artist and subject, weaving between conversations and demands with a newfound confidence. "One chocolate tart, two pistachio macarons, and a latte!" I call out, my voice cutting through the chatter as I plate the delicate desserts. There's a joy in the rhythm, a dance of flavors and smiles that fills the bakery to the brim with life.

"Don't forget the sprinkles!" Ethan chimes in from behind the counter, his eyes twinkling as he reaches for a jar filled with colorful confetti. I shoot him a mock glare, but the corners of my lips betray me, curving into a smile that mirrors his enthusiasm. The sprinkles, he insists, are the secret ingredient to making our pastries feel like celebrations.

In between the hustle, I catch snippets of conversations drifting from the tables. A mother is teaching her daughter how to pick the perfect pastry, while an older couple reminisces over shared memories tied to sweet treats. Each moment captured in the bakery feels like a slice of life, a reminder of how food brings people together. I think of the moments I've spent here—how every pastry created tells a story, from the first flour-dusted attempts to the polished masterpieces we present today.

Amid the delightful chaos, I spot Mia at the corner of the café, her phone pressed to her ear, gesturing animatedly. Her laughter booms over the chatter, and I can't help but feel grateful for her unwavering support. Mia is the heartbeat of this place, the one who reminds me that behind every successful venture lies a team fueled by shared passion and camaraderie. I've watched her juggle her own art projects while nurturing the bakery, her spirit an unyielding force that propels us both forward.

As the rush begins to ebb, I step outside for a moment of reprieve, the crisp autumn air wrapping around me like a familiar embrace. The leaves are just beginning to change, their vibrant hues painting the sidewalks in shades of orange and gold, and I feel a sense of renewal stirring within me. It's the perfect backdrop for reflection, and I take a deep breath, inhaling the scents of the season—earthy, invigorating, alive.

My thoughts drift back to Ethan. Just last night, we spent hours brainstorming new ideas for our menu, bouncing concepts off each other with a fervor that felt electric. There's something uniquely invigorating about collaborating with him, and I cherish how he challenges me to push beyond my comfort zone, to innovate rather than conform. Yet the more I uncover the layers of his personality, the more I feel that familiar thread of uncertainty—Emma's shadow looming ever so slightly in the background, whispering doubts that I desperately try to silence.

I pull my phone from my pocket, scrolling through messages until I stumble upon a photo from the art show. It's a candid shot of Ethan and me, both laughing, paint-splattered aprons proudly worn, our creations proudly displayed behind us. I can almost hear the laughter that filled the air that night, the joy that radiated from each brushstroke and baked good. It was a night where everything felt right, and I want to hold onto that feeling forever. But the reality of Emma's presence still haunts me, a specter of my past, and I wonder if my burgeoning connection with Ethan is as fragile as spun sugar, capable of dissolving at the first hint of pressure.

Returning inside, I'm met with the buzz of conversation and the soft clatter of dishes. "How's it going out there?" Mia asks, her brow raised as she wipes her hands on her apron.

"Refreshing," I reply, trying to shake off the lingering doubts. "Just soaking in the moment."

"Good. We need to savor these little victories. Speaking of which..." Her eyes dance with mischief. "Have you seen the reviews? They're glowing!"

My heart flutters at the mention of reviews. The local food critic had stopped by last week, a culinary deity in our small town whose approval could catapult our bakery to the next level. The thought of his review—a cascade of praise for our art-inspired pastries—fills me with hope. "I haven't had a chance to check yet. Are you serious?"

"Absolutely! I'll show you." She whisks her phone from her pocket, scrolling rapidly until she finds the article. As she hands it to me, my eyes scan the words, and warmth spreads through my chest. It's not just the accolades; it's the acknowledgment of our vision, our passion poured into every bite.

"This is incredible," I whisper, trying to absorb the weight of it all. "We did this, Mia. Together."

"Of course we did! And it's just the beginning. I can see a line out the door in our future!"

As we stand there, the bakery alive with the sounds of laughter and clinking cups, I realize how deeply I want to protect this—my bakery, my artistry, and this burgeoning relationship with Ethan. I want to build a life where creativity flourishes, where every day brings a new opportunity to dream and create without the chains of doubt binding me.

With renewed determination, I glance over at Ethan, who is entertaining a group of children, expertly balancing a tray of cupcakes as they giggle in delight. He catches my eye and flashes that radiant smile, a reminder that we are on this journey together, no matter the shadows that linger. There's something comforting in the certainty of his presence, the way he seems to anchor me amidst the chaos.

"Hey, do you think we should plan a special event for the bakery?" I propose, the idea blossoming in my mind like a perfectly frosted cake. "Something to celebrate our success and bring the community together?"

Mia's eyes widen with excitement. "Yes! A baking class, maybe? We could invite everyone to join us in making their own pastries, showcasing our techniques. It would be fun and engaging!"

I nod, the thought sparking more ideas. "We could pair it with local art, invite artists to display their work here, and make it a true celebration of creativity!"

Just then, Ethan approaches, his eyes dancing with interest. "What's this about a celebration? I'm all in, as long as there's a cupcake tower involved."

"Count on it," I say, my heart racing at the thought of this collaborative endeavor. "We're thinking about hosting a baking class with local artists and showcasing our creations. You in?"

He grins, his enthusiasm palpable. "Absolutely. I can't wait to bring our vision to life. Just imagine the community coming together, creating something beautiful!"

And in that moment, I feel a surge of hope. The past may echo with uncertainty, but right now, I'm surrounded by laughter, warmth, and the promise of what lies ahead. Together, we're crafting not just pastries but a vibrant tapestry of dreams and connections. The bakery is no longer just a place to work; it's a haven of creativity, a canvas where our aspirations blend and rise like dough in the warmth of the oven.

As we dive into planning, ideas swirling like sprinkles in a whirlwind, I feel the chains of doubt loosen their grip. With Ethan, Mia, and the bakery's buzzing atmosphere, I embrace the adventure, knowing that the sweetest confections often emerge from the most unexpected ingredients. Together, we'll whip up a future filled with flavor, joy, and endless possibilities, ready to savor every moment.

Chapter 21: Stirring the Pot

The bell above the door chimed with a gentle tinkle, a sound that had become a familiar anthem in the symphony of my days at Luna's Sweet Retreat. Sunlight poured through the large bay windows, painting the room in soft hues of gold, while the scent of freshly baked cinnamon rolls swirled in the air like an invisible ribbon, wrapping around each customer who wandered in. It was a Sunday morning, a bustling time in our little corner of the world, where the clamor of conversation intertwined with the occasional laugh, and the clinking of ceramic cups echoed like delicate chimes in the background. I stood behind the counter, my hands dusted with flour, kneading dough that had taken on a life of its own, responding to the rhythm of my movements.

As I worked, I let my mind drift, savoring the blissful chaos that defined my life here. Each roll of dough was a reminder of the journey I'd embarked upon—leaving behind the sterile office cubicle for the warmth of ovens and the sweet laughter of customers. I glanced around, absorbing the vibrant energy of the café. In one corner, a young couple shared furtive glances over a slice of our famous red velvet cake, the cream cheese frosting glistening like pearls on a delicate necklace. In another, a group of friends laughed over their coffee, their joy infectious, bubbling up like the froth on their cappuccinos.

Just as I was about to roll the dough into perfect spirals, my phone buzzed on the counter, its vibration breaking through the harmonious sounds around me. I wiped my hands on my apron, intrigued by the unfamiliar number flashing on the screen. Curiosity tinged with trepidation gnawed at me as I answered. The voice on the other end was smooth, polished, and bursting with excitement. They were from a well-known lifestyle magazine, eager to feature

Luna's Sweet Retreat in an article spotlighting rising bakeries across the country.

My heart raced, a frenzied dance within my chest, matching the rhythm of my thoughts. This could be it—an opportunity to put our name on the map, to elevate our little bakery from the cozy nook of this charming street to the larger canvas of the culinary world. As I spoke, my voice was laced with a confidence I didn't fully feel, but the anticipation bubbled over, spilling out in enthusiastic phrases and promises of delectable treats. Each mention of our signature pastries felt like a secret I was eager to share, an invitation to join us in our sweet sanctuary.

I hung up, my hands trembling slightly, a mixture of excitement and disbelief coursing through me. This was the moment I had envisioned countless times, where Luna's Sweet Retreat transformed from a quaint bakery into a beloved destination. I spun around to find Ethan, my partner in both baking and life, leaning against the counter, his arms crossed and a smile playing on his lips. My excitement ignited his, but as I began to relay the details of the call, I noticed a flicker of uncertainty flash across his face.

Ethan had always been my rock, his gentle demeanor balancing my effervescent energy. But beneath that surface, I had learned over the years, lay a depth of experience that had weathered more than its fair share of storms. The thrill of our impending exposure tugged at him, revealing an undercurrent of fear that whispered of past failures. He had once stood in a spotlight of his own, only to have it dim when the pressures of expectation crashed around him. As I shared my enthusiasm, I could see that while he was happy for us, a part of him recoiled, haunted by shadows that lingered longer than I realized.

"I'm so excited!" I said, my voice high and airy, buoyed by the prospect of what lay ahead. "This could be everything we've dreamed of, Ethan. Just think of the customers we could reach!"

His smile faltered slightly, the worry etched into the lines of his forehead deepening. "I know, but what if we can't handle it? What if we disappoint people again? I don't want to let you down."

His words hung in the air, heavy with unspoken fears, and I felt my heart twist at the vulnerability he displayed. "Ethan, we're in this together," I reassured him, stepping closer, my hands gripping the edge of the counter as I leaned in. "We've built something amazing here, brick by brick. This is just another step forward, and I believe in us."

He nodded, but the doubt remained, a shadow lurking behind his hopeful facade. I took a moment, my thoughts swirling like the icing I'd once piped onto our cakes with such finesse. I wanted him to feel the same excitement I felt, to revel in the possibility of success, but I also understood the weight of his past. It was a delicate dance, one I had learned to navigate with care.

"Let's not think about what could go wrong," I suggested, my voice steady and warm. "What if we focus on what we can create? The joy we bring to people through our baking? Every pastry we make is a piece of us, and the world deserves to see that."

Ethan's eyes flickered with a spark of hope, and I could see the tension begin to ease from his shoulders. I took a step back, allowing him space to breathe, to process, to envision the future without the chains of fear dragging him back into the shadows.

As the café buzzed around us, I felt a sense of urgency build within me. I wanted this, not just for me, but for us. I was ready to embrace the chaos that came with growth, to savor every moment, even the messy ones. Because after all, the most beautiful cakes were often the ones with unexpected layers, crafted with love and a sprinkle of resilience. The thought of Luna's Sweet Retreat stepping into a new chapter, one filled with promise and adventure, made my heart soar like the buttery pastries rising in the oven. The scent of possibilities lingered in the air, rich and inviting, and I was determined to make this leap, hand in hand with Ethan, into the sweet unknown that awaited us.

The sun dipped lower in the sky, casting a warm glow through the café windows, igniting the swirls of flour that danced in the afternoon light. I glanced at Ethan, who now stood by the mixing station, fingers absently tapping against the counter as if to the rhythm of his own anxiety. The aroma of vanilla and rich chocolate hung in the air, a fragrant balm that usually soothed us both, but today, it seemed to amplify the tension brewing between us. I could sense his turmoil like a distant storm threatening to wash away the sunshine we had so carefully cultivated.

"Why don't we celebrate?" I suggested, hoping to infuse some levity into the moment. "Let's whip up something special to mark this occasion. How about a batch of our signature macarons?" I loved the delicate little confections, each one a small masterpiece of color and flavor, a testament to our shared artistry. Besides, I knew the rhythmic act of creating would ease his mind and perhaps open the door to the excitement I felt bubbling beneath the surface.

Ethan sighed, his eyes still lingering on the mixing bowl, where the remnants of yesterday's batter clung stubbornly to the sides. "Macarons? Those are a lot of work, aren't they?" He raised an eyebrow, a hint of mischief flickering across his features, but I saw the apprehension lurking just beneath.

"Exactly! A lot of work means a lot of distraction," I replied, leaning into the counter, my enthusiasm practically radiating. "We'll channel all this energy into something beautiful—let's show the world what we can do!" The words spilled out before I had a chance to second-guess them, fueled by the intoxicating idea of being featured in a magazine that could bring Luna's Sweet Retreat into the limelight.

A moment of silence lingered between us, thick with possibility. Then, with a reluctant chuckle, Ethan grabbed an apron from the hook by the door, his movements a little more sprightly now. "Okay, but you're the one who's going to get the egg whites whipped to perfection. I'll handle the almond flour, though we both know I'm really just pretending I know what I'm doing."

We worked side by side, our laughter punctuating the air like the beat of a favorite song. As I whisked the egg whites, watching them transform from glistening liquid to fluffy peaks, I couldn't help but steal glances at Ethan. He was an artist in his own right, his focus sharpening as he measured ingredients with a precision that belied his earlier doubts. I watched as he poured the almond flour into the bowl, the golden grains cascading like a fine sandstorm, each grain a small victory over the doubt that had threatened to envelop us.

"Hey," I said, breaking the comfortable rhythm of our tasks. "You know that article isn't just about the bakery. It's about us, our journey, and how far we've come. They want to highlight the heart behind the treats." I smiled, trying to share the warmth blooming inside me. "You're part of that heart, Ethan. This isn't just my dream; it's ours."

He paused, the whisking slowing as he turned to me, eyes searching mine as if trying to decipher a language only we could understand. "Do you really think people will care about our story?" His voice was softer now, stripped of bravado.

"Absolutely," I replied, stepping closer, the scent of lemon zest from the bowl before us mingling with the sweet anticipation hanging in the air. "We've poured our souls into this place. The late nights, the laughter, the moments when we thought we might burn down the kitchen—those are the stories that connect us to our customers. They'll see us in the treats we create."

Ethan nodded slowly, a hint of a smile breaking through. "Alright, let's make these macarons," he said, the spark of determination igniting in his eyes once again. "But if they turn out terrible, I'm blaming you."

"Deal!" I laughed, the sound echoing off the walls, a joyful melody of camaraderie that I hoped would drown out the remaining echoes of fear that lingered in the corners of his mind.

As we folded the vibrant mixture of colors and flavors together, a kaleidoscope of possibilities began to emerge. We piped the batter onto sheets lined with parchment paper, my heart racing at each swirl that formed, perfect circles of pastel beauty that awaited their transformation in the oven. "Can you imagine if we get a huge following?" I mused, leaning back to admire our handiwork, a dozen perfectly piped macaron shells staring back at us like tiny, colorful suns. "People lining up for our creations, raving about them online."

Ethan chuckled, his laughter warm and rich. "Or, you know, we could become a meme if they taste terrible." He wiggled his eyebrows, a playful spark igniting in his gaze, and I couldn't help but playfully nudge his shoulder.

"Stop it! They're going to be amazing!" I retorted, my voice half-joking but laced with determination. "We're going to create something that makes people feel good, something they'll want to share. That's the essence of what we do, isn't it?"

After sliding the trays into the oven, the heat enveloped us, wrapping around our bodies like a comforting blanket. I could see Ethan relaxing into the moment, his shoulders dropping away from his ears, the tension melting like butter on a hot skillet.

As we waited, the café filled with the unmistakable scent of baking, a rich tapestry of flavors intermingling, a signal of the deliciousness that awaited us. We chatted idly, reminiscing about the early days when Luna's Sweet Retreat was just an idea, a dream sketched on a napkin. I shared the memories of those late nights, fueled by takeout and ambition, the electric feeling of turning a vision into reality.

Finally, the timer chimed, and my heart raced as I pulled the trays from the oven. There they were—our creations, golden-brown and delicately domed, the promise of sweetness resting upon the counter. I glanced at Ethan, who leaned in closer, his eyes sparkling with curiosity and hope. "They look perfect," he whispered, as if afraid to disturb the magic of the moment.

"Let's fill them," I said, grabbing the pastry bags filled with vibrant ganache and buttercream. The task transformed into a dance, each filled shell representing a piece of our journey, a testament to our commitment to not only each other but to the dream we had nurtured.

As we finished, I placed a completed macaron into Ethan's hands, a little piece of our heart and soul wrapped in vibrant colors. "Here's to us," I toasted, my voice a soft melody filled with affection. "No matter what happens next, we've already won."

Ethan raised his macaron, a smile breaking across his face as he took a bite. The moment was perfect, a sweet intertwining of dreams and reality. The taste exploded on his tongue, rich and indulgent, a promise of what was to come. As he savored it, I couldn't help but believe that this was just the beginning of our story—one where fear and doubt could never dim the sweet light of our dreams, where every bite would echo with the laughter and love that built Luna's Sweet Retreat from the ground up.

The bakery hummed with life, the chatter of patrons blending harmoniously with the gentle clinking of cups and saucers. With each passing moment, the warm scent of freshly baked goods intertwined with the rich aroma of coffee, creating an inviting atmosphere that wrapped around me like a comforting embrace. I stood behind the counter, watching as our loyal customers enjoyed their treats, their faces lighting up with delight. A little girl clutched a cupcake adorned with colorful sprinkles, her eyes wide with joy, while a couple shared a slice of our chocolate cake, whispering sweet nothings between bites. Each smile ignited a spark within me, a reminder of why I had poured my heart into Luna's Sweet Retreat.

As the afternoon sun spilled through the windows, casting playful shadows on the rustic wooden floors, I caught a glimpse of Ethan in the back, expertly frosting a tray of cupcakes. The concentrated furrow of his brow made him appear deep in thought, yet I could see the faintest hint of a smile tugging at the corners of his mouth. It was these moments—watching him lose himself in the creative process—that made my heart swell with pride. He was my partner in every sense, and together we had built something beautiful, layer by layer, just like the cakes we crafted.

But as I moved around the counter, placing fresh pastries in the display case, my mind wandered back to the magazine call. The prospect of being featured in such a prominent publication was exhilarating, yet I couldn't shake the anxiety that flickered like a candle flame within me. I knew that for every moment of excitement, there lay the shadow of doubt. Ethan's earlier words echoed in my mind, the weight of his past failures looming like a thundercloud over our budding success. I wanted to lift him, to remind him of the triumphs we had already achieved, but I also understood that the road ahead might be fraught with challenges.

"Hey, Luna!" A voice broke through my thoughts, and I turned to see Marissa, a longtime customer and friend, waving enthusiastically as she approached the counter. Her presence always brought a jolt of energy, her vibrant personality a perfect match for the creativity we celebrated in the bakery.

"Hey, Marissa! How's your day going?" I asked, my voice brightening as I wiped my hands on my apron.

She leaned over the counter, her eyes gleaming with excitement. "I just heard about the magazine feature! That's amazing! I'm so proud of you guys!"

I beamed at her support, but beneath my smile lay a flicker of uncertainty. "Thanks, Marissa. It's all still sinking in, to be honest. I just hope we're ready for it."

Her laughter rang out, a sweet sound that danced through the café. "Ready? You've been ready since day one! You and Ethan are the best thing that's happened to this town. Just wait; this will be the start of something huge."

Her words wrapped around me like a warm hug, and I felt a renewed sense of determination surge within. "You really think so?" I asked, my voice barely above a whisper.

"Absolutely! Just look at how far you've come. You started with a dream and a tiny space, and now look at this!" She gestured around, taking in the bustling café and the array of delectable treats lining the shelves. "This is just the beginning. The world needs to know about Luna's Sweet Retreat!"

Marissa's infectious enthusiasm bolstered my spirits, and I glanced back at Ethan, who was now placing the finished cupcakes on the display. I caught his eye, and a smile broke across my face, a genuine reflection of the joy I felt in that moment.

As the afternoon rolled into evening, the café slowly emptied, leaving behind the last lingering notes of laughter and the comforting hum of conversation. The day had been a whirlwind, but as the final customers departed, I took a deep breath, allowing the quiet to settle over us like a soft blanket. The faint sound of the bell chimed as I locked the door, sealing the outside world away for the night.

Ethan and I worked side by side, cleaning up the remnants of the day, our movements synchronized like a well-rehearsed dance. The golden light from the overhead fixtures cast a soft glow on the countertops, illuminating the scattered flour and sprinkles that marked our creative territory.

"Let's do a test run on those macarons tomorrow," Ethan suggested, breaking the comfortable silence. "I want to make sure they're perfect before we send samples for the article."

"Great idea!" I exclaimed, my heart fluttering at the thought of perfecting our new creation. "And what if we add a twist? Maybe a passion fruit filling to balance the sweetness?"

His eyes lit up at the suggestion, a flicker of excitement overshadowing his earlier doubts. "That sounds incredible! I can already picture the colors—a little tropical explosion!"

The prospect of creating something new ignited a spark between us, and the shadows of doubt that had once hovered over Ethan seemed to dissipate. We laughed and bounced ideas off each other, discussing flavor combinations, colors, and presentation as if we were artists about to unveil our latest masterpiece. In that moment, the weight of the magazine feature transformed into a canvas for our creativity, a way to showcase not just our skills, but the essence of who we were as a team.

As the evening deepened and the stars twinkled outside the window, I felt a sense of clarity wash over me. We were more than just a bakery; we were storytellers, sharing our journey with every whisk of a mixer and every sprinkle of sugar.

By the time we finally locked up for the night, our hearts were lighter, filled with the promise of what tomorrow would bring. I glanced at Ethan, who was stacking the last of the dishes, a look of determination etched on his face. He caught my gaze, and a knowing smile exchanged between us spoke volumes of the unbreakable bond we had forged.

"Ready for the spotlight?" I teased, a playful lilt to my voice.

Ethan chuckled, the sound deep and warm. "You know what? I think I am. Let's give them a show they won't forget."

As we stepped out into the cool night air, the world felt different, imbued with possibility. I could already envision the bakery bustling with new customers drawn in by our feature, each of them discovering a piece of themselves within our treats. The journey we had embarked upon together was a testament to our resilience and creativity, a delicious blend of flavors that was uniquely ours.

Under the vast expanse of stars, I realized that this was more than just an opportunity—it was a celebration of everything we had built, a chance to share our love for baking and the joy it could bring to others. With Ethan by my side, I felt ready to embrace whatever came our way, to savor the sweetness of our shared dreams, and to face the challenges ahead with courage and laughter. Together, we would rise, just like the warm pastries we baked, ready to take on the world, one delightful bite at a time.

Chapter 22: An Unexpected Challenge

The bell above the bakery door jingled softly as I pushed through, the sound a comforting reminder that I was stepping into my sanctuary. The scent of freshly baked bread and sweet pastries enveloped me, wrapping around my senses like a warm embrace. Each morning, I marveled at how the sun's golden rays danced through the glass-paned windows, illuminating the flour-dusted surfaces and glistening pastries that lined the display cases. My little haven sat nestled on a charming street in a quaint town, where life moved at a pace that felt both nostalgic and exhilarating.

I glanced around, taking in the familiar sight of my small kitchen bustling with activity. My hands moved instinctively, kneading dough as I pondered the upcoming magazine feature. It was a golden opportunity, a chance to showcase not only my baking but the heart and soul that I poured into every creation. My loyal customers often said that my baked goods tasted like love, a notion that warmed my heart. But as excitement bubbled within me, it was tempered by the simmering unease in my chest, gnawing at the corners of my mind.

Ethan stood at the counter, a mop of unruly curls falling into his eyes as he stacked boxes of freshly baked cookies. His presence was a comfort, his laughter a melody that played in the background of my thoughts. Yet, lately, I sensed a subtle shift in our dynamic—a flicker of uncertainty behind his bright smile. The pressure of the magazine feature hung heavy in the air, and while he always encouraged my ambitions, I could see the burden weighing on him. The last thing I wanted was for my dreams to cast a shadow on the light of our relationship.

As I rolled out pastry dough, my mind drifted to the invitation I'd received the night before—a chance to compete in a prestigious baking competition that promised not only recognition but a substantial prize that could elevate my bakery into a local legend. The allure was intoxicating, the thought of standing in front of judges, my creations twinkling with hope and ambition. But as I considered it further, a knot formed in my stomach. Would this be a step toward my dreams or a chasm that would deepen the divide between Ethan and me?

My fingers froze mid-knead, contemplating the stakes. I could almost hear the soft whispers of my own insecurities echoing back at me. Would I risk everything I cherished for the chance of fleeting glory? I could envision the glances exchanged between Ethan and me, laden with unsaid words and heavy with unspoken fears. The thought unsettled me more than the idea of failure in the competition.

With a determined breath, I pulled my thoughts back into focus, reminding myself of the joy that baking brought me—the laughter shared over failed attempts, the sweetness of creating something from nothing. If I entered the competition, perhaps it would spark something in Ethan too, reigniting his confidence in both himself and our journey together. As I flicked flour off my apron, I made my decision.

"Hey, Ethan!" I called out, the excitement bubbling within me as I wiped my hands on my apron. He turned, his curious eyes meeting mine. "I got an invitation to compete in that baking competition!"

A flicker of surprise crossed his face, quickly followed by a smile that made my heart flutter. "That's amazing, Jess! You've got to do it!" His enthusiasm was infectious, wrapping around me like a comforting shawl, yet his eyes held a hint of uncertainty. I caught the way he hesitated, as if weighing the implications of my decision.

"Yeah, but..." I began, searching for the right words to express the turmoil in my heart. "I don't want this to come between us. I know how hard you've been working too."

He stepped closer, his warmth radiating off him like the sun breaking through clouds. "You can't let fear hold you back. This is your moment, Jess. You deserve to shine."

But his words didn't fully soothe my worries. I could see the shadows of self-doubt crossing his features. Ethan was a talented baker in his own right, but he'd been feeling overshadowed by my burgeoning success. The magazine feature felt like a spotlight trained on me, and I feared the glare might blind him instead of illuminating our path forward together.

As the evening drew near, I found myself back at the kitchen counter, the air thick with the aroma of baking bread. I watched as Ethan meticulously decorated a batch of cupcakes, his focus a testament to his passion. Each swirl of frosting was a stroke of art, yet I could see the flicker of uncertainty in his brow. I longed to reassure him, to remind him of the talent he held just beneath the surface, yet the competition loomed like a shadow over our shared dreams.

"Do you remember the first cupcake you ever made?" I asked, hoping to lighten the mood. A smile broke across his face, and the tension in his shoulders eased a fraction.

He chuckled, shaking his head. "How could I forget? I think I ended up with more icing on my hands than on the actual cake!"

The warmth in his laugh pulled at my heartstrings, igniting a spark of hope that maybe, just maybe, we could navigate this challenge together. I reached out, squeezing his hand gently, the connection grounding me. "Let's tackle this, Ethan. Together."

We spent the evening perfecting recipes, each creation a testament to our teamwork, a melody woven between our laughter and flour-dusted hands. The competition was a chance for me to stretch my wings, but it also became a canvas for us to paint our story—a reminder that in the vibrant tapestry of life, each thread mattered.

With my heart fluttering with anticipation and a newfound determination, I took a deep breath, ready to embrace the whirlwind ahead. The competition awaited, but so did the love and laughter we shared in our little bakery—a love I refused to let dim. As the oven timer chimed, I couldn't help but feel that perhaps, in chasing my dreams, I was only drawing Ethan and me closer, intertwining our destinies like the sweet aroma of baking bread in the air.

The following days passed in a flurry of flour and fervor, each morning starting with the sun casting golden rays through the bakery windows, illuminating the tiny flecks of dust that danced in the air like fairies at play. The magazine feature loomed large on the horizon, a shimmering promise of exposure and recognition, while the impending competition lurked like a mischievous imp at the edges of my thoughts. My heart was a kaleidoscope of hope and anxiety, each emotion clashing yet blending into a vibrant tapestry of determination.

With every batch of croissants I pulled from the oven, the crisp, buttery aroma wafting through the air, I found myself immersed in a rhythm that felt familiar and comforting. The way the dough transformed under my hands was nothing short of magical, and each pastry held a piece of my heart. Yet, the challenge of balancing the excitement of the competition and the pressure of the magazine feature tugged at me, reminding me that I wasn't just crafting pastries—I was also piecing together a delicate relationship.

Ethan and I spent our evenings huddled together at the bakery, prepping for both the upcoming feature and my competition. The workspace was alive with creativity; our laughter bounced off the walls as we exchanged playful banter while frosting cupcakes and layering cakes. Yet, beneath the joyous surface, I sensed a shift in our connection. He wore an encouraging smile, but I could see the worry lines etched across his forehead, the way his fingers occasionally stilled over the piping bag as he fought his own insecurities. I wanted to reassure him, to tell him that we were in this together, but each time I opened my mouth, the words tangled in my throat like overcooked spaghetti.

One evening, as I mixed a rich ganache, Ethan leaned against the counter, his arms crossed, his expression thoughtful. "You know, I always thought I'd be competing alongside you, not just supporting from the sidelines." His voice held a tinge of wistfulness, like a forgotten melody longing to be played again.

I paused, the whisk suspended in mid-air, realizing how deeply his words cut. "Ethan, you are my rock. I couldn't do any of this without you." I set the whisk down, wiping my hands on my apron as I moved closer to him, seeking to bridge the growing gap. "But you know how much this means to me. The magazine, the competition... it feels like my chance to finally show what I can do."

He nodded, a flicker of understanding in his eyes, but the uncertainty still lingered. "I get that, Jess. I really do. It's just... sometimes I feel like I'm not enough." The vulnerability in his admission struck me, a jolt of recognition. I, too, had battled my own doubts and fears, yet here was my partner, feeling inadequate beside my ambitions.

Stepping into his space, I grasped his hands, my palms warm against his cool skin. "You are more than enough. You make this bakery what it is. Remember those caramel tarts you created? They had customers lining up outside! We wouldn't be here without your magic." I watched as a smile broke through the fog of worry, his eyes lighting up like the bakery at dawn.

As the days flew by, I found myself pouring all my energy into perfecting my competition entries, inspired by the little victories we shared. The anticipation swirled around me like flour in the air, a dizzying mixture of excitement and anxiety. Each time I prepared a new recipe, my heart raced at the thought of what lay ahead, yet I couldn't shake the undercurrent of fear that perhaps this competition would lead me to a fork in the road, separating Ethan and me.

The night before the competition, the kitchen buzzed with an electric energy, filled with the warm glow of fairy lights strung overhead, casting a cozy ambiance. I felt as if I were standing on the precipice of something extraordinary, but the doubt still clawed at me. Would this be a turning point, or would I find myself standing alone in the spotlight?

Ethan and I worked late into the night, a symphony of clattering pans and muffled laughter echoing around us. I finished the last of my creations—a tower of intricately layered cakes, each one adorned with delicate sugar flowers, as vibrant and intricate as my feelings for Ethan. I felt a swell of pride as I stepped back to admire our work, a vision of colors and textures that came together beautifully.

"Are you ready for this?" Ethan asked, his voice low and filled with warmth, as he leaned against the counter, studying my masterpiece. I nodded, my throat suddenly tight, unable to find the words to express the whirlwind of emotions inside me.

"Let's make a pact," he said, a grin tugging at his lips. "No matter what happens tomorrow, we celebrate afterward. If you win, we celebrate. If you don't, we celebrate. Deal?"

A laugh bubbled from my chest, breaking the tension like a ripe fruit bursting in sunlight. "Deal." I held out my pinky, and he wrapped his around mine, sealing our agreement with a promise—a promise that regardless of the outcome, we would face the future together, hand in hand.

As I lay in bed that night, sleep eluding me, I listened to the distant sounds of the town settling down for the night. The comforting hum of life outside my window washed over me, weaving a blanket of serenity. I felt Ethan's presence beside me, his steady breathing anchoring my thoughts. In that quiet moment, I knew that whatever awaited me the next day, it was not the competition that mattered most. It was the love and support we offered each other, the shared laughter in the kitchen, the dreams we wove together. The competition might test my skills, but it would not define me.

As dawn broke, casting a warm glow across the world, I rose with a renewed sense of purpose. Today would be about more than just me; it would be a celebration of us, our journey together, and the sweet possibility that lay ahead. The bakery was not just my dream but ours, and as I stepped into the kitchen, ready to embrace the day, I felt a spark of hope igniting within me. With every beat of my heart, I knew we could conquer whatever challenges awaited us, side by side, united in our love for baking and each other.

The day of the competition dawned bright and clear, with the sun spilling over the horizon like melted butter cascading from a warm biscuit. I felt an electric charge in the air, a promise of new beginnings mingled with the palpable tension that came from standing on the edge of the unknown. The bakery hummed with life as Ethan and I prepped our final entries, the soft clatter of utensils and the sweet aroma of vanilla wafting through the air like a comforting blanket.

As I layered my final cake with precision, a familiar flutter of excitement mingled with apprehension coursed through my veins. I caught Ethan stealing glances at me, a playful smirk dancing on his lips, yet I could see the concern lurking in the depths of his dark eyes. "You've got this," he said, his voice steady, though I sensed an undercurrent of vulnerability behind his words. "Just remember to breathe."

His support felt like a lifeline, yet beneath it lay an unspoken weight. I could almost hear the quiet echoes of his doubt reverberating through the room. Did he believe he was less than enough, somehow overshadowed by my rising star? The thought gnawed at me, casting shadows over the thrill of the day ahead.

With the final touches complete, I stepped back to admire my creation—a cake of striking beauty, layers of raspberry and lemon interspersed with rich cream, crowned with delicate sugar blossoms that glimmered like jewels in the light. It was a celebration of flavors, a representation of my journey thus far. Yet, as I prepared to transport it to the venue, I felt a pang of hesitation. Would this cake symbolize a victory or a growing chasm between Ethan and me?

Arriving at the competition venue—a stunning historic building draped in ivy, its elegant façade reminiscent of a bygone era—sent a rush of adrenaline through me. The atmosphere buzzed with anticipation, a mélange of aromas and sounds weaving together as contestants hustled about, their eyes sparkling with determination. Each one of us carried the weight of dreams and desires, hopes and fears, as we set our creations on display, making our way to the waiting judges who would ultimately hold our fates in their hands.

Ethan and I navigated the crowded hall, my heart pounding like the rhythm of a snare drum. "What if I freeze up?" I asked, my voice barely a whisper against the cacophony around us.

"Then just remember why you started. You bake because it makes you happy, right?" he replied, his eyes steady on mine. "Channel that joy. It's all that matters."

His words filled me with warmth, like a freshly baked loaf rising in the oven, and I clung to that feeling as we prepared for the judging. I watched as competitors crafted elaborate towers of confections, their skill evident in every delicate layer and frosting swirl. My cake, while beautiful, felt like a simple song amidst a symphony, and doubt threatened to creep in again.

Yet, when the time came to present my creation to the judges, I found an unexpected calm washing over me. The nervous energy morphed into excitement, and as I stepped forward, I focused on the joy of sharing my passion rather than the fear of judgment. "This cake is inspired by the sweet summers of my childhood," I began, my voice steady and clear, "where flavors were vibrant, and laughter filled the air like the smell of fresh bread."

As I spoke, I caught glimpses of Ethan in the crowd, his face a blend of pride and support, and the sight grounded me. The judges listened, their faces softening as I painted vivid pictures with my words, each brushstroke of my narrative deepening the connection between my cake and the essence of my journey.

Once my presentation concluded, the judges eagerly sampled my creation, their eyes widening with delight. "The balance of flavors is exquisite," one judge exclaimed, nodding approvingly. I beamed, the warmth of their praise igniting a spark deep within me. The thrill of sharing my passion—of being seen and appreciated—melted away the weight of my earlier doubts.

As the judging wrapped up, I made my way back to Ethan, who enveloped me in a warm embrace. "You were incredible," he murmured into my hair, his breath tickling my ear. The tension that had coiled around us seemed to dissipate like steam rising from a fresh batch of pastries. For a moment, everything felt perfect, as if the universe had aligned in our favor.

However, as the day wore on and the judges deliberated, whispers of the competition's outcome began to swirl through the room. I caught snippets of conversation, the anxious chatter of my fellow contestants mingling with the crackling energy of anticipation. Each tick of the clock felt like a countdown to the unknown, and despite the initial euphoria, a nagging sense of dread began to creep in.

Finally, the moment arrived, the judges took the stage to announce the winners. My heart raced as they began to call out names, each syllable falling heavy in the air. With each passing second, my hopes fluctuated like the flame of a candle, flickering between light and shadow. When they finally reached the grand prize, I held my breath, my heart a wild drum in my chest.

"And the winner is..." The pause seemed to stretch into eternity, the air thick with suspense. "Jessica, for her stunning raspberry-lemon layer cake!"

For a heartbeat, silence enveloped me, the world blurring into a whirlwind of colors and sounds. Then, the roar of applause broke through like a wave crashing on a shore, pulling me into the euphoria of the moment. I staggered forward, overwhelmed by a rush of disbelief and joy, accepting the gleaming trophy from the judges.

Ethan's cheers rose above the crowd, his voice a clarion call of support that reached deep into my soul. I spotted him, his face alight with pride, and in that instant, all the worries and fears I had harbored melted away. We shared a triumphant glance that spoke volumes—this victory was ours, a testament to the strength of our bond amidst the challenges we faced.

As I stood before the audience, the trophy cradled in my hands, I realized that this wasn't just about winning a competition. It was a celebration of everything we had built together—a partnership rooted in support, love, and shared dreams. The bakery, the magazine feature, and the competition were threads in the rich tapestry of our lives, each one woven intricately into the other.

In that moment of triumph, I made a silent promise to cherish our journey together, to nurture the dreams we both held dear. As the cheers enveloped me, I caught Ethan's gaze again, and the look we exchanged was one of understanding—a shared acknowledgment that we were stronger together, ready to face whatever lay ahead, side by side.

As the sun dipped below the horizon, painting the sky in hues of pink and gold, I felt a surge of gratitude for the life we were building—a life filled with sweetness, laughter, and the promise of many more adventures yet to come. The road ahead might be uncertain, but together, we would navigate the twists and turns, savoring each moment like the finest dessert, rich and layered with flavor. With Ethan by my side, I knew that the best was yet to come.

Chapter 23: A Taste of Competition

The morning sun filters through the sprawling trees lining Main Street, casting dappled patterns of light on the cobblestone path. The air is rich with the scent of freshly baked pastries and the distinct tang of artisanal breads, mingling with the sweet perfume of blooming magnolias. I can hear the laughter and chatter of the crowd as it swells in the distance, creating a symphony of excitement that thrums in my chest like the beat of a drum. Today is not just another Saturday in our quaint little town; it's the day of the annual culinary competition, and the energy is palpable, electrifying even the air I breathe.

As I weave my way through the throngs of people, my heart races with every step, fueled by the vibrant banners that flutter above me in the warm breeze. The lively colors—rich reds, sunny yellows, and deep blues—paint the festival grounds, each hue capturing the essence of summer's glory. Stallholders display their wares with pride, showcasing pies bursting with ripe berries, towering cakes dripping with creamy frosting, and jars filled with local honey that sparkles like liquid gold. Every stall feels like a doorway to a different world, each offering its unique treasure, yet my focus remains steadfast on my own little corner of this bustling festival.

I arrive at the contest area, where the smell of sugar and spice wraps around me like a comforting embrace. Tables are adorned with elegant cloths, their surfaces gleaming under the warm sun, each one ready to host the culinary masterpieces that will soon take center stage. I can see the other competitors moving about, a mixture of familiar faces and newcomers, all sporting determined expressions as they prepare for the day's challenge. The competitive spirit hangs thick in the air, yet beneath it, there's an undercurrent of camaraderie—a shared love for the art of baking that binds us all together.

My heart swells with pride as I pull out my ingredients, arranging them methodically on the table. The delicate lavender buds, their purple hues vibrant against the white flour, exude a soothing aroma that instantly transports me to my grandmother's garden. I remember how she would tell me stories as we picked the flowers, her voice laced with warmth and wisdom, infusing every memory with a sense of belonging. I pour my heart into the mixing bowl, allowing the rhythmic motion of whisking to guide my thoughts. This lavender-infused cake, with its honey glaze, is not merely a dessert; it's a piece of my soul, a tribute to the memories that have shaped me.

As the clock ticks down, I feel Ethan's presence in the audience, his steadfast support enveloping me like a warm blanket. Just the thought of him grounds me, dispelling the butterflies swirling in my stomach. I can almost feel his eyes on me, encouraging me to push through the final moments of preparation. I steal a glance toward the crowd, searching for him among the sea of faces. There he is, leaning against a wooden post, a charming grin plastered on his face, his dark hair tousled by the breeze. Our eyes meet, and in that fleeting moment, a silent promise passes between us, a reminder of the journey we've embarked upon together.

With my cake finally in the oven, I take a moment to breathe, absorbing the lively chatter around me. The judges, a panel of local culinary stars, mingle with the spectators, their presence a reminder of what's at stake. I can see their discerning gazes scanning the tables, assessing the creations with the same intensity as an art critic examining a masterpiece. I tuck a loose strand of hair behind my ear, the warmth of the sun kissing my skin, as I remind myself that today is about more than just competition. It's about expressing who I am through my baking, about sharing my passion with the world, and, most importantly, about celebrating the journey that has led me here.

The aroma of my cake wafts through the air, a fragrant melody that dances with the scents of cinnamon and vanilla from nearby stalls. As the timer buzzes, I pull the cake from the oven, its golden top slightly domed, gleaming like a summer sunset. The honey glaze glistens as I drizzle it atop the still-warm cake, a delicate layer that promises a burst of sweetness with each bite. I place it on the table, stepping back to admire my creation—a labor of love that embodies my hopes and dreams.

As the judges approach, I can feel my heart pounding in my chest. Their expressions are inscrutable as they take their seats, and I fight to keep my hands steady, reminding myself that I've poured every ounce of effort into this moment. One by one, they take a bite, and a hush falls over the crowd, an almost reverent silence that amplifies the tension. I hold my breath, my mind racing as I watch their reactions. A nod here, a smile there, and I can feel the warmth of validation blooming in my chest.

When they finally share their feedback, my heart soars. Their praise washes over me like a gentle tide, filling me with a euphoric sense of accomplishment that lights up my entire being. Yet amidst the joy, a bittersweet feeling settles in the pit of my stomach, whispering reminders of the dreams I'm chasing. As I glance at Ethan, a flicker of concern crosses his face, a reflection of the reality we both know—my ambitions might one day take me far away from him. The thought lingers like the last notes of a beautiful melody, leaving behind a sweet ache that resonates within me. Today is a celebration, but it's also a reminder that every choice I make carries weight, threading our lives together in ways that are both wondrous and daunting.

The crowd's applause lingers in the air, a gentle wave of appreciation that sweeps over me, momentarily lifting the weight of my thoughts. I stand there, bathed in the warm glow of the spotlight, my heart a wild drumbeat echoing in my chest. Each clap seems to pulse with a life of its own, mingling with the scents of sugar and lavender that still envelop me. It's exhilarating yet terrifying, a paradox that dances at the edges of my mind.

As I step back from the judges, my thoughts drift toward the future. The echoes of their praise intertwine with the doubts that surface like pesky weeds in a garden I've worked so hard to cultivate. What comes next? The whispers of possibility are intoxicating, and yet they carry the weight of change, each scenario threaded with the bittersweet knowledge that my path might lead me to distant horizons, away from the familiarity of this town—and away from Ethan.

While the judges deliberate, I allow myself a moment to savor the atmosphere, to absorb the vibrant life around me. Nearby, a child giggles, her laughter like chimes in the wind as she reaches for a sample of strawberry shortcake, her fingers smudged with frosting. I can see the baker behind the stall, a middle-aged woman with flour-dusted hands, beaming as she hands out tiny slices, each piece a token of her labor. The joy on the child's face is a mirror of my own; it reminds me that food is more than sustenance. It's a language of love, a bridge between souls that transcends the ordinary.

Ethan's figure looms larger in my mind, his unwavering support a soothing balm to my frayed nerves. As he threads through the crowd, his presence is magnetic; he's like a lighthouse in a storm, guiding me back to shore. I watch as he greets the familiar faces, exchanging laughs and playful jabs, his charisma effortless and magnetic. Yet when our eyes lock again, I see a flicker of something deeper—a question, perhaps, or a shared understanding that we're both grappling with the weight of dreams and the fear of what those dreams might cost us.

The judges finally convene, and the hush that falls over the crowd feels monumental. I can see their deliberation etched on their faces, each wrinkle and crease a testament to their experience. One judge, an older man with spectacles perched on his nose, lifts his fork, gesturing for silence. The crowd leans in, breath held like a collective secret. I force a smile, willing my heart to calm as I stand there, a statue carved from anxiety.

"Today's competition showcased an incredible array of talent," he begins, his voice steady and warm. "But one dish stood out—not just for its flavors, but for the story it tells." My breath catches as he continues, praising the delicate notes of lavender that dance within the cake, and the way the honey glaze glistens like a promise on the plate. As he speaks, I can feel my heart soar, the joy bubbling up like champagne, effervescent and exhilarating.

The announcement of the winner feels surreal, like I'm watching it unfold in a dream. When they call my name, a rush of disbelief crashes over me. I'm enveloped in applause, the sound echoing in my ears like a sweet symphony. For a moment, the world blurs around me, and I can hardly comprehend what's happening. The thrill of triumph and the sting of uncertainty swirl together, a tempest within my chest. I walk toward the judges, each step feeling both heavy and light, a paradox I can hardly fathom.

As I accept the award, the golden trophy glimmers in my hands, reflecting the sunlight that spills across the festival grounds. I raise it high, the weight of it grounding me even as my heart floats above the chaos. I'm overwhelmed with gratitude, yet beneath it all lies the unshakeable feeling that this is only the beginning. There's a path stretching out before me, twisting and turning in ways I can't yet fathom. With each opportunity, I sense a potential widening chasm between Ethan and me, the distance marked not by miles but by dreams pulling us in different directions.

Later, as the sun dips low on the horizon, painting the sky with strokes of pink and orange, I find a quiet moment to reflect. The festival winds down around me, the sounds of laughter and celebration fading into the soft rustle of leaves and the distant chirping of crickets. I make my way to a secluded corner, a small bench tucked beneath an oak tree, its branches sprawling overhead like protective arms.

Ethan joins me, his energy a vibrant contrast to the twilight around us. He plops down beside me, his smile radiant, though I can sense the tension simmering beneath the surface. "You were amazing out there," he says, his voice warm and inviting. His admiration washes over me, a soothing balm to the frantic thoughts swirling in my mind.

"Thank you," I reply, my voice soft. "But it feels strange, winning like this. There's so much uncertainty ahead." I gaze at the trophy resting in my lap, its polished surface reflecting not just my victory but the crossroads I now face.

"I get that," Ethan says, his expression thoughtful as he leans back, looking up at the canopy of leaves swaying gently in the evening breeze. "But you've earned this, and whatever comes next, you'll figure it out. You always do." His words are a lifeline, tethering me to the present moment even as my mind races ahead.

"It just feels like a double-edged sword," I confess, my voice barely above a whisper. "This competition, it opens doors, but what if those doors lead me away from you? From here?" The reality of my dreams—so vivid and beautiful—also threatens to pull me from the life I know, the life I've built alongside him.

Ethan turns to face me, his expression unwavering. "You deserve to chase those dreams," he says, his tone earnest and reassuring. "And if you need to go, I'll be here, cheering you on. I want you to fly, even if it means letting go."

His words are both a comfort and a weight, the promise of support tethered to the fear of loss. The sky darkens above us, stars beginning to twinkle like distant hopes, and I realize that while the future may be uncertain, the strength of our connection can illuminate the way forward. We share a moment of silence, our thoughts intertwining like the branches above, a fragile yet beautiful tapestry of dreams and realities, longing and love.

The celebration swells around me, the laughter and cheer creating a symphony of joy that vibrates through the evening air. I clutch the trophy against my chest, its cool metal a comforting weight, grounding me amid the swirling thoughts of what the future might hold. Each applause rings in my ears, a reminder of the victory that feels, at once, exhilarating and haunting. As I absorb the moment, my gaze drifts back to Ethan, who stands at the periphery, his expression a mix of pride and contemplation.

"Let's grab some food," he suggests, breaking into my reverie, his smile brightening the shadows of uncertainty. It's an invitation that seems simple, yet it carries the promise of connection, of shared experiences that we've woven into the fabric of our lives. Together, we navigate the vibrant marketplace, the sounds of sizzling meats and the sweetness of caramelized popcorn beckoning us like sirens.

As we approach a food stall draped in cheerful yellow, the enticing aroma of barbecue fills the air, wrapping around us like a cozy blanket. The vendor, a jovial man with a bushy beard, leans over the counter, his face lighting up at our approach. "You two look like you just won the lottery!" he calls out, laughter dancing in his voice. I can't help but laugh along, the lightness of the moment momentarily dispelling the shadows of doubt.

"Just a little baking competition," I reply, still buzzing from the adrenaline. "But it felt pretty big."

"You have to celebrate! Two pulled pork sandwiches coming right up!" The vendor sets to work, his hands moving deftly, expertly layering the succulent meat with tangy barbecue sauce.

As we wait, I glance at Ethan, who watches the vendor with a fond smile, a hint of nostalgia flickering in his eyes. "You used to come here all the time, didn't you?" I ask, intrigued.

"Every summer. My friends and I would race to see who could eat the most funnel cakes before we burst," he chuckles, his laughter bubbling up like soda pop. "We were pretty much unstoppable."

"Unstoppable? Care to share how you're not bursting now?" I tease, nudging him playfully.

"I'm pacing myself," he grins, his eyes sparkling with mischief. "Or at least trying to."

The vendor hands us our sandwiches, their warm aroma wafting through the air, rich and smoky. We settle on a nearby bench, the wood worn smooth by countless conversations and shared laughter. As I take a bite, the explosion of flavors sends a thrill through me—tender meat slathered in sweet sauce, paired with crunchy coleslaw that cuts through the richness. It's perfection, a burst of summer joy that mirrors the festival surrounding us.

"So, about that trophy," Ethan says, wiping a smudge of sauce from the corner of his mouth. "What are you going to do with it?"

I contemplate the question, the trophy's weight shifting in my lap as if it bears the weight of my dreams. "I don't know yet," I admit. "Maybe I'll keep it as a reminder that I can chase my dreams, no matter where they lead."

Ethan's expression turns serious, and I can sense the undercurrents of unspoken words. "You know, if you decide to go far away, it doesn't mean I won't be here," he says quietly, his gaze unwavering. "You have to do what makes you happy, even if it pulls us in different directions."

I nod, swallowing the lump in my throat as his words sink in, carving a path through my uncertainty. The reality of our potential futures, entwined yet divergent, hangs heavy in the air between us. "I want to bring you along for the ride," I whisper, vulnerability creeping into my voice.

"You know I'm always going to support you, no matter what. Just promise me you won't forget where you came from," he replies, his sincerity washing over me like a comforting wave. "You've built something beautiful here, and wherever you go, that part of you will never change."

His words weave a thread of hope through my heart, a gentle reminder that while the future may be unknown, the bond we share can weather any storm. I look around at the festival—the laughter, the joy, the way the lights twinkle like stars come down to Earth—and realize that this place is a tapestry of my past, intertwined with the promise of what could be.

As the sun dips below the horizon, painting the sky in strokes of gold and violet, the festival lights flicker to life, casting a magical glow over the grounds. We stroll hand in hand, weaving through the crowd, taking in the sights and sounds that envelop us like a warm embrace. Street performers juggle and dance, their antics eliciting laughter from children who race around, their innocence a stark contrast to the complexities of adulthood that weigh heavily on my heart.

We pass a stall where a group of artists demonstrates their craft, splashes of paint brightening the canvas with bursts of color. I pause, captivated by the chaotic beauty they create, a perfect metaphor for my own life—the way I'm trying to balance dreams and relationships, each stroke a choice that shapes the picture of my future.

"Do you ever think about art?" I ask Ethan, curious. "Like, how each piece tells a different story?"

"Absolutely," he replies, his eyes glinting with understanding. "Just like baking. Every recipe has its own narrative, and you add your unique twist. You know, that's what makes your lavender cake so special—it's infused with your memories."

His words resonate deeply, and I feel a flicker of resolve spark within me. I want to tell my story, to let the world know that while I may chase my dreams, my roots will always anchor me. "I guess

I need to remember that, don't I?" I muse, stealing a glance at the vibrant canvas, realizing how interconnected our experiences are, how each moment shapes us.

Ethan squeezes my hand, and in that simple gesture, I feel the weight of our shared history, the laughter, the struggles, the love that has grown between us. "Just promise me that when you're up there chasing the stars, you'll remember that I'll always be your biggest fan, no matter where life takes us," he says, his voice steady and unwavering.

"I promise," I say, the vow slipping from my lips with an ease that surprises me. I don't know what the future holds, but I do know that wherever I go, I want Ethan by my side, whether physically or in spirit.

As we meander back through the festival, the world around us glimmers with possibility. Each booth we pass tells a story—of community, of creativity, of dreams both realized and yet to be born. The night stretches out before us, a canvas waiting to be painted with laughter, connection, and the kind of magic that comes from shared experiences.

With every step, I feel lighter, as if the burdens I've carried have begun to dissipate into the night air. The dreams that once seemed daunting now feel within reach, and the bittersweet tang of ambition mingles with the sweetness of love. And as the lights twinkle like stars overhead, I embrace the unknown with a heart full of hope, ready to create a masterpiece of my own.

Chapter 24: Frosting and Fissures

The air hung thick with the sweet scent of buttercream and the intoxicating aroma of vanilla bean as I navigated the bustling kitchen, where every surface was cluttered with the remnants of a baking frenzy. Flour dust motes danced in the beams of the overhead lights, swirling like little fairies caught in a whirlwind of sugar and ambition. My heart raced, not just from the caffeine coursing through my veins but from the palpable energy of competition swirling around me. This was the Sweetheart Bake-Off, a showcase of talent, dreams, and culinary wizardry, held in a charming, historic barn on the outskirts of a quaint town, where the local cherry blossom trees stood sentry, their delicate pink petals fluttering like confetti in the spring breeze.

Each workstation was a kaleidoscope of color and chaos; sprinkles glimmered like jewels, and vibrant fruits were piled high, ready to be transformed into decadent confections. It felt as if I had stepped into a wonderland where sugar reigned supreme, and yet, beneath the cheerful clatter of mixing bowls and the hum of conversation, an undercurrent of tension flowed. The excitement of the competition was tinged with an unspoken pressure, a weight that pressed down on my chest, threatening to stifle the very joy that had brought me here.

Ethan had been my anchor throughout this whirlwind of whisking and baking. His laughter, like a soft melody, had wrapped around me, offering solace amid the fray. But lately, I sensed a change. The vibrant spark in his eyes had dimmed, replaced by a cloud of doubt that hung over him like a stormy sky. It gnawed at my insides, turning my joy into a bittersweet ache. The late-night talks that used to last until dawn, filled with dreams and laughter, had dwindled into heavy silences that echoed louder than any conversation ever could.

One evening, after the sun had dipped below the horizon, painting the sky with hues of lavender and gold, I found him staring out the window, his hands stuffed in his pockets, his shoulders hunched as if trying to shrink into the very fabric of the world. The faint glow of the kitchen lights cast a warm halo around him, but I felt the chill emanating from his retreating figure. My heart ached, a tightening sensation that urged me to reach out and bridge the widening gap between us.

"Ethan," I began softly, my voice almost lost in the ambient sounds of clinking utensils and muffled laughter from our fellow competitors. He turned, his expression guarded, like a deer caught in headlights. "What's going on? You seem... distant."

He hesitated, his gaze flickering away, as if searching for an escape in the shadows of the room. I felt a mixture of frustration and concern boiling within me, but I kept my voice steady, a steady beacon in the tumultuous sea of uncertainty. "You can talk to me, you know. I want to understand."

Finally, he exhaled, the breath escaping him like a deflating balloon, leaving behind a frail version of the vibrant man I had known. "It's just... I feel like I'm losing myself in all this," he admitted, his voice barely above a whisper. "You're so talented, so driven. Sometimes, it feels like I'm just here, a ghost in your shadow."

His honesty struck me like a lightning bolt, illuminating the darkness that had begun to envelop us. I moved closer, placing my hand gently on his arm, grounding him with the warmth of my touch. "You're not a ghost, Ethan. You've always been my partner in this. Without you, it would feel like a half-baked cake—lopsided and lacking flavor."

He chuckled softly, a sound that seemed to lift a little of the weight from his heart. But the flicker of a smile quickly faded, replaced by a look of vulnerability that tugged at my soul. "It's hard to see that when the spotlight is on you. I can't help but worry that I'll never measure up."

The truth in his words resonated deeply within me, intertwining with my own insecurities. My ambition, which had once felt like a radiant beacon, now appeared to cast a shadow over him. I stepped back, reflecting on the delicate balance we had created, the tightrope we walked between support and self-worth. "I never want you to feel that way. Your success is my success. We're in this together."

The kitchen buzzed around us, the chaos of sugar and flour swirling into a cacophony of sound, yet all I could focus on was the quiet moment we shared. In that space, a realization dawned on me. It was easy to get lost in the excitement of competition, but the most vital ingredient in our recipe was the connection we shared. The love and partnership that had blossomed amidst the flour and frosting was what truly mattered.

As we stood there, the lights of the barn flickering like stars trapped in the wood beams above, I saw a glimmer of hope in his eyes. "I just don't want to drag you down," he murmured, his vulnerability stark against the backdrop of our ambitious surroundings.

"You could never drag me down," I reassured him, the words pouring out with an honesty I hadn't fully grasped until that moment. "You lift me up. Let's focus on what we create together, not just what we achieve individually." The warmth of his smile ignited a flicker of determination in my heart, a reminder that the competition was merely the stage upon which our shared journey unfolded.

In that moment, we forged an unspoken pact, one that transcended the pressures of the bake-off. As we returned to our tasks, I felt the weight begin to lift, replaced by the joy of collaboration. Together, we would blend our strengths like the perfect frosting, each layer adding depth to the other. And just like that, with a sprinkle of sugar and a dash of laughter, we began to carve out a path forward, hand in hand.

The air hung thick with the sweet scent of buttercream and the intoxicating aroma of vanilla bean as I navigated the bustling kitchen, where every surface was cluttered with the remnants of a baking frenzy. Flour dust motes danced in the beams of the overhead lights, swirling like little fairies caught in a whirlwind of sugar and ambition. My heart raced, not just from the caffeine coursing through my veins but from the palpable energy of competition swirling around me. This was the Sweetheart Bake-Off, a showcase of talent, dreams, and culinary wizardry, held in a charming, historic barn on the outskirts of a quaint town, where the local cherry blossom trees stood sentry, their delicate pink petals fluttering like confetti in the spring breeze.

Each workstation was a kaleidoscope of color and chaos; sprinkles glimmered like jewels, and vibrant fruits were piled high, ready to be transformed into decadent confections. It felt as if I had stepped into a wonderland where sugar reigned supreme, and yet, beneath the cheerful clatter of mixing bowls and the hum of conversation, an undercurrent of tension flowed. The excitement of the competition was tinged with an unspoken pressure, a weight that pressed down on my chest, threatening to stifle the very joy that had brought me here.

Ethan had been my anchor throughout this whirlwind of whisking and baking. His laughter, like a soft melody, had wrapped around me, offering solace amid the fray. But lately, I sensed a change. The vibrant spark in his eyes had dimmed, replaced by a cloud of doubt that hung over him like a stormy sky. It gnawed at my insides, turning my joy into a bittersweet ache. The late-night talks that used to last until dawn, filled with dreams and laughter, had dwindled into heavy silences that echoed louder than any conversation ever could.

One evening, after the sun had dipped below the horizon, painting the sky with hues of lavender and gold, I found him staring out the window, his hands stuffed in his pockets, his shoulders hunched as if trying to shrink into the very fabric of the world. The faint glow of the kitchen lights cast a warm halo around him, but I felt the chill emanating from his retreating figure. My heart ached, a tightening sensation that urged me to reach out and bridge the widening gap between us.

"Ethan," I began softly, my voice almost lost in the ambient sounds of clinking utensils and muffled laughter from our fellow competitors. He turned, his expression guarded, like a deer caught in headlights. "What's going on? You seem... distant."

He hesitated, his gaze flickering away, as if searching for an escape in the shadows of the room. I felt a mixture of frustration and concern boiling within me, but I kept my voice steady, a steady beacon in the tumultuous sea of uncertainty. "You can talk to me, you know. I want to understand."

Finally, he exhaled, the breath escaping him like a deflating balloon, leaving behind a frail version of the vibrant man I had known. "It's just... I feel like I'm losing myself in all this," he admitted, his voice barely above a whisper. "You're so talented, so driven. Sometimes, it feels like I'm just here, a ghost in your shadow."

His honesty struck me like a lightning bolt, illuminating the darkness that had begun to envelop us. I moved closer, placing my hand gently on his arm, grounding him with the warmth of my touch. "You're not a ghost, Ethan. You've always been my partner in this. Without you, it would feel like a half-baked cake—lopsided and lacking flavor."

He chuckled softly, a sound that seemed to lift a little of the weight from his heart. But the flicker of a smile quickly faded, replaced by a look of vulnerability that tugged at my soul. "It's hard to see that when the spotlight is on you. I can't help but worry that I'll never measure up."

The truth in his words resonated deeply within me, intertwining with my own insecurities. My ambition, which had once felt like a radiant beacon, now appeared to cast a shadow over him. I stepped back, reflecting on the delicate balance we had created, the tightrope we walked between support and self-worth. "I never want you to feel that way. Your success is my success. We're in this together."

The kitchen buzzed around us, the chaos of sugar and flour swirling into a cacophony of sound, yet all I could focus on was the quiet moment we shared. In that space, a realization dawned on me. It was easy to get lost in the excitement of competition, but the most vital ingredient in our recipe was the connection we shared. The love and partnership that had blossomed amidst the flour and frosting was what truly mattered.

As we stood there, the lights of the barn flickering like stars trapped in the wood beams above, I saw a glimmer of hope in his eyes. "I just don't want to drag you down," he murmured, his vulnerability stark against the backdrop of our ambitious surroundings.

"You could never drag me down," I reassured him, the words pouring out with an honesty I hadn't fully grasped until that moment. "You lift me up. Let's focus on what we create together, not just what we achieve individually." The warmth of his smile ignited a flicker of determination in my heart, a reminder that the competition was merely the stage upon which our shared journey unfolded.

In that moment, we forged an unspoken pact, one that transcended the pressures of the bake-off. As we returned to our tasks, I felt the weight begin to lift, replaced by the joy of collaboration. Together, we would blend our strengths like the perfect frosting, each layer adding depth to the other. And just like that, with a sprinkle of sugar and a dash of laughter, we began to carve out a path forward, hand in hand.

The kitchen, once a sanctuary of laughter and shared dreams, had morphed into a battleground of unspoken fears. Each day blurred into the next, the moments ticking away like grains of sand slipping through an hourglass, each grain heavier than the last. The cacophony of clattering pans and the mingling scents of melting chocolate and toasted pecans became a constant reminder of the competition, a reminder that success was dangling just out of reach. My thoughts drifted, flitting between recipes and techniques, but my heart was tethered to Ethan, who stood there like a shadow, his brilliance dulled by doubt.

The morning light filtered through the barn's large windows, illuminating the dust motes that floated lazily in the air. I stood at my workstation, the vibrant colors of my ingredients an affront to the dullness that seemed to hang over us. I mixed batter, my hands moving mechanically as I struggled to find the rhythm we once shared. The hum of the kitchen buzzed around me, voices rising and falling, but all I could hear was the silence between Ethan and me, a chasm that threatened to swallow us whole.

I glanced over at him, standing across the room with a bowl of frosting, his brow furrowed in concentration. He was meticulously whipping air into the mixture, but I saw the tension in his shoulders, the way his lips pressed together in a thin line. It was as if he was sculpting not just frosting but a façade, one that masked the turmoil brewing inside. The specter of inadequacy loomed over him, and I knew it was time to bridge the gap.

"Let's take a break," I suggested, the words tumbling from my lips with a mix of hope and desperation. I saw him hesitate, the flicker of doubt crossing his face like a shadow, but he eventually nodded, his smile tentative, as if unsure of its place in this fray.

We stepped outside into the fresh air, the sun warming our skin like a balm. The spring breeze carried the sweet scent of cherry blossoms, a fragrant reminder of life blooming anew. The world outside felt alive, vibrant, a stark contrast to the unease inside the barn. We wandered a little away from the clamor of the bake-off, settling onto a sun-drenched bench beneath a tree heavy with blossoms. The petals fell like soft confetti around us, swirling in the gentle breeze, transforming our surroundings into a whimsical paradise.

"Look at those petals," I mused, reaching out to catch one as it floated past. "It's as if nature is celebrating."

Ethan chuckled, a sound that still held a trace of hesitation but felt a little more genuine. "Yeah, or it's just trying to distract us from the chaos inside."

I leaned back, tilting my head to watch the branches sway. "Maybe it's doing both. A reminder that even in the midst of competition, there's beauty. And it's not just about winning."

He fell silent for a moment, his gaze drifting to the ground as he pondered my words. I could see the wheels turning in his mind, wrestling with the notion that beauty could exist alongside pressure. "I guess I've been so focused on the outcome that I forgot to enjoy the process," he admitted, finally looking at me with a vulnerability that made my heart ache.

"That's the thing," I replied softly, "The process is where the magic happens. The laughter, the mistakes, the late nights where we end up covered in flour—it's all part of the experience. Winning is just a cherry on top."

His eyes softened, and for the first time in what felt like ages, the distance between us began to shrink. "You always have a way of reminding me of what really matters," he said, the sincerity in his voice sending warmth through me.

We sat there, cocooned in the fragrance of blossoms and freshly cut grass, our fingers brushing against each other in a gesture that felt both innocent and charged with something deeper. The world around us faded, the worries and stresses of the competition fading into a distant hum as we found solace in our shared connection.

With renewed spirit, we returned to the kitchen, the once oppressive air now filled with possibility. We worked side by side, the rhythm of our movements syncing as we tossed ideas back and forth, our laughter mingling with the sounds of clanging pots and pans. It was as if we had stepped back into our bubble, where the pressures of the bake-off faded away, and we could simply be ourselves.

As the hours ticked by, we transformed our creations into culinary masterpieces, each dessert reflecting not only our skills but our renewed partnership. I poured vibrant hues of color into my batter, while he meticulously crafted elegant designs with his frosting. Each swirl and sprinkle spoke of our journey, a testament to the resilience we had built together.

As we decorated the final layers of our cakes, I glanced at him, a warm smile playing on my lips. "I think we make a pretty good team."

He raised an eyebrow, the corner of his mouth quirking up into a smirk. "Pretty good? We're like peanut butter and jelly. A classic combination."

I laughed, shaking my head. "Classic? More like a wild experiment that somehow turned out deliciously."

Ethan's laughter echoed through the barn, bright and infectious, igniting a spark within me. It felt like a breath of fresh air after a long, stifling silence. We finished just in time to present our confections to the judges, the aroma wafting from our creations enveloping us in a sweet embrace.

The moment we placed our cake on the judging table, I felt a rush of pride. Win or lose, I realized, we had already triumphed in so many ways. This journey had taught us the importance of vulnerability, of leaning into our fears and doubts. As we stood shoulder to shoulder, watching the judges taste our creations, I knew that this was just the beginning of something extraordinary. Together, we could tackle anything life threw our way, frosting and fissures be damned.

Chapter 25: Breaking Down Walls

The moment I stepped into the bakery, I was enveloped by the familiar embrace of warm, sugary air and the comforting hum of the ovens working tirelessly in the background. The vintage charm of the place radiated a nostalgic glow; its polished wooden countertops reflected the soft flicker of fairy lights I had draped over every available surface, their twinkling luminescence casting playful shadows that danced across the flour-dusted floor. It was a sanctuary of comfort, filled with the quiet symphony of whirring mixers and the gentle rustle of parchment paper being prepared for the cookie battalions I planned to unleash.

With a steady heartbeat thrumming in my chest, I arranged the ingredients like a painter preparing their palette. The flour, a snowy mountain; the sugar, crystalline and bright; the eggs, glistening orbs of promise. Each item was a note in a grand melody I hoped would harmonize perfectly with Ethan's lingering doubts. I longed for this evening to become a bridge, spanning the chasm that had widened between us, leaving me grasping at shadows of what had once been.

As I added a sprinkle of cinnamon to the mixing bowl, I heard the familiar jingle of the bell above the door. The sound sent a cascade of warmth through my chest, an invitation that both thrilled and terrified me. I turned to see Ethan, his tall frame silhouetted against the dusky backdrop of the evening. He wore the same well-loved hoodie that I remembered from our early days, its fabric slightly faded but somehow still a part of him. The way he stepped inside, hesitating just for a moment, reminded me of a deer venturing out from the safety of the woods. I couldn't help but smile at the sight of him.

"Hey," I said, my voice light, as if I were inviting him to join me in some secret adventure. "Welcome to my surprise baking night."

He grinned, though the edges of his smile appeared tentative, as if he was unsure whether to engage or retreat. "This is... impressive," he said, taking in the ambiance with a slow sweep of his gaze. "You went all out."

With a playful flick of my wrist, I gestured to the various bowls and utensils sprawled across the countertop. "I needed to set the stage for our culinary masterpieces," I teased, trying to draw him closer with levity. "Come on, let's make some magic happen."

As he stepped beside me, the air shifted subtly. Our shoulders brushed, a fleeting contact that sent a shiver of recognition between us. I could feel the weight of unspoken words lingering like the scent of vanilla that filled the space, and for a moment, the past few weeks felt suspended in time. We were still us—beneath the layers of misunderstanding and hurt lay the essence of what we shared, vibrant and true.

We began to measure flour, a tactile dance of ingredients spilling between our hands, and I watched as Ethan's initial hesitance began to melt away. He poured sugar into the bowl with an easy confidence, his laughter bubbling over as we exchanged playful banter. Each chuckle was a tiny victory, a small reminder of the chemistry that once bound us together, a connection that I had desperately missed.

"So, what's your favorite cookie?" I asked, as I rummaged through the pantry, the sound of canisters clinking together providing a backdrop to our growing intimacy.

He paused, a thoughtful frown settling across his brow, his fingers absentmindedly brushing against the edge of a measuring cup. "Honestly? I'm a sucker for chocolate chip. Classic, I know, but there's something about the gooey chocolate and the warm dough that just feels... right."

"Classic is never boring," I countered, enthusiasm bubbling in my chest. "It's timeless, just like us."

The moment hung delicately in the air, and I could see the flicker of surprise in his eyes at my words. The walls we had built around our hearts seemed to tremble slightly, yearning to crumble. I watched as he took a deep breath, the tension in his shoulders loosening.

"What about you?" he asked, his voice softening. "What's your favorite?"

"I'm a bit of an adventurous baker," I admitted, a grin creeping onto my lips. "I love experimenting. Maybe snickerdoodles today, with a dash of cayenne for a kick. Sweet and spicy, just like life."

"Now that sounds like a dangerous combination," he said, his brow raising with intrigue. "But I like it."

We began to mix the dough, flour dusting our cheeks and laughter echoing off the walls like a forgotten song rediscovered. With each pass of the whisk, with every scoop of dough, I felt the ice between us slowly thaw. I challenged him to a flour fight, and, with mock indignation, he threw a small handful at me, causing a riot of giggles to spill from my lips. It felt liberating, each burst of laughter shattering the heavy remnants of silence that had defined our recent days.

As the cookies baked, the rich aroma enveloped us, and we settled into a comfortable rhythm, side by side, swapping stories and dreams. Ethan shared his aspirations of owning a restaurant, his voice earnest and earnest. It was a vulnerability that ignited something deep within me—a spark that mirrored the warmth of the oven as it worked its magic. I could see the dream dance in his eyes, a flickering flame that had been nearly snuffed out by the weight of our misunderstandings.

"You really want to do that?" I asked, my heart swelling with admiration. "You'd be incredible at it. Your passion is contagious."

He chuckled softly, a hint of shyness creeping into his demeanor. "I've always loved cooking. It's like art, but you get to eat the canvas."

As the cookies emerged from the oven, golden and fragrant, I felt a swell of hope blossom in my chest. Maybe, just maybe, this night could be the turning point we desperately needed. We plated the cookies, a colorful array of warmth and sweetness, each one a testament to our effort. And as our hands brushed again while reaching for the same treat, a spark ignited between us, too bright to ignore.

In that moment, under the soft glow of the fairy lights, our laughter mingling with the lingering warmth of freshly baked cookies, I leaned in closer, our breath mingling in the cool air. With every ounce of courage I could muster, I tilted my head, and as our lips met in a tentative kiss, it was as if the world around us melted away. The past weeks faded into oblivion, and all that remained was the sweetness of this connection, warm and promising, a new beginning wrapped in sugar and spice.

The kiss lingered in the air between us, a tentative promise as sweet and rich as the cookies cooling on the counter. I pulled back, searching Ethan's face for any sign of what this moment might mean, my heart thumping like a restless drummer in a parade. He looked just as startled as I felt, eyes wide and a playful smile tugging at the corners of his mouth, the flickering fairy lights casting a soft glow that illuminated the lines of uncertainty etched across his brow.

"Wow," he murmured, still breathless from the kiss. "That was... unexpected."

"Unexpected good or unexpected bad?" I asked, my voice teasing but my heart fluttering nervously. I didn't want to breach this new, fragile territory we were navigating, and the last thing I wanted was to scare him away again.

"Definitely good." His grin widened, revealing the charming dimple that I had always found so endearing. "In fact, I think it's the best thing that's happened tonight. But then again, those cookies look pretty promising, too." He gestured toward the cooling rack, his playful banter filling the space where my anxiety had settled.

We moved toward the counter, the cookies arranged like little golden trophies, each one a small victory in our mission to reclaim the warmth we had lost. I couldn't help but laugh as I grabbed a spatula, using it as a prop in our ongoing game. "What do you think? Should we celebrate with an official taste test?"

"Only if we can go for the biggest cookie first," he replied, eyes sparkling with mischief.

"Deal." I handed him the spatula, our fingers brushing again, igniting another spark that sent warmth coursing through my veins. The simple act of sharing this moment felt monumental, each laugh serving as a balm for the wounds we had both been nursing.

As we broke into the cookies, the gooey chocolate chips melted like little bursts of joy on our tongues. It was blissful, rich and warm, like coming home after a long journey. We sat side by side on a stool that creaked under our weight, the bakery humming softly with life around us. Each bite was a reminder of how easily we fit together, how laughter and sweetness could bridge the gap left by unspoken fears.

"I think I could eat an entire batch of these," he said, wiping a smear of chocolate from the corner of his mouth with the back of his hand. The action was so adorably casual, so him, that I couldn't help but smile.

"Then you'd have to share with me," I said, nudging him playfully. "There's no way I'm letting you get away with a cookie heist."

Ethan chuckled, a sound that rang like music in the air. "Fair enough. But if I'm sharing, I'm making you promise that you'll help me experiment with new recipes. I've got a few ideas swirling around in my head."

The thought of collaborating with him sparked an exhilarating thrill in my chest. "I'd love that! What have you been thinking?"

"Well," he began, his voice dropping to a conspiratorial whisper as if sharing a top-secret plan. "I've been dreaming about a spicy chocolate chip cookie—something that starts off sweet but hits you with a kick at the end. Something that leaves an impression."

"That sounds amazing!" I leaned in closer, captivated by his enthusiasm. "What inspired that?"

Ethan hesitated, a shadow passing over his features. "I don't know. Sometimes I feel like life is too... predictable. I want to create something unexpected, just like that kick in the cookie. I want to surprise people."

His vulnerability hung between us, fragile yet potent. I realized that this was the glimpse of the man behind the wall, a glimpse I had been yearning to see. In that moment, the light of the bakery seemed to glow a little brighter, illuminating the hope that flickered in his eyes.

"Then let's do it together," I encouraged, my voice steady and sincere. "Let's make every cookie a little surprising."

As we dove back into baking, the rhythm of our laughter intermingled with the clattering of bowls and the steady hum of the ovens. The air was filled with the heady scent of vanilla and chocolate, and as the next batch baked, I felt an overwhelming sense of ease. We moved in tandem, a well-practiced duet, as though we had been doing this forever. The physical space between us began to dissolve, replaced by a closeness that felt like home.

Between mixing and measuring, our conversation drifted to our lives beyond the bakery walls. He spoke of his childhood dreams, how he used to watch his grandmother whip up culinary wonders in her cramped kitchen, her laughter ringing out like music. I shared my own tales, of late nights spent crafting recipes in my tiny apartment, trying to transform simple ingredients into something magical.

As the final batch emerged, we stepped back, surveying our work. "We really did this," I marveled, disbelief and joy swirling in equal measure. The counter was a mosaic of cookies, each one unique, a testament to our shared efforts and blossoming connection.

"Yeah," Ethan replied, pride swelling in his voice. "And I think we might just have created something special."

The atmosphere crackled with possibility, and as I leaned in to steal another kiss, this one deeper and more passionate, I felt the walls that had separated us begin to crumble, leaving a path wide open for new beginnings. The sweetness of the moment enveloped us, mingling with the warm, comforting scent of baked goods that lingered in the air. It was a night of rediscovery, an affirmation that we were not defined by our struggles but rather by our ability to rise above them.

Time lost its meaning in that cozy little bakery, the world outside fading into obscurity as we immersed ourselves in laughter, cookies, and the sweet music of hope. With every cookie we shared, with every moment spent side by side, I felt the ties that bound us growing stronger. We were building something beautiful from the remnants of our past, weaving together threads of shared dreams and aspirations into a tapestry that promised a brighter future.

And as the last crumbs disappeared, I couldn't help but believe that perhaps this was just the beginning of a delicious adventure, one filled with spice, sweetness, and a touch of unpredictability, just like life itself.

The evening unfurled like the delicate petals of a blooming flower, each moment filled with the sweet scent of our creations and the laughter that had begun to weave us back together. We stood shoulder to shoulder, the once-familiar intimacy resurfacing as we rolled out dough and cut it into whimsical shapes—stars, hearts, and even a questionable rendition of our beloved cat, Luna. The kitchen became our stage, where the trials of the past transformed into a backdrop for the joy we were rediscovering.

"Okay, here's a challenge," Ethan declared, an impish glint lighting his eyes. "Let's see who can make the best animal cookie."

"Animal cookies? Is that your secret weapon?" I shot back, unable to hide my grin. "You think you can out-bake me?"

With an exaggerated wink, he replied, "Just you wait. Prepare to be amazed." His confidence was infectious, and as we both dove into our respective cookie creations, I felt a sense of playful competition bubble between us.

The dough was warm beneath my hands as I shaped it, my fingers working deftly. As I sculpted a peculiar rendition of a cat, I couldn't help but steal glances at Ethan. His focus was unwavering; he was meticulously molding a dinosaur, each tiny detail a testament to his artistic flair. The sight of him in this moment, so absorbed in his work, sent a rush of affection through me. I wanted to remember this feeling—the way the air shimmered with possibility and how hope seeped into every crevice of the bakery.

With the timer ticking away in the background, we continued our friendly banter, the bakery transforming into a sanctuary where we could laugh freely. "I think I'm onto something here," Ethan declared, lifting his dinosaur cookie triumphantly. "Meet Spike, the most fearsome cookie in existence."

"More like Spike, the adorable cookie," I laughed, inspecting his creation with exaggerated scrutiny. "Are you sure you're not secretly aiming for a cookie zoo instead of a restaurant?"

"Cookie zoo!" he repeated, his laughter joining mine in a joyous symphony that echoed through the kitchen. "What a concept. You know, I could serve cookies shaped like all sorts of animals. Think of the possibilities!"

"Only if you promise to wear a chef hat that looks like a bear," I teased, reaching out to poke his cheek playfully. The moment our laughter died down, I felt a warmth bloom between us, an invisible thread tethering our hearts, solidifying this newfound connection.

With a final flourish, I popped the cookies into the oven and turned to face him. "Okay, Mr. Future Restaurant Owner, what's the first dish you'll serve?"

He hesitated for a moment, a contemplative look crossing his face. "Definitely something that combines flavors. Like a sweet and savory pizza with figs and goat cheese, topped with a drizzle of honey."

"Fig pizza? You're a culinary wizard," I replied, my curiosity piqued. "How did you come up with that?"

"It just came to me one day, watching my grandma bake. She always believed in mixing unexpected ingredients. I want to carry that legacy forward, to create dishes that surprise people."

The sincerity in his words washed over me like a warm tide. It was clear that his dreams were not just idle fantasies; they were rooted deeply in a rich tapestry of memories and aspirations. This was more than just about food; it was about heritage, family, and creating connections through shared experiences.

"I think you'll do it," I said softly, looking into his eyes. "You have this spark, Ethan. You make people feel things."

The moment hung suspended, the air thick with unspoken emotions. He held my gaze, his eyes reflecting the flickering fairy lights, their warmth mirroring the burgeoning trust between us. Just then, the oven timer beeped, cutting through the silence like a jolt of reality. We both turned, and a wave of anticipation washed over us as I pulled open the oven door, releasing a cloud of aromatic steam that curled into the air like tendrils of our shared hopes.

"Look at those!" I exclaimed, pulling out the tray filled with golden-brown cookies, their edges crisp yet invitingly soft.

"Not bad, not bad at all," Ethan said, leaning closer to inspect my creations. "I think Spike might be in trouble."

"Spike will always have a special place in my heart," I replied, affection lacing my voice. "But let's face it, I am the reigning champion here."

We both dug into the cookies, the first bite igniting a wave of flavor that sent our taste buds into a dance. The sweetness of the chocolate mingled with the buttery dough, creating a symphony of deliciousness that demanded second helpings.

"What's next on our agenda?" he asked, licking his fingers with an unabashed glee that made me laugh.

"Well, we could always try our hands at decorating these little masterpieces," I suggested, gesturing to the array of colorful sprinkles and icing. "The more ridiculous, the better."

Ethan's eyes sparkled mischievously. "I'm in. Let's turn these cookies into the most epic cookie menagerie anyone has ever seen!"

With a newfound enthusiasm, we set to work, transforming our baked creations into vibrant works of art. I squeezed out bright pink icing in a wobbly line that resembled a rainbow; Ethan followed suit with electric blue, creating a rather flamboyant cat that looked like it had just stepped out of a candy factory. We were no longer simply baking; we were creating a narrative of joy, each cookie a character in our unfolding story.

As the cookie decorating reached a fever pitch, I glanced out the bakery's window, noticing the moonrise casting a silvery glow over the sleepy town. The world outside seemed distant, yet peaceful, almost like a cozy backdrop to our little sanctuary.

"Hey," I said, looking back at Ethan, who was fully absorbed in placing googly eyes on his latest cookie creation. "Do you ever think about what life will look like in a few years?"

He paused, his hand stilling as he considered my question. "I do. I imagine having a small restaurant with an open kitchen, where people can see everything happening. A place filled with laughter, where families gather over good food and create memories."

I smiled, the vision he painted warming my heart. "That sounds perfect. I can already picture it—community tables, laughter echoing off the walls, and the delicious aroma of baked goods wafting through the air."

"What about you?" he asked, his curiosity piqued. "Where do you see yourself in a few years?"

I hesitated, wondering if I dared to dream aloud. "I want to create something impactful—something that brings people together, just like this," I said, gesturing around the bakery. "A space where people can learn, grow, and share. Maybe a bakery that also serves as a community center for aspiring bakers."

Ethan nodded, his eyes shining with admiration. "I can see that happening for you. You have a way of making people feel welcome. This place is proof of that."

The sincerity of his words sent a rush of warmth through me, and I felt a profound sense of connection—a bond that was now stronger than before. As we decorated the last cookie, the playful banter dwindled into a comfortable silence. In that moment, surrounded by colorful icing and remnants of laughter, I realized that this was not just a baking night. It was a celebration of our resilience, a reminder that together, we could create something beautiful.

As the night drew to a close, we stepped back to admire our cookie masterpieces, a silly array of decorated treats that represented the whimsicality of our journey. The bakery, once a mere backdrop, had transformed into a haven of laughter and connection. I felt a renewed sense of purpose swelling within me, intertwined with the realization that our individual dreams could intertwine and flourish together.

"Ready for the big taste test?" Ethan asked, holding up one of the most outrageous cookies—a bright blue dinosaur with sprinkles for scales.

"Absolutely," I replied, unable to suppress my laughter. "But you know what? Let's share one last cookie together."

We each took a half of the dinosaur cookie, our fingers brushing once more. As we took a bite, the world outside faded further into obscurity, and the sweetness of our shared dreams filled the space between us. I felt a profound sense of hope, as if the walls that had once separated us were now nothing but a distant memory, replaced by the promise of new beginnings and a future rich with possibility.

In that moment, I knew we were no longer just Ethan and I, two individuals navigating the complexities of life. We were a team, united by laughter, dreams, and a sweet, sticky connection that would carry us forward. And as we stood in the warmth of the bakery, surrounded by the remnants of our creations, I couldn't help but believe that together, we could face whatever challenges lay ahead, one cookie at a time.

Chapter 26: A Bitter Rivalry

The sun dipped low over the horizon, casting a warm amber glow that spilled through the tall windows of our bakery, illuminating the shelves lined with an array of pastries. The air was thick with the intoxicating scent of fresh bread, the kind that made you feel like you'd just returned home after a long, arduous journey. My fingers were dusted with flour, and I savored the sweetness of success as I rolled out the dough, each movement a testament to countless hours spent perfecting our craft. This little haven, nestled between a flower shop and a vintage bookstore on the bustling streets of Savannah, Georgia, was more than just a business to me; it was a dream carved into reality, a sanctuary where every croissant and tart whispered stories of love, laughter, and resilience.

But just as I began to believe that my world had stabilized, Emma waltzed back in, her presence as vivid and jarring as a bolt of lightning on a clear day. She strolled through the door with a confidence that felt almost tangible, the sound of her heels clicking against the polished wooden floor echoing like an ominous warning. I had thought I was rid of her influence—her sultry laughter and mischievous glances—but here she was, just when I had started to breathe easy, ready to stir the pot once more.

"Evelyn!" she exclaimed, her voice dripping with feigned sweetness, "Isn't it simply delightful to see you again?" Her eyes sparkled with an allure that could ensnare even the most steadfast heart. I felt a pang of annoyance mingled with wariness as I wiped my hands on my apron, forcing a smile that felt more like a grimace.

"Emma," I replied, trying to keep my tone light. "What brings you here?" The question hung in the air, heavy with unspoken words and lingering tension. Ethan, my partner and the love of my life, was at the counter, his gaze flickering between us, his brow furrowed in unease. He was the calm to my storm, but even he couldn't mask the unease that had begun to settle like dust over our sanctuary.

"I have an idea," Emma said, her voice smooth like chocolate ganache, the hint of mischief playing at the corners of her mouth. "What if we joined forces? Our talents combined could create something extraordinary, something the people of Savannah have never seen before." She leaned in slightly, her presence a magnetic force that threatened to pull Ethan into her orbit. My heart sank as I registered the glimmer of temptation in his eyes, a flicker of nostalgia for the ease with which she navigated the world, always knowing exactly what to say.

I straightened my back, summoning every ounce of confidence I could muster. "Emma, I appreciate your offer, but I think we're doing just fine on our own," I said, my voice steady despite the storm brewing within me. The weight of her gaze was palpable, and I could feel the tension spiraling as she leaned back, crossing her arms with an air of defiance.

"Are you sure?" she challenged, tilting her head slightly, her raven hair cascading over her shoulders like a dark waterfall. "You could be missing out on something incredible. Think of the possibilities! Imagine a bakery that not only caters to the sweet tooth but also offers savory delights—a fusion of flavors that would capture the heart of this town." Her words flowed like syrup, sweet and thick, attempting to wrap around Ethan's thoughts, trying to sway him toward her vision.

I felt my heart race, the protective instinct flaring within me. I glanced at Ethan, searching for reassurance, but his expression was clouded with uncertainty. He admired Emma's creativity, her fearless ambition, but I wasn't about to let her charm us into a partnership that could unravel everything we had built. "We have a vision for this bakery, Emma. One that doesn't involve you," I said firmly, hoping to slice through the tension that had thickened like dough left to rise too long.

Her lips twisted into a smirk, a combination of amusement and irritation. "You really think you can do this alone? Without my expertise? You've only just begun to make a name for yourself in this town." The barb hit home, and I felt a rush of defiance surge through me. This bakery was my heart and soul, a canvas where I painted my dreams with flour and sugar, not some fleeting venture to be manipulated by her whims.

"I'm not doing this alone," I countered, gesturing toward Ethan, who was now visibly tense, his hands gripping the edge of the counter. "We have built something special together. We're a team."

Emma's gaze flicked to Ethan, and I felt the air crackle between them, an electric tension that only intensified my resolve. I refused to let her rekindle a rivalry that could shatter our fragile peace. "This isn't just about business," I added, my voice steady and firm. "It's about what we've created here. It's personal."

Her laughter rang through the bakery, sharp and hollow, and for a moment, I thought I might see a glimpse of vulnerability behind her bravado. "Personal? Sweetheart, in this world, everything is business. You might think your little bakery is immune to competition, but trust me, it's not."

The dismissal stung, but I stood tall, defiance flaring in my chest. "Maybe, but I'm not going to compromise my dreams just to prove a point." I looked at Ethan again, desperate for him to understand. He was my anchor, and I needed him to stand beside me against the storm that was Emma.

The silence hung thick, the tension palpable as Emma's eyes flickered back to me, the challenge unspoken. I had laid down my gauntlet, but I couldn't shake the feeling that this wasn't over. A rivalry had sparked, and with it, the looming question of whether we could weather the impending storm. My heart raced, but I refused to be intimidated; my love for this bakery, for Ethan, burned brightly, a flame I would fight to protect.

The door swung shut behind Emma with a definitive click, yet her presence lingered like a shadow in the soft afternoon light. I could still feel the weight of her words hanging in the air, a challenge cloaked in the guise of an offer, teasing me to reconsider what I held dear. I let out a shaky breath, gripping the edge of the counter as if it were my only lifeline, my mind swirling with uncertainty. Ethan remained silent, his eyes clouded, revealing a flicker of something I couldn't quite place—was it admiration, intrigue, or perhaps a hint of doubt?

"Evelyn," he said finally, his voice low and thoughtful, cutting through the thick silence that enveloped us. "Are you sure about this? She does have a point—her ideas could really push us forward." The doubt in his tone was like ice water poured over the warmth of my resolve. I took a step back, trying to gauge his thoughts. "Think about the extra exposure, the people we could reach together."

"Together," I echoed, the word tasting bitter on my tongue. I ran my fingers through my hair, trying to tame the whirlpool of emotions that threatened to spill over. "But at what cost, Ethan? Do you really want to bring her back into our lives?" The memory of late nights spent unraveling her schemes, the way she'd manipulated situations to her advantage, ignited a fire within me that I struggled to contain.

He sighed, a sound heavy with the weight of a thousand unspoken arguments. "I just think it's worth considering. It could bring something new to our bakery, something fresh."

"Fresh?" I snapped, my heart racing. "She doesn't know anything about what we're doing. She'd be an anchor, not a sail." My words hung between us, sharp and biting, but beneath the anger, a ripple of fear threaded through my veins. What if he was right? What if my stubbornness was blinding me to an opportunity? I didn't want to admit that the notion of Emma's return, her dazzling smile, and infectious laughter could light a spark of creativity that we desperately needed.

"Look," he said, his tone softening as he took a step closer, "I just want what's best for us. For the bakery." He reached for my hand, and I felt the warmth of his palm seep into my skin, grounding me amidst the chaos. "Let's just think it over. No harm in exploring possibilities, right?"

I met his gaze, searching for reassurance, but found only the reflection of my own doubt. "Ethan, I'm not sure I can just forget everything we've gone through with her. This is our bakery. It's not just a business to me; it's home."

His brow furrowed, the tension between us palpable. "I understand that, but maybe we could make it work. With some boundaries."

"Boundaries," I repeated, the word feeling weak in my mouth. I thought of Emma, the way she glided through life with effortless grace, her laughter ringing like chimes in the breeze. She was a tempest, unpredictable and fierce, and I had no desire to be swept up in her whirlwind again. "Do you really think she'd respect boundaries? This is Emma we're talking about."

A silence fell between us, a chasm I feared might swallow the very foundation of what we had built together. I turned away, trying to collect my thoughts, the world outside our bakery fading into a blur of color and sound. I could see families strolling past, children laughing and chasing one another, unaware of the storm brewing just beyond the glass. The warmth of the golden sun bathed our sanctuary, but inside, I felt the chill of doubt creeping in, an unwelcome visitor lurking in the corners of my mind.

The delicate chime of the doorbell pulled me back to the present as a young couple entered, their eyes lighting up at the sight of the confections on display. I plastered on a smile, determined to reclaim the warmth of my sanctuary, the place that had been my refuge and my pride. "Welcome to Sweet Flour," I greeted, my voice bright and welcoming despite the turmoil raging inside.

As they approached the counter, I felt Ethan's gaze lingering on me, a mix of concern and admiration. I busied myself with the pastries, arranging them with the precision of a painter framing a masterpiece, each tart and muffin crafted with love and intention. I could hear the couple's laughter, their shared joy infectious, and I realized how much I cherished this connection—the way food could bring people together, forge bonds that transcended the chaos of life.

Yet, as I handed them their order, Emma's words echoed in my mind, and I could feel the tension that had settled over our bakery like a heavy fog. My heart sank with the realization that I was not just fighting for the integrity of our business; I was fighting to protect my heart, my home, and the love I shared with Ethan.

When the couple left, the door chimed again, and I turned to Ethan, ready to voice my thoughts. But before I could speak, he held up a hand, his expression shifting from concern to determination. "You're right," he said, his voice steady. "We can't let her take this from us. This is our space, our dream, and we've worked too hard to let anyone in who doesn't have our best interests at heart."

Relief washed over me, a wave of warmth that enveloped me in its embrace. I stepped closer, closing the distance between us. "So we agree? No partnerships?"

He nodded, the weight lifting from his shoulders. "No partnerships. Just us."

The moment hung in the air, fragile yet powerful, and I felt an overwhelming surge of gratitude for the bond we had forged amidst the flour and sugar, amidst the laughter and tears. We were a team, imperfect yet unwavering, navigating the wild terrain of dreams together. I leaned in, my heart soaring, knowing that whatever storms lay ahead, we would face them side by side, fortified by love and a shared passion that was indomitable.

With newfound clarity, I turned my gaze back to the window, watching as the sun dipped below the horizon, painting the sky in hues of orange and purple. The streets of Savannah were alive with the hum of evening, and I felt a sense of peace settling over me. We would chart our own course, without interference, and together we would create a legacy that was wholly ours, one bite at a time.

The days that followed were steeped in a tension that clung to the air like the sweet scent of vanilla in the bakery. I threw myself into the rhythm of kneading dough and whipping cream, each action a form of therapy, a way to drown out the nagging doubts that crept into my mind like unwelcome guests. Despite the comforting routine, Emma's shadow loomed larger than the oversized stand mixer in our kitchen, a specter reminding me of her earlier visit and the allure of her proposition.

Ethan and I worked diligently side by side, but I could feel the unspoken words dancing between us, a tightrope we both hesitated to walk. Whenever I caught his gaze lingering a moment too long on the door, my heart would flutter, a mix of anxiety and resentment. I had no doubt that Emma could charm him with her ideas, her enthusiasm, her zest for life. But did he see beyond that façade? Did he truly grasp the implications of what partnering with her might mean for us?

One Saturday afternoon, we hosted a small event to introduce our new line of artisan breads—a nod to my grandmother's age-old recipes. The sun poured through the large front windows, bathing the room in a golden glow as laughter echoed through the space. Families gathered around tables draped in white linen, the air thick with the scent of freshly baked focaccia and rosemary-infused olive oil. I watched as parents laughed with their children, each of them breaking pieces of warm bread, the sound crackling like the gentle pop of fireworks on a summer night.

Amidst the hustle and bustle, I caught sight of Emma as she strolled down the street, her figure effortlessly drawing the eyes of passersby. She paused outside, glancing in, and for a heartbeat, the world around me stilled. I felt my pulse quicken as I caught the way she straightened her back, her eyes sparkling with mischief, undoubtedly aware of the effect she had on everyone around her.

Ethan noticed my shift in focus, his brow knitting together. "Are you alright?"

"I'm fine," I replied too quickly, my tone betraying the tension within. "Just... distracted."

He followed my gaze, and I saw a flicker of concern cross his face. "Maybe we should invite her in," he suggested, his voice cautious, careful not to incite another flare-up.

The thought made my stomach churn. "Why would we do that?" I shot back, the words sharper than I intended. "We've built this space for ourselves. This isn't a stage for her performance."

"Evelyn," he began, but I interrupted him, the heat of my frustration igniting a fire within me.

"Look, Ethan, I don't want to turn this into some competition. This is our moment, and she doesn't get to barge in and steal our spotlight. Not now, not ever."

I could see the conflict waging in his eyes as he struggled to reconcile my fiery defensiveness with his desire to remain neutral. "I understand that, but it might help to show her we're not afraid of her. We can coexist."

"Coexist?" I huffed, the irony of his suggestion not lost on me. "It's not about coexisting; it's about protecting what we have. If we invite her in, it sends a message that we're open to her ideas, and I refuse to play her game."

The argument hung in the air, tension thick enough to cut with a knife. Ethan finally nodded, his shoulders slumping slightly, and for a moment, I felt a pang of regret for the fire I had wielded. I knew that his heart was in the right place, always striving for harmony, but I couldn't shake the feeling that any interaction with Emma would only serve to complicate our lives further.

Later that evening, as the last customers filtered out and the door swung shut with a soft jingle, I leaned against the counter, letting the stillness wash over me. "We did well today," I said, trying to break the tension that had hung over us all day. "The turnout was better than expected."

Ethan smiled, his face lighting up in a way that made my heart skip. "It really was. I think people are starting to recognize what we're doing here."

I met his gaze, and in that moment, I felt the weight of my fears begin to lift. "And it's only going to get better," I added, feeling a surge of optimism.

As we cleaned up together, our laughter filled the space, a comforting sound that reminded me of why I had fallen in love with him in the first place. I handed him a damp cloth, our fingers brushing, igniting a spark that traveled up my arm, grounding me in the reality that we were in this together, come what may.

But just as I was beginning to feel that comforting bubble enveloping us, the unmistakable chime of the doorbell echoed through the empty bakery, shattering the fragile moment. My heart sank as I turned to see Emma gliding through the door with a smile that was all too familiar.

"Good evening, lovelies!" she announced, as if she had stepped into her own personal spotlight. The room felt charged with tension again, as if the air itself recoiled from her presence.

"Emma," I said, forcing the word out as my stomach twisted in knots.

"Just thought I'd drop by and see how the event went. Heard it was quite the success." She leaned against the counter, a calculated casualness about her.

"Thanks," I replied, my tone clipped, unwilling to grant her the satisfaction of engaging in a conversation about her potential comeback.

"Seems you two have been doing quite well without me," she remarked, her voice smooth, yet sharp enough to slice through the atmosphere. "But imagine what we could do together."

I exchanged a glance with Ethan, the apprehension palpable between us. "We're happy with our direction, Emma," he said cautiously, a diplomatic tone coloring his words.

"Are you?" she challenged, her gaze flicking back and forth between us. "Because it seems like you're both just a bit on edge."

"We're fine," I shot back, irritation creeping into my voice, but the truth was I could feel the walls tightening around me, a storm brewing on the horizon.

"Why not let me take you on a little adventure?" she proposed, her tone teasing, mischief glinting in her eyes. "We could scout out some ideas, get the creative juices flowing. It would be fun!"

"No, thank you," I said firmly, the words leaving my mouth with a strength I didn't entirely feel.

Her smile faltered, but only for a moment, replaced quickly with a mask of amusement. "Suit yourselves. Just remember, opportunities don't come knocking every day."

As she turned to leave, I felt a wave of relief wash over me, but it was quickly replaced with a tinge of dread. I glanced at Ethan, who wore a look of confusion. "Did I handle that right?" I asked, my heart racing as I tried to reconcile my emotions.

"You did," he assured me, though I could see the shadows of doubt flickering in his eyes.

The door swung shut behind her, and I exhaled deeply, feeling the tension slowly release its grip. But the unease settled back into my chest as I knew this wouldn't be the last time Emma would try to tempt us.

"I won't let her ruin this for us," I murmured, the resolve igniting within me. Ethan nodded, a silent promise exchanged between us, our hands brushing against one another, reinforcing the bond we had forged.

Outside, the sun began to set, casting long shadows across the cobblestone streets. I knew that while Emma might have flitted in and out of our lives like a fleeting breeze, the love and determination we shared would be the anchor we needed. Together, we would navigate the challenges ahead, forging a path that was distinctly ours, crafted with care and infused with the sweetness of our dreams. No rival could ever overshadow the bond we had built, and as long as we stood united, our future was bright, filled with the promise of what was yet to come.

Chapter 27: Tangled Threads

The warm scent of vanilla and cinnamon swirled around me like a comforting embrace as I stepped into the bustling bakery, the heart of our small town. Light streamed through the large glass windows, illuminating the flour-dusted countertops and the array of pastries waiting to be artfully adorned. The clatter of pots and pans mixed with the gentle hum of conversation, creating a melody of activity that filled the air. I took a deep breath, letting the familiar scents wrap around me, each inhale a reminder of why I had chosen this path. Yet, despite the bustle, a heaviness settled in my chest, an unshakable tension that had taken root after my confrontation with Emma.

Emma's words echoed in my mind, her disappointment sharp and stinging, a reminder that choices come with consequences. I had felt justified in my actions, standing firm in my convictions, but now, as I watched flour billow in the air and sugar crystals glisten like tiny diamonds, I questioned if my choices had been selfish. I shifted my gaze toward Ethan, who stood at the other end of the counter, his usually vibrant spirit dimmed by an invisible weight. His hands moved mechanically, rolling out dough with a precision that lacked its usual flair. There was a time when we had danced around the kitchen, flour flying like confetti, laughter spilling from our lips, but now the light seemed to flicker, wavering under the strain of our dreams colliding.

"Hey," I called softly, my voice barely rising above the cacophony of mixing bowls and chatty customers. He didn't respond, his brow furrowed in concentration, or perhaps something deeper—an anxiety that had become a familiar visitor since the magazine feature was announced. I crossed the room, the soles of my shoes squeaking against the polished tile, and leaned against the countertop beside him. "You okay?"

Ethan's gaze remained fixed on the dough as if it held the answers to questions neither of us dared to voice. He sighed deeply, the sound a mixture of resignation and frustration. "I don't know, Nora. I thought I was ready for this, but... now it feels like I'm drowning in expectations." The admission hung in the air, heavy and tangible. I reached out, resting my hand on his forearm, feeling the warmth of his skin beneath my fingers, a grounding force in the chaos swirling around us.

"You're not alone, you know. We're in this together," I reassured him, though my own uncertainty clung to the edges of my words. The magazine feature loomed over us like a giant wave, ready to crash down, but the reality of our collaboration had morphed into a source of stress rather than the joyful creation we had envisioned. I could see the tension etched in the lines of his face, the weight of unfulfilled dreams pressing down on his shoulders, and it broke my heart to witness it.

Ethan finally turned to me, his hazel eyes searching mine for a glimmer of understanding. "What if I'm not enough? What if the magazine decides we're not worth their time?" Each question was a dagger, piercing through the protective bubble I had created around my own insecurities. I could feel the corners of my mouth turning down, a frown creasing my forehead as I contemplated his fears.

"You're more than enough," I declared, my voice steadier than I felt. "You have talent, vision, and passion that can't be bottled up. Remember why we started this in the first place?" I searched his eyes, willing him to see the truth I was trying to convey. "This bakery isn't just a place for pastries; it's our dream. Let's focus on what we love, not what we fear."

His lips curled into a reluctant smile, and I felt a flicker of hope ignite between us. "You always know what to say." The compliment warmed me, even as I felt the tightness in my chest loosen just a fraction. It was a small victory, yet the emotional current running between us felt deeper than the sweet whispers of encouragement. It was a raw and vulnerable moment, both of us stripped down to our bare insecurities, revealing the tangled threads of our aspirations and fears.

With a newfound resolve, we began to work side by side, the weight of unspoken worries lifting as laughter punctuated our tasks. The rhythm of our collaboration shifted, becoming more fluid and intuitive, as if the kitchen itself had wrapped us in its embrace. We rolled out pastries, each swirl of dough reminding me of the tangled mess we often found ourselves in—yet there was beauty in that mess. I handed him a brush, and together, we painted golden egg wash over the pastries, transforming them into little pieces of art that would soon emerge from the oven, crisp and fragrant.

"I know we can do this," I murmured, glancing up at him as he gently brushed the dough. "Let's not forget that the joy is in the making, not just in the outcome." Each stroke of the brush felt like a metaphor for our journey—an intricate dance that required both of us to be present and engaged, savoring the process rather than fixating on the destination.

As the oven timer chimed and the sweet aroma of baking pastries filled the air, I caught Ethan's eye and felt a wave of determination wash over us. We stood there, side by side, caught in a moment that felt suspended in time, where the chaos of our thoughts faded into the background, leaving only the shared warmth of our aspirations. The bakery, with its worn wooden counters and walls that had witnessed our laughter and tears, felt like a sanctuary. And in that sanctuary, I knew we could face whatever came next, as long as we faced it together.

With the last of the pastries emerging from the oven, golden and glistening, the bakery transformed into a haven of warmth and delight. I couldn't help but let out a small laugh as Ethan attempted to balance a towering platter of freshly baked croissants. "Careful!"

I called, my voice laced with amusement as I watched him wobble, arms outstretched like a tightrope walker. He caught my gaze, and the corners of his mouth quirked into a grin, the kind that crinkled his eyes and dispelled some of the weight that had been resting on his shoulders.

"Who knew pastry could be so perilous?" he quipped, carefully lowering the platter onto the countertop. Each croissant looked like a little crescent moon, soft and flaky, their buttery aroma wafting through the air, inviting everyone to indulge. The bakery was now alive with customers, each drawn in by the enchanting scent that seemed to weave a spell of comfort and nostalgia. I relished in the vibrant atmosphere, yet the shadow of my earlier confrontation with Emma lurked in the back of my mind, a reminder that not all was well in my world.

As I moved through the bustling space, I spotted Mrs. Thompson, our beloved regular, her silver hair shimmering under the light as she eagerly approached the counter. "Oh, dear, you've outdone yourselves!" she exclaimed, her voice carrying the warmth of a grandmother's embrace. I smiled, soaking in her enthusiasm as I served her a croissant, watching her face light up with delight. It was moments like these that grounded me, reminding me of the purpose behind all our late nights and early mornings.

"Thank you, Mrs. Thompson! I hope you enjoy it!" I called out, feeling a surge of pride as she took a bite, her eyes closing in bliss. But as I turned back to Ethan, the smile faded slightly. I could sense the tumult beneath his surface, a storm brewing in the depths of his hazel eyes. The laughter and chatter around us felt like a cocoon, wrapping us in comfort, yet I knew the outside world loomed beyond, waiting to pounce on our vulnerabilities.

In the quiet lull that followed, I found a moment to step outside for fresh air, the cool breeze brushing against my flushed cheeks. The bakery, nestled in the heart of town, stood amidst brick buildings and leafy trees, their leaves beginning to turn golden with the approaching autumn. I leaned against the cool metal railing outside, closing my eyes, letting the sounds of laughter and clinking plates drift away as I gathered my thoughts.

"Hey, you okay?" Ethan's voice broke through the moment, and I opened my eyes to find him standing beside me, concern etched into his features.

"I think I'm just overwhelmed," I admitted, exhaling slowly. "With everything that's happened… It feels like the walls are closing in." The vulnerability slipped out before I could rein it in, the openness of our earlier conversation making it easier to share my burdens.

Ethan shifted closer, the warmth radiating from him, offering a solace I desperately needed. "It's okay to feel that way. I mean, look at us! We're about to be in a magazine, and it's terrifying. Sometimes I feel like I'm just trying to keep my head above water." His honesty resonated deeply, the acknowledgment of our shared struggle bringing us back to the same page, the tangled threads of our fears intertwining like a complex tapestry.

"Why do we put so much pressure on ourselves?" I asked, my voice barely a whisper, yet the question hung heavy between us, echoing the struggles we both faced. It was a struggle that had grown more palpable with every late-night brainstorming session and every moment of self-doubt that had crept in like an unwelcome guest.

"Because we care," he replied, a softness lacing his words. "And that's what makes it all worthwhile, right? If we didn't care, we wouldn't feel so much. Maybe we just need to remind ourselves of that every once in a while."

The sincerity in his voice pierced through the fog of my worries, offering a glimmer of clarity. It felt as if we had formed a pact in that moment, a commitment to navigate this journey together, no matter how tangled it became. I wanted to cling to that thought, to let it envelop me like the comforting embrace of a beloved blanket.

"Let's celebrate the little victories," I suggested, a smile beginning to return to my lips. "Like finishing that batch of pastries without any disasters. Or getting through the day without a panic attack."

His laughter rang out, rich and genuine, and I felt the tension between us ease slightly. "I can get on board with that. A toast to our pastry triumphs!" He raised an imaginary glass, and I joined in, mimicking the gesture with an exaggerated flourish that made him chuckle even harder.

The laughter lingered in the air, weaving through the bustling bakery, and I felt a renewed sense of determination blossoming inside me. We weren't just two people trying to juggle dreams; we were a team, and together, we could weave our fears into something beautiful.

As we returned inside, I could feel a shift in the atmosphere, a lightness replacing the heaviness of the past few days. Customers continued to filter in, their faces bright with anticipation. I joined Ethan behind the counter, and we began working in sync, laughter flowing between us like the rhythm of a well-rehearsed duet. He played off my playful banter, adding his own witty remarks, and the bakery felt alive, pulsing with energy as we created together.

In that lively space, the bakery felt like a canvas, and we were the artists, painting our dreams with flour and sugar. The evening turned into a symphony of clinking dishes and sweet melodies, a reminder that in the midst of our fears and doubts, joy could still be found. Each pastry we crafted held a piece of our story, a testament to our resilience and creativity.

As the sun dipped below the horizon, casting a warm glow through the windows, I felt a sense of peace wash over me. The path ahead might still be tangled with uncertainty, but for now, we were creating something real and beautiful together, and that made every moment worth it.

The sweet smell of baked goods enveloped the bakery like a soft embrace as we slid into a new rhythm, our worries momentarily sidelined by the act of creation. Customers flowed in and out, each face a unique tapestry of delight and nostalgia. I watched as a father and his young daughter shared a moment over a chocolate eclair, the girl's laughter ringing out like chimes in the gentle breeze. These simple joys were what fueled my passion, grounding me amidst the uncertainty that danced at the corners of my thoughts.

Ethan was immersed in his work, the delicate artistry of his hands creating intricate designs atop our latest batch of pastries. The way his brow furrowed in concentration was captivating, and I found myself momentarily lost in the sight of him. His hair was tousled, flour dusting the tips, a testament to the long hours we had both poured into our shared dream. As I assisted him, our arms brushed occasionally, sending tiny sparks of electricity that were hard to ignore. It was a reminder that we were not just partners in business; there was something deeper, something unspoken between us that often tangled itself within our professional conversations.

The hours slipped away, each tick of the clock bringing us closer to the magazine feature, yet also closer to the inevitability of Emma's words. I had spent countless nights replaying our confrontation, the sharpness of her disappointment reverberating in my mind. What if I had made a grave mistake? What if the choice to stand up for my values meant sacrificing relationships that once felt unbreakable? With each passing day, those thoughts grew heavier, an anchor pulling me down into the depths of my doubts.

"Do you ever think about what happens after this?" Ethan's voice cut through my spiraling thoughts, drawing my focus back to the present. He had stepped away from the counter, leaning against it as if it were the only thing keeping him grounded. "What if the magazine feature goes well, and we suddenly find ourselves... successful?" The way he spoke the word "successful" felt both thrilling and terrifying, like standing on the edge of a precipice, ready to leap but unsure of what awaited below.

"Then we keep going, right?" I replied, forcing a buoyancy into my voice, though my heart raced with uncertainty. "We create more, dream bigger. That's what we've always wanted."

"Sure, but what if it changes everything?" His question lingered in the air, heavy with implications. "What if we lose sight of why we started this in the first place?"

I leaned back against the counter, crossing my arms as I pondered his words. The bakery had begun as a haven, a space where creativity flourished, and the chaos of life faded into the background. Yet, the specter of success loomed large, casting shadows that threatened to distort our vision. "Then we remind ourselves," I suggested slowly, "of what brought us here. The joy of baking, the people we serve, and the passion we have for this craft."

"Like our little victories?" he prompted, a spark of mischief igniting in his eyes.

"Exactly! Each pastry is a victory, a testament to our hard work." I grinned, grateful for his ability to shift the mood. "We could make a whole wall of them—'Victory Pastries,' and each one can have a little plaque detailing its triumph. Like a Hall of Fame for baked goods!"

Ethan chuckled, the sound resonating like music, the tension easing in our shared laughter. "I can see it now—each pastry framed with a little bio. 'This croissant was born from an intense brainstorming session fueled by too much coffee and not enough sleep.'"

"Or the chocolate cake, created after a minor existential crisis," I added, our playful banter easing the weight in my heart.

In that moment, we reclaimed our joy, our laughter echoing through the bakery as customers joined in, drawn by our infectious energy. With each shared joke and light-hearted moment, I felt the heaviness of my thoughts begin to lift, if only slightly.

As the sun dipped lower in the sky, painting the bakery with warm hues of orange and gold, I noticed Emma's figure framed in the doorway. Her silhouette was striking against the backdrop of the setting sun, but the warmth I felt was quickly overshadowed by the uncertainty that tightened my chest. She hesitated, scanning the bustling room, her expression unreadable. I wondered if she had come to confront me again, to remind me of the fragility of our relationships in the wake of ambition.

Ethan caught my eye, sensing my hesitation. "You got this," he whispered, an encouraging smile breaking through my doubts. I took a deep breath, smoothing my apron, steeling myself for whatever interaction lay ahead.

Emma stepped inside, the bell above the door tinkling softly as she approached the counter. "Hey," she said, her voice softer than I had anticipated. There was no anger, no confrontation, just a tinge of vulnerability that mirrored my own. "I wanted to talk."

"Of course," I replied, my heart racing. "Can we grab a table?"

We settled into a cozy nook by the window, the glow of the sunset spilling over us like a soft blanket. I could feel Ethan's watchful presence lingering in the background, a silent pillar of support as I faced the complexity of my relationship with Emma.

"I'm sorry for how I reacted before," she began, her gaze fixed on the wooden table between us. "I just—I don't want to lose you." The admission hung in the air, heavy with unspoken feelings and fears.

"I know," I said gently, my voice barely above a whisper. "I didn't mean to push you away. I just felt like I had to stand up for myself."

"I get it," she replied, finally looking up. The vulnerability in her eyes caught me off guard. "I just didn't expect you to challenge me. I thought we were on the same page."

"That's the thing," I said, my heart racing as I bared my own feelings. "We are on the same page, but I also have my own dreams. I want to make this bakery a place where we can thrive, and sometimes that means making hard decisions."

She nodded slowly, the tension in her shoulders easing slightly. "I want that too. I guess I just thought—maybe selfishly—that our friendship would come first."

"Friendship is important," I assured her. "But we can have both. Our dreams don't have to come at the cost of our relationship. Let's find a way to make it work."

The warmth of understanding enveloped us, and I could feel the air shift as the weight of miscommunication began to lift. There was a road ahead that would undoubtedly be paved with challenges, but perhaps we could navigate it together, our friendship intertwining with our ambitions like the delicate threads of a beautifully woven tapestry.

As we continued to talk, I could sense Ethan in the background, listening quietly, his presence a reassuring anchor. The sun finally dipped below the horizon, leaving a soft twilight glow in its wake. We shared laughter, vulnerability, and dreams, weaving a tapestry of our lives together, stitching our friendship with the resilience that had blossomed through adversity.

In that moment, I realized that life, like baking, was an unpredictable journey. Each choice, each victory, and even the occasional failure contributed to the masterpiece we were creating. As the bakery buzzed with energy and warmth, I felt hopeful, ready to face whatever came next, both in my relationships and in our shared dream. We were building something beautiful, and for the first time in a long while, I believed we could do it together.

Chapter 28: The Final Whisk

The scent of warm vanilla and fresh berries danced through the air, wrapping around me like a comforting blanket as I surveyed the bustling bakery. Each pastry displayed on the glass cases glistened under the soft, golden light. The bakery had become my sanctuary, a place where I could pour my heart into every dough and sprinkle love onto every dessert. But today, a restless energy pulsed beneath the surface, a current of tension that threatened to pull me under. The magazine feature was looming, a glittering opportunity that could elevate our humble bakery from the quaint corners of my small town into a culinary spotlight.

I meticulously arranged the delicate tarts, each one adorned with a glossy layer of glaze that caught the light like a prism. They were a tribute to summer, bursting with colors reminiscent of a painter's palette—deep ruby reds, sunny yellows, and rich purples. Just as I set the last tart into place, my phone buzzed, slicing through the sweet melody of the bakery. The name on the screen sent a shiver down my spine. It was Ethan, my partner in both life and the bakery, his voice crackling with an urgency that made my stomach drop.

"Jules," he began, a tremor threading through his words, "it's Sarah. She's... she's in intensive care."

The world tilted beneath my feet, and I stumbled backward, my breath hitching in my throat. Sarah, my best friend, my confidante, the sister I had chosen, was in a battle I had never been prepared to face. "What do you mean?" I managed to whisper, each syllable dragging along the weight of my fear.

"Just come to the hospital, please. I don't know how much time we have," Ethan urged, his voice a lifeline in the storm. Without thinking, I dropped the pastry bag and dashed out of the bakery, the bell above the door chiming a dissonant farewell. The sun beat down on my skin as I rushed to my car, the heat soaking into my worry-laden thoughts.

The hospital loomed ahead, a stark contrast to the sunny streets of our town, its sterile walls a reminder of the fragility of life. The scent of antiseptic hit me like a slap as I entered the building, the cheerful chaos of the bakery feeling like a distant memory. I navigated through the maze of white walls and linoleum floors, my heart pounding in my chest. Each step echoed like a drumbeat of despair, propelling me forward even as my feet felt leaden.

When I finally reached her room, the door stood slightly ajar, revealing a scene that made my breath hitch again. The soft beeping of machines filled the air, a rhythmic reminder of Sarah's fight. She lay there, her vibrant spirit now muted beneath the harsh glare of fluorescent lights. Tubes snaked around her, a tangle of wires and gadgets that held her to this world, and I felt a wave of nausea crest within me. My heart ached at the sight; this wasn't the girl who had danced through life, her laughter ringing like bells in the quiet of my darkest days.

I stepped inside, my body heavy with dread. "Hey, it's me," I whispered, pulling a chair close to her bedside. I clasped her hand, cold and fragile, and a familiar warmth coursed through me. "You've got to wake up. We have things to do, remember? The magazine is coming, and I need you to taste-test my tarts. I can't do this without you."

Tears pricked at the corners of my eyes, but I fought them back, determined to be the anchor she needed. I squeezed her hand tighter, imagining the warmth returning to her fingers. "You were always the brave one, Sarah. You taught me how to face the world, and now I need you to teach me again. Just open those beautiful eyes of yours. Please."

The silence in the room was a suffocating blanket, wrapping around my chest and squeezing until I could hardly breathe. I spent what felt like hours recounting our adventures, the summer nights spent chasing fireflies, the baking marathons that filled our kitchen with laughter and flour, the promises we made under starlit skies. I hoped that my words could weave a thread of comfort through the cacophony of machines and the sterile air.

Outside the window, the world continued its dance. The sun cast golden rays across the city, illuminating the trees that swayed gently in the breeze, a stark contrast to the weight of grief pulling at my heart. I felt a pang of longing for the days when everything seemed simple, when our biggest worry was whether to add more chocolate chips to the cookies or keep them classic.

As the hours slipped away, I settled into the chair, my eyes never leaving Sarah's face. The room was a cocoon of sterile sounds, but my heart thudded in time with her breaths, each rise and fall a reminder of her resilience. I could almost hear her voice, teasing me about my habit of overthinking, urging me to stay positive, to keep fighting.

With the weight of uncertainty pressing down on me, I closed my eyes for just a moment, surrendering to exhaustion. In that fleeting escape, I saw a vision of the bakery, the laughter of children enjoying their treats, the smell of freshly baked goods mingling with the sweet notes of summer. I imagined Sarah there beside me, her smile lighting up the room.

When I finally opened my eyes, the room was darker, shadows creeping in as night began to weave its tapestry of stars outside. I blinked away the heaviness, the haunting worry that clung to my thoughts like smoke. The only sound was the steady beeping of the machines, a metronome of hope that reminded me she was still here, still fighting.

"I won't give up on you," I murmured, my voice a vow that hung in the air. The world may be swirling in chaos, but here, with her, I would hold the line against despair. With each passing moment, I knew I had to be her strength, her voice, the spirit that wouldn't let her fade. The bakery awaited, a reminder of the dreams we had built together, dreams that still shimmered like sugar in the light. And I would fight for them. I would fight for her.

The room, cloaked in soft shadows, was an oasis of silence punctuated only by the mechanical symphony of machines, a constant reminder of Sarah's fragility. Each beep and whirr wrapped around me, creating a rhythm that echoed my heartbeat, resonating in tandem with the anxiety swirling within me. I refused to leave her side, pulling my chair closer as I took in every detail—the gentle rise and fall of her chest, the wisps of hair that had fallen across her forehead, and the fragile way her fingers lay intertwined, as if seeking an anchor.

I leaned in, the cool air of the hospital room contrasting sharply with the warmth of my worry. "You always were the stubborn one," I murmured, hoping the sound of my voice could pierce through the haze of unconsciousness that enveloped her. "Remember that time we tried to bake the giant chocolate cake and it collapsed like a sad soufflé? You insisted on salvaging it, turning it into truffles. I think we ended up with a pile of chocolate goo that was still better than most cakes." I chuckled softly, the sound mixing with my tears. My words were a fragile lifeline, an attempt to tug her back from the precipice.

As the hours trickled by, time seemed to blur, the moments stretching into a languid expanse where reality shifted. I stared at the walls, painted in clinical white, and imagined them transforming into the warm hues of our bakery—the bright yellow walls adorned with quirky art, the shelves brimming with confections that sparkled like jewels. The laughter of customers, the chatter of friends over steaming mugs of coffee, the familiar clink of utensils against plates filled with my creations. Those memories washed over me, a balm against the chilling reality that threatened to consume us.

Outside, the world transitioned from the golden light of day to the deep indigo of night, the stars winking through the window as if urging me to hold on to hope. I shifted in my seat, fatigue seeping into my bones, but I pressed on. "You know, they say the bakery is going to be featured in a big magazine. Can you imagine? All those people finally getting to taste your favorite lemon meringue tarts? I've been working on perfecting the recipe—adding a hint of lavender to the filling. I know you'll love it."

I wished I could see her eyes light up, hear her laughter bubbling forth as we exchanged ideas, as we had countless times before. It was those small moments, the shared joy of creation, that had cemented our friendship. I grasped her hand tighter, willing the warmth of my spirit to seep into her.

Just then, a soft knock on the door startled me from my reverie. A nurse entered, her presence a gentle reminder of the reality we faced. She wore a kind smile, her eyes crinkling at the corners as she adjusted the monitors. "How is she?" I asked, my voice barely above a whisper, as though raising it could disturb the fragile balance of life in the room.

"She's stable for now," the nurse replied, her tone reassuring but laced with the reality of the situation. "We're doing everything we can. Just keep talking to her. It's important."

I nodded, grateful for her encouragement, and returned my focus to Sarah, my heart swelling with a mix of determination and dread. The soft sounds of the nurse's footsteps faded into the background as I continued to recount our adventures. "You remember the time we went to that farmer's market and got caught in the rain? I was convinced we would drown, and you just laughed, spinning in circles with your umbrella. We ended up with enough strawberries to last a month."

The room shifted with the weight of memories, my words wrapping around us like a soft embrace, creating a cocoon against the harsh realities outside. I leaned forward, speaking not just to fill the silence but to fill the spaces of fear that hung in the air like fog. "You've always been my rock, Sarah. The steady force that kept me grounded. Now it's my turn to be yours."

As night deepened, exhaustion began to tug at my eyelids. I fought against it, desperate to remain present, but the gentle pull of sleep was relentless. Just before I succumbed, a soft groan broke the silence, and my heart jolted. "Sarah?" I whispered, my pulse quickening with hope. I leaned in closer, my breath caught in my throat. Her eyelids fluttered slightly, and I felt a spark ignite within me, a flicker of the resilience that had always defined her.

"Jules?" The sound of her voice was faint but unmistakable, a whisper of the vibrant spirit I knew. "What... where am I?"

Relief flooded through me, warm and intoxicating. "You're in the hospital, but you're going to be okay. I'm right here," I replied, my voice thick with emotion. "You scared me so much, but I knew you were still fighting."

She blinked slowly, her eyes struggling to adjust to the light. A faint smile tugged at the corners of her lips, and I could see the spark of life returning to her. "You're talking about cake again, aren't you?"

"Always," I chuckled, the sound a mixture of laughter and tears. "I was just telling you about the lemon meringue tarts and how they're going to blow everyone's mind."

Her smile widened, a beacon of light piercing through the darkness of the past hours. "You have to save me a slice," she insisted, her voice still weak but laced with determination.

"Only if you promise to get better. I need my partner in crime back," I replied, squeezing her hand, warmth rushing through our connection.

With each passing moment, the fear that had clutched at my heart began to loosen its grip. Sarah was still with me, her indomitable spirit beginning to re-emerge from the depths of uncertainty. The machines around us became a backdrop to our reunion, the sterile room transformed into a sacred space filled with hope.

As the night wore on, I settled into the rhythm of her breathing, a soothing lullaby that washed over my racing thoughts. I knew the road ahead would be long and fraught with challenges, but I also knew we would face them together. The bakery, with its tantalizing aromas and sweet memories, waited for us. Together, we would create not just pastries but a legacy of resilience and love.

In that moment, as I watched Sarah's eyes grow heavy with sleep, I made a silent vow. No matter what it took, I would fight for her, for our dreams, and for the sweetness of life that awaited us both.

The soft hum of the hospital room had morphed into a comforting lullaby, each beep of the monitor syncing with the rhythm of my heart, a steady reminder that Sarah was still with me. The dull glow of the nightlight cast a warm halo around her, softening the harsh lines of the medical equipment. As I watched her rest, I felt an overwhelming sense of gratitude for her presence, however tenuous it seemed. I clung to that gratitude like a lifeline, fighting against the fear that threatened to engulf me again.

It was in those quiet moments that I allowed myself to drift, to wander through memories that painted our friendship in vivid strokes. I remembered the day we first opened the bakery, the sun streaming through the windows, illuminating the flour-dusted counters and the colorful array of pastries that adorned the shelves. We had stood in awe, surrounded by the sweet scents of vanilla and chocolate, our hearts swelling with hope. "This is it, Jules," she had said, her eyes sparkling with mischief and determination. "We're going to make magic here."

Magic, indeed. The bakery had become a sanctuary for so many in our town—a place where dreams rose alongside the bread, where laughter mingled with the aroma of freshly brewed coffee. I could almost hear the familiar jingle of the bell above the door as customers entered, each one a part of our tapestry. From the elderly couple who shared a slice of cake every Tuesday to the group of young artists who set up shop at the corner table with their sketchbooks and coffee cups, our little haven was a refuge for souls seeking sweetness in their lives.

But in the stillness of this hospital room, I felt the enormity of what was at stake. Without Sarah, our dreams risked fading into shadows. The thought was unbearable. I reached for her hand, tracing the lines of her palm with my fingers, willing her strength to return. "I can't do this without you, Sarah," I whispered, my voice trembling with vulnerability. "You're the heart of this place. It's not just about the pastries; it's about us."

A soft sigh escaped her lips, and for a fleeting moment, I thought I saw her eyes flutter. My heart raced, hope igniting within me. "You know, we could make a lemon meringue tart so good that it could revive anyone," I said, my voice buoyed by the thought. "We'd just need the right ingredients—lots of love, a pinch of laughter, and maybe a dash of your stubbornness to ensure it turns out perfectly."

As the night deepened, a soft glow emerged in the dimness—a flicker of life in her spirit that I hoped would grow. I had nearly succumbed to exhaustion when a familiar sound broke through the quiet—a gentle knock, followed by the unmistakable scent of lavender and chamomile. It was Ethan, his weary face lighting up at the sight of us. "I thought I'd find you here," he said softly, moving to stand beside me.

"Did you bring food?" I asked, my stomach growling in protest. The hospital cafeteria's offerings had been unkind to my appetite. He chuckled, and I could see the warmth in his eyes as he pulled out a carefully wrapped container. "Only the best for my two favorite ladies."

"Are you sure I'm still your favorite?" I teased, raising an eyebrow at him.

"Always," he said, his gaze drifting to Sarah, where a fragile light lingered in her expression. "I wouldn't be here without the two of you."

As Ethan settled into the chair beside me, he opened the container to reveal a feast of finger sandwiches, pastries, and my favorite raspberry macarons. The simple act of sharing a meal brought a semblance of normalcy to the chaos surrounding us. We nibbled quietly, my mind half on the food and half on the myriad of thoughts swirling like whipped cream in a mixer.

"Have you thought about the magazine feature?" Ethan asked, his tone casual, but I could sense the weight behind his words.

"I have. But honestly, it feels so trivial now. What if she can't be there?" I let the words tumble out, my heartache spilling like melted chocolate. "What if everything we've worked for crumbles without her?"

"Jules," Ethan said, his voice steady. "Sarah wouldn't want you to stop because of her. You have a gift, and you've built something beautiful together. She's a fighter, and so are you."

His words settled around me like a warm embrace, rekindling the flicker of hope. I looked at Sarah, her face still pale but undeniably serene, and a surge of determination washed over me. "You're right. We'll get through this," I declared, a fierce conviction igniting within my chest. "I'm not letting our dreams die, and I know Sarah wouldn't want that either."

As if sensing the shift in energy, Sarah stirred slightly, her brow furrowing. I leaned closer, my heart racing. "We're here, Sarah. Just squeeze my hand if you can hear me." A moment later, I felt her fingers move, the faintest of squeezes igniting a wave of relief.

"I knew you could hear me," I whispered, tears pricking at the corners of my eyes as I shared a glance with Ethan. "You're stronger than you realize."

The hours slipped by, the delicate interplay of worry and hope weaving a tapestry of resilience around us. I filled the silence with tales of our bakery, recounting the stories of our customers, the flavors we'd explored, and the laughter that permeated our days. I spoke of the magazine and how we were finally going to be recognized for our hard work. As the dawn began to break, painting the room in hues of soft lavender and pink, I felt the darkness lift ever so slightly.

With the sun climbing higher, a nurse peeked in, her expression one of warmth. "Good morning! I see our girl is waking up," she said cheerfully. "How are you feeling today, Sarah?"

"Like I could use a pastry," came Sarah's raspy voice, surprising us all. The room erupted into a mix of laughter and tears, a beautiful chaos that signaled the return of the vibrant spirit we all adored.

"You heard that, right?" I grinned, my heart swelling. "You'll have the finest pastry this town has ever tasted."

The nurse chuckled, and with a gentle nod, she noted Sarah's progress. "That's the spirit! We'll get you some more comfortable pillows and your favorite blanket. Just keep talking to her. You're doing wonderfully."

Ethan and I exchanged glances, a shared understanding passing between us. Our bond, like the baked goods we cherished, was crafted from the finest ingredients—love, laughter, and resilience. The promise of recovery wrapped around us, a bittersweet reminder that we would need to face the world again, but this time, together.

As the day unfolded, the sun streaming through the window, I felt the warmth of new beginnings. The bakery awaited us, its doors ready to open wide once more. And though the path ahead would be fraught with challenges, I knew we would face them hand in hand, baking not just for ourselves but for the countless souls seeking solace in our treats. Each pastry would tell our story, a testament to survival, friendship, and the undeniable magic that could arise from the darkest of days.

With Sarah's hand still clasped in mine, I dared to dream once more. The magazine feature, the tarts, the laughter—they were all still within reach. And with every beat of our hearts, I felt certain of one thing: our dreams, like the best recipes, were crafted from love, resilience, and a sprinkle of hope. Together, we would rise again, baking our way into a bright future, one delectable creation at a time.

Chapter 29: Reflections in the Dark

Sitting in the dim hospital room, the hum of fluorescent lights is a far cry from the comforting warmth of the bakery, where the scent of vanilla and freshly baked bread once wrapped around me like a beloved blanket. I lean back against the cold, sterile wall, the paint chipped and faded, as if it, too, has seen better days. The sterile scent of antiseptic fills the air, mingling uncomfortably with the whir of machines, each beep and sigh reminding me that life teeters on the edge of hope and despair. Outside, the sun sets slowly, casting an amber glow through the half-closed blinds, creating stripes of light that dance on the floor like memories flickering through my mind.

Ethan's face flashes before me, a beautiful collage of joy and concern, and I'm suddenly struck by the gravity of what's transpired. The world beyond this hospital room has become a blur, a distant echo of laughter, flour dust, and the soft chatter of patrons enjoying their coffee and pastries. I realize that my relentless pursuit of external success—a dream that once filled me with purpose—has led me to this moment of isolation. In my fervor to rise above, I neglected the very roots that nourished my spirit. I missed birthdays, skipped out on dinners, and traded late-night conversations for endless deadlines. What good is success if the people I love slip through my fingers like sugar through a sieve?

I close my eyes and picture the bakery: the worn wooden counter where customers linger, sharing stories and smiles, the laughter of children as they sample cupcakes, the way the early morning sun dances off the glass display case filled with colorful confections. Those moments feel like treasures, each one a note in the symphony of my life. And yet, here I am, trapped in a moment of despair, a poignant reminder that I am but one note in a much larger score, yearning to play in harmony with those I cherish.

When the clock ticks away the minutes and my own reflection in the window reveals dark circles under my eyes, the nurse enters with a clipboard, her kind demeanor a balm to my frayed nerves. She checks the IV line, her movements practiced and sure, but her eyes linger on me for a moment longer. "You're doing the right thing by being here," she says softly, her voice an anchor in this turbulent sea. "Sometimes it's hard to remember what matters most." I nod, her words resonating within me like a sweet melody, a reminder that my journey is not just about the destination but also about the people who walk alongside me.

Hours pass like molasses, thick and unyielding, as I contemplate the weight of my choices. I reach for my phone, my fingers hovering over Ethan's name, the warmth of his love a beacon in the growing darkness of uncertainty. I send a quick text, my heart racing with each word. "I'm thinking of you. Can you come?" A few moments later, the reply comes, swift and reassuring. "On my way."

The anticipation fills the space around me, transforming the sterile walls into something more vibrant, more alive. I can almost hear the creak of the bakery door, the familiar jingle of the bell announcing his arrival, the way he always greets me with that crooked smile that lights up his face. As I wait, I replay our moments together—lazy Sunday mornings spent creating towering stacks of pancakes, his laughter echoing against the walls of our home. Those simple joys remind me that life's richness lies not in accolades or achievements, but in the warmth of connection, the shared silence of understanding, and the comfort of belonging.

Finally, the door swings open, and there he stands, a figure wrapped in shadows and light, a fierce guardian of my heart. His eyes search for mine, a storm of emotions swirling within them, and I can see the worry etched across his brow, like an artist's brushstroke on canvas. He crosses the room in an instant, his arms enveloping me in a cocoon of warmth that melts the coldness of the hospital air.

In that embrace, I feel the pulse of our love, steady and unwavering, a rhythm that reminds me we are not just surviving but thriving together.

"I was so worried," he whispers, his breath a soft caress against my ear. I lean into him, my heart fluttering like a bird finally freed from its cage. In this moment, the cacophony of machines and hushed voices fades away, leaving only us—tangled together in this messy, beautiful life.

"I'm sorry for everything," I confess, pulling back to look into his eyes. "I let everything else overshadow what really matters. I don't want to lose us." My words tumble out in a rush, filled with the urgency of my realization. His grip tightens, and I can see the understanding in his gaze, a mirror reflecting my own fears and hopes.

"I've been thinking, too," he admits, a hint of vulnerability creeping into his voice. "It's easy to get caught up in the hustle, but we have to make sure we're in this together. I want to build a future with you, one that includes all our dreams, not just mine or yours."

As we stand there, the hospital room fades into the background, and I feel a renewed sense of purpose bloom within me, as if the flowers of our dreams are finally breaking through the surface, ready to thrive. I realize that love is not just about shared moments of happiness but also about weathering the storms together, hand in hand. And in that understanding, I find the strength to face whatever lies ahead.

As the evening deepens, the golden light of the setting sun gives way to the cool embrace of twilight. The fluorescent hum of the hospital room recedes into the background, replaced by the soothing rhythm of Ethan's breath beside me. Together, we sink into a comfortable silence, our fingers interlaced as if we are two vines, entwined and stronger together. The vulnerability in the air is palpable, a delicate web spun from our shared fears and desires, and

I can feel the tension melting away like ice cream under the summer sun.

"Let's go home," Ethan finally suggests, his voice low, almost reverent. The words hang in the air, an invitation to step beyond these sterile walls and back into the world where laughter echoes off bakery walls and the aroma of fresh bread beckons with the promise of comfort. I nod, a smile breaking free, lighting up my face like a candle igniting in the dark. Home—the word carries a weight of familiarity, warmth, and love that I long to return to.

The drive through the streets is a patchwork quilt of memories, each turn revealing a different moment we've shared. The bakery, my sanctuary, stands at the corner, its windows aglow with soft, inviting light. As we step inside, the familiar scents envelop me like a hug. The laughter of the late-night bakers drifts from the back, where flour dust dances in the shafts of golden light filtering through the window. This is where my heart lies, amidst the whir of mixers and the rhythmic kneading of dough—a symphony of creation and connection.

I move toward the counter, fingers trailing across the cool surface as if greeting an old friend. Behind the counter, my trusted team is bustling about, their energy a lively melody that fills the space. They pause as I enter, their faces brightening with recognition and relief, and I can't help but feel a rush of gratitude. This is my family, the people who have stood by me, pouring their hearts into each cupcake and croissant, who have witnessed my triumphs and failures with unwavering support.

"Hey, boss! You're back!" one of the bakers calls, his flour-dusted apron a testament to his commitment. The others nod in agreement, their smiles wide and genuine. "We saved you a piece of the new chocolate torte!"

Laughter spills from my lips, a sound I didn't realize I'd missed so much. "I'll take it!" I reply, and as I step further inside, I feel the weight of my worries dissipating. In this vibrant space filled with creativity and camaraderie, I can breathe again.

Ethan stands a little to the side, watching me with an expression that oscillates between admiration and amusement. I can see him appreciating the way my spirit comes alive in this setting. It's in the way I engage with my team, my hands animated as I describe the vision I've long held for our bakery. "We're going to introduce a new line of seasonal pastries," I say, the ideas bubbling forth like the yeast in our dough. "Pumpkin spice éclairs, cranberry-orange scones, and maybe even a spiced apple tart." My excitement is infectious, and I see nods of agreement and eager smiles on their faces.

As I delve into the plans, I glance at Ethan, who leans against the counter, his arms crossed, a proud smile playing on his lips. In that moment, I realize that he is not just my partner in life but also my partner in passion. We share this dream of nurturing our little corner of the world, a place where sweetness reigns and every pastry tells a story. The realization brings warmth to my heart—a promise that we are building a life not just together, but for those around us as well.

After a whirlwind of laughter and chatter about the new creations, I find a moment to pull Ethan aside. The kitchen buzzes with energy, and I feel the warmth of the oven at my back. "I've been thinking," I begin, hesitating just enough to gauge his reaction. "About us, about this place. I want to create not just a bakery, but a community."

His gaze sharpens, curiosity igniting in his eyes. "What do you mean?"

"Picture this: workshops where we teach kids how to bake, community events to support local artists, maybe even hosting a 'pay what you can' day to give back to those in need," I explain, my heart racing with the possibilities. "I want our bakery to be a safe space for everyone—a place where people come not just for the pastries but to feel like they belong."

Ethan's brow furrows as he processes my words. I can see him considering the challenges, the logistics, the potential impact. And then, slowly, a smile spreads across his face. "I love that idea. We could really make a difference."

His support ignites a spark of determination within me. We stand together in that cozy kitchen, amidst the clatter of mixing bowls and the gentle hum of conversation, united in a vision that reaches beyond ourselves. As we dream together, I can almost see the bakery blossoming into something even greater—a hub of creativity and compassion, where every pastry is a gesture of love, and every event strengthens the fabric of our community.

Hours pass in a blur of flour and frosting, laughter and ideas. The outside world fades away, leaving just the rhythm of our teamwork—a choreography perfected over countless nights spent together, crafting sweet delights. As the night wears on and the last batch of pastries cools on the rack, Ethan and I exchange glances filled with understanding and excitement.

When we finally lock up the bakery, the moon hangs high in the sky, casting a silver glow over the world outside. I feel lighter, as if I've shed the weight of my past mistakes, allowing hope and joy to seep in like the first rays of dawn. Hand in hand, we walk into the cool night air, a promise of a future rich with possibilities stretching before us. We step into the unknown, ready to embrace whatever comes our way, knowing that as long as we have each other, we can face anything life throws our way.

The soft glow of the moonlight spills through the bakery's window, casting delicate patterns of light and shadow across the flour-dusted counter. As we lock up for the night, the warmth of the kitchen lingers in the air, filling my senses with the sweet fragrance of vanilla and caramel. Outside, the world is draped in silence, a blanket of tranquility settling over our little corner of the city. I lean against the cool glass, looking out at the quiet streets illuminated by flickering lamplights, my heart swelling with gratitude and determination.

"Let's celebrate," Ethan suggests, breaking the silence that envelops us. His smile is infectious, brightening the dim corners of the bakery as he pulls a couple of glasses from the shelf. "We've got a new plan, a new direction. I think we should toast to that."

I nod enthusiastically, the idea of celebration making my heart race. It feels fitting—a small ritual of acknowledgment for the rebirth of our dreams. While he pours sparkling cider into the glasses, I can't help but marvel at how effortlessly he moves through this space that is so familiar to me. Each action, from the precise pour to the way he wipes a nonexistent smudge from the counter, speaks of our shared history, the comfort of companionship that has blossomed over late-night baking sessions and flour fights.

With glasses raised, we toast under the soft light, the bubbles dancing merrily as if echoing our hopes. "To new beginnings," I say, my heart pounding with excitement and anticipation. "And to building something beautiful together."

"To new beginnings," he replies, his eyes gleaming with the same fervor I feel coursing through my veins. We sip the bubbly drink, laughter bubbling up between us like the yeast in our dough. It's a moment of pure joy, a reminder that amidst life's chaos, we can carve out pockets of happiness, celebrating the small victories that lead to grand transformations.

After we finish our toast, Ethan takes my hand, his warmth radiating through me, and we step outside into the crisp night air. The city hums with life around us, a gentle symphony of distant laughter and the soft rustle of leaves. I take a deep breath, inhaling the freshness that comes with the night, and let my mind wander back to the plans we've discussed. The thought of workshops and community events fills me with a sense of purpose, a promise to not just make our bakery a haven of pastries but a sanctuary of belonging.

As we stroll through the familiar streets, I imagine how our bakery could transform into a bustling hub, a gathering place where families could create memories and friendships could blossom over warm pastries and shared experiences. I see kids bustling about in the kitchen, their hands smeared with flour as they learn to roll dough and decorate cupcakes. I can picture the smiles on their faces as they taste their creations, a moment of triumph in their eyes.

"What's going on in that brilliant mind of yours?" Ethan's voice pulls me from my reverie, and I can't help but smile.

"I was just thinking about all the possibilities," I say, my excitement bubbling over. "Imagine the community events—baking contests, seasonal markets. We could even host local artists to showcase their work."

His eyes light up, and I can see his mind racing to catch up with mine. "And we could partner with local schools to teach kids about healthy eating and cooking," he adds, his enthusiasm matching mine. "There's so much we could do."

As we continue walking, our ideas flow freely, weaving a tapestry of dreams that seems to stretch as far as the horizon. With each step, I feel the weight of uncertainty lifting, replaced by a shared vision that pulls us closer together. We navigate the streets like explorers charting a new course, our laughter echoing in the night as we lay the groundwork for our future.

Arriving at the bakery the next morning, the golden sun pours through the windows, casting a warm glow over everything. The space feels alive, ready to embrace our plans. Ethan and I jump into action, moving as a well-rehearsed duo, flipping the sign from "Closed" to "Open," the familiar jingle of the bell signaling the beginning of a new day.

As customers trickle in, I feel the energy of the bakery shift. The scent of coffee wafts through the air, mingling with the sweet aroma of pastries fresh out of the oven. The first family walks in, their faces lighting up at the sight of the colorful display. "What's new today?" the mother asks, her eyes sparkling with anticipation.

I smile brightly, feeling a rush of pride. "We have pumpkin spice éclairs and cranberry-orange scones!" I declare, my voice infused with the enthusiasm that has bubbled within me since the previous night.

As I share our new offerings, I can see Ethan engaging with the customers, his charm effortless, drawing them into the warmth of our bakery. He makes them feel seen and valued, just as he does with me. Watching him interact with them, I am reminded of the true heart of our venture—not just the pastries, but the relationships we forge along the way.

The day flows seamlessly, laughter and chatter intertwining with the sounds of clinking plates and sizzling pans. Between serving pastries and answering questions, I find moments to jot down ideas for our upcoming workshops. The vision is taking shape; it feels like we are piecing together a jigsaw puzzle, each idea a vibrant piece fitting into a larger picture.

As the day winds down, the golden light of dusk begins to filter through the windows once more. We take a moment to catch our breath, leaning against the counter, our hearts full. "Today was incredible," Ethan says, his eyes shining. "I can already see how much this means to our customers."

I nod, my heart swelling with pride. "It's just the beginning," I reply, a sense of determination coursing through me. "Together, we can create something truly special."

In that shared moment, standing side by side, I realize that our journey is not just about baking but about forging connections that transcend the kitchen. It's about building a community where every person feels valued, every story is welcomed, and every dream is nurtured. I can feel it in my bones—this is what I was meant to do.

With the sun dipping below the horizon, the bakery glows warmly, a beacon of hope and happiness in the heart of the city. Ethan takes my hand, and as we look around at the life we've created together, I know that no matter what challenges lie ahead, we will face them side by side, united in purpose and love, ready to embrace the future with open hearts.

Milton Keynes UK
Ingram Content Group UK Ltd.
UKHW041822201024
449814UK00001B/52

9 798227 612236